## "Make a scene, if you must.

"I will curse loudly and swear you have insulted all of France. Think of the scandal, mademoiselle. An international affront. The disgrace to your country!"

Now he was invoking patriotism? The man was shameless! It only made Elizabeth more determined to refuse. She tapped her fan against her chin in thought. There must be some way to vanquish him. "If you force me to dance, I shall be powerless against your brute strength, true enough. But I'm quite sure I'll faint in the middle of the dance floor."

Noël laughed at that. "Faint? *You?* Who would believe it? But if that should happen—alas!—I would be forced to loosen your bodice. For your own good, of course." He dropped his insolent gaze to her bosom.

"You wouldn't!"

"I would."

Yes, he would, she thought grimly....

Dear Reader,

Welcome to Harlequin Historicals, where the new year could be any year—from the turn of the twentieth century to one as far back as our talented authors can take us. From medieval castles to the wide-open prairies, come join our brave heroines and dashing heroes as they battle the odds and discover romance.

In Barbara Faith's first historical, *Gamblin' Man,* Carrie McClennon's simple life is turned upside down by a notorious saloon owner.

*Jasmine and Silk,* from Sandra Chastain, is set on a Georgian plantation soon after the American Revolution.

Louisa Rawlings's *Wicked Stranger* is the sequel to her *Stranger in My Arms,* and tells the story of the second Bouchard brother.

A luckless Southern belle finds herself stranded in Panama in Kristie Knight's *No Man's Fortune.*

Four new adventures from Harlequin Historicals. We hope you enjoy them all.

Sincerely,

Tracy Farrell
Senior Editor

# Wicked Stranger

## Louisa Rawlings

# Harlequin Books

TORONTO • NEW YORK • LONDON
AMSTERDAM • PARIS • SYDNEY • HAMBURG
STOCKHOLM • ATHENS • TOKYO • MILAN
MADRID • WARSAW • BUDAPEST • AUCKLAND

If you purchased this book without a cover you should be aware
that this book is stolen property. It was reported as "unsold and
destroyed" to the publisher, and neither the author nor the
publisher has received any payment for this "stripped book."

Harlequin Historicals first edition January 1993

ISBN 0-373-28757-7

WICKED STRANGER

Copyright © 1993 by Sylvia Baumgarten.
All rights reserved. Except for use in any review,
the reproduction or utilization of this work in
whole or in part in any form by any electronic,
mechanical or other means, now known or
hereafter invented, including xerography,
photocopying and recording, or in any information
storage or retrieval system, is forbidden without
the permission of the publisher, Harlequin Historicals,
300 E. 42nd St., New York, N.Y. 10017

All the characters in this book have no existence
outside the imagination of the author and have no
relation whatsoever to anyone bearing the same name
or names. They are not even distantly inspired by any
individual known or unknown to the author, and all
incidents are pure invention.

®: Trademark registered in the United States Patent
and Trademark Office and in other countries.

Printed in the U.S.A.

---

## LOUISA RAWLINGS

has written eight historical romances, several under the pseudonym of Ena Halliday. Interested in France since her high school days, she has set most of her books in that country. She has received awards for her books from the Romance Writers of America and *Romantic Times*. When her four children were younger, she enjoyed a suburban, domestic life: PTA, gardening, gourmet cooking and sewing her own clothes. With the children grown and gone, she and her husband find more time for traveling and attending the opera. They now live happily in a Manhattan apartment.

To Deena Mazer
What better time than in a book about
loving brothers to acknowledge a dear sister,
a superb actress, a friend and companion,
a partner for the difficult times,
and—most precious of all—
co-keeper of Hilda's rare flame.

# Prologue

"Twins? Egad, *monsieur,* more than twins. You're as like as two currants in a plum pudding!"

Noël Bouchard shrugged and smiled at the Englishman, tossed his gloves into his riding hat and placed them on a table in the large, elegantly furnished vestibule of the château. He answered in the man's own language, his English softened by the melodious accent of his native French. "I can assure you, sir, that my twin brother Adam would not be so reckless and uncivil as to go riding when you have an appointment with him." He bent his head in the direction of the sunny March day beyond the windows. "I, on the other hand, would be willing to snub your king and mine, and insult every minister in both courts, for the freedom to ride on such a glorious afternoon. It would..." He stopped as a musical laugh floated down the staircase behind him. He turned and smiled warmly at the woman who came toward them, still laughing.

*"Mon Dieu, quelle absurdité,"* she said, shaking her head. "I beg you, Sir Alfred," she continued, lapsing into English, "pay no attention to my brother-in-law Noël. He tries to appear more roguish than he is."

Noël kissed the woman on both cheeks and affected an aggrieved frown. "Will you tell all my secrets, Charmiane?"

The Englishman took Charmiane's fingers in his and bowed low over them, while discreetly keeping his eyes from straying below her chin; the awkward gesture made him look like a turtle peering out of its shell. "You're looking splendid, *madame la comtesse*. Burn me if you're not. Months since I've had the pleasure of your company. You're..." He harrumphed loudly and tugged at his cravat. "You're well?"

Charmiane suppressed a smile as Noël rolled his eyes behind the Englishman's back. The man was far too proper to openly acknowledge Charmiane's advanced state of pregnancy, though her fashionably high-waisted pink gown, billowing over the rounded swell of her body, scarcely concealed her condition. Her raven hair was bound loosely and framed her face in charming informality. She looked like a fragile Madonna out of a Renaissance painting, soft and glowing with maternal radiance.

Noël sighed. A remarkable woman. She'd been Adam's wife for four years, and he wondered when he'd stop feeling envy for his twin brother. Charmiane was beautiful and gracious, and she presided over Adam's household like a princess. He felt a stab of regret. If only...

Fool! he thought a moment later. What was he thinking of? His brother was rich, titled, an important personage in the court of France: the Honorable Adam Bouchard, Comte de Moncalvo, for many years general under the Emperor Napoleon, now councillor of state to the restored monarch, Louis XVIII. He possessed this magnificent château, a town house in Paris, honor and esteem—all the result of half a lifetime of distinguished service in the army. Absently Noël rubbed at his leg. All *he* had to show for his mere seven years under Napoleon's command was a scarred leg that ached when it rained. Even if Charmiane had had a twin of her own, what could he offer her? The life of a wanderer? No permanence, no future. Rented rooms and rented horses, in every corner of the globe. Adam had often said that he'd rent the food he ate, if he could, to keep from tying himself down, from taking responsibility. Noël sighed again. Perhaps it was just as well that Charmiane had married Adam.

"Sir Alfred," said Charmiane, "why don't you go straight up without waiting for Adam's secretary? My husband is in his sitting room."

Noël smirked. "*Sitting* room? I have no doubt Brother Adam is standing at attention even now, eager to do his duty. *Mon Dieu.* I shall never understand a man's need to spend his life on work."

"Yes. Ahem. Quite so." Disconcerted, the Englishman shifted the briefcase under his arm and turned toward the stairs. "Perhaps Monsieur de Moncalvo and I can work out these trade agreements and have something to show our respective ministers. Your servant, *madame. Monsieur.*"

Charmiane waited until the Englishman had disappeared up the wide staircase before allowing herself a soft giggle. "Really, Noël, I never saw anyone who so glories in a wicked reputation as you do!"

Noël pushed back a lock of dark blond hair that had fallen across his broad forehead and tried to look solemn. "It isn't easy, I can assure you. It's simple enough to win someone's approval, you understand. A few disarming smiles, a sweet compliment or two." His blue eyes twinkled merrily. "Ah, but to convince someone that you're completely unredeemable . . . *that's* an art."

She clicked her tongue. "You haven't changed since the first time we met. Still playing the devil with great delight. Are you so afraid of being loved?"

He laughed, though he found himself unable to meet her direct gaze. "For more than a season at a time? Good God, yes! Love, like life itself, is to be tasted. Savored fully. And then one moves on to something new, someone new, to keep from getting . . ."

"Touched too deeply?" Charmiane finished, with more than a little irony.

"Bored," he drawled. "Do you know how many women I haven't loved yet? It was fortunate for you that Adam found you first. For all that I adore you, my dear Charmiane, I should have been inconstant and restless within a year."

Charmiane put her hand on his arm. Her eyes were unexpectedly serious, soft with understanding. "Perhaps someday—if you allow yourself to love with all your being—it will be different."

Noël turned away sharply. It had suddenly become impossible to look at her for another moment. It was not that he was in love with her—or ever had been, he supposed, beyond an initial attraction to her beauty and grace. But the sight of her—love and happiness and serenity radiating from her face—tore at his heart, surprising him with a rush of emotion. Charmiane and Adam. They made him feel like an outsider, an empty intruder hoping to fill himself with the warmth of their love.

Damn! he thought. He must be getting old. Thirty-nine a week ago, he and Adam. And now he was in danger of falling into the mire of self-pity, stricken with regrets. Questioning a life that had been eminently satisfying until now.

The silence had become awkward. "Aren't you going riding?" Charmiane asked at last.

Noël willed away the unwelcome doubts. "I wanted to see Bazaine before I go. He mentioned something about a few hands of cards before dinner." He chuckled. "He's still hoping to get back the fortune I won from him the other night."

"What a wicked influence you are on that poor man! A loyal, efficient secretary. Adam's steady right hand for fifteen years. I don't know what either of us would do without him to run our affairs. But you've been here scarcely three weeks, and he's a changed man. Do you know he even told a joke this morning after breakfast? A particularly silly joke. I thought Adam would fall off his chair in astonishment."

Noël nodded in satisfaction. "Good! Brother Adam needs a little stirring up once in a while. Keep him from becoming a complacent married man."

Charmiane's green eyes sparkled with the enjoyment of their banter, but she managed to look insulted. "Oh! Complacent? Do you now intend to corrupt my husband? I see I'll have to give a party and invite all the eligible young women I know."

Noël affected an expression of horror. "No! Spare me! Anything but eligible women panting for a husband!"

Charmiane snorted. "I should like to see the woman who could trap *you*. She'd have to— Oh, here are Madame Nogare and the children."

Noël turned. A stout woman, in the cap and apron of a nursemaid, had come into the vestibule. In her arms she held a squirming child of two and a half with pale brown hair and pink cheeks; a little boy, perhaps a year older, trailed beside her, clutching her skirt in his fist. His curls were spun gold, touched with red where the light hit them, and his smile was shy but beautiful.

Noël dropped to one knee and held out his arms to the elder child. "Good afternoon, Martin."

"Uncle Noël!" The boy skipped forward and threw himself at Noël, who picked him up and swung him around in a giddying circle. Martin's eyes were round with wonder. "We saw soldiers in the village. Lots of them. With big shiny hats."

"Did you? Well, now, I think we might look for a little soldier's hat in a shop. Just for you. Would you like me to buy one?"

Martin nodded vigorously and pointed to the other child, who was still fidgeting in his nurse's arms. "And Fabien, too?" asked Martin. "He needs a soldier's hat."

"Of course. Fabien, too."

Charmiane shook her head. "Really, Noël. How you spoil those children."

Noël looked abashed. "Sorry. Do you mind?"

"May I have the hat? Oh, say yes, Mama. Please." Martin's voice was soft and pleading.

Charmiane laughed. "I don't know which one of you looks more hangdog. Very well, Martin. Your Uncle Noël may buy you the hat."

The boy grinned as Noël set him on his feet. "I'll look like Papa. In the painting upstairs."

Fabien began to whimper and squeak. Madame Nogare shifted him to one ample hip. "If you please, Madame, let me take the children up for their naps. It's been a long morning."

"Of course." Charmiane kissed the two boys and stroked Fabien's hair.

Solemnly Noël saluted Martin in his best military style and nodded at the child's answering salute. "Off to your nap, little soldier. We'll go to the village tomorrow for those hats," he said, and watched the boy scamper after the nursemaid, taking the stairs with as much agility as his solid little legs would allow. A beautiful child, he thought. Sweet and serious, thoughtful beyond his years. A child to be proud of.

Charmiane's soft voice came from behind Noël. "Do you regret it?"

Noël watched the boy maneuver the last of the stairs, then turned to Charmiane. "He has Martine's coloring."

"But are you sorry?"

"That I gave him up? Good God, no." He forced a laugh. "Can you imagine me raising a child? The child of a camp follower? With the blot of illegitimacy to his name, to boot?"

"You could have adopted him. Instead of allowing us to do it. He's still a Bouchard either way."

Noël shrugged and reached for his riding hat and gloves. "Let him be a Bouchard with roots. I'm scarcely a shining example. Tell Bazaine he'll have to wait till tomorrow to avenge himself at the card table. I feel like a very long ride." Clapping his hat on his head, he strode into the sunshine.

He rode like a man bedeviled, spurring his horse as though demons followed behind. But of course there was no escaping his thoughts. Four years. Four years since Martine—inconstant, unfaithful, weary of waiting for him to return from the endless battles—had run off with another soldier. A momentary blow to his pride, but not much more. Or so he liked to tell himself now. Martine had been his companion when he'd needed a woman; he'd been her benefactor and protector at every army bivouac. He hadn't even known about the child. Not until later, when he'd gone looking for Martine after his last campaign in 1814 and Martine's mother had thrust the infant's basket into his hands with a terse "If you be Bouchard, this is yours."

It had been right to let Charmiane and Adam take Martin. He didn't regret that. The boy had a home, a loving family, and Adam's own son, Fabien, for companionship. He did feel a twinge of remorse, aware that it had taken him three years to return from his wanderings to see his son. Still, the regret was minimal, and he could endure it.

What was new, and unexpected, was the pride he felt at the sight of the boy. The heart-swelling emotion, that rush of joy and wonder that made him painfully aware of his loss. Made him consider whether the devil-may-care Noël who'd so mindlessly handed over his son to others wasn't a bit of a fool.

And guilt. Dear God, *that* was new. Wrenching, agonizing guilt that tore at his guts. He saw his son, and imagined his future. Martin looked upon Adam and Charmiane as his parents, called them Mama and Papa. He thought Fabien was his younger brother, and looked forward to welcoming Charmiane's baby as a new sibling. But there would come a time when he'd have to learn the truth. Or at least the embellished truth that had been told to the servants and Parisian society: that he was adopted, the child of one of Adam's late war comrades. And that, though he could legally call himself a Bouchard, Adam's title and holdings would eventually go to his true heir, Fabien. A bitter truth for Martin, growing up as the eldest and assuming it would all be his someday.

Noël reined in his horse and stared across the hills at the lengthening shadows. The still-wintry landscape was as bleak as his heart, for all the bright sunshine. Adam would see that Martin's future was financially secure, of course. No need to worry on that score. Still, *he* was the boy's father. There ought to be something he could do, some way to give the boy a legacy. His true father's legacy.

Noël tapped his horse's flank and started down the ridge. The ride had done him good. He had a plan in mind. It was time to act on it.

It wasn't until after dinner that night that he broached the subject to Adam. Not that he needed—or wanted—his brother's help. If he was going to do the thing at all, he ought to do it himself. Still, Adam had always been the responsible twin, while he'd gone his carefree way. It would be helpful to hear what Adam had to say about his idea. It was a big step for him, after all. It wasn't the risk that bothered him; hell, he'd been a gambler all his life. But the damn thing was so... so *permanent*. Once he'd taken on the burden, there'd be no turning back, no blithe abandonment of the scheme while he moved on to something new.

"That was a superb dinner, Charmiane," he said. "It's a wonder Brother Adam hasn't grown stout these past few years." The three of them had retired to the snug library, with its high-backed leather armchairs that faced the hearth and the welcoming fire.

Charmiane set a decanter of cognac and several glasses on a small table between Adam and Noël. "I'll see you comfortable, and then I'm off to bed," she said. She fetched a box of aromatic cigars and offered it to the two men. When they'd made their choices, she took a taper off the mantel, ignited it from a smoldering log and lit their cigars, lingering before Adam to smile tenderly. "Don't sit up half the night talking. Not if you're going to ride to Chantilly to buy horses in the morning."

About to put away a sheaf of papers in the desk, Adam's secretary, Charles Bazaine, paused. An imposing man, with hair and mustache the color of steel, he'd been Adam's aide-de-camp until a severe battle injury had left him unfit for military service. Now he wore a large black patch over one eye, which served to accentuate the piercing brilliance of his remaining eye. He shook his head in disapproval. "More horses? Where will you put them all, *monsieur le comte?*"

Adam shrugged apologetically. "I can't resist, when Noël is here. He always had a better eye for horseflesh than I did. The best animals in the stable are the ones he bought on my behalf. Don't frown like an old woman, Bazaine. I'll only buy one or two."

"Monsieur Noël will get his usual commission?"

Noël laughed. "Which I'll double, you old paper-pusher, as soon as you can find time for a few hands of piquet."

Bazaine sniffed, making for the door. "*Double?* A few francs that I allow you to win. Out of the goodness of my heart."

Noël's mouth twitched in amusement. "If you wish to think so. But your 'goodness' paid my passage to the United States three years ago." He scratched at his chin in thought, his expression bland and innocent. "I haven't been to Tahiti in years. Do you suppose you could oblige me, Bazaine?"

Ignoring that parting shot, Bazaine inclined his head toward Charmiane. "May I see you to your suite, *madame la comtesse?*"

Charmiane wished the brothers a final good night, blew a kiss to Adam and left the room with Bazaine, who closed the door behind her.

Adam took a deep puff of his cigar and leaned back in contentment. "You didn't really sail to America just on your winnings from Bazaine, did you? The truth, now."

"Well, you understand I had my final pay. From when my regiment was disbanded in '14. And the captain of that particular vessel was a gambling man. And a very bad card player. I had the best cabin aboard his ship."

"But what madness! What if you'd lost?"

Noël helped himself to another glass of cognac. "I haven't forgotten how to haul on a line. Remember the year I worked aboard that merchantman down the coast of Africa?"

"You were a great deal younger then," said Adam dryly.

"We get older and better." He grinned wickedly and glanced at Adam's angular form and features, still as trim as his own. "At least I do."

"And what do you propose to do now?"

"I thought I'd stay here at Bonneval for another week or so, and then be on my way."

Adam scowled. "You intend to leave so soon? I know you don't like to stay in one place for long, but..." He gave a deep sigh. "Three years, Noël. Will we wait another three years before we see you again? Stay a little longer. At least until Charmiane is delivered of her child." His smoky blue eyes were dark with sincerity, reminding Noël again of the bond of twinship between them, that special connection that vibrated with unspoken affection and fellowship. It had never wavered.

Noël looked into the crackling fire. "You don't need me here," he growled. "It's time to go. I'm restless."

"But are you content with your life?"

Noël made an attempt at a laugh. It was a hollow sound. "Of course. Haven't I always been?"

"Did you ever find out what happened to Martine?"

"Good God, why should I? The last time I saw her was in Strasbourg, before she ran off with Hautecoeur. Poor devil. Killed at Leipzig, with half his regiment of hussars. I never even learned the name of the man Martine finally married. Only that he didn't want my son."

The air was heavy with a melancholy that seemed to affect them both. They smoked in silence for a long while, filled with their own memories, with a sense of the passage of time. At last Adam leaned forward and tossed the remains of his cigar into the fireplace. "Damn it, Noël, what will you do now? Waste your time? Teach French in America? Or dancing?"

Noël chuckled. "I've already done that. Remember? Years ago, in Philadelphia. The female pupils were charming, as I recall. One or two of them were amenable to learning other things, as well.... Now don't look at me that way, brother. *Two* sober and serious Bouchards would have been more than the world could endure." He cast a sidelong glance at Adam, debating with himself. What the devil. If he was going to discuss his plans with his brother, it might as well be now. "As a matter of fact, I'm thinking of going into the shipping business." He ignored Adam's look of surprise and hurried on. "On that trip over to America three years ago, I met a Dutch sea captain who'd had his vessel blown from under him in a gale. By chance, I met him again just last month. In New York, before I sailed for France. He has a small shop in the port, selling canvas and tackle. But he wants a ship again. And he knows where to find a cheap one. It's full of water and needs a little repair. But it can be made seaworthy."

Adam stared at him. "The deuce! Shipping? What do you know about shipping?"

Noël laughed. "Not a damn thing. But the furs coming out of Pennsylvania and Ohio would bring top prices in Le Havre. I've met a few trappers in my travels. When I went by flatboat down the Ohio River. And if we can't get enough furs, we'll fill up the hold with whatever cargo we can. Exchange it in the Caribbean for goods for France. Steenboch—my Dutch captain—thinks we should sail under the French flag. Not the American."

"Because of the English treaty with the United States last year."

"Yes. American ships can't sell their goods in English ports. That would mean that half the West Indies markets would be closed to us."

Adam frowned into his glass. "It could be a good scheme, and I assume your Dutch captain can see to the repairs. But how the deuce do you intend to finance it?"

"With my exceeding charm, of course. I think I can find a few bankers, here in France and in New York, who'd be willing to make the investment. And, wonder of wonders, I've actually begun to save a little money."

Adam swore softly. "You're mad. You've no experience of the trade."

"You've been calling me irresponsible for years. I thought you'd be delighted with my transformation."

"Let me back you, then. I can afford—"

"No!" Noël started to rise, his eyes flashing. Then, with a rueful smile, he subsided into his chair. "Sorry, brother. But this is my scheme."

"Noël, for God's sake, let me do *something*."

He grinned. "You can wish me well. I thought I'd go to Le Havre next week and see what I'd have to do to register a ship."

"Let me give you letters of introduction, at least. I know a few bankers and officials in Le Havre."

Noël wavered, fighting his pride. It was only a small favor that Adam offered. Still . . .

Adam held up his hand. "Before you refuse me, I should warn you, I'd want a favor in return. I've been reluctant to ask you. But you've given me the opportunity."

Noël eyed him with curiosity. Adam was as proud and independent as he. Perhaps more so. And now to ask for a favor . . . "What do you want of me?"

"The twin game. We haven't played it for a long time."

Noël smiled, recalling many a childhood escapade. He and Adam had become quite adept at taking one another's place, adapting one another's mannerisms to dodge a punishment, take an examination, confound a schoolmaster. "You want me to take your place?"

"There's a meeting in Paris next week. At the Hôtel de Ville. A trade conference with foreign merchants and investors. I've already told them I planned to send Bazaine in my stead. He's as familiar with the complexities of the trade laws as I am. But now there's to be a reception on the final night." Adam's mouth twisted in disgust. "And General Bouchard is expected to put in an appearance. Uniformed, beribboned and bemedaled. There's no way I can avoid it." He shook his head. "But Charmiane is very close to her time. Her last delivery was difficult and premature. I hate to leave her alone."

"I'd do anything for that beautiful wife of yours. You know that. But what am I to say to your friends at the reception?"

"There won't be any. Mostly foreign dignitaries and passing acquaintances. Even if they think something's odd about General Bouchard, they won't be able to discern the reason."

Noël couldn't resist the impulse to tease Adam. "And if someone should become suspicious," he said, "I'll look away and frown and clear my throat. As you do. You're very good at keeping people at a distance when you want to, brother."

A raised eyebrow was Adam's only acknowledgment of his brother's salvo. "Bazaine would be at your side all evening, of course,'' he went on smoothly. ''In case there were people and details you'd be expected to know. Will you do it?''

''My impersonation in return for your letters of introduction?'' Noël hesitated. Adam clearly thought his shipping scheme was worthy, but chancy. He had to agree. To refuse his brother's small offer of help under those circumstances would be the height of proud folly. And if Adam's name could open a few doors... ''Why not?'' he said.

Adam leaned forward in his chair. ''Are you sure?''

Noël laughed. ''I'm sure. To tell you the truth, brother, I'm delighted that you've finally learned to put your heart above duty, at least once in a while. You're becoming more like me every day!''

''I'll go mad, Bazaine. I truly will, if I have to stand here and look solemn for much longer.'' Noël tugged at the stiff military collar of Adam's uniform. It certainly was splendid, with its gold braid and epaulets against the dark blue tunic, its red sash of the Legion of Honor, the breastful of medals. But the music for dancing had been playing for a quarter of an hour now, and his feet in their elegant leather pumps tapped impatiently on the marble floor. ''I think I've met everyone of importance, haven't I? Let me enjoy myself now. I don't need a nursemaid for that. Haven't you something that you want to do? Cultivate a charming supper partner, perhaps?''

Bazaine smiled thinly at what had been meant as a gibe. Married briefly as a young man, he'd long since found more satisfaction in his work. ''Well,'' he said, rubbing thoughtfully at his single good eye, ''there is that Spanish minister you met before. We've had fruitful discussions all this week, he and I. Perhaps I should make sure that we've come to a meeting of the minds. It will make General Bouchard's future correspondence that much more effective. You're sure you don't need me?''

''Name of God, what an old woman you can be! You've pointed out Adam's acquaintances here tonight. Now that we've exchanged greetings, I intend to avoid them for the rest of the evening. And enjoy myself."

Bazaine continued to look uneasy. "With restraint, if you please, Monsieur Noël. The count will have to live with whatever you do tonight."

"I won't gamble, if that's what you mean." Noël glanced around the large reception room of the Hôtel de Ville. It was magnificently furnished, with paintings and statuary and swagged velvet draperies at the windows. The center of the hall was crowded with whirling couples dancing to the strains of a lively waltz. Along the sides of the room, clusters of brightly gowned women laughed behind their fans. "I won't gamble," he said again. "Not when there are more delightful opportunities." He smiled his admiration at a blonde who danced by in the arms of her partner, and was gratified to see her turn her head and acknowledge his smile with a flutter of her eyelids.

Bazaine grunted. "You're the Comte de Moncalvo this evening, lest you forget."

"I'll not forget. Nor compromise Adam's name. But, good God, man, I'm not a saint! And neither should Adam behave like one. A discreet flirtation or two can only enhance his reputation as a gentleman. And then I..." He stopped and stared across the room at a group of people who had just come in. "My faith! Who are those two beauties?"

They were without doubt the most beautiful women in the room, he decided. Not blushing young girls whose dewy charms would pall after the first few minutes of empty-headed discourse, but women. In their early twenties, he supposed. The taller of the two was slender and graceful, with an elegant carriage, dark brown hair and delicate facial bones; the shorter, while not so refined of feature, had a soft, rounded form, a pale peach complexion and a well-shaped head surmounted by bright copper curls. Their gowns were in clear pale tones that complemented their distinctive coloring; the slightly flared hems were short enough to display trim ankles and dainty feet. They were enchanting.

Noël dragged his eyes away from them long enough to survey the other members of their party: an older couple, and a woman in a dark dress who lingered at the doorway, as though she were reluctant to enter the room. The gentleman had fading red hair and an interesting face—pleasant, but somewhat plain. Noël frowned at Bazaine. "Did I meet that man earlier?"

Bazaine shook his head. "No. Josiah Babcock. A banker from the United States. I haven't seen him at many meetings this week. His wife and daughters, they say, keep him occupied with shopping trips."

Noël returned his gaze to the first two women and stared unabashedly. He couldn't remember the last time he'd been so entranced by beauty. Not even Charmiane... He watched in fascination as the young women smoothed their long kid gloves and self-consciously patted their curls. Their cheeks were pink, as though they'd come in from the chill night. "They've only just arrived, it would seem."

"Yes. It's the latest fashion with young women. They come late enough to a soirée to avoid the tedium of introductions, and early enough so the eager gallants are still fresh for dancing." Bazaine's voice betrayed his disapproval of the new ways, which he clearly found the height of bad manners.

Noël took a moment to assess Mrs. Babcock. A plump woman, though still handsome. Her glossy dark hair was set off by several silk roses tucked into the curls. "I can see where the daughters get their looks." He smirked at Bazaine. "Since you seem to know more gossip than I would have believed of you, perhaps you can tell me the names of those two charmers."

"I'm afraid you'll be disappointed, Monsieur Noël. They both have husbands. Left behind in New York, I believe, while Mr. Babcock took his women on the grand tour."

"Husbands? Why should that disappoint me? I told you, I'm only interested in harmless pleasures tonight. A dance. A smile." He waited until Bazaine's stern expression had softened before delivering the coup de grace. "Perhaps a kiss or two," he added innocently, and was delighted to hear

Bazaine sputter beside him. "What shall I do, Bazaine," he said, laughing, "when I'm far away in America and have no one to twit? Now come and introduce me to those women before they get away."

"Hmph! I'll not be a party to any of your mischief, Monsieur Noël."

"What mischief? I have the Frenchman's wicked reputation to uphold. The Americans expect it."

Bazaine made a grumbling sound in his throat, though he couldn't quite keep the corners of his mouth from twitching.

Noël sighed. "But if you'll not oblige me, I'll introduce myself. Mr. Babcock won't mind, I'm sure. Americans don't stand on ceremony as we do. Damn!" he exclaimed. Across the room, two gentlemen had stepped forward and made their compliments, and were now escorting the Babcock sisters onto the dance floor.

"Too late," crowed Bazaine. "It must be your advancing years that have slowed you. The bees on that side of the room have already found the honey. I doubt the Babcock women will have a dance left for you by the time you marshal your waning powers of seduction."

Noël grinned. "*Touché.* I'll..." He stopped, the smile fading from his face. The woman in the dark dress had moved forward to stand beside Mr. and Mrs. Babcock. Noël had ignored her before, in favor of the two beauties. Now he was struck by her appearance. To begin with, she was exceptionally tall and thin. Not slender—that was too flattering a description. Thin, and lamentably so. She moved with grace and dignity, but her thinness made her movements appear slightly awkward; her sharp-boned coltishness reminded Noël of an unsteady foal just learning its way in the world. My God, he thought. Doesn't she eat anything?

Her dark red hair stamped her as another Babcock daughter, but she had been far less fortunate than her sisters. Where they were exquisitely beautiful, she was plain. Her features were regular and ordinary—not unattractive or ugly, to be sure, but plain. Unremarkable. Very much her father's child. She seemed older than her sisters by several years, but it was difficult to tell. Her dark chestnut hair, parted in the middle, was drawn back into a tight knot, without a single curl to soften the harsh line of her coiffure, the angular thrust of her jaw and pointed chin. Her unflattering dress was a deep prune color, simple and unadorned, which only accented her thin hips and modest bosom. She held her mouth in a tight line, and her white-kid-gloved hands were pressed primly together. Everything about her was severe, old-maidish, austere and unbending.

No, thought Noël, not quite everything. Oblivious to her mother chattering beside her, the Babcock woman watched the dancers as they circled the room. It was impossible for Noël to see the color of her eyes from this distance, but their expression was unmistakable. Soft and melting, they overflowed with longing—the aching desire to be on that dance floor, to be held in a man's arms, to dance to the dizzying strains of a glorious waltz. Her pain, her yearning, reached out to touch Noël. He felt a wild impulse to comfort the wounded soul behind that stern façade.

He muttered an oath. Surely it was one of God's small, cruel jokes: in a world filled with mirrors, to give a woman like that two exquisite sisters. "That one, Bazaine. Another Babcock daughter, I presume?"

"The eldest, I believe. Elizabeth."

"Married, like her sisters?"

"No. A spinster."

"Damn. It doesn't seem fair, does it? That unfortunate creature."

To Noël's surprise, Bazaine began to chuckle. "Save your pity. That 'unfortunate creature' has been the subject of lively gossip all week. She's a virago. A hellion, they say. Not even her father seems able to control her. She's quarreled with the porter of her hotel, smashed a plate of food over a waiter's head..."

Noël stared at Elizabeth Babcock with renewed interest. In spite of Bazaine's words, he was certain of the pain he'd read in the woman's eyes. "I don't believe you."

Bazaine shrugged. "She claimed the waiter was insolent. She seems to dislike men in particular. She took her riding crop to an American gentleman who tried to speak to her as she rode in the Bois de Boulogne the other day. And only this afternoon she had a young English dandy tossed out of her hotel suite. She accused him of being a fortune hunter, only after her dowry."

Noël threw back his head and laughed in delight. "By my faith! *That* is a woman I want to meet!"

# Chapter One

He was far more handsome than any man deserved to be.

Elizabeth Babcock scowled across the room at the Frenchman in the dark blue uniform. Handsome and arrogant, with a chestful of decorations and a smug conceit in his smile. He was a man of importance, that was certain. Less than two years after the Battle of Waterloo, only a brave soldier or a skillful politician would have risen to such prominence. There weren't many who had found favor with both Napoleon and the restored king. It was enough to make her hate him at once—that air of male self-confidence and superiority. But, of course, that wasn't the only reason.

"Oh, Bessie! Now he's looking at *you*."

Elizabeth turned and glared at her mother. "That's only because Rose and Caroline have begun to dance," she said, with an edge of bitterness in her voice.

Martha Babcock fluttered her graceful hands. "Oh, don't be foolish. He's speaking to that other man. The one with the eye patch. Perhaps he's just learned that your sisters are married, while you . . ."

"A spinster with a dowry, Mother?"

Mrs. Babcock looked pained. "Eligible, my dear. Merely eligible." She reached over to Elizabeth's gown and smoothed a ruffle on the short puffed sleeve. "I wish you'd consent to wear a padded corset, Bessie. You're so thin. It doesn't hurt to show a well-rounded bosom, you know."

"Don't do that," said Elizabeth through clenched teeth. "I'm quite content as I am. I'm not a side of beef at the market!"

"Perhaps a little bit of crumpled paper in your bodice, then. To show your figure to advantage."

Elizabeth's eyes flashed dangerously. "Stop it! Let a man want me for what he sees, or not at all."

Moving near enough to catch the end of the conversation, Josiah Babcock scowled at his daughter and puffed in exasperation. "Confound it, then let him see you smile once in a while. As your sisters do."

Elizabeth curled her hands into fists. She could feel the fury building in her. Was she to endure it forever? To have Caroline and Rose thrown in her face for the rest of her life? Father never stopped talking about them. Their husbands, their happy lives, their good fortune, their agreeableness as daughters. He never spoke of their beauty, but she could see it in his eyes, the way he compared her to Caroline and Rose. And found her wanting.

On the other hand, Mother seldom spoke of the other girls to Elizabeth, and her eyes took on a misty tenderness every time she looked at her eldest daughter. Somehow that was even worse. Elizabeth felt sometimes as though she were drowning in her mother's pity, suffocating under her mother's useless but well-meaning advice. Poor Bessie. Poor, plain Bessie Babcock. A trial to them in every way. Sometimes she felt so hemmed in she wanted to scream aloud. If only she'd been born a man, with a man's freedom. Five years. Five years before she'd turn thirty and come into her money. Then she could fly away.

But . . . five long years. Sometimes she wondered if it wouldn't be easier just to marry the first man whose head was turned by the prospect of a dowry of ten thousand dollars.

"You have such a sweet disposition," said her mother, her voice soft and tentative with conciliation. "If you'd only allow it to show."

"*Sweet?* Stuff and nonsense! I am as I am," she said, "and with reason. I shall never again endure the humiliation of—'' She took a deep breath, willing herself to remain calm. ''Now, I swear by old Beelzebub, if I must listen to another word tonight about finding myself a suitor, I'll turn on my heel and leave!'' She emphasized her determination by slapping her closed fan against her palm.

Mrs. Babcock flinched. ''Now, now, my dear...'' Her quivering voice trailed off.

Mr. Babcock sighed in helpless resignation. ''Just try to be civil tonight,'' he begged. ''It's our last night in Paris.''

''My stars!'' Mrs. Babcock stifled a gasp with her fan. ''He's coming over here, Bessie. I told you he admired you.''

Elizabeth looked up in alarm. The French officer was ambling toward them, threading his way past the dancers on the floor. He continued to smile in that maddening way. As though he were thoroughly aware of his assets, thought Elizabeth in disgust.

She examined him as if he were a specimen on a scientist's table. He was very tall, and his uniform fitted him to perfection. His face was strong and lean, with a firm jaw and high cheekbones. And he moved like a tiger, with the grace the comes only with the self-assurance of maturity.

Elizabeth felt a cold premonition at sight of him. Rot and nonsense! A foolish weakness. He was only a man, after all. Shallow, lustful, thoughtless, no doubt—like all men. Wanting nothing more than a pretty face, or a fortune. Or both. She couldn't understand why *this* one made her feel uneasy.

He stopped in front of her father and bowed. His eyes were a pale, clear blue, with an odd sooty ring framing the azure. ''Please to forgive my presumption, Mr. Babcock,'' he said in French. His voice was deep and resonant, with an intimacy of tone that belied his formal words. ''I believe you met my secretary this week. Charles Bazaine.''

''Of course.'' Mr. Babcock nodded in pleasure, responding to the man in his rather clumsy French. ''I thought I saw you talking with Monsieur Bazaine a moment ago. You must be General Bouchard.'' He saluted the other man with a bow of respect, then made a proprietary gesture toward his women. ''May I have the honor to present my wife and daughter? Mrs. Babcock. Miss Elizabeth Babcock. And this gentleman, ladies, is the esteemed General Bouchard, Comte de Moncalvo.''

Martha Babcock giggled like a schoolgirl and gave a little curtsy. "General. *Monsieur le comte*. What an honor."

The general took her hand in his. "The honor is mine, *madame*." He bowed over her gloved hand and pressed his lips lightly to her fingers. Then he straightened and turned to Elizabeth. "*Mademoiselle?*" The warm smile deepened.

This was the general's prelude to wangling an introduction to her sisters, no doubt, Elizabeth thought to herself. Well, just because her parents were prepared to make a fuss over him was no reason she had to! "*Monsieur,*" she said coldly, refusing either to extend her hand or bend her knee.

Mrs. Babcock sidled closer and gave her daughter a nudge with her fan. "Bessie, for heaven's sake, make your compliments," she whispered in English.

Elizabeth scanned Bouchard's face. His expression hadn't changed. Clearly the man didn't understand English. She condescended to smile at him. "My mother just asked me to curtsy to you, *monsieur,*" she explained in French. "But we're democratic in America. Every person is considered equal." She held out her hand in a bold gesture, challenging him to shake hands; it was a somewhat unrefined form of greeting that had become increasingly popular in the United States, especially among the men.

She'd meant it as an affront, but he seemed not to notice. Instead, he responded to her offer with alacrity, extending his own hand. He made no concession to her sex, but clasped her hand with all the vigor he'd give a man. His fingers were solid and warm through her glove. "Enchanted, *mademoiselle,*" he said. "But I suspect one would have to search far to find *your* equal." While Elizabeth was still pondering whether he'd meant that as a compliment or an insult, he moved quickly. He released the handshake, pulled her hand to his lips and kissed her fingers with a loud smack. Then, still holding fast to her hand, he stared into her eyes and grinned in triumph.

The scamp! she thought, and pulled back her hand.

"Bessie, please," said her father.

"I please myself, Father," she replied in English. "Why should I bother to be civil to this French peacock with all his decorations?" She smiled sweetly at Bouchard to disguise the venom of her words.

He returned her smile and responded in flawless English. "I can assure you, *mademoiselle,* there is a sad story behind every medal and ribbon."

It took her only a moment to recover from the shock. After all, he wasn't the first man she'd insulted, and he certainly wouldn't be the last. "Pray don't bore me with any stories, *monsieur.* In French or in English."

His blue eyes flickered with momentary annoyance, but he continued to smile. "Rudeness is the same in any language, *mademoiselle.*"

"In plain English," she muttered, "go to the devil, *monsieur.*"

Mr. Babcock reddened at the exchange. With a look of despair toward his daughter, he cleared his throat loudly and made an attempt to restore harmony. "We should make every effort to speak in *monsieur le comte*'s language, Bessie," he said, returning the conversation to French. "After all, we're guests in his country."

"Then we should do all we can to please him," said Elizabeth, in her most honeyed tone. "Shall I run and fetch Caroline and Rose? To meet *monsieur le comte?* I couldn't help but notice how carefully *monsieur* was watching them from across the room." It had set her teeth on edge to see it.

"No," said Bouchard. His voice was unexpectedly serious. Intimate, even. "Had I planned to meet your sisters, I should have done so. I came, rather, to meet you."

Mrs. Babcock began to giggle again. It wasn't often that Elizabeth received such flattering attentions—and from such an important person—and she intended to make the most of the opportunity. She slipped her hand through her husband's arm. "Come, Mr. Babcock. Our presence isn't required here. Isn't that that nice Monsieur Dubois across the room? The one we met in the Tuileries Gardens?" Before Elizabeth could stop them, they had sailed around the dancers toward Dubois, leaving her at the mercy of the Frenchman.

He began with the usual trivialities. "One trusts you are enjoying Paris, *mademoiselle*. Have you been in the city for any length of time?"

Elizabeth tilted her chin at a haughty angle. Perhaps, if she was indifferent to the man, he'd lose interest and go away. "Beg pardon?" she asked. Her voice was as cold as ice.

Instead of being driven off by her frosty response, he chose to misinterpret it. "I fear I've spoken too rapidly for you to follow, *mademoiselle*," he said slowly and distinctly. "Would you be more comfortable if I speak to you in English?" He smiled and switched to her tongue. "*Alors,* we speak in English. I would not wish to put you at the disadvantage."

It didn't make it any easier for her—the realization that his English was more facile than her French. And he clearly wished to emphasize the point, the sly devil, pretending to change languages out of mere politeness. "*Monsieur,*" she said, her eyes flashing. "I would be most comfortable if you didn't speak to me at all!"

"*Mon Dieu,* but your eyes are extraordinary."

"What?" She gaped at him, taken aback by the sudden shift in the conversation.

His voice had become a soft murmur. He didn't seem to be mocking her; his very sincerity left her at a loss for words. "Extraordinary," he repeated. "I wonder I did not notice them at once. Such a beautiful color. Not blue. Nor yet quite purple. There is a flower...*pensée,* we call it. It lives deep in the woods, hiding from the sight of man. But to wander under the trees in the spring, and kneel and push aside a bush...and to see glowing there the violet blossom, the soft brilliance of it...*Pah!*" He laughed ruefully. "My English makes it sound clumsy. But your eyes...they are like that flower. Beautiful and rare."

Elizabeth trembled. Wasn't this how it always began, a man's seduction? With soft words, a gentle voice, a tender earnestness that disguised his true motives? And this Bouchard seemed to be a man skilled in the art—all the more dangerous. She turned her head aside so that he could no longer look at her eyes. Or perhaps it was to keep herself from being drawn into his spellbinding gaze. "Go away, *monsieur*," she said sharply. "I'm not at all interested in your fanciful sallies into botany. Go away."

"*Mais non.* I shall not. I came to meet you in the first place because I wished to ask...do you waltz, *mademoiselle?*"

"Of course I do," she snapped. "We're not all provincial clodhoppers in America."

"Forgive me. I did not choose my words with care. I should have said, *will* you waltz?"

"Certainly not. The knowledge of the dance doesn't necessarily equate with the execution of it. In plain English, I don't want to."

"How strange. Watching you from across the room, I would have guessed that you wished very much to dance."

Was that condescension she heard in his voice? Pity? It was not to be endured! "Even if I did," she said pointedly, "I certainly wouldn't wish to dance with you."

"Are you afraid of me, *mademoiselle?*"

She sneered her contempt. "Afraid of you? Why should I be afraid of you?"

His smile had lost none of its warmth, though his blue eyes twinkled with mischief. "My point exactly. Why indeed? So why do you refuse? I merely want to dance. I do not plan to ravish you."

The rascal! He'd said that deliberately, hoping to embarrass her, no doubt. "Are you surprised to see I'm not turning red at your words, *monsieur?* Like a blushing rose?"

He laughed aloud. "I have already discovered that the rose has thorns. The only surprise for me would be if you accepted my invitation without a fight."

He was altogether too smug for her taste. "What do you mean by that?" she demanded.

"I mean that I think you would quarrel with *Saint-Pierre* at the gates of heaven."

She gave him a withering glance. "Don't be absurd. If I quarreled with Saint Peter, he might deny me entrance. And then I'd have to go to the other place, where I'd surely find you."

He grinned. "A paradox. For how could it be hell for me, if you were there?"

She tapped her foot in impotent fury. The man was impossible! She scowled at him out of the corner of her eye. "Do you mean to torment me all evening?"

"No. I mean to kiss you. Before the night is out."

She gasped in stunned surprise, feeling the blood rush to her cheeks.

He smiled his delight at the effect of his words. "Ah. You *do* blush, I see. Very charming. Very... feminine."

"Oh!" She could scarcely contain her rage. "Because my female weaknesses betray me from time to time is no cause for you to puff up like a crowing rooster! I also blush when the fire is too hot."

He dropped his gaze to her lips, and his voice to a husky murmur. "Then you had best run away for now, Mademoiselle Babcock. For my fire will surely burn you."

She swallowed hard. His eyes had darkened to a smoky blue, like the haze over distant and mysterious mountains, drawing her with a strange power. His lips were sensuous and finely formed—they held the promise of sweet delights. She felt the hot flush creep up again from her bosom to her neck and cheeks, a burning tide that brought with it shame and fear. And that worst of all emotions—the one to be dreaded, to be kept buried in her heart at all costs. Desire. Consciously she fought the forbidden urges. Hadn't her experience with Jack given her enough grief for one lifetime?

"You're a wicked devil and a rogue, *monsieur!*" she exclaimed. She snapped open her fan and turned on her heel, wondering whether she was making a strategic retreat or running for her safety.

He laughed softly behind her. "Until later, *ma chère.*"

An impossible man, she thought, making for the farthest corner of the room. He grinned like an imbecile and called it charm! She watched the dancers from behind the refuge of a marble column, aware that Rose and Caroline hadn't stopped for a moment, obliging a steady stream of admirers on the dance floor. Bouchard seemed to have vanished. It gave her an odd thrill of satisfaction to know that he hadn't immediately gone running to her sisters when he left her side.

Ridiculous! she thought a moment later. Why should I care?

Half a dozen liveried footmen had come into the reception hall and were now moving among the crowd, quietly indicating to the guests the large double doors that led to the room where supper was to be served. Mr. and Mrs. Babcock hurried over to rejoin Elizabeth. She noticed that they diplomatically avoided all mention of the absent General Bouchard.

Leaving the great hall, they passed through a wide corridor; on either side were doors leading to several smaller reception rooms. Through the open doors Elizabeth glimpsed tables set for cards, a wall full of books, sofas clustered for intimate conversation. Just outside the dining salon, the maître d'hôtel waited with a seating list in his hand; as he inquired the name of each guest, a footman was summoned to escort the guest to his place.

"I wonder if you'll be seated with us, Bessie," said Mrs. Babcock. "I know Rose and Caroline will be with that English banker, Mr. Tierney, and his two handsome sons. He told Mr. Babcock earlier this week that he planned to arrange it." She smiled at Elizabeth in that maddeningly tender-eyed manner and patted her hand. "Never mind, my dear. You'll be just as happy with your father and me."

At the door, Mr. Babcock gave their names. "Mr. and Mrs. Babcock. Miss Elizabeth Babcock."

The maître d'hôtel nodded and smiled. "Ah, yes. Mademoiselle Babcock." He snapped his fingers and beckoned to a footman. "Show Mademoiselle Babcock to her chair."

To her astonishment, Elizabeth found herself ushered to the principal table in the room—a sweeping horseshoe-shaped table that sat on a raised platform and looked out upon some two dozen large round tables. Though each table was set with gilded candelabra and giant bowls of flowers and fruits, the principal table was the most splendidly furnished. In the center was a gigantic centerpiece of carved nymphs and goddesses holding swags of fresh roses in their outstretched arms. Before each guest's place was a dazzling array of silver and glassware, and the porcelain plates were a brilliant blue rimmed with pure gold.

Elizabeth scanned the filling room and saw that her parents had been seated at a remote table in the corner, and were staring at her in wonder and surprise. Surely there had been a mistake, she thought. Perhaps she should speak to the maître d'hôtel.

She heard a soft laugh at her shoulder and whirled to see Bouchard smiling down at her. "How fortunate that chance has thrown us together again, *mademoiselle*."

"*Chance*, General Bouchard?"

He tried to look shamefaced, but the grin kept breaking forth. "Well, I did speak to Bazaine, you understand."

"The privilege of rank, no doubt," she said with a sniff. "The great General Bouchard, who commands men and rides roughshod over women."

"Not at all. With or without these epaulets, I tend to do as I want. It makes life so much more interesting, *n'est-ce pas?*" He held Elizabeth's chair for her. "*Mademoiselle?*"

"And if I don't choose to sit here with you?"

He shrugged good-naturedly. "It is too late, in any event. Look over there, where your mother and father are seated. You see the woman in the blue gown? The one with her... How do you say it in English? Her nose out of joint? That is Mrs. Johnson. Her husband—unhappily indisposed this evening—is secretary to Mr. Gallatin, your American minister here in France. She expected to be seated here, you understand. Alas. *Quelle mésaventure.* Someone has made an error." He spread his hands in a gesture of helplessness. "Of course, I have already arranged to send her flowers in the morning, with my apologies on behalf of the entire French delegation. So you see? You may as well sit here. She will not forgive us tonight, no matter what I do.''

It had all been said so charmingly that Elizabeth found her mouth twitching with the urge to smile. He was still a man, and dangerous. But she couldn't remember the last time she'd found anyone's company so stimulating. After a moment's hesitation, she took the chair he held out for her, careful not to appear to be capitulating too readily. He introduced her to the gentleman sitting on her other side, a financier from Bordeaux.

During the first few courses, as the waiters came and went with platters of food, she divided her conversation equally between the two men, discussing such neutral topics as the weather, the risks of sailing across the Atlantic at this time of year, the exquisite color of the hothouse roses that graced the table. She found that if she could prevent Bouchard from touching on personal matters that made her uncomfortable, he was really quite interesting, even amusing. They weren't precisely friends, but at least the truce held. Until the dessert course.

Bouchard watched the waiter take away Elizabeth's half-filled plate. He turned to her and frowned. ''I know that stoutness is out of fashion with the ladies, but, *grand Dieu,* you eat like a bird.''

It was far too personal an observation for a gentleman to make. ''That's none of your affair,'' she said with some heat. ''I eat enough to satisfy my hunger.''

His eyes were soft and warm on her face. ''Poor little one. Do you find no joy in food?'' He put his hand on her thin arm in a gesture of tender sympathy. ''Do you find no joy in life?''

She shook off his burning touch. Drat him! She hadn't let a man get close to her for a very long time. What made Bouchard think he had the right to come knocking on the door of her soul, demanding entrance?

Deliberately she turned and smiled at her other dinner companion. ''Your museums here in Paris hold the finest collections I've ever seen, *monsieur.*'' They discussed the treasures of the Louvre at some length; Elizabeth tactfully refrained from bringing up the point that the museum owed its magnificent collection to Napoleon's having plundered every capital in Europe. "I've spent every day this week on visits to your museums," she added with pride. It had been her one enjoyment—the artistic delights of Paris. While Caroline and Rose shopped and received visitors.

"Not every day, surely," said Bouchard. "I hear that sometimes you fended off your countrymen in the Bois de Boulogne."

"Paris seems to be a city full of gossips," she said, turning to skewer Bouchard with a malevolent stare. "Did they also tell you why I struck the man with my riding whip? He had the effrontery to think that if he smiled and kissed my hand often enough, I wouldn't notice that he was a threadbare, money-grubbing little worm!"

Bouchard laughed. "Why is it I have concluded you do not care much for men?"

"I find you all loathsome, fickle, selfish. Scarcely worth a first glance, let alone a second."

"Ah, but to be glanced at from those lovely eyes...so sparkling in their anger. To be scorned by that curling lip, while one longs to see it smile..."

"Save your pathetic attempts at charm for someone who has no discernment."

If she'd hoped he would crumble before the onslaught of her sharp words, she was disappointed. He threw back his head and laughed in delight. "But you are so much more a challenge for my... How did you say? My pathetic attempts at charm? Well, perhaps I can win you over when we are dancing."

She clenched her teeth in a cold fury. "I will *not* dance with you." It had become a point of honor. Nothing would persuade her to change her mind. She turned her attentions to the man from Bordeaux and steadfastly refused to have anything more to do with Bouchard. When the meal was ended, she slipped out of the dining room and hurried back to the great hall. Perhaps she could convince her father to send for a fiacre to take her back to the hotel.

She wandered the large room as the music for dancing resumed. Her parents didn't seem to be about. After a fruitless search, she concluded that they must be in one of the smaller rooms. She was about to seek them there when she saw General Bouchard bearing down on her, a resolute look on his face. In a panic, she cast her eyes toward a row of gilded chairs against the wall. If she could just reach one of them, sit down... He couldn't be so ungentlemanly as to drag her to her feet in front of the whole company!

Her desperate, hasty glance had revealed her intentions. Bouchard moved more quickly than she, putting himself between her and the safety of the chairs. His mouth twitched. "Our dance, *mademoiselle?*"

Now there was no escaping him. "Why are you doing this?"

"Because you are the most spirited woman I have met in a long time, Elizabeth Babcock."

Oh, he was skillful! Even in the way he said her name—his soft French accent and deep voice making the staid "Elizabeth" sound like a rhapsody. "Is there a purpose behind your empty flattery?" she demanded.

The triumphant grin faded to a smile of warm sincerity. "*Ma chère mademoiselle,*" he said, "there are things I could say that *would* be empty flattery, and we both know it."

Though he clearly hadn't meant his words to hurt, she couldn't help but feel the familiar pain. No. He was honest, at least. He hadn't falsely praised a nonexistent beauty. "You're not as shameless as some," she conceded.

"Is that why the English dandy was shown your door this afternoon?"

She felt naked before him. She'd never before regretted losing her temper when she found it necessary. But confronted by his probing eyes, she wished she could take back this whole week of quarrels and thoughtless outbursts. "Did the gossips of Paris camp outside my door?" she said bitterly. "The English dandy was a fortune-seeking flatterer who seemed to think I didn't own a mirror."

"But a mirror would not capture your fire." He held out his arms. "Come and dance with me. Please."

"I will not."

He stepped closer. Elizabeth noticed the crinkles around his eyes from frequent laughter. "*Mademoiselle,*" he said, "I am going to put my arms around you and take you out onto that dance floor."

She gulped. There was hard determination behind his gentle smile. "If you do, I'll make a scene, I'll—" She found herself stammering, as much from nervousness as from pique.

He shook his head. "Make no mistake, *ma petite.* I will do the waltz with you in my arms. Whether you cooperate or I am compelled to hold and carry you like a stubborn child, it is all the same to me." He shrugged. "I fear the ill opinion of others as little as you seem to. Make a scene, if you must. Let them think me a rascal. What does it matter? Indeed, if you make a scene, I will curse loudly and swear you have insulted all of France. Think of the scandal, *mademoiselle.* An international affront. The disgrace to your country!"

Now he was invoking patriotism? The man was shameless! It only made her more determined to refuse. She tapped her fan against her chin in thought. "If you force me to dance, I shall be powerless against your brute strength, true enough. But I'm quite sure I'll faint in about a moment. In the middle of the dance floor."

He laughed at that. "Faint? *You?* Who would believe it? But if that should happen—alas!—I would be forced to loosen your bodice. For your own good, of course." He dropped his insolent gaze to her bosom.

"You wouldn't!"

"I would."

Yes, he would, she thought. She resigned herself to the inevitable; she nodded her reluctant consent. Immediately, he gathered her in his arms and swept her into the swirling intricacies of the waltz. Still sulking at her defeat, she tried at first to step on his toes, to stumble deliberately, but he was too fine a dancer. It was impossible to resist his strength and grace. She might not be a willing partner—her compressed lips and slight frown attesting to her vexation—but her body responded to the lilting rhythm of the dance, prodded by his firm, guiding hand at her waist.

"This is not so unpleasant, *n'est-ce pas?* Now, if only I can persuade you to smile and truly enjoy the waltz."

"Stuff and nonsense. It's merely a dance."

He scowled. "Merely a dance? No! It is a waltz. It is a dance to feel the joy of life! *Joie de vivre.* The blood stirring in your veins. What are bodies for, if not for pleasure? To feel alive. Three years ago, at the battle of Laon, I took half a dozen saber cuts to my leg. They said I might be a cripple for the rest of my days. I remember only regretting that it would steal from me the joy of the waltz." His blue eyes shone, brilliant sapphires glittering with zestful fire. "Come, Elizabeth Babcock. *Come.* Yield to the dance." His voice was soft and cajoling.

She stiffened in Bouchard's embrace. Yield to me, Jack had said. And what had it earned her? Shame and betrayal and abandonment. She would not be seduced again. Not for an hour. Not for a moment. Not even for a dance. "I'm growing quite weary," she said, in her chilliest tone. "Have you had enough, *monsieur?*"

He stopped abruptly in the middle of the dance floor. "Why do you resist with such stubbornness?" he growled. "*Bon Dieu,* I do not ask you to surrender to me. Only to the dance. You *do* want to dance. I saw it in your eyes when you first came in. You are light in my arms, like a feather. I think you must be a graceful dancer. But when you bend all your energies to anger, not joy, how is one to tell?"

His outspoken brashness was not to be endured. How dare he presume to read her thoughts! "I warn you, *monsieur...*" She dropped her hand from his shoulder in a gesture of finality. Perhaps he would release her at last.

"Look," he said, as the other dancers continued to swirl around them. "Observe those women. There is not a one who has your proud bearing. Come. Shall we set the tongues of Paris to wag again by showing that the difficult Mademoiselle Babcock is also the most wondrous dancer here tonight?"

After this week of disasters and humiliations, it was a challenge she couldn't ignore. And she *was* a good dancer. Even Jack had said so. It was the only time—dancing—when she didn't feel awkward about her height, her gangling arms and legs. She nodded and returned her hand to Bouchard's shoulder. He tightened his hold on her waist and spun her away.

He was a superb dancer. She was caught in the magic of the waltz almost as soon as she gave in to it. She felt as though she were floating over the polished floor, her slippered feet scarcely touching the smooth marble. It was thrilling, dizzying, to spin and twirl in his embrace, to feel the warmth of his hand, the strength of his arm. She was breathless and giddy, the reigning queen of the ball, dancing with the most handsome man in the room. An unexpected laugh burst from her throat; she threw back her head in wild abandon. She fought the impulse to cry out to him, Hold me fast, or I shall fly away in utter joy!

The waltz was ended. She rocked for a moment in his arms, clinging to him while she regained her equilibrium and caught her breath. "Upon my oath," she murmured, "but it surely would have been a tragedy for you to be crippled, Monsieur Bouchard."

He gave a little bow. "A generous sentiment. Thank you for that. You should dance more often, Elizabeth Babcock. It makes your eyes sparkle. They are very seductive when they sparkle like that." He grinned. "And dangerous. A man might fear for his safety."

She had forgotten—in the glories of the waltz—what a rogue he could be. She slapped away his arm to release herself from his embrace. "How is it you manage always to overstep the bounds, *monsieur?*" She marched resolutely toward the door. "Your dance is over. There will not be another. I intend to send for a carriage at once."

He caught up to her as she made her way down the corridor. "*Grand Dieu!* You are a very difficult woman, *mademoiselle.*" He clamped his hand firmly on her elbow.

"Let me go."

He shook his head and quickened his pace to keep up with her hurrying steps. "You surely should be danced with, at least once a week. To keep your eyes shining," he said cheerfully.

She was sputtering in indignation. "Curse you, let me go!"

With a tug on her arm that allowed for no opposition, he steered her into one of the side rooms off the passageway. The room was empty, its several card tables deserted. He pulled her close, holding her body tightly against his own and bending her back over his arm. "You most certainly need to be kissed. And often," he said, and pressed his lips against hers.

She wanted to fight him. She truly did, she told herself. But she was bent so far backward that for the first moment she could only concentrate on trying to keep her balance. And then, as his lips touched hers, it was all she could do to keep from collapsing in a trembling heap upon the floor. He was as skilled at kissing as at dancing. His mouth moved softly on hers, coaxing her lips to yield. Gentle and caressing, with a light pressure that made her shiver. And when she could no longer resist, and allowed herself to respond, he deepened his kiss, sucking her lower lip in between his own two with a passionate ferocity that wrung from her a soft moan. Her head was spinning, her senses in a whirl, as though she were still caught up in the rapture of the waltz.

Blast him! The rage came with the return of her common sense. What was she doing? With an enormous effort, she tore herself out of his arms. "You…you…" There were no words to express her fury—at his audacity, at her weak-willed submission to this overbearing man. She raised her hand to slap his face, but he checked the blow, his hand an iron clamp about her wrist.

He chuckled in delight. "*Formidable! C'est une tigresse!*" At his words, she cried out and tried once more to hit him with her free hand, but he grabbed that, as well. "Oh, no," he said in a menacing tone. "You will not."

Though he continued to smile, Elizabeth felt a moment's thrill of fear. "You may let me go," she said, with as much dignity as she could manage. "I won't try again to strike you. I'm not a fool to risk my person with a brute like you."

He hesitated, wary, then dropped his hands and stepped back. Seeing that she made no fresh moves to attack him, he grinned and folded his arms against the medals on his chest. "You remind me of a horse I had once—a wild spirit that only needs a little taming and gentling."

She was suddenly aware that they were quite alone, and she gave full rein to her sharp tongue. Her voice rose in fury. "Rot your soul!" she cried. "You arrogant, self-satisfied, puffed-up..."

"Bravo!" He applauded with enthusiasm.

"Oh!" She whirled to a shelf and snatched up a small porcelain statue. "You monster, you...you..."

He smiled broadly. "Frog? Is that not what you Americans call a Frenchman, when you wish to offend?"

"You're not a frog," she said, curling her lip. "You're a toad, a snake, a low-minded worm." She raised the statue over her head and aimed for his smirking face.

He pretended to look horrified. "I beg you, no! This is the Hôtel de Ville, *mademoiselle*. The town hall, as you would say in your country. And that is the property of the city of Paris."

"Since you're a man of such influence and importance, General Bouchard, I'm sure you can—"

"Ahem!"

Elizabeth whirled to the loud cough that had come from the open door. Bouchard's secretary, Bazaine, stood there, his one good eye widening in disbelief. "Ahem," he said again. "*Monsieur le Comte!*"

Bouchard had the decency to look shamefaced. "Have I forgotten myself, Bazaine? And disgraced my title?"

"Monsieur le Comte de Moncalvo will survive this momentary lapse, I'm sure," said Bazaine dryly. "I came to tell you that Monsieur d'Arcy wishes to say good-night."

"Yes, of course," said Bouchard. Elizabeth stared at him in surprise. He seemed to have been transformed. The rogue had once again become the general, the proper official who had greeted her father with such formality hours before. He came toward her, reached out and gently removed the statue from her fingers. He took her hand and pressed it to his lips. He paused, scanned her face with his piercing blue eyes, then bowed deeply. "*Adieu*, Elizabeth Babcock," he said. "A pity we shall not meet again. There is a woman hiding behind all that fury, I think. I should have liked to search for her." He straightened and turned. "Come, Bazaine. If I'm to start for Le Havre in the morning, I, too, should begin to say my farewells. Do you agree?"

Bazaine looked relieved. "I do indeed, *monsieur*."

The moment they had gone, closing the door behind them, Elizabeth sank onto a divan, trembling in every muscle and nerve of her body.

She would stay here until the ball ended. She would be safe. Tomorrow they were leaving for the coast, and the ship that would take them home to New York. She breathed a soft prayer. Thank heaven.

She put her hand to her mouth, still feeling the throbbing of her swollen lower lip, the pressure of his kiss. The mad desire to be held and kissed again. Curse him forever. He was the most dangerous, wicked man she'd ever met, the sort of man who would break her heart if she didn't guard it with care.

He reminded her of Jack.

## Chapter Two

The April wind blowing strongly across the East River wharves smelled of spices and tea, of strange lands and exotic ports. It reminded Elizabeth of those carefree childhood years—before Father had become quite rich—when they'd lived above Grandpa's shop at the end of Wall Street. She had welcomed her parents' neglect then, their everlasting preoccupation with Rose and Caroline. While Mother fussed over their dresses and fripperies, and Father worried that he might never earn enough to dower them as they deserved, Elizabeth had been free. Free to wander the docks of South Street from one end to the other, to poke among the bales and barrels of cargo, to perch on a tar-smeared coil of rope and watch an old sailor carve a bit of whalebone into a magical pipe or comb or shoe buckle.

Elizabeth turned from contemplating the harbor of New York to look at her parents and her sister Rose. How smugly contented they were, watching the world pass by the carriage windows as though they were above it all. They had long since chosen to forget those humble years. Father sported a new beaver top hat, and a diamond-and-citrine pin adorned his black silk cravat. Mother and Rose were wearing the expensive spring outfits they'd bought in Paris: Mother in a deep gold satin pelisse with an abundance of frills and pleatings and ribbon loops, Rose in an emerald-green gown of heavy silk that set off her copper curls to perfection.

Elizabeth glanced down at her own new pelisse, purchased at Mother's insistence from the same French dressmaker. The latest color, she'd been told—"tea leaf"—but it was identical to the ordinary shade of grayish green she'd worn in the past. The only difference between this and her old American gowns, as far as she could see, was several thousand francs! And for what? The fashions of the day didn't really suit her. All they did was call attention to her thinness, her unremarkable features.

Rose's sweet, childlike voice cut into her reverie. "Oh, Bessie, do please pull up the carriage window. The breeze is doing such mischief to my bonnet."

Reluctant to lose the harbor scents, Elizabeth hesitated, then obliged her sister. Ah, well. If I looked as attractive in a bonnet, she thought, appraising Rose's green satin hat, with its halo of white lace framing her face, I shouldn't want to be blown about, either. There was no malice in the thought. Though she often felt bitterness and anger at other people's reactions to her beautiful younger sisters, she bore Rose and Caroline no ill will. They had no control over the bountiful gifts nature had bestowed upon them. Any more than she could blame fate for her own lack of beauty.

For what seemed like the hundredth time, Rose pulled off one kid glove and admired the jeweled ring on her finger. "Wasn't Edward sweet to think of me while we were away?"

"So thoughtful," cooed Mrs. Babcock.

Mr. Babcock nodded. "You're a fortunate young woman, Rose, to have found a husband worthy of you."

That was certainly true, thought Elizabeth. Edward Welling was young and dashingly handsome, gentle and kind, with prospects for a fine future. He and Rose had been married for almost two years, yet he still behaved like a bridegroom, doting on his doll-like wife with a tenderness that made Elizabeth's heart ache with envy and longing.

This afternoon was one more example of his thoughtful consideration. While the Babcock family had been abroad, Edward had left his previous place of employment—the countinghouse of a large shipping company—and taken a new position, at a better salary, as a clerk in a small law of-

fice. The family had been home less than two weeks, and
hadn't yet resumed their social obligations, but Edward had
begged them to call upon him at the law firm. Modest, yet
proud, he wished them to see in what esteem he was held by
his new employers. And, in turn, he would be honored to
present his beautiful wife and her family to the senior law
partner.

It had been a pleasant visit, in fine offices on the second
floor of one of the new commercial buildings the Scher-
merhorn family had built on Fulton Street, adjoining the
wharves. And then, stammering like a schoolboy, Edward
had presented the ring to his wife. It had been weeks in the
planning and crafting, he'd said, and had only just arrived.

Rose beamed at her ring once again. "What a surprise.
And in front of all those people! Dear Edward. Isn't it
clever? Caroline says anagram rings are so fashionable now.
I'm sure Mr. Scantlebury was most impressed by Edward's
good taste."

It was indeed clever, Elizabeth had to admit to herself.
The ring, a narrow gold band, was set with four small stones
in a row—ruby, onyx, sapphire and emerald. In the current
mode, the first letter of each jewel was intended to spell out
a name or a tender sentiment.

Mrs. Babcock smiled dreamily. "So romantic of Edward." And then, seeming to realize the effect of her words
on her eldest daughter, she reached forward and patted
Elizabeth's hand, her eyes soft and moist. "Someday, Bessie. Never you fear."

Elizabeth glared at her mother and pulled her hand away.
"I'm sure I can survive without a piece of jewelry spelling
out my name," she snapped. "*Elizabeth* is rather too long
for it. I should need to be trundled about in a barrow in order to wear the blasted thing!"

Mr. Babcock cleared his throat loudly in an attempt to
forestall an outburst from his daughter. "I thought, since
we're here at the waterfront, we might stop in on Mr. Lawson. He's been urging me to come round and talk about
some business with my bank. And I know he's always most
eager to entertain you ladies at tea." Without waiting for a

reply, he rapped on the roof of the carriage with his walking stick and called out to the coachman. "Pike slip. At once."

"I'm sure Mr. Lawson will be sorry not to see Caroline, as well," said Mrs. Babcock. "I swan, since Stephen bought that country house for Caroline, we never get to visit as we used to."

"New York is growing," said Mr. Babcock. "They've already laid out the streets. Stephen's house will be on Sixty-third Street someday. Not so far away, when you think of it like that."

"It is to me," said his wife with a pout. "I don't know why Stephen couldn't have kept their house in the city, as well. So near... Just next door..." Her voice trailed off into a sigh of regret.

"Make my excuses to Mr. Lawson," said Elizabeth. "I don't care for any tea. I'll wait outside until you've finished your visit."

"But you *can't,*" bleated Mrs. Babcock. "Such an insult to Mr. Lawson. His family has been in New York for generations... It isn't proper."

Elizabeth's eyes flashed dangerously. "I'll do as I choose. It's a bright spring day. I'd much prefer to watch the ships in the harbor than sit in a stuffy office listening to an old man talk business. No matter how exalted his family connections!"

Mr. Babcock's voice was mild, but his words held reproach. "Lawson was very kind to you, Bessie. Willing to be a friend to the Babcocks when you needed it."

Elizabeth was unable to meet her father's gaze. She didn't give a fig for propriety, but she knew her obligations. "Yes, of course," she conceded. "I'll only stay outside for a few minutes, and then I'll join you."

Rose stared out the window at the lively port: the ships, the groaning wagons with their goods, the stacks of crates and boxes, the stevedores and merchants and sea captains. She wrinkled her perfect little nose in distaste. "But what can you possibly *do* out there, Bessie? So noisy and dirty."

"I'll watch the ships. I'll..." She turned to Mr. Babcock, her voice suddenly dark with anguish. "Father, why can't I have my dowry now?"

"Bessie!" Mrs. Babcock gave a little squeak. "That money is for when you marry!"

She dismissed her mother with an impatient toss of her head. "I intend to remain a spinster. Well, Father?"

Mr. Babcock rolled his eyes in exasperation. "Sometimes I think you don't appreciate the value of money in the bank, Bessie. My father was just a common soldier when he left London. It took years of hard work and saving before he could afford the Wall Street shop. Years more before I could buy into the bank. Your dowry is for you to make a future with a husband. So that your children can go to fine schools, and have more than I did. That's why my father loved this country. A family—even a lowborn family—can advance through the generations. I won't see you throw away your dowry at twenty-five merely because you haven't the sense to know what's best for you!"

"A man like Jack, you mean?" she cried. The shrill words seemed to bounce against the walls of the carriage. Mrs. Babcock flinched at her tone, and Mr. Babcock swore softly.

Oblivious to the sudden turn in the conversation, Rose looked at her sister. Her innocent blue eyes opened wide with the contemplation of the unthinkable. "But what would you do with your dowry, Bessie, if you weren't married?"

Elizabeth's mouth curled in a sardonic smile. "I'd run away to a strange land. Wear nothing but palm-leaf skirts. Teach heathen children to speak English, and mate with a savage from the South Seas." A foolish, frivolous answer, meant to shock her family. In truth, she really didn't know what made her feel so discontented. Nor what would be the balm for her indefinable pain. She shrugged. "Find life. Adventure."

Mr. Babcock grunted and folded his arms across his chest. "There will be adventure enough for you, miss, when you settle down with a husband and children. And don't tell me there isn't a man out there for you! But for your temper, you'd have had half a dozen suitors since Jack..." He stirred uncomfortably and clamped his mouth shut.

"Left me standing at the altar?" Elizabeth finished. "Do you know it will be five years next month? I think of him when the lilacs bloom in May." Her voice was heavy with sarcasm. "Didn't you tell me that *he* was the man for me? The proper Englishman. A true gentleman. Grandfather would have been so proud. And all the rest of that balderdash."

"He was a scoundrel. Took all of us in. But one man's villainy shouldn't be enough to turn you away from all men."

"Listen to your father, my dear." Mrs. Babcock's smile of pity had returned, curdling Elizabeth's soul. "We have faith you'll find a man worthy of you."

"Oh!" Elizabeth felt as though she'd suffocate if she stayed a moment longer. She pounded on the top of the carriage with a clenched fist. "I'm getting out here. I'll walk the rest of the way and join you at Mr. Lawson's." She swung out of the carriage as the footman opened the door, then turned back to her mother. "If you have such faith, Mother," she said, "why did you and Father find it necessary to double my dowry after Jack left? Five thousand for your beautiful Rose and Caroline. Ten for your plain Bessie, disgraced and abandoned. Clearly damaged goods in the eyes of New York society." She turned on her heel then and stalked away across the cobblestones of South Street. The sea breezes were a welcome relief on her burning cheeks.

The harbor seemed particularly busy this afternoon. Schooners and merchant vessels moved in and out, their decks crowded with passengers and sailors; customs agents frowned over ships' manifests, pacing and shouting orders; street peddlers hawked their wares. Elizabeth was overwhelmed by the sense of people going places. While she was frozen in time, never to breathe again, never to *feel* again, never to be free.

Though she'd looked forward to it, she hadn't felt free on their trip abroad. There had been no adventure, no excitement. Father had concerned himself with meeting important people, Rose and Caroline wished only to shop, and Mother had a horror of every detour, every intriguing side trip, that Elizabeth suggested. Suffocating. Constricting. And then they had gone to Paris. And, Paris being what it was, the word had gone out to every adventurer drawn to the capital by the expectation of wealth that the rich American spinster was, no doubt, panting for a husband.

"Blast them all," said Elizabeth aloud, startling a dirt-smudged street urchin nearby. There was no difference, as far as she was concerned, between European adventurers and American fortune seekers. They were all greedy, dishonest, treacherous men. The enemy, who must never, ever discover in her a spark of feminine weakness. Whom she must keep at a distance with her sharp tongue, as she had managed to do for the past five years. Except—she felt her heart quicken with an unwelcome emotion—except that arrogant Frenchman. General Bouchard had assuredly been more dangerous, maddening and impossible than any man she'd ever met. Including Jack.

Jack. It was astonishing how the memory of him could still bring such pain. She saw him now in her mind's eye, the way he'd looked the night they met: darkly handsome, with his neat mustache and his clipped British way of talking that bespoke pride and confidence and generations of good standing in society. It was even hinted that he could boast Hampshire aristocrats among his forebears. Elizabeth hadn't believed her luck—that of all the young women at Caroline and Stephen's first-anniversary party, she had been chosen by the likes of Mr. John Cochran as his companion for the evening. At twenty, she had already learned to her sorrow that a plain woman was expected to be content with plain, uninteresting men. Caroline, on the other hand, had been married at eighteen to the distinguished, successful, wealthy and thirty-year-old Stephen Stowe. The catch of the season. And Rose, just turned seventeen that February of 1812, had already had so many offers she'd vowed to wait for years before she married—it had been too difficult for the frivolous butterfly to light on one man.

But Jack Cochran had chosen the wallflower, Elizabeth.
The rising young Englishman, with a modest shipbuilding
establishment on the Brooklyn shore, had chosen Josiah
Babcock's plain daughter. He had rushed her off her feet,
escorted her to every fashionable party and ball, brought her
little presents and flowers and sweet poems tied up in pink
ribbons. A splendid man, in every way.

Elizabeth had never known such happiness; she had lain
in bed at night, too buoyed to sleep, thinking it must all be
a dream. The gossips of New York had smiled and whispered behind their fans all that spring. Jack had been so
charmingly obvious and indiscreet in his courtship.

They had fixed the wedding date for the middle of May.
Though there wasn't much time for planning, Mother had
driven herself to make elaborate arrangements, and the great
day had dawned: two hundred guests arriving in a line of
carriages, Trinity Church banked in flowers, the ballroom
of the City Hotel set for a banquet.

The fresh blossoms in Elizabeth's wedding wreath had
withered and collapsed in a sad heap of petals before she'd
allowed herself to admit that Jack would never take his place
beside her at the altar. He was gone. Father and Stephen,
sent to fetch the truant bridegroom, had discovered his
rented rooms empty and bare, his business sold the day before to a shipbuilder from Boston, and only the departure
schedule of a London-bound packet, left carelessly in his
office, to suggest his whereabouts.

Overcome with shame and humiliation, Mother, Caroline and Rose had taken to their beds, while the derisive
gossip swirled around the family name. And when it was
learned that Jack had sold his business at a loss and had left
behind a mountain of debts, everyone had whispered that
something shocking must have occurred between the affi-
anced parties to send Mr. Cochran away so precipitately. For
surely the Babcock dowry would have saved his fortunes.
Father had raged and cursed and sworn he'd pursue Cochran and sue the scoundrel for breach of promise on Elizabeth's behalf, but Stephen had convinced him that the
scandal would die down more quickly if they did nothing.

Besides, Stephen had said, she was probably better off without the blackguard.

Not even the beginning of the war with England in the following month could still the gossips, though a growing anti-British sentiment had gradually turned the prevailing attitude of scorn and derision toward Elizabeth to one of pity.

In the beginning, she'd gone on as she had before the advent of Jack Cochran: going to lectures, taking her solitary promenades along Broadway, riding out on Bloomingdale Road in the glory of the spring. Surely it was an ugly nightmare, and she would waken. But nothing, in the end, could keep reality from sifting into her numbed brain and heart. Through her bewilderment at Jack's treachery, the shame and agonizing pain, she had been driven to search for his reasons for leaving. And to arrive at what must be the truth. It was a secret suspicion she shared with no one.

It was too simple merely to dismiss Jack as a fortune hunter. That might have been his original plan in choosing her—to save his ailing business. But ultimately the fault had been hers. She knew it with a certainty. Not only had she been born with less beauty than her sisters, but nature's lack of generosity extended to those traits that couldn't be seen. Clearly she was deficient in femininity, charm, warmth, lovableness—all those qualities a man sought in a wife. At the eleventh hour, and faced with financial difficulties that marriage and Elizabeth's dowry would have relieved, Jack still had found her not worth the sacrifice of his life, his future, his freedom.

But after several months of blaming herself, Elizabeth's quiet resignation had turned to rage. Against Jack, against all men who used women badly. Her always volatile spirit had become a bristling wall of fury, like the fortresses of old, studded with spears to impale any man who dared to approach her. The gossips said that Banker Babcock would never have enough money in this world to persuade a man to marry his foul-tempered daughter.

"All to the good," she muttered, turning toward the neat brick building at the end of Pike Street that held Mr. Lawson's offices and countinghouse. The Babcock carriage was already there, but empty. Only the coachman and footman remained, chatting idly while they watched a large, weather-beaten sloop maneuver into the slip.

Elizabeth hesitated. It was very tempting to linger and watch the seamen unload their cargo, but her duty prevailed. Mr. Lawson deserved civility. He was her father's friend, though his background—his family had been early settlers in New York—set him socially far above the Babcocks and their nouveau riche ilk. Nevertheless, the day after Elizabeth had been jilted by Jack, Mr. Lawson had called upon Mr. Babcock and offered for Elizabeth's hand in marriage. It had been a warmhearted gesture, and she had been grateful for his gallantry, even as she had refused his charity. She knew his feelings for her were paternal and nothing more. And—given her own state of mind—she knew she couldn't be a loving wife to him. There was no point in ruining both their lives merely to save her reputation. He had never offered again.

The tea party was as tedious as Elizabeth had feared. Her parents couldn't stop fawning over Mr. Lawson, listening with exaggerated attention to everything he said. Rose—in her usual fashion—was so distracted by trivialities that she didn't seem to follow much of the conversation. And Mr. Lawson, a ship owner with several merchant vessels in his fleet, was unusually low in spirits. Business hadn't improved much in the past two years, even though the war with Britain was over and the ports were open again. Perhaps he was getting old, he said with a sigh, touching his graying hair. That topic reminded Mrs. Babcock of an ailing friend, and they spent the next half hour discussing sick friends and the difficulties of aging.

At last the visit was over. The Babcocks stood outside on the cobbled street, waiting for the coachman to bring their carriage round. The nearby sloop had begun to disgorge its passengers. A man appeared at the top of the gangway, shielding his eyes against the glare as he scanned the waterfront. He was quite tall, and his broad-shouldered coat and pantaloons—snugly fitted, in the European manner—left no doubt of the vigor and strength of his form. He wore no hat, and the sun glinted on a casual shock of blond hair. He looked vaguely familiar; as he turned toward the Babcocks, he dropped his hand and smiled in recognition.

"Oh, criminy," whispered Elizabeth.

"My stars, Bessie!" exclaimed Mrs. Babcock. "Isn't that your French general?"

"He's not *mine,* Mother," she said, casting a panicky glance toward the safety of the carriage. "We only sat together at dinner that night."

"And danced," said Rose. "I saw you."

Mrs. Babcock beamed in pleasure. "Danced, too? Bessie, you never told me!" Before Elizabeth could stop her, she had raised her handkerchief in the air and was waving it wildly. "Halloo! *Monsieur!*"

"Oh, for the Lord's sake," said Elizabeth, signaling frantically to the coach, "let's go home!"

"Where are your manners, Bessie?" muttered Mr. Babcock. "The man has already seen us."

And remembers us, she thought with a sinking heart. His smile had been accompanied by that self-satisfied twinkle in his eyes, that look that she remembered so well. He clearly recalled *everything* about that unfortunate night. But as he moved down the gangway and sauntered over to where they stood, she saw that he was no longer smiling. Indeed, his expression was as bland and impersonal as though they were strangers to him.

He stopped in front of Mrs. Babcock and inclined his head. "*Madame?* Did you wish to speak to me?"

His cool formality flustered Mrs. Babcock. "I only wished... That is... *Monsieur*..."

Mr. Babcock cleared his throat. "The Babcocks. We met in Paris. Remember?"

The blue eyes narrowed for a moment. Then the man smiled apologetically and shook his head. "No. I fear not, *monsieur.* Babcock, you say?"

"But you're Bouchard, aren't you?" Mr. Babcock wasn't accustomed to being snubbed. "See here, my man, we met at the Hôtel de Ville."

"Of course. I understand now. Alas." Bouchard shrugged; it was a charming, Gallic gesture. Elizabeth remembered how much she'd hated him that night. "You have mistaken me, *monsieur,*" he went on. "It must have been my twin brother you met in Paris."

"But you're the Count de Moncalvo. The general."

He shook his head again. "Not I. Permit me to introduce myself. I am Noël-Victor Bouchard. Ordinary citizen of France. No titles, no honors. It was my esteemed twin brother you met in Paris. May I infer from your warm greeting that he made a profound impression upon you?"

Blinking in confusion, Martha Babcock struggled to accept this new bit of information. "Your... twin was very gracious to us that night. In particular to Bessie, here."

"Bessie?" Bouchard turned and smiled at Elizabeth. She felt her pulse beating wildly somewhere beneath her left ear. "Then I feel I almost know you," he said. "Will you do me the honor to present me to your family, *mademoiselle?*"

Elizabeth could scarcely believe what was happening. She swallowed her fury with the greatest effort and introduced her family in turn, watching in disbelief as the scoundrel Bouchard maintained his pretense of never having met them before.

"What brings you to New York, Monsieur Bouchard?" asked Mr. Babcock.

"Please. Now that I am in your country, I prefer to be called *Mister* Bouchard. You are democratic here. There are no distinctions, *n'est-ce pas?* I am here on a piece of business that I hope to conclude within a few months. I... Oh, *pardon.*" He turned toward the gangway of the sloop. "The mate wishes me to gather my belongings. You will excuse me?"

"Can you imagine?" said Rose, wide-eyed, as Bouchard strode away. "He looks so much like his twin, the general."

"Twin, my foot!" exclaimed Elizabeth. "By the living jingo, I've never seen such brazen gall in all my life!"

Mrs. Babcock looked uncertain. "Do you think he's really the count?"

"I'll swear to that," said Elizabeth with finality.

Mrs. Babcock sighed. "Well, I'm *almost* sure he recognized us. At least for a moment."

Mr. Babcock frowned. "Now, ladies. I'm sure the general has his reasons for wishing to remain incognito while he's on our shores. If he chooses to play the part of a humble twin brother, it's not for us to question him. Nor to noise it around."

Mrs. Babcock's eyes shone. "Oh, but I wish I could tell Elvira Beedle. Imagine! A real French count and war hero in our midst, and we were the very first to greet him as he stepped ashore. What a feather in one's cap if our set should learn of it!"

"Now, now, Mrs. Babcock," warned her husband. "I'm sure we'll see a great deal of him in the next few months. In the meantime, we must respect the man's desire for anonymity. Perhaps he prefers it for his safety in a foreign land. I remember they said in Paris he's very rich. That could put him at risk with the wrong sort of people. If you *must* tell his secret, you should caution our friends to go along with his fiction. He is never to be called by his title. We must all act as though we believe he's only who he says he is. A simple Frenchman looking to advance a business venture."

"Yes, of course," said Mrs. Babcock, somewhat crushed by the need to exercise social restraint. "But surely the count—"

"Hist!" cried her husband. "He's coming back."

Bouchard moved toward them, carrying a large valise. He had clapped a jaunty top hat on his head, and he smiled in that irritating way that raised prickles on the back of Elizabeth's neck. "I despise swaggerers," she muttered.

Bouchard put down his valise and bowed solemnly. "Mr. and Mrs. Babcock. Mrs. Welling. Miss Babcock." Did Elizabeth only imagine that his voice dropped seductively at her name? "It has been my pleasure to make your acquaintance," he continued. "I trust we shall meet again before I leave your fair city." He glanced down the street, looking for a porter with a pushcart.

"Where do you intend to stay, Mr. Bouchard?" asked Josiah Babcock.

"There is a boardinghouse that has accommodated me on my brief visits to New York in the past."

"Not the City Hotel?" asked Rose in surprise. "Everyone of importance stays there."

"I have no doubt they do," he responded. "But, since I am unimportant and wish to save my money, I prefer a modest boardinghouse."

His pretended humility was enough to make Elizabeth gag.

"See here, why don't you stay with us?" said Mr. Babcock, to Elizabeth's horror. "We have a large house on Warren Street, near City Hall Park. Convenient to your business, I'm sure."

Mrs. Babcock clapped her hands together in delight. "Oh, yes! What a clever idea, Mr. Babcock. We have a fine spare bedchamber, Mr. Bouchard. I'm sure you'll be quite comfortable there for as long as you're here in the city."

Bouchard frowned in perplexity. "But it is such an imposition. I have been in your country before, and have grown accustomed to your American hospitality, but you are too kind."

"If it would make you uncomfortable," said Elizabeth quickly, "perhaps you ought not to consider the invitation after all."

Mrs. Babcock gasped. "Bessie! For shame. Mr. Bouchard might get the idea that you don't want him."

Bouchard ducked his head to hide a smile, and when he looked up at Elizabeth, only the sparkle in his eyes betrayed his amusement. "Why should I ever imagine such a thing? Still—" he turned to Mr. Babcock with a genuine smile of gratitude "—your kindness is extraordinary."

Mr. Babcock looked pleased with himself. "Perhaps I wish to repay your brother's kindness in Paris. He particularly honored our daughter Elizabeth with his presence during much of the evening. He even seated her next to him at the principal table. A singular honor. Eh, Bessie?" Mr. Babcock stared hard at Elizabeth, waiting for her to remember her manners and be polite to their guest.

Elizabeth clenched her fists so tightly that she felt the stitching give way on one of her gloves. To think of this man a guest in her parents' house—! For weeks, possibly *months*. She disdained to smile. "Your brother's behavior was...consistent with that of his sex," she said contemptuously. Let him take that for what he would!

He raised a quizzical eyebrow, but said nothing.

Mrs. Babcock leapt hurriedly into the awkward silence. "What my daughter means to say, I'm sure, is that your brother behaved in every way like a gentleman."

This time Bouchard didn't bother to hide the smile. "I'm very pleased my brother's conduct met with *mademoiselle's* approval."

*Approval?* Of a stolen kiss snatched by a brute and a ruffian? Elizabeth felt as though she'd explode in another minute.

Mr. Babcock indicated the coach that now awaited its passengers. "Shall we go?"

There was room for Bouchard's valise next to the footman in back, but the carriage had been designed for four passengers, not five. Mr. Babcock proposed to sit up front, beside the coachman, a suggestion that filled Elizabeth with abhorrence. Since Mother and Rose were already seated side by side, that meant *she* would have to sit next to the vile Bouchard.

"I'll sit outside," she cried, and scrambled up beside the coachman. "I prefer the fresh air."

Mr. Babcock huffed and scowled up at her. "Must you always be difficult, Bessie?"

Bouchard grinned. "No. *Mademoiselle* is wise. It is indeed a fine day to take in the air." He tossed his hat inside the carriage, reached up and swung himself easily into the seat beside Elizabeth. The coachman was small and the seat was wide, but they were dreadfully crowded all the same. Bouchard pretended not to notice how closely their bodies were pressed together, nor how Elizabeth had begun to quiver. He smiled and leaned his head close to hers. "Comfortable?" His voice was low and intimate, with only a hint of mockery. Before she could reply, he frowned, leaned close again, and took a deep and audible sniff. "Superb! A lovely perfume, *mademoiselle.*"

"It's just soap," she snapped.

"But it is very pleasant." He inhaled again. A lock of his hair tickled her cheek. "You chose a soap that gives you the fragrance of a summer meadow. *Très charmant.*"

Elizabeth stiffened. If she held herself quite rigidly on the ride home, perhaps she wouldn't notice the warmth of his arm against her shoulder, the strength of the hard-muscled leg pressing nonchalantly into her thigh.

With a look of wild desperation, she gazed at the team of horses as the coachman cracked his whip over their heads. She had never before prayed so hard for a speedy trip home.

# Chapter Three

"Good morning, Mr. Bouchard." The two matrons simpered up at Noël from beneath their parasols.

Noël reined in his rented horse, tipped his hat and smiled back at them. "*Mesdames.*" He glanced down the length of Broadway, white with drifting cherry blossoms and warmed by the May sunshine. "A beautiful day for a stroll. A day matched only by your charms," he added, and was pleased to see the two women turn to each other and giggle like country maidens.

American men, he thought wryly, don't know the first thing about making their women feel like women. Perhaps it was the rawness of this new land that made them rough and crude. Even the educated ones, the ones with money and power, seemed more comfortable in the company of men—with their chaws of tobacco, their whiskey and water, their unending talk of business and politics—than among the civilities of the drawing room.

He replaced his hat, nodded again at the ladies and resumed his ride. Still, he mused, when it came to hospitality, the Americans had no equals. He still couldn't quite believe it. During the past five weeks in New York, he'd scarcely had to put his hand in his pocket for a single expense that wasn't related to his business. Not only had the Babcocks anticipated his every need, but their friends had received him into the social life of the city as though he were visiting royalty! There had been balls and soirées and supper parties, evenings at the theater and afternoon concerts.

He'd been catered to, fawned upon, sought out by the men and gushed over by every female old enough to wear her hair up. He'd managed—once—to take the Babcocks to dinner at the City Hotel at his own expense, which made him feel a little less beholden to them, at least.

But perhaps, he thought with a sharp prick to his pride, he was paying for all that adulation and attention in a way that his hosts couldn't begin to guess. Far too often he'd noticed he was introduced as the twin brother of the great General Adam Bouchard, Comte de Moncalvo—as though the family connection alone were enough to make him the success of the season, with hostesses vying with one another to have their invitations accepted by him. For a classless society, the Americans were certainly preoccupied with class! He tried to tell himself it didn't bother him, but it wasn't completely true; maybe he was still too sensitive to the reminders of Adam's success, and his own unfulfilled expectations for success.

"*Grand Dieu!*" he swore aloud. Such pessimism on such a fine day! In truth, he should feel as confident as he did when he sat down to a game of cards. The gamble seemed to be paying off. Everything was going well for him, so far.

It had begun in Le Havre, with Adam's connections. With no more than an idea and his enthusiasm, he hadn't been able to secure an out-and-out loan, of course. But several French bankers had been sufficiently impressed with his scheme to give him letters of credit for a few New York banks, guaranteeing their financial support once they were assured that he could take possession of the ship and repair it. He'd even found an importer of furs in Le Havre who was eager to supply French hatmakers with good beaver pelts. It had taken all his charm and powers of persuasion, but he'd convinced the man to invest hard cash in the venture. Between that and the money he'd been putting aside from his gambling profits, he knew he could manage the four thousand dollars that Captain Steenboch had said the battered old ship would cost to buy. He'd get the repair money in New York, God willing.

Not that he wasn't confident. Even before he'd left France, he'd sent a message on to Steenboch in New York, telling him to start making plans. He'd even included a letter to be forwarded to a trading post in Ohio—to a fur trapper he'd met on his travels—asking if he had pelts to sell. By the time he'd arrived in New York, the ship had been waiting. A beauty. Or it would be, when the hull was emptied of water and the repairs were made. A pretty little schooner of a hundred and fifty tons. He'd almost wanted to name it *Martin,* but that had seemed premature and impolitic; he'd settled on *L'Espérance. The Hope.*

Noël urged his horse to a comfortable trot and beamed in remembered satisfaction. It had taken no time at all for him to secure investors here in New York. The ship was well on the way to becoming seaworthy. He'd spent this morning with Steenboch at the shipyard, admiring the sleekness of the hull, her trim lines. Steenboch surely had an eye for a bargain, that wily old Dutchman! He might still need another loan before he was through; he probably couldn't afford a full cargo of furs, and he'd need to buy other goods and supplies, and hire a crew. But he wasn't worried. If all went well, he'd be able to prove to himself once and for all that—despite *Maman*'s warnings that he'd come to a bad end—he could be as successful as Adam.

He pulled out his pocket watch. Good. Just after noon. He had time to stop at a tavern for a bite of food before heading out of the city to the Stowes' country house overlooking the East River. They'd been there for a week now. He and the Babcocks, and their daughters Rose and Elizabeth. Rose's husband, Edward, had had to stay at his job in the city all week, but—this being Friday—he was expected for the weekend. Bearing presents, no doubt. He treated his wife like a princess, and never failed to spend a great deal of money on her. Even to Noël, with his carefree ways, it seemed shortsighted and wasteful: the Wellings were still living with the Babcocks, until Edward should become more established.

The Stowes were gracious hosts, with all the grace that money could buy, but Noël didn't think he liked them very much. Stephen Stowe had made his fortune importing tea, but he made it very clear he held both the English and the French responsible for the embargoes and blockades and privateering of the past dozen years which had so adversely affected his business. On the whole, Noël found him unpleasant—sour and sullen much of the time.

And jealous of his young and beautiful wife. Caroline Babcock Stowe was exquisite. Probably the most magnificent creature Noël had ever met. Tall, dark-haired, cleareyed, with a perfection of features that was nothing short of miraculous. It was a pity she knew it. She behaved as though she expected the world to stop spinning on her account. And she flirted outrageously, seeming to demand the attention she felt was her due. But sometimes, when Noël caught a glance of Stephen Stowe's face, dark with anger, he wondered if she wasn't flirting simply to make her husband jealous. *He* certainly hadn't made an effort to encourage her. Despite her beauty, he was beginning to think there was less to her than met the eye.

As for Rose, he had dismissed her almost at once. He found childish innocence cloying. And how long could a man look at a beautiful face without wishing there were something behind it?

Elizabeth, now . . . by God, what a challenge! Everything to her was cause for a battle. It had kept his blood stirred all these weeks, fencing with her. The temper, the sharp tongue. A challenge that taxed his wits. Certainly he wasn't about to cringe, as her mother did, or back away in exasperation—her father's favorite dodge. And his instincts told him that to engage her in a shouting match—as Stephen occasionally did when she touched upon topics he thought were beyond a woman's purview—was a waste of time and energy.

In an odd way, he rather enjoyed her spirit, foul-tempered though she could be. He sometimes wondered what had made her that way. Certainly her animosity toward fortune hunters was out of all proportion. After all, though a Frenchwoman always came with a dowry and had no choice of husbands, an American woman, dowry or not, had more freedom to reject her suitor if she chose. But Elizabeth never gave any man a chance. She attacked before she even knew the enemy. He'd remarked it more than once in the past few weeks. The woman seemed to feel that the very fact of his masculine gender was enough to condemn a man, without even finding out if he was after her money.

To outwit her had become a game with him. They attended a concert—he secretly arranged with an usher to sit beside her, grinning as she fumed. They went to a ball—he maneuvered her into dancing with him. And, though she always made a point of telling him that he didn't dance nearly as well as his brother, the count, he knew she enjoyed the dance. And when they went to the horse races at the New Market on Long Island, he'd wait until Elizabeth bet on a horse before placing his own bet on the same animal. She never failed to change her wager—most often to her loss—just to disagree with him.

He reined in his horse at a promising-looking tavern on Bloomingdale Road. As long as he reached the Stowe estate before two, he'd be in time. He chuckled softly. Poor Elizabeth Babcock. She must be completely bewildered by now. All this week, when she'd set out on a daily ride, he'd joined her, blithely ignoring her frowns, her protests. After the third morning, she'd arbitrarily changed her hour of riding, clearly hoping to avoid him. And still he'd be waiting for her just outside the stable. Morning, afternoon. What difference? He laughed aloud. It had cost him a whole dollar to bribe the Stowe stableboy to keep him informed of every change in her plans.

It was wicked of him, but he delighted to see the look of surprise and outrage on her face. Her fury usually lasted through at least ten to fifteen minutes of sharp-tongued insults. It kept him quick and ready, matching her riposte for riposte. He wasn't sure he didn't goad her on just to see her eyes sparkle with life when she was vexed.

Then—like a wild horse broken to the saddle—she'd settle down and they'd ride together. And he, who had spent half his life with horses and riders, in and out of the cavalry, would watch in awe and admiration as that thin, awkward woman became a sylph in motion. She took the jumps straight and tall, she held her saddle with ease, she controlled the horse with firm hands and a murmured word or two. It always surprised him, that strong gentleness in her. She was a creature of constant revelations, forever catching him unaware with something new and unexpected in her personality.

He'd thought these busy weeks would be difficult, with his unaccustomed business worries preying on his mind. But, thanks to Elizabeth Babcock, the days had flown by. He was having a wonderful time.

He glanced up at the sky. High, wispy clouds lay like gentle feathers across the blue vault. It would rain tonight, perhaps. Certainly tomorrow. They wouldn't be able to sit on the lawn after supper, watching the boats pass on the river. Maybe he'd challenge Elizabeth to a chess match. She was an intelligent player, but if he could get her to lose her temper it would cloud her judgment.

He laughed again. It was an unfair advantage, but...what the devil! Those violet eyes were magnificent in fury.

"My riding crop, Billy, if you please." Elizabeth adjusted herself in the sidesaddle and arranged the skirt of her light brown riding habit so that it wouldn't catch her in its folds, should she fall. She tucked a stray wisp of her dark red hair under her silk toque and reached down for the proffered crop.

She loved riding in the country. The long meadows, the dusty country paths, the shady groves. It wasn't the same in the city, clattering over the cobblestones and dodging carriages and wagons merely for a few moments of solitary pleasure out on Bloomingdale Road. She smiled; it was a grin of smug contentment. And today she'd particularly enjoy her ride in the country. Without that devil of a Frenchman!

Why he'd suddenly taken it into his head to ride with her this week was more than she could imagine. Especially since she'd made her feelings about his company quite plain that first morning. And still he'd persisted. She chuckled softly, ignoring the groom's look of surprise at her unaccustomed good humor. Today she'd outwitted that scoundrel Bouchard. Be dashed if she hadn't! He didn't expect to return until four, he'd said. By which time she would have taken her ride and returned. Alone. She'd tell him tonight after supper and watch him nurse his defeat.

As usual, Bouchard was seeing to his business down at the shipyard today. Well, good riddance for a few hours. The less time he had to spare, the less opportunity he had to torment her.

She gave a light tap to her horse's flank and moved out into the sunshine. She followed the fence enclosing the stableyard, went through the gate and turned west, away from the river. There were orchards in that direction. The air would be sweet with the scent of blossoms. She could...

"Good afternoon, Mademoiselle Babcock."

Elizabeth jumped in the saddle and swung her head around. Noël Bouchard sat his horse not ten paces behind her and grinned like the devil himself. "How did you do that?" she cried.

He was clearly pleased with himself, the wretch! "The coincidence of our meeting?" he asked. "What does it matter? I am here. Shall we ride together, since we seem to have met so fortuitously?"

"Fortuitously?" She tapped her riding crop angrily against her gloved hand. "You *knew* I'd ride at two!"

He opened his eyes wide in clear blue innocence. "*Mais non.* How could I know?"

She didn't know whether she was angry at his impudence or frustrated at having been outwitted once again. She thrust out her lower lip in a sullen pout. "I explicitly waited until after you'd said you were going to be in the city all day. Only then did I tell Billy privately to ready my horse for two and—" She gasped. "Billy! Blast his treason. *He* told you! I'll..."

Drawing his brows together to offset the merry twitch of his lips, Bouchard interrupted her. "No, no. Have pity on the boy. He only told me under extreme duress."

That alarmed her. Despite her pique at Billy's betrayal, she was really rather fond of him. A good boy. "You brute," she sputtered. "Duress? Did you hurt him?"

He sighed and shook his head. "It was worse even than that. I forced him take money in exchange for the information." The grin broke through unchecked.

"Oh!" she sputtered, then changed her tack. Perhaps she could shame him with his dishonesty. "You said you'd be gone all day," she said accusingly. "At least till four."

"*Grand Dieu!* Do not believe a Frenchman, *mademoiselle*. We are wicked prevaricators, all."

His enjoyment of his game only added to her fury. "Heaven alone knows why my parents decided to take you in," she snapped. "If it were up to me, I'd turn you out neck and heels!"

He frowned, his blue eyes as dark and shadowed as the distant clouds beyond the sunshine. She didn't believe the emotion for a minute. "Why do you not like me, Elizabeth Babcock?" he asked.

Why, indeed? On the whole, he'd been gracious and kind all these weeks. Thoughtful in his concerns for her. Then why did she fear that he was laughing at her? That his gentle teasing was a cover for darker, more selfish motives? Like every other man's. "Why have you insisted on dogging me all this week? Why don't you ride with Caroline or Rose?" Her words were like a sharp attack, thrown up to challenge him. Or to protect herself.

"Does it not occur to you that I might enjoy to ride with you? You are a superb horsewoman, *mademoiselle*."

He *was* mocking her. She'd have sworn to it. "Do you compliment all the women you ride with?" she said in disgust.

"*Mon Dieu.* All the women? Is that jealousy I hear in your voice?"

"Jealousy?" She snorted. "You flatter yourself. Merely because every ninny in New York has thrown herself at your feet these past weeks is no reason for you to think that I'd count myself among them! With or without your insincere compliments.'' The very thought of the legion of beautiful women he'd attracted was enough to turn her stomach.

This time the frown was genuine, tinged with impatience. ''You think it an insincere compliment, Mademoiselle Babcock, when I say you ride well? Pray do not insult me. I spent too many years in the cavalry, among good riders and bad, not to recognize skill at manège when I see it. Now, if you can stop behaving like a prig for a little while, I should like to ride with you.''

She opened her mouth to protest—loudly—then reconsidered. She *had* behaved foolishly all this week. It was only a ride, after all. And she'd allowed her annoyance at being bested by the man to keep her from admitting the truth to herself. She liked riding with him. She enjoyed his company, even when he goaded her into a temper. These past few weeks she'd found herself listening for his footsteps on the stair of her father's house, eagerly awaiting the zest with which he burst into a room and filled it with life, with his spirited presence. And when he looked at her, smiled in that intimate way, it was easy to pretend for a few moments that plain Bessie Babcock had captivated the most handsome, eligible man in all of New York.

Still, it rankled that he'd won again today. Especially since he was clearly aware of her vexation. She nodded coldly, regally. ''You may ride with me, Mr. Bouchard. I shall permit it.''

A raised blond eyebrow, arching into the broad expanse of tanned forehead, was his only acknowledgment of her haughty tone.

They set out on their ride, crossing a broad meadow and climbing a hill to the top of a wide plain. Spread before them were fields and orchards and stands of trees. The oak tree buds, slowest of all to welcome spring, were just breaking, and the apple trees had begun to show pink clusters. The cherry and pear trees were already in full bloom; the warm air was fragrant with their aroma. The breeze had freshened, and some petals had begun to fall, drifting before them like a pale pink-and-white carpet laid down for their pleasure.

Elizabeth glanced at Noël Bouchard out of the corner of her eye. He rode like a man born to the saddle, with an easy, elegant bearing that still retained an aspect of his military training. She frowned. Usually his enjoyment of their ride was written plain on his face, but today his expression, beneath the shade of his top hat, was somber and distant. She felt an unfamiliar pang of remorse. She'd scarcely been civil to him, and perhaps his business concerns weighed upon him. Though it certainly wasn't what she was accustomed to, she made an effort to say something nice to him. "You're a fine rider yourself, Mr. Bouchard. The cavalry, you said? One can see it in your bearing."

He turned and smiled, and the sun seemed to shine more brightly. "A compliment from you, Elizabeth Babcock? That is something to be treasured. Thank you."

Somehow she knew he wasn't teasing her this time. It emboldened her to continue the conversation. "Did you see any of the great battles we read about here?"

"Yes. All but Waterloo. My regiment was disbanded in 1814, and I had left France and the army long before the emperor's return from exile. But I fought at Wagram, Borodino, Moscow, Leipzig. And many others that history will speak of, no doubt."

Elizabeth stared in awe and envy. The names were magic to her. She had followed the course of the Napoleonic Wars in the newspapers, filled with longing to know the excitement of life that a man took as his due. And Bouchard had been there. Her eyes shone at the thought. "It must have been thrilling!"

The expression he turned to her was dark and sad. "It was…inhuman," he said softly. "I do not like to talk about it."

"Oh, but …"

He laughed; it was a gentle laugh, deep with understanding. "I suppose war seemed thrilling to me, as well, when I was twenty-five."

She felt her face burn. Twenty-five. A spinster's age. It had become a source of embarrassment to her. To be twenty-five and unmarried. Other girls married at eighteen or nineteen. "How do you know my age?" she demanded.

A careless shrug. "I asked."

"That was presumptuous of you. Not gentlemanly at all!"

He grinned. "I know."

The impudent dog! His knowledge of her age gave him an advantage that made her uncomfortable. "How old are you?" she asked, scowling.

"How old do you think?"

With a look of withering contempt in her violet eyes, she pretended to assess him. Of course, she'd long since decided he was probably about Stephen Stowe's age. Thirty-five or so. But she was still seething at his effrontery. To ask a woman's age behind her back! Only this arrogant Frenchman would have the gall. And now he was smiling in self-congratulation. "I think you're..." She hesitated. "You're close to fifty," she announced in clear tones.

He looked neither surprised nor insulted. He threw back his head and began to laugh. "Then I'm old enough to be your father. *N'est-ce pas?*"

She rolled her eyes. "Heaven protect me."

"You would not like me as a father, Elizabeth Babcock. I would send you to your room without supper every time you had a tantrum." He ignored her gasp of outrage and shook his head. "No. That would not be wise. You are too thin to go without supper." He grinned. "But there are other ways to tame a headstrong child. At least in my country. A firm hand, vigorously applied... Do you understand me?"

She understood him perfectly. And—despite his continued good humor—the mental picture his words conjured up was too humiliating to be allowed without a challenge. "How do you say 'pig' in French, *monsieur?*" She raised her riding crop and swung it at his face.

Laughing, he dodged the blow, and the whip merely caught his top hat and knocked it from his head. His blond hair glinted in the sunlight. "A most difficult child," he said genially, and smiled with the warmth of an indulgent parent.

She felt her insides turn to jelly. He was beautiful and seductive and she hated him. This time, the slash of her whip caught his horse's flank. The animal snorted, reared, and took off at a gallop through the orchard. Elizabeth watched it careening among the trees with a surge of satisfaction that turned to unease in another moment. Bouchard was a skilled horseman. Why didn't he rein in, control the beast?

Just then he rocked unsteadily in the saddle and cried out—a shout of surprise and helplessness. His boots slipped out of the stirrups, and he thrust wildly with his feet to regain his toehold. He turned once to glance in dismay at Elizabeth, threw up his hands and toppled to the ground.

Oh, criminy! thought Elizabeth. What have I done? He lay very still on his back, long limbs spread amid the green grass and pale flower petals. Filled with dread, Elizabeth urged her horse forward. Perhaps he'd hit his head. Maybe he was dead! She drew near and slid from her saddle, bending over him in concern. His eyes were closed, the long lashes brushing against the sharp planes of his cheeks. "Mr. Bouchard!" she cried. "Noël."

He opened his eyes and frowned as though he were in pain. "How sweetly you say my name, Elizabeth," he whispered.

"I'm so sorry. I didn't mean..." She stopped abruptly as the look of pain became a grin of triumph.

"In the cavalry," he said, in a normal voice untouched by distress, "I had one horse I trained to fall *with* me. It was very convenient in the middle of a battle, with cannonballs flying about."

"What?" she shrieked. He'd been shamming, the villain! She raised her fists to pound on his chest. He grabbed her wrists and rolled over with her, pinning her beneath him. She felt her riding hat crush against the back of her head. "Let me go," she cried, writhing furiously.

Bouchard was still smiling. "Since I'm only thirty-nine, and certainly not old enough to be your father, I am most fortunate. There is no better way to tame a woman than with a kiss.''

She ceased her wild struggles and stared up at him, feeling the panic build in her. Why did he have to be so perfect? His face, his deep, stirring voice. His mouth. He'd kissed her in Paris, and she'd dreamed of it for weeks, yearning—like a moth drawn to a flame—for that which could destroy her. Oh, treacherous body that filled with desires even as she fought to deny them! There was no life, no future, for her in submitting to a man. He would take his kiss and stir her hungers, then go away. What else would he want? She had no illusions. There was nothing else she could offer a man—not beauty or charm or any of the things other women could offer. She was a moment's amusement. A little sport, and nothing more. ''Please don't,'' she whispered.

The smile faded from his face, to be replaced by a look of gentle bewilderment. A cherry blossom drifted from an overhead tree and alighted on her cheek. He bent low and blew it away. His soft breath made her shiver. He frowned. ''Who are you, Elizabeth Babcock?''

''Let me up. Please.''

He released her wrists, stood up and helped her to her feet. The concern on his face was too close to pity.

Pity. It was the one thing Elizabeth couldn't endure. Tinder to her inflammable temper. She slapped at his steadying hands. ''Let me go, I said!'' She turned to her horse and mounted it quickly. She felt for her riding hat, pulled it from her head and tossed it at Bouchard's feet. ''And you've ruined my hat, you beast. Don't they teach you manners in your country?'' She kicked at her horse and galloped off.

Noël watched her ride away, his brow furrowed thoughtfully. Strange, he thought. Most women in those circumstances secretly longed to be kissed, pretending distress or pique only for the sake of propriety. At least until the first kiss. After which they usually were so eager and forward that he had to decide how far he himself wanted to go. There had even been a few—*very* few, thankfully—who had been genuinely angry at being forced to surrender to a kiss.

But Elizabeth... He'd expected a battle royal. At the very least, a stream of insults. Instead, she'd lain beneath him like a wounded animal, trapped and fragile. Was it fear he'd read in those beautiful eyes? And if so, why? Was she so innocent that a mere kiss frightened her? His experiences had taught him that American women, by and large, were less comfortable with the ways of the flesh than Frenchwomen. But even by those standards, Elizabeth was uncommonly apprehensive.

He'd heard it said that prudery often made women seem more cruel than they were. Perhaps a fear of men, a fear of her own womanliness was the source of Elizabeth's rage and hostility. Growing up with those exquisite sisters, with parents who tried to ignore her, how could she have learned to value herself, let alone to value herself as a woman?

*"Grand Dieu,"* he muttered aloud. Why the devil should he care? He had his future to think of. He had Martin to think of. His son. He had no time for a woman. Most especially not a bad-tempered one who was beginning to get under his skin, like a burr on his saddle. No. He would put her out of his mind.

He looked up at the sky. The clouds were beginning to gather, dark and purple and stormy as Elizabeth's haunting eyes. It would rain tonight.

## Chapter Four

"Will you have more wine jelly, Noël? It's one of my pet recipes that I gave to Mama's cook." Caroline Stowe smiled across the dinner table at Noël Bouchard, her soft eyes shining.

From her seat at the end of the table, Elizabeth watched her sister with a combination of envy and admiration. How fine Caroline looked today, with her dark hair framing her delicate features, her expensive gown accenting a fashionably rounded bosom. How dazzling the smile she gave to Bouchard. Elizabeth frowned at a sudden thought. But when had she begun calling him "Noël," her voice soft and musical as she said his name?

"Thank you, no, Madame Stowe," said Bouchard. "It was delicious, but I am content."

Well, thought Elizabeth with an odd kind of relief, at least he's not returning the familiarity. Not with Stephen glaring at him, at any rate. They were gathered in the large dining room of the Babcock house on Warren Street, celebrating Mrs. Babcock's forty-fifth birthday with a small family dinner. Edward Welling had been excused early from his position at the law firm to join his wife, Rose, at the festivities, and Stephen and Caroline had made one of their infrequent trips into the city in honor of the occasion.

"Some roast quail, then?" Caroline persisted. "I swan, you've eaten so little you'll soon be as skinny as Bessie."

"I have had quite enough, thank you!" Bouchard's voice was unexpectedly sharp.

Elizabeth looked at him in surprise. It wasn't at all like him to answer in such a rude way. Couldn't he see that Caroline was only trying to be gracious? And now she was hurt, that was clear. Her pale lips trembled. She moistened her napkin in her glass of water and dabbed delicately at her temples. Stephen, sitting to her right, coldly ignored her distress. Poor Caroline, thought Elizabeth. With her charm and beauty, she didn't deserve to be treated badly by a single man, let alone two.

Edward signaled to the servant and helped himself to another portion of quail. "If you worked as hard as I do," he said to no one in particular, "you'd get mighty hungry. Mr. Scantlebury is a regular slave driver."

Seated beside him, Rose smiled at her husband; it was a smile of warmth and adoration. "You poor dear." She patted his hand.

What a handsome couple they are, thought Elizabeth, remarking once again how Edward's dark good looks complemented Rose's flame-haired beauty. And as devoted to each other as the day they'd married.

Mr. Babcock frowned. "Scantlebury's a decent man, Edward, and don't you forget it. Now that President Monroe has taken the oath of office, there's talk that Scantlebury might have a place in Washington politics. He grew up with Vice President Tompkins right here in New York."

"I didn't know that." Stephen Stowe leaned forward in his chair, his shrewd and intelligent eyes narrowing. With his sharp features and his sleek, graying hair, he always reminded Elizabeth of a ferret. "It might pay for me to get to know Scantlebury better," he went on. "They keep raising the duties on tea until I think it would be cheaper to grow my own souchong in New York than buy it off a ship from China. But with a voice in Washington..."

"Well, we're a growing country," said Elizabeth. "All those settlements to the west. We need the revenue from imports. I read that two-thirds of all the duties in the United States come through the port of New York alone."

Stephen looked at her in disgust, then deliberately turned his head away as though she were invisible. "Shall we save this conversation for after dinner, gentlemen? When the ladies have left the room?''

Elizabeth pressed her hands to the sides of her chair until her arms ached. She mustn't lose her temper on Mother's birthday. ''Are you trying to tell me I'm not welcome in this conversation, Stephen?'' she said tightly.

He took a sip of wine and dabbed at his lips with his napkin. There was condescension in his every movement. ''My dear sister-in-law,'' he said, sounding tired or bored, ''I've been trying to tell you for years that you've never understood a woman's place in a man's world.''

Eyes flashing, Elizabeth reached for the heavy saltcellar and started to rise in her chair. Birthday or not, she wouldn't endure Stephen's insult without a counterattack. Let other women follow along like sheep. She wasn't about to learn her ''place'' if it meant deferring to the likes of Stephen Stowe!

But Noël Bouchard had already stood up and moved quietly around behind her. She felt his hand on her shoulder. It was both a comfort and a firm restraint. She was unable to move further. ''Surely you are not a fool, Monsieur Stowe,'' said Bouchard softly. ''*Alors,* you cannot have failed to notice that Mademoiselle Elizabeth is a woman of keen intelligence. She deserves more than to be relegated to the sitting room with her workbasket and sewing.''

Elizabeth subsided in her chair and relinquished the saltcellar. It was all she could do to keep her jaw from dropping open in surprise.

Stephen snorted. ''For a people who've all but descended into anarchy in the past thirty years, you Frenchies are very democratic when it comes to women.''

Bouchard resumed his seat. He shrugged as though Stephen's obvious attempt to rile him had meant nothing. ''Democratic?'' he said. ''Not at all. We are, rather, autocratic. Very aware of a woman's place. But it is not the same for us as it is for you.'' He stared across the table at Elizabeth and grinned unexpectedly.

Blast his hide, she thought. A woman's place? She was remembering their ride of last week, when she'd lain beneath him on the grass. And he remembered too—the beast! If she'd been feeling grateful because of his defense of her before Stephen, that spark of gratitude was quenched by his conceited smirk.

Bouchard's smile stiffened and became cold as he returned to Stephen. "Perhaps the difference between you and a 'Frenchy,' *monsieur,* is that we do not find a woman's intelligence to be a threat to our manhood."

Stephen turned as ruddy as the wine jelly on the plate before him. Caroline looked pleased, but Mrs. Babcock fluttered her hands nervously at the sudden tension in the room. "Oh, Mr. Bouchard," she said in a high, rapid tone, "do tell us about France. It's always so interesting."

"Yes, do," said Caroline, her voice low and intimate. She seemed not to notice that her husband was working himself into a jealous fury. "Do speak of your country. Noël," she added pointedly. Stephen made a growling sound in his throat.

Bouchard stared out at the still-bright day beyond the tall windows. His face was sad and remote in the golden glow of the late-afternoon sun. "I do not like to talk of France. It reminds me of my responsibilities. Sometimes it is very pleasant to feel free, bounded only by this moment in time."

"Yes, of course," murmured Mrs. Babcock, and Rose clucked her tongue in sympathy.

Criminy! thought Elizabeth. In another moment her mother would be weeping for the poor burdened aristocrat, who only longed to play at being one of the common folk! Wasn't that what their queen, Marie Antoinette, had wanted, dressing as a milkmaid at Versailles while the peasants starved in the streets of Paris? "How do you continue to escape your burdens, Mr. Bouchard?" she asked with sarcasm.

"I laugh them away," he said darkly. Then he shrugged and smiled. "And the world is wide. A man should see it all, if he can."

"Surely a man should settle down sooner or later," said Mr. Babcock, with such a crafty expression that Elizabeth wondered if he was playing matchmaker again. The thought set off alarm bells in her head.

"Of course," replied Bouchard. "The pull is always there. The longing for permanence. When a man wearies of wandering, as he must. Wearies of strange places, strange faces..."

"Strange women?" challenged Elizabeth, remembering with a certain resentment the crowds of females who followed him at every ball and dinner party.

He seemed surprised by her hostility. "That, too," he said. "*Certainement*. But if a man is wise, he will finally choose a woman lively enough to keep him faithful."

"If fidelity is in any man's nature," said Elizabeth bitterly.

"Alas, Elizabeth Babcock," he said. "Such a cynical view in one so young."

She had no answer for that. She spent the rest of the meal in silent withdrawal. For she knew that Edward was faithful to Rose. And Stephen, for all his unfounded jealousy of Caroline, was devoted to her. It wasn't Caroline's fault that she attracted admirers with her great beauty. Perhaps if she gave her husband a child he'd feel more secure in her love. But that hadn't happened in the six years they'd been married, and even Mother had ceased prying into the reasons why. Still, her sisters were happy in their marriages, indulged by doting husbands.

Only plain, jilted Bessie Babcock had cause for cynicism when it came to men.

They retired to the parlor after dinner. Since it was Mrs. Babcock's birthday, the gentlemen eschewed the usual "men's talk" around the dining room table and joined the ladies at once for coffee. While the men chatted and leaned against the mantel, all the women—except Elizabeth, who detested handwork—pulled out their sewing and sat in contentment as the twilight dimmed the room. A servant came in and began to light the candles.

Edward smiled at Bouchard. "I say, Mr. Bouchard, do you have that deck of cards on you?"

Noël patted his waistcoat pocket. "Of course. A hand of piquet?"

Elizabeth, who had been restlessly pacing the room, stopped and turned. "Be careful, Edward," she said. "Mr. Bouchard is a sly devil at the game. I noticed when he was playing with Father the other day. He didn't announce a tierce on purpose, just to fuddle Father. He took every trick after that."

Bouchard looked at her in pleased surprise. "You play piquet?"

"Not for years. I was good at it, too. I used to play with Grandpa, for straws. But everyone else said it was unseemly for a lady to gamble," she finished. It had been one of the small disappointments of her awkward adolescence, never to find anyone to play cards with after Grandpa had died.

Mr. Babcock cleared his throat. "My father was a wicked influence on you, Bessie. Confound me if he wasn't. Mr. Bouchard," he went on, "can I interest you in the sideboard and its refreshments?" He crossed the room and poured himself a whiskey and water.

Stephen was still smarting from his set-to with Bouchard at dinner. "Of course," he said. "Every Frenchy likes his tipple."

"Are you determined to insult me tonight, *monsieur?*" Bouchard's voice was like ice.

Stephen took a belligerent step forward. "Damned Frog," he muttered.

Mr. Babcock reacted in alarm. "Stephen! Please remember that Mr. Bouchard is a guest in my house."

"I don't give a damn. I'll have my say." He glared at Bouchard. "I don't like you, sir. I don't like the way you look at my wife. I don't like your country or anything about it. As far as I'm concerned, your country and its continental system damn near ruined my trade. We could just as easily have gone to war with you Frenchies as with John Bull. And with reason. As for your high-handed Napoleon and his empire, I wouldn't trade all that glory for one inch of America—free, sovereign and independent!"

Bouchard's eyes shone like blue sapphires. Elizabeth hadn't thought he was capable of such contained fury. "It is right that you should be proud of your country, *monsieur*. But I am equally proud of mine! Though I did not have to serve, I fought in the emperor's army, and shed my blood with pride. You are my junior by several years, I believe. But did you risk your life for your country in the late war with Great Britain? Or did you sit in your countinghouse and complain of your declining trade while young men died on your behalf?"

Elizabeth looked from one tight face to the other. In another moment they'd be at each other's throats, and no one quite seemed to know what to do. For a change, her temper might prove useful. She whirled to the sideboard, picked up a tumbler and flung it with all her might into the cold fireplace. "Blast and hellfire!" she cried. "Business and politics! Is that all you men can talk about? I want to go for a walk before it gets dark. Mr. Bouchard, you will please accompany me." When he hesitated, dragging his angry glance from Stephen for only a moment, Elizabeth stamped her foot. "Will you refuse me?" she said.

Bouchard wavered, but at length he agreed with a nod. He turned to Mrs. Babcock and gave a little bow. "I regret this scene on your birthday, *madame*." A servant was sent upstairs to fetch his top hat and Elizabeth's gloves and bonnet, and they set out.

The soft twilight of early June glowed pink against the cobblestoned street, and the sweet air was scented with the first roses. They turned onto Broadway and passed City Hall Park, going south, toward the older part of the city. They walked for several blocks without exchanging a word. Elizabeth could see that Bouchard's face was still hard and stony with suppressed anger. She felt the need to do something. Say something. "Mr. Bouchard," she ventured, then "Noël," when he didn't immediately respond.

"You should not have interfered," he growled. "I could deal with Stowe in my own way."

"Twaddle! How? With pistols at dawn, or some such nonsense?"

He glanced at her, grinned and relaxed. "I think you did it to prevent a fight that would have forced me to leave your house. And your companionship." The grin deepened. "Should I credit such tender sentiments, Elizabeth Babcock? I did not think it possible."

It almost seemed a compliment, the way he said it. "Do you think I'd care if the earth swallowed you up?" she said scornfully.

"But if I were gone, who would keep you from losing your temper with your brother-in-law? And destroying a very handsome *salière?*"

"You needn't be smug about it! I returned the favor."

He thought about that for a moment. "So you did," he conceded. "And I thank you. I should never permit myself to get angry at Monsieur Stowe. He is a man, like many Americans I have met, who allows his pride in this new country to make him narrow-minded and hostile to foreigners. It is both a strength and a weakness in your national character. Well, I shall attempt to apologize to Monsieur Stowe in the morning."

"I don't think it will matter. You won't be invited back to the country. Stephen can be very cruel and childish when he's riled."

"Then we shall never ride again together? *Quelle catastrophe.*"

Elizabeth glanced quickly at his face. In the deepening twilight, it was difficult to see whether he was serious or merely teasing her in his maddening way. "You can always ride out on Bloomingdale Road to where it stops being paved."

"No. I should prefer that we ride together. A long day, under the trees. What perfection. And then...there are several secluded inns where we could spend the night..."

She whirled to face him, sputtering in indignation. "You lecherous devil! You scoundrel! You—" She stopped, seeing the look on his face. "You said that on purpose, didn't you?"

He contrived to look innocent. "I? I meant separate rooms, of course. Evil is as evil thinks, we like to say in my country." He shook his head, the wicked smile scarcely contained. "Oh, Elizabeth Babcock, how wanton of you to misread a simple remark. I shall be compromised in another moment. And on such a fine June evening!"

Elizabeth smiled in spite of herself. How could she be angry when he was so amusing? And besides, it was indeed a beautiful night. Sweet and warm and magical, in a way that filled her with gladness, as though the most wonderful events had happened, were about to happen, were destined to happen in her life.

They were nearing the Bowling Green, a fenced-in oval of grass laid out with paths and containing the remains of the statue of King George III that had been torn down during the Revolution. It was a popular spot for promenading. The streets around it were thronged with people enjoying the mild evening. A lone lamplighter worked his way up Broadway, igniting the lamps as he passed so that they filled the streets with a golden glow. Several small carriages rumbled by; they were open to the soft night air, and the merry laughter of their passengers floated on the breeze. It reminded Elizabeth of the Babcock festivities. "I think Mother enjoyed her birthday," she said. "It was fortunate that Edward could come on time."

Bouchard stopped and stared at her. "Fortunate? But your father arranged it with Monsieur Scantlebury. Did you not know?"

"No. I thought that Edward himself..."

"I doubt that Monsieur Welling has the... What is the word you use here? Gumption?"

She felt the need to defend her brother-in-law. For Rose's sake. "But he brought a lovely gift. Mother adored the shawl. Rose wants one, too, and Edward says he'll buy it as soon as the shop opens tomorrow."

Bouchard snorted but said nothing.

She frowned. "Is that meant to be disapproval? Don't French husbands buy their wives presents?"

"Edward would be wiser to save his money and find a home of his own. Where his wife can learn to be a woman, not the child of her parents."

"What a stupid thing to say. *I'm* the child of my parents, as well."

"No." He turned to her and put his hands on her shoulders. "You are a woman. Rose is a child. Greedy and self-interested, like all children, if her husband continues to indulge her."

She didn't know what vexed her more—his insult to her dear sister, or his brazenness in touching her in public without her leave. She compressed her lips in anger. "Kindly do not hold me."

He stared for a moment, then dropped his hands and bowed. "As you wish, *mademoiselle.*" Though he seemed to defer to her, there was scarcely humility in his deep, arrogant voice.

They continued their walk in frosty silence. But his remarks about Rose had upset her. He'd always seemed to enjoy her family's company. "I suppose you don't like Caroline, either," she said sulkily.

He shrugged. "Caroline is a flirt."

"She is not! It's only that she's so beautiful. She can't help it if men—"

He laughed sharply. "Can't help it? I doubt there is anything Caroline does that is not calculated. It was not my wish to do so, but I think I could have become an intimate of your charming sister the first day I met her. I would not be surprised if that was why Stephen moved her out of the city. To keep her from mischief."

"Oh, you arrogant popinjay. You puffed-up lothario! You smug, overbearing—" Her eyes filled with tears of rage. "My sisters are the sweetest, dearest, nicest creatures in the world! I won't have you speaking ill of them because you dislike them."

He swore softly in French. Elizabeth didn't know the translation of the words, but she guessed they were quite wicked. "I do not dislike your sisters," he said with a sigh of exasperation. "But, my foolish Elizabeth Babcock, they are merely beautiful. Not paragons of virtue. Do you think that beauty is the sum total of a woman? Or that a man sees nothing more?"

"It has been my experience," she said with some bitterness.

"Then you have known the wrong men." He stopped, turned and pushed her face-framing bonnet off her head. It dangled between her shoulder blades, held by its wide ribbon ties. He tilted her chin upward with one slim finger.

"What are you doing?" Her voice was unsteady, a tremulous croak.

"I wish to prove you wrong," he said, and bent his head to take her lips.

"In the middle of the street?" she squeaked.

"Night has fallen. Who will see?"

It had to be pity and nothing else that prompted his desire to kiss her. By the lamplight, she could see it in his eyes, could read it in a syrupy tenderness of manner that made her want to gag. She bared her teeth like a cornered jungle cat. "If you try to kiss me," she said, "I'll kick your shins."

He laughed in delight and slipped his other hand around her waist. "Do your worst. Like it or not, I intend—" He stopped as a scream tore the night air.

Elizabeth broke from his embrace, and they both turned to see what was the commotion. An empty carriage with a single horse was circling round and round the Bowling Green, out of control. A wild-eyed man, waving a coachman's whip, ran behind it, shouting at the top of his lungs. The louder he yelled, the more the horse's panic grew. It snorted, shook its mane and increased its frenzied pace. The carriage swayed wildly and careened around the green, scattering terrified walkers in its path. A woman shrieked and fainted, and a young man, in imminent danger of being trampled, dived headlong into a shrub.

"*Le diable!*" Noël raced toward the Bowling Green, losing his top hat along the way. He vaulted the fence, dashed across the lawn and scrambled to the top of the far fence, positioning himself at some distance in front of the hurtling carriage. Just before it reached him, the carriage swerved for a moment; its large, heavy wheel glanced off a little flower girl and sent her flying into the air. She fell back to the ground and lay twitching among her ruined bouquets. Elizabeth gasped in horror and rushed forward.

Bouchard had waited, perched on the fence, and now he made his move. As the horse galloped past him, he leapt onto its back and tangled his fingers in its harness, tugging with all his might to bring the animal to a standstill. It bucked wildly, nearly toppling its determined rider, then came to an abrupt halt. While the stunned onlookers gaped or chattered in nervous relief, Noël soothed the overwrought beast with soft words and a firm hand.

Elizabeth had already reached the crumpled child and knelt beside her. One little arm was twisted at a grotesque angle, and blood covered the front of her ragged gown. She looked at Elizabeth, her large dark eyes filled with fear and trembling tears.

"Mama?" she whispered. "Will God take me now?"

Elizabeth gulped, seeing the extent of the child's injuries. "No, no, little one," she murmured. "Don't be afraid."

"Hold me, Mama."

Elizabeth hesitated, afraid to cause more distress. But the child seemed already to be beyond pain, her broken body numbed by the severity of her injuries. As gently as she could, Elizabeth gathered the girl into her arms, crooning a tuneless lullaby that seemed to bring comfort to the child and still her frightened sobs.

Noël Bouchard was at her elbow. "Elizabeth. Let me take her now."

"No!" She glared fiercely at him and pressed the little girl more closely to her breast. Her hands—through her gloves—felt warm and damp with blood. "Find a doctor, for the love of God." He nodded and moved away.

After a while, she seemed to lose all sense of time, all her energies bent to the fragile bundle in her arms, as though her strength alone could will the child to live. The girl's hiccuping sobs subsided into soft moans that broke Elizabeth's heart. She was aware at last that Noël had returned to her side and was urgently speaking her name.

"Elizabeth. *Elizabeth*. Here is a doctor. He lives just there."

She looked up. An elderly man was holding out his hands. "Give Mary to me, ma'am. I'll take her to my surgery."

She would as soon have given up her life as relinquish the child at that moment. She felt an odd, personal responsibility—as though the little girl were hers alone. "No, I'll carry her," she said. With Noël supporting her, she struggled to her feet, cradling her burden.

The child had grown ominously quiet, but still she murmured words of comfort and cheer. "We'll have you fit in no time, Mary," she said, placing the girl on the table in the doctor's surgery as he directed.

The doctor straightened from his brief examination. "I'm afraid not, ma'am. Mary's gone."

It was not to be borne! She stamped her foot in frustrated anger. "What do you mean, gone? Of course she's not. You're a doctor. Fix her!"

He sighed. "I'm a doctor. I'm not the Almighty."

"Twaddle!" She fought to deny the truth, fending off reality with her rage. The child *couldn't* be dead. It wasn't fair. "Blast you! If you'd only—"

"Elizabeth. Come." Noël put his strong hands on her shoulders and gently tried to guide her from the room. "Will there be money for a burial?" he asked the doctor. "If not, I should be pleased to—"

"No, no. I'll see to it. I know the family well. Poor but hardworking. Mary's been on that corner every evening for a year. Heartened my patients with her bouquets and her sunny smile. I'll see to it." He sighed again. "Such a misfortune." He looked at Elizabeth. "But you're covered with blood, ma'am. You'll find a washbasin and towels in the next room."

While Noël watched in concern, Elizabeth pulled off her gloves and scrubbed at her hands, clicking her tongue in consternation over her ruined gown. It was easier to focus on the mundane, to think about a soiled gown instead of the broken little body in the next room. She glanced at Noël. He was looking at her as though he'd never seen her before.

"Criminy!" she burst out. "What is it? Is my face green, or something?"

He smiled tenderly. "Your eyes are soft with compassion. I remember seeing a Madonna in a church painting with eyes like that."

"Stuff and nonsense. You blaspheme with such talk." She took a deep breath. Despite her rigid self-control, she was beginning to shake. She dried her hands and threw down the towel. "Madonna, indeed! A Madonna would have been able to..." The shaking was becoming a series of violent spasms that tore through her. She choked and blinked back the welling tears. "Able to save...poor Mary." She collapsed into Noël's waiting arms, sobbing out her grief and helplessness.

"There was nothing you could do, Elizabeth." His arms were firm around her, warm and comforting.

She wept until the pain had drained away, leaving her calm and once again in control of her faculties. She was aware that Bouchard still held her in his strong embrace, that he had begun to kiss the top of her head. That she was altogether too comfortable in his arms. Who knew what further liberties he might take in another moment if she didn't stop behaving like a ninny? She shook free of his enveloping arms. "Don't think that this stupid moment of weakness entitles you to think we're the best of friends now, Mr. Bouchard," she snapped.

He nodded his head solemnly. "Of course not. I should never presume such an idea."

She brushed at her hair. Several unruly wisps had come loose from her severe topknot, and she pushed impatiently at them. "I must look a sight. Not even a bit of pomade for my hair—and just look at my bonnet!" She untied the ribbons and held out her straw hat, crushed beyond repair when Noël had held her so tightly.

"*Quel sacrifice.* I have not yet replaced your riding hat. Now I see I owe you a bonnet, as well." He smiled, but it was a peculiar smile, filled with hidden meanings. The smoky blue eyes drew her in, made her feel as warm and protected as she had when she'd been in his arms.

He must be feeling remorse because of the ruined hats, she thought. Or pity at her tears. She wished he'd stop staring. It made her so uneasy. He reached out and brushed a lock of hair from her temple. She shivered at his gentle touch, and cursed her weakness at the same time. Pity. Yes, of course. What else could it be? He was the handsomest, bravest man in all of New York. She the plainest of women. It was best for her to remember that, before she was hurt again.

## Chapter Five

"Tontine Coffee House, if you please." Noël settled himself in the hired carriage and frowned. He seemed to be doing a great deal of frowning lately. He looked around at the lovely June day, the sun glinting off the East River, the cloudless, clear blue sky. As sweet a day as a man could want. Yet he'd scarcely noticed it.

He sore softly. Was this how men lived their lives? Being thrifty and sensible and worrying about where the next moneys were coming from? Had he exchanged his carefree life of a rover and a gambler for this? The need to frown on a perfect June day? He sighed. Well, perhaps in some ways his mad scheme wasn't a complete denial of his past. God knows it was the biggest gamble he'd taken in all his days!

But this time the gamble was different. For the first time in his life, he was scared. Maybe it was because of his responsibility to Martin, maybe because—deep down—he'd always been afraid to measure himself against Adam's success. And maybe he was beginning to feel his age, losing that sense of invincibility that had seen him through bloody battles and reckless gambles and daredevil, carefree escapades. He only knew that this scheme had come to mean more to him than he cared to admit.

And Steenboch was no comfort. As filled with worries as a clucking old woman. Noël turned about in the carriage and looked back toward the shipyard at Corlear's Hook. He could just see the tops of the masts of *L'Espérance*. At least a month until the repairs were finished, and costing more every day. With more expenses to come. There were supplies to buy, and there was a crew to hire. They'd be short-handed at fifteen men, but it couldn't be helped. He couldn't afford a larger crew. Not if he had to give them an advance on their pay when they signed on.

And then there was the cost of the cargo. Without an established reputation, he couldn't get a cargo on credit. No merchant would do business like that, no matter how persuasive his arguments. It would probably mean another bank loan, and he'd already solicited the soundest banks in the city.

He'd long since abandoned his original plan of filling the hold of the ship entirely with furs. Not at thirty thousand dollars for a full cargo of mixed animal skins! He'd buy enough from his Ohio trapper to satisfy the importer in Le Havre. Convince him that he could supply quality furs on a regular basis. Then, if all went well this trip, he'd persuade the fur importer to finance a full load for the next voyage. For the rest of the cargo, he'd been thinking about taking on a load of perishable foodstuffs for the West Indies. He could realize a quick profit in the islands, pick up a new cargo cheaply—maybe tobacco or indigo—and carry it back to France to sell along with the furs.

But he'd still need more money first. Steenboch, already concerned at the rising costs, had begun to mutter about a hidden cove out on Long Island where a ship could pick up contraband cargo. No questions asked. No record on the ship's manifest. And devil take the customs agents.

Well, he wasn't ready to consider that yet. He still had money. And the good favor of New York society. If his meeting with Josiah Babcock went well, perhaps Babcock could help him arrange for a consortium of businessmen to buy shares in the venture. It would mean sharing his profits, but at least it wouldn't add to his indebtedness should the whole scheme fail.

No, damn it! He wouldn't fail. He couldn't. He owed it to Martin. He closed his eyes, picturing the sturdy little boy. He'd been haunted by a recurrent daydream lately. An absurd idea, but it wouldn't go away. He would take Martin on his knee, tell him that *he* was his father. Then he'd bring the boy home to live with him. A real home, like the one Martin was used to. With love, permanence, a father and a mother.

He groaned and opened his eyes. That was always where the dream ended. A mother. A wife. And how could he afford a wife for years and years? A woman needed the assurance of savings, of money in the bank, not the chanciness of this gamble.

A wife. He sighed. A wife like... Elizabeth. Strange that she should have come instantly to mind. She wasn't the kind of woman he usually sought out—agreeable beauties who gave their lips and their bodies with passionate nonchalance. Who expected nothing in return except laughter and a skillful lover. Simple relationships that suited the impermanent life he led.

There was nothing simple about Elizabeth. Difficult and vexing. An adversary. Scarcely a woman to bring a man tranquillity!

But there was something about her. Her fire. Her independence. Even her wickedly sharp tongue. Yes. He'd enjoy a woman with her spirit. He frowned. And her tenderness. That had surprised him. He hadn't stopped thinking about it all week—her fiercely maternal concern for the little flower girl. And that sweet fragility in her, whenever she let down her guard. He remembered the first moment he'd seen her in Paris—watching the dancers with pain-filled eyes. Remembered how he'd wanted to comfort her. To make her smile. He was delighted with the lively, spirited Elizabeth. He hated boring women. But that other Elizabeth...

Ah, well. He wished he had the time and the money to find that other Elizabeth. It was clear she saw nothing wrong in her mother's pity, her sisters' haughty superiority merely because of their looks. Yet, in a hundred subtle ways, the whole family never stopped reminding her that she was thin and plain, a disappointment to them all. And, for all her fierce pride, she accepted their patronizing as her due.

She was an intriguing challenge. He wished he had the luxury to take her dancing every night and watch her eyes shine, to praise her till she glowed, to make her feel valued for herself alone. To touch the Elizabeth who lurked behind those beautiful eyes.

The carriage slowed, then stopped at the corner of Water and Wall Streets. Noël paid the coachman and mounted the broad steps of the Tontine Coffee House, nodding in greeting to several acquaintances who lolled on the broad veranda. Josiah Babcock was already waiting inside. He motioned to Noël from a sunny corner table and raised his glass of whiskey in welcome.

"I've taken the liberty of ordering you a cognac rather than coffee," he said. "For such a formal meeting as you requested, it only seemed right." His eyes twinkled. "Though I've been speculating on your reasons ever since you asked me here."

What the devil is he smirking for? thought Noël. He kept his affairs to himself. There was no way Babcock could know he hoped for more money. "Business is business," he said. "As a guest in your house, I feel a certain need to keep the two aspects of my life separate. *N'est-ce pas?*"

"I don't mind saying you're entirely welcome in my house, Mr. Bouchard. I trust you've enjoyed your stay so far?"

"Very much so, thank you. You and your family have been most gracious."

Josiah Babcock beamed. "You like my family, then?"

"Your wife and daughters are charming, *monsieur.*"

"Stephen has made his peace with you, I trust?"

"A momentary disagreement, *monsieur.* Nothing more."

"And...Elizabeth? What is your opinion of her?"

Noël sipped his cognac and smiled. Absurdly, the thought of Elizabeth warmed him almost as much as the drink. "A most spirited young woman. Clever and lively. I find her company stimulating."

"You don't find her—ahem—her high spirits daunting?"

"If you mean her occasional sharp temper..." He shrugged. "Not at all."

Babcock sighed and brushed at a wisp of fading red hair. "She was always a high-strung child. Firstborn, you understand. And of course I'd wanted a son. I felt differently when Caroline and Rose were born. Only natural."

"But you have *three* remarkable daughters," said Noël tightly. Did every damn fool in that family see no farther than the pretty noses on Caroline and Rose's faces?

"Yes. Well. Caroline and Rose have happily learned to be charming and agreeable. But I'm sure if Bessie made the effort..."

The man's disparagement of his eldest daughter was beginning to grate on him. "Elizabeth has other estimable qualities."

"It doesn't—forgive me if I speak frankly—it doesn't lessen your esteem that she's so plain?"

Noël swore to himself. "There are no plain women. Only clumsy men. With a little care and affection, Elizabeth could bloom like a rose." It seemed late in the day to teach the man how to be a loving father. But he felt the need to enlighten the fool. "Perhaps you have never given Elizabeth the opportunity to display her fine qualities. But the man who wins her will be fortunate indeed."

Babcock leaned back in his chair and patted his paunch. "And rich. I've decided on a dowry of fifteen thousand."

"That is extraordinarily generous of you, *monsieur.*" And indiscreet, he thought. Did Babcock share that information with everyone?

"You think so? Generous?"

Noël laughed ruefully. "I should consider myself a lucky man to have that sum come with a bride."

Babcock cleared his throat. "See here, Bouchard. Let's stop beating around the bush. I assume you asked me here to offer for Elizabeth."

"'Offer for'? *Pardon?* I fear I am unfamiliar with that term."

"Ask for her hand in marriage, of course. Mrs. Babcock and I haven't failed to notice how attentive you've been to her these past two months."

Noël almost choked on his drink. "Marriage? *Grand Dieu!*"

Babcock frowned. "Have I mistaken the situation, Bouchard?"

Noël stared out through the large arched windows. Marriage. Marriage to Elizabeth Babcock. With fifteen thousand in the bank as insurance should his shipping scheme come to nothing. It would take him years to raise new money to pay off his debts, should he fail. But at least Elizabeth could live off the dowry. She wouldn't suffer.

Marriage? he thought again. Good God, it was madness! Why was he even considering it? He *was* fond of her, of course. No denying it, when he thought about it. She'd brightened his days here in America. Recalling all the gay parties and balls, he realized he'd enjoyed them most when she was nearby to do battle with him, to surprise him with her rapier wit, to look at him with those limpid amethyst eyes.

He laughed softly. What the devil! All of life was a gamble, wasn't it? "No, *monsieur,*" he said. "You have not mistaken the situation. I should very much like to marry your daughter Elizabeth."

"Dash my buttons!" Babcock slapped the table in delight and motioned to a waiter. "That calls for another drink, sir."

"Wait." Noël had been thinking. In France, a man made his arrangements with the lady's father, and that was that. But this was America, where women were more independent. And Elizabeth—God knows!—the most independent of all. "Perhaps we should keep our celebration until after Elizabeth agrees, *monsieur.*" And there was one thing more. Of primary importance, if he and Elizabeth were to have a chance for happiness. He hadn't forgotten her suspicions of every suitor who came her way. "I want you to tell her," he said, "that I am very fond of her. That I trust that fondness can ripen into love. And that I *do not* intend to touch her dowry." Let her be assured at the outset that he wasn't a fortune hunter.

"No, of course not, Mr. Bouchard. I quite understand. We're agreed, then?" At Noël's nod, he offered his hand in a firm handshake. "Now," he said, "since you're to be my new son-in-law, it seems only fair that I should make an investment in your company. Say...ten thousand dollars? Would that be agreeable to you?"

"Agreeable?" Noël croaked. He was reeling in shock. In the space of ten minutes, he'd acquired a wife and a generous loan—and he wasn't sure which surprised him more.

They spent the next fifteen minutes making arrangements for the wedding and the transfer of funds. Despite Noël's misgivings, Mr. Babcock insisted that he and Mrs. Babcock should break the news to Elizabeth. Noël had the uneasy thought that they intended to coerce her into agreeing. "She must be willing," he warned with a scowl.

"Of course. You have my oath on that."

In the end it was decided that the marriage would be held in a little more than two weeks' time, since Noël would be leaving for France as soon as his ship was readied. He wondered at Babcock's haste, at his insistence on a small, intimate ceremony. He would have thought—given their clear desire to be quit of Elizabeth—that the Babcocks would trumpet their success from the top of their City Hall, rather than bundle off their daughter in a hurried, clandestine wedding. If he were not sensible of Elizabeth's wariness toward men, he would wonder if there was a less than chaste reason for such speed.

They set the wedding day for the last Friday in June. Noël emphasized again that he wanted Elizabeth to be told that her dowry wouldn't be touched by him. The less financial concerns entered into the discussion, the more secure she would feel. "I count on your discretion, *monsieur*," he said.

"Don't be silly, my boy. She'll be delighted. Every woman wants to be married. Now, let's have another round of drinks."

Noël was back on the street in less than an hour, striding up Water Street with an involuntary lilt to his step that dis-

gusted him when he stopped to notice. Fool! he thought.
He'd just taken on another burden. Tied himself down with
another care. He should be feeling *some* unease. He should
be frowning like a businessman, planning how he'd spend
Babcock's investment and where to find the best cargo for
the voyage.

Instead, he kept seeing Elizabeth's face before him. Those
eyes. That rigid mouth that had softened under his when
he'd kissed her in Paris. She'd yielded in his arms, trembled with a passion that had nothing to do with Adam's title or splendid position. She'd responded to the man, not the
uniform. It gave him hope for the future. He'd touched her
in Paris, seen a glimmer of the woman he knew was there
within her. If he'd done it as Adam, he could do it again as
Noël.

He looked up and caught sight of himself in a shop window. Grinning like an imbecile. Noël Bouchard, he thought,
you are mad!

*"Marriage?"* Eyes flashing, Elizabeth hurled a pillow
across the parlor with such force that the crystal drops on
the chandelier tinkled in the sudden draft. "You've sold me
to that—that *Frenchman,* like a cow brought to market?"
she cried.

Mr. Babcock tugged at his thinning hair in exasperation.
"Confound it, he didn't *pay* for you."

Her lip curled in scorn. "No. You paid for him."

"Nonsense. In fact, he assured me that he doesn't intend
to use your dowry."

"Hmph! That's what Edward said when he married Rose.
But he went through her money in a right hurry."

Mrs. Babcock wrung her hands and sighed. "Now, Bessie. Have a little charity. Edward is still trying to establish
himself."

"All men are the same. Only looking after their own in-
terests." Including her father, who was clearly eager to see
her out of his house. The thought of his betrayal made her
blood boil. She'd rejected every suitor her parents had sent
her way. And now, suddenly, to have the choice made for

her, the arrangements concluded behind her back! Well, they weren't concluded as far as *she* was concerned. She moved impatiently around the room, spending her fury in restless pacing. "And in only two weeks? Such shameful haste!"

"It's merely because Mr. Bouchard hopes to sail for France before the end of July."

"And you want to snare him before he can change his mind," she said with a sneer. "Well, I won't have him. Not in two weeks or two years. And you can tell the rascal so!"

"He wanted you to know he's quite fond of you. Come, Bessie, doesn't that count for something?"

"If he's so fond of me, why does he find it necessary to accept my dowry?"

Mr. Babcock huffed loudly. "Must you always be difficult? I told you he said he won't use it. He made a special point of telling me that. Maybe he wants to have the dowry for you to spend on yourself."

"Ha! Ten thousand dollars sitting in his very own bank, and he doesn't intend—" She stopped. At her words, Mrs. Babcock had reddened and looked nervously toward her husband. "What is it?" demanded Elizabeth. "It *is* ten thousand, isn't it?"

Mrs. Babcock gave a little squeaking sigh. Her large eyes held a plea for understanding. "Now, Bessie, you're not getting any younger, you know."

"Oh!" Her mother was impossible. She glared at her father. "I want to know how much it cost you to be rid of me!"

Mr. Babcock muttered an oath and shook his head. "The less you know about business matters the better off you'll be, young lady."

She clenched her fists and dropped her voice. "If I have to ask Mr. Bouchard himself, I swear to you I'll see that everyone in New York learns how much you paid."

Mrs. Babcock gasped. "Mercy me, Bessie! Think of the scandal, the shame!"

A bitter laugh escaped her lips. "Shame? After Jack deserted me, I drank my full measure of shame. There's nowhere lower for me to sink. Now, how much, Father?"

He shrugged in resignation. "I offered a dowry of fifteen thousand."

She leaned against a chair, clinging to its back to keep from swaying. She felt as though she'd been hit in the pit of her stomach. Fifteen thousand. Three times what Rose and Caroline had needed to win husbands. "And that's all?" she said weakly, praying the earth would swallow her up.

"No." A reluctant admission. "I promised to invest money in his shipping venture."

"How much?"

"Ten thousand dollars."

"And he accepted it all, without a protest." She felt her disappointment like a tight cord twisted around her heart. Bouchard was a wicked devil, a tormenting rogue who'd vexed her many a time. Still, she'd somehow thought that he wasn't quite like other men. She grimaced in anger. "You can just go and tell Mr. Bouchard that I wouldn't have him if he were served up to me pickled and stewed in a soup tureen. I'm going to my room. Have them bring supper to me, Mother. No. Never mind. I couldn't swallow a mouthful tonight." It was true. Though she hadn't eaten since lunch, she felt a lump of discomfort within her, like an undigested green apple, that seemed to grow with every new revelation of her unworthiness. "Oh, Father!" she burst forth in a cry of pain. "How could you? Do you care so little for me?"

Mr. Babcock strode to her and put his arms around her. It was an awkward, uncharacteristic gesture. "Bessie. I want you to be happy. Don't you know that? If I'd found him, I would have choked Jack Cochran with my bare hands for breaking your heart the way he did. Bouchard is a good man. He cares for you. He hopes to be worthy of your love someday. That's not such a poor beginning for a marriage, is it?"

"Love?" she whispered, wide-eyed, moving out of his embrace to sink into a chair. "He used that word?"

"He seems very happy with the prospect of marriage to you. He was delighted when I proposed it."

Her father's unfamiliar tenderness had begun to warm her, calming her fears. Now she paused, suddenly aware of what he'd said. "*You* proposed it?"

"No, I didn't!" he exclaimed, disconcerted. "That is . . . You misunderstand. It was simply that I . . . helped him along. He spoke of you in the warmest manner. I took the next logical step. I asked him if he wanted to marry you. He said yes."

She jumped up, her temper returning in a great rush of anger and humiliation. "You tempted him with the offer of twenty-five thousand dollars, then trapped him into asking for my hand. Did you suppose he'd refuse when you managed it so adroitly? Bah! He's a money-grubbing toad, like all the rest!"

Mr. Babcock threw up his hands in despair. "You'll be the death of me yet, Bessie."

Mrs. Babcock stared at her daughter in bewilderment. "I don't understand why you keep accusing Mr. Bouchard of being interested in your dowry. He may be thrifty and penny-wise. He certainly lives modestly. And he's prudent. Mr. Babcock, you yourself said so—that a prudent man prefers not to use his own money on a risky venture. But, my stars! Have we all forgotten who he is? A *count,* Bessie. A very rich count. That's why he doesn't need your dowry."

By the living jingo, thought Elizabeth. She'd almost forgotten that. Bouchard had always been so open in his manner, so generous and democratic, that it was easy to forget he was an aristocrat. It cast a whole new light on the present state of affairs. Her anger began to fade, to be replaced by a new thought. "But if he doesn't need the money, why didn't he refuse it?"

"Nobility has a peculiar sense of honor," said Mr. Babcock. "Old World ways. Perhaps he thought it would be an insult to you if he refused the dowry."

The green-apple lump within her was beginning to dissolve. "Do you think so? I never thought of that." She managed a tentative smile.

Mr. Babcock beamed in relief. "Then you're agreed to the marriage?"

"I suppose so."

Mrs. Babcock clapped her hands. "Oh, Bessie! I just this minute realized it. You'll be a *countess.*"

That gave her pause. "Upon my oath—so I shall."

Mrs. Babcock was warming to her theme, her voice rising with excitement. "I wonder when he's going to reveal his identity to us? Will he expect you to live in France, do you think? Father heard he has a great château in the country. Do you think he'll—"

Mr. Babcock shook a stern finger at his wife. "Now, Mrs. Babcock. I expect you to hold your tongue. Until the man is ready to tell us more, we'll respect his masquerade."

Mrs. Babcock clucked loudly. "Didn't you ask him *anything* of importance while you were negotiating this afternoon?"

"Confound it, what could I say without revealing that we've always been aware of who he was? Besides, that will be for Bessie to ascertain, as she learns to know him better." He turned to his daughter. "Now, if you're decided, Elizabeth, Mother and I will go upstairs and send Mr. Bouchard down to you."

She hesitated, then nodded in agreement, wondering if she was making a dreadful mistake.

Mrs. Babcock fluttered like a butterfly in a field of flowers. "There's so much to do! We can't get a proper trousseau in two weeks, but when he takes you to France... Oh, Bessie! The gowns. The linens and laces! I'll call on Mrs. Hudson for your wedding dress, I think. She does fine work. And we can have the reception right here in the house. St. Paul's Church would be best for the ceremony. Don't you think so? Trinity Church holds too many...unfortunate memories. I think your sisters—"

Mr. Babcock put a firm hand on his wife's arm. "Come, Mrs. Babcock. I'm sure Mr. Bouchard would like to speak to Elizabeth now."

"Yes, of course." Still fluttering, she allowed her husband to steer her from the room.

Left alone, Elizabeth paced nervously. She paused, staring at her reflection in a small, mirrored candelabra on the wall. Her sharp-boned cheeks seemed more drawn than usual, and her eyes were dark with uncertainty. She should be happy. After her torments of the past five years, she was embarking on a new voyage. A new beginning. With a new man. He was handsome, rich, titled—a dream come true. Every woman in New York would envy her; it was a fitting revenge for the years of gossip and pity she'd endured since Jack had gone away.

Yes, she should be happy. Then why did a finger of doubt scratch so relentlessly at her insides? She looked again at her face in the mirror. Plain Bessie Babcock. Now to be a countess? It was too improbable. She wasn't beautiful like Caroline, or sweet and gay like Rose. She sighed. If Bouchard wasn't marrying for the money, why in the name of Beelzebub did he want *her?*

"Elizabeth."

She turned. Noël Bouchard stood in the doorway, smiling at her. He seemed to fill the room with his presence, a self-assurance and sophistication that was distinctively European. He'd long since adopted the American style of clothes, putting aside his snug pantaloons for trousers, his tailcoat for a simple frock coat with a high-standing collar. But even when he was dressed that way, his fine, strong figure, long legs and elegant bearing served to emphasize his natural superiority over other men. It only increased Elizabeth's uneasiness. There *had* to be a reason behind his proposal. "Please come in, Mr. Bouchard."

The smile deepened. "You must call me Noël, now."

She hadn't noticed before that there was a small dimple beside his mouth when he smiled. But surely he was aware of it. Aware of his devastating charm. He'd captivated every woman in New York, and he'd probably left behind a string of heartbroken females in France. She had a sudden thought. Perhaps *that* was why he wanted to be married. To protect himself from the assaults of too many women. Or— given a Frenchman's inclinations toward married women, as the gossip in Paris seemed to suggest—perhaps he wanted a wife of his own to give him the appearance of decency while he pursued other men's wives. Whatever his reason, he wasn't to be trusted. Not when he swaggered into the room looking as satisfied as a cat with a bowl of cream!

"Are you pleased?" he asked. His confidence set her teeth on edge. He clearly expected a flattering response. As though she should be grateful for her good fortune in catching him, the arrogant dog!

"Perhaps 'resigned' is a better word," she said tartly. "With you and my father plotting behind my back, I can scarcely feel pleased."

He frowned. "But you agreed, *n'est-ce pas?*" At her reluctant nod, the smile broke through once more. "Come, Elizabeth. It will be a great adventure."

She sniffed in disdain. "Adventure? So is setting off into the wilderness without a compass. But I see no great joy in it."

He laughed. "I will teach you to know joy."

His eyes were as blue as an April sky, and the deep resonance of his laughter made her breath catch. There had to be a reason why this perfect man would choose her. "There's no sense in it, either," she said. Better to have it out now, before she risked her heart again. "Why do you want to marry me?" she asked boldly.

His tone was sober and thoughtful. "Shall I say it is because you come with a large dowry? Is that what you want to hear? So you can be confirmed in your low opinion of men? Shall I say that you are sensitive to children, which bodes well for the family I hope to have?" He smiled tenderly. "Or shall I say that it is because of the sadness I see in your eyes?"

She dropped her gaze at once. "What a buffleheaded thing to say. Am I now to be pitied?" she muttered.

"No. Cherished and loved, I hope." His eyes swept her body in a frank appraisal that made her painfully aware of her thin arms, her small bosom. "And desired," he added.

She ground her teeth together. The man was shameless, with his feigned sincerity. "You lie most unconvincingly."

"And how do you lie? With your hair unbound on the pillow? Your mouth soft, and waiting to be kissed? I should like that."

She squealed and leapt forward. "How dare you mock me!"

He moved aside. "It was not mockery, Elizabeth. I do find you desirable. You have a pleasing shape. Not full, but pleasing. And you are straight and tall, with a natural grace." He regarded her with a look that seemed to hold genuine approval; then he grinned. "I shall tell you a secret. Short women, bouncing along beside me, have always made me feel like a gamekeeper with a rabbit in tow."

The picture his words suggested to her mind was so absurd she began to giggle. "You're a very wicked man," she said, softening.

"No doubt. And you're a vexing woman. We are well matched, I think." He crossed to the sideboard and poured two small glasses of Madeira. "Perhaps I want to marry you for your spirit, your fire."

"My bad temper," she said ruefully. "Is that what you mean?"

"The one thing I have dreaded was a dull wife." He laughed; it was an open, rich laugh, bubbling with the joy of life. "*Le bon Dieu* knows you will never bore me with a sweet and submissive disposition!" He proffered one of the glasses. "Come. Let us drink to a good bargain struck."

She accepted his offer, but her thoughts were churning as they drained their glasses and set them down. "Do you think you'll leave for France in July?"

"I hope to, if all goes well."

"And I?"

"I fear it is impossible for me to find a suitable house before I go. I trust it will not be too taxing for you to stay with your parents until I return. Three months, at the most."

"And what will you do? Where will you go in France?" She deliberately kept any guile from her voice. Perhaps she'd learn where his château was.

He raised an eyebrow in surprise. "Go? Unless I must visit Paris on business, I intend to stay in Le Havre until we sail again." He chuckled wickedly, his eyes twinkling. "And then I shall fly back to your side, my superb Elizabeth. Eager for a fresh battle." He frowned suddenly, as though a stray thought had crossed his mind. "I do not like that they call you Bessie. I shall speak to your family."

"Don't you have nicknames in France?"

"Of course. But *Bessie?* Never. Let me think. Elizabeth." His French made the *Z* an *S,* and the final sound a *T.* Elizabeth had always found it seductively musical, the way he said her name. "Elizabeth," he said again. "Lis. That is *lily,* in my language. Liselle. Lisette. Lisbet." He nodded in satisfaction. "Yes. Lisbet. I shall call you that. A nickname should be pretty and soft, bespeaking a woman's grace. The beauty in her eyes."

She turned away from his searching gaze. "Rot and nonsense."

"It makes you uncomfortable when a man says something nice to you?"

"Perhaps I don't believe what men say." She'd turned back and threw the words at him like a challenge, expecting a sharp rejoinder.

Instead, he reached out and stroked the side of her cheek with a gentle finger. "How very sad for you," he murmured. "But I shall teach you to believe."

She felt her mouth grow dry at his touch. So soon? she thought. So soon her stupid passions would betray her? No! She mustn't allow it. Not again. Had she learned nothing from Jack?

She didn't know if other women were as foolish, as susceptible to a man, as she. She knew only that Noël Bouchard mustn't learn how easily she could be ruled by tender words, a soft caress, a few kisses. At least not until after they were safely married. Mother always said a man was more agreeable with a marital bond to temper his dictatorial impulses.

She stepped away from the temptation of Noël Bouchard, like a skittish animal evading a trap. "I'm sure Mother will be waiting dinner for us. Shall we go in?"

His mouth twisted in amusement. "Such haste to leave me, Lisbet? First, give me a kiss to seal our bargain."

"If you must." She moved closer—keeping her body rigid—lifted her chin and kissed him formally on each cheek.

"I asked for a kiss," he said. "Not a salute."

"I don't know how things are done in France, but here in the United States a betrothed couple is expected to observe the proprieties."

He frowned and reached out to gather her into his arms. "*Grand Dieu,* I shall not compromise you! But I expect something more than a kiss you would give your grandmother."

"Not until we're married," she said primly, moving away from his grasp.

The frown deepened. "Is this to be a battle, Elizabeth? Over a kiss that we will both enjoy? Don't be childish. Come to me now."

A kiss they'd both enjoy? she thought. Such smug arrogance! This was not a battle. By the living jingo, it was *war*. "No," she said. "I shall not!"

"Indeed you will." He rapped out the words in a cold, low voice. She saw the flash of determination in his eyes, the set of his steely jaw.

She stamped her foot in anger. "If you think I intend to meekly obey you simply because you and my father have forged this little agreement, you'd better think again. I consented to be your wife. Not your possession, despite what you may have expected of me." She smiled tightly. "Now, please excuse me. I'm sure Mother wants to discuss my wedding dress. Perhaps I'll have something designed on the lines of a Greek slave, dragged into captivity by an arrogant Roman. Or Frenchman, as the case may be. A marauding Frenchman, who isn't content with plunder in his own country, but must cross the ocean to plunder on our shores. Or did you come here because the women in France had already tired of your treacly charm and abandoned you?"

She could tell by the look on his face that she'd scored a direct hit to his masculine pride. His color darkened, and a taut muscle quivered along the edge of his jaw. She gave an insolent little curtsy. "By your leave, Mr. Bouchard." She tossed her head, turned on her heel and made for the door.

She heard his step behind her, followed by the clamp of his hands on her shoulders. He spun her around, pulled her savagely against his powerful body, and attached his mouth to hers. It was a hard, angry kiss—too hurtful, too cruel, to stir any emotion in her save outrage. She struggled in his fierce embrace. When she could take no more of it, she squeaked in protest beneath the tyranny of his mouth.

He lifted his head from hers. His eyes glinted with a dangerous light. "The first thing I will teach you, my Lisbet," he growled, "is how to be civil."

She trembled, her outrage replaced by a sudden cold fear. Jack had broken her heart. Would this man destroy what was left?

With a cry, she wrenched herself out of his arms and fled the room and his overbearing presence.

# Chapter Six

St. Paul's Church, sitting serenely on Broadway near City Hall Park, was a splendor of pink and cream, with gilded Greek columns, crystal chandeliers, and a soaring Palladian window behind the altar. Usually a quiet oasis, this Friday afternoon it was filled with the rustle of silk-gowned ladies, the low murmurs of gentlemen, and the nervous silence of anticipation.

From his vantage point near the late President Washington's pew, Noël surveyed the scene. There was something almost barbaric in a marriage service, he decided. It reminded him of some of the native customs he'd seen in the South Seas: onlookers gathering, licking their chops, hungrily waiting for the sacrifice. He would have preferred a simple civil ceremony. He regretted not having insisted on that. He regretted even more that there had been no time for an exchange of letters with Adam. In an odd way, he'd wanted his twin's blessing for the giant step he was taking.

Not that he regretted taking the step. It was a gamble, of course; it was an adventure. But he was used to that—the unknown tomorrow that had always brought zest to his life. And he cared for Elizabeth. That was important in a marriage.

They hadn't seen much of each other this past couple of weeks. There had been a few prenuptial parties in their honor—the kind of honor fit for a king, he thought uneasily—with noise and gaiety and fawning acquaintances. But beyond that, he'd been down at the harbor most of the time, inspecting the final repairs to *L'Espérance*, shopping for the cargo he could buy with Babcock's investment, arranging for their honeymoon trip. And Elizabeth and her mother had been busy with the nuptial arrangements: the gown, the wedding gifts, the reception that was to be held at the Babcock home after the ceremony. All too silly and unimportant, to his way of thinking—especially when Mrs. Babcock's flurries and nervous shrieks had become an almost daily occurrence.

He'd wanted Steenboch for his groomsman, but the grizzled captain had given him a disgusted look and said he'd rather be taken by a press-gang than wear a starched neckcloth and stand up in church. Even if it was for "M'soo Noël." Faced with the choice of one of his two brothers-in-law-to-be, Noël had diplomatically settled on Stephen Stowe: Stephen was the senior relation, and choosing him would keep peace in the family.

Noël crossed the aisle, ignoring the admiring whispers of the ladies, and stepped into a small anteroom at the back of the church. He nodded to Mr. Babcock, and to Rose, Caroline, and their husbands, reassuring them with his smile that he was no more nervous than a bridegroom was expected to be.

He pulled out his watch. Nearly four. Elizabeth should be arriving soon with Mrs. Babcock. He was curious to see her mood. Since the day of their betrothal she'd been cold and distant, scarcely speaking to him, arranging for them always to have a chaperon so that they'd never be alone together. Finding reasons not to dance with him at the evening parties. As though she still hadn't forgiven his domineering kiss that day. Or as though she were genuinely afraid of him.

For his part, it still surprised him—the surge of anger he'd felt when she'd refused to kiss him. He'd wanted to wring her neck. Until that moment, he'd thought he merely enjoyed their battles in a lighthearted way; he'd viewed them as nothing more than games that challenged his intelligence, his understanding of women. Now he wasn't so sure. He didn't know when she'd begun to reach his deeper emotions, to nag at a part of him that he'd always ignored. But he didn't like it. It made him feel helpless, vulnerable. He hadn't asked her for a kiss since that day. He didn't want a battle that might make him lose control of his emotions again.

Well, perhaps everything would be resolved once they were married. Her resistance to the kiss might simply have been fear and prudery, a maidenly innocence that he'd soon overcome. He'd have to be very gentle and tender with her, teaching her not to be afraid of his touch, his body. God knows he didn't want a frightened, weepy, hysterical virgin on their wedding night.

The organist began to play softly; the choir filed into the upper gallery. From the open door of the anteroom, Noël could see that the front pews of the church were filling rapidly. It had been a mild day for the end of June, but now the heat of so many bodies pressed close was making the church uncomfortably warm.

Standing possessively beside his wife, Stephen Stowe began to grumble. "Damn it, I hope Elizabeth doesn't intend to be late," he said, and tugged at his collar in annoyance.

Caroline sighed, her lower lip thrust out in a sullen pout. "I just know my dress will be wilted before anyone can see it. You'd think Bessie would try to be a little thoughtful of others."

Rose swirled daintily, admiring the sway of her embroidered skirt. "You should have chosen worked muslin, as I did. It doesn't show the creases." She smiled at her father and slipped her arm through his. "Isn't it pretty, Papa? It was very expensive, and Edward was a dear to let me have it." She blew her husband a kiss and was answered by a shy, blushing smile from Edward.

Josiah Babcock beamed with pride. "Both my girls look lovely today."

There was a loud sigh from the doorway. Mrs. Babcock stood there, her face damp with perspiration, and fluttered her hands. "I'm so put out. I've only just had a note saying that my second cousin Albert can't come from Albany after all."

"It doesn't matter, my dear." Mr. Babcock went to his wife and patted her hand. "I never liked Albert anyway." He looked over her shoulder toward the open church door. "Bessie is still in the carriage?"

"No. She wasn't finished with her toilette. She told me to go without her. I've sent the carriage back to wait for her."

"Oh, bother!" cried Caroline. "You'd think *this* time she'd be eager to arrive early."

"Caroline!" Stephen scowled a warning to his wife and took her by the elbow. "Since we have the time, perhaps we should make an effort to greet the guests."

"Excellent idea," said Mr. Babcock. "We'll all go." He gathered in his family and shepherded them toward the door. He glanced back at Noël. "Will you mind being left alone?"

"Not at all, *monsieur.*" In truth, Noël had begun to tire of their conversation. The mindless chatter of the family only served to remind him that he was tying himself to *them*—good God!—as well as to Elizabeth, for the rest of his life.

"I'll stay with Noël," said Rose. "I can never think of anything to say. At least not to anyone old enough to be my parents."

She waited until everyone had left the room, then turned to Noël with a coy smile. "*You* didn't say I look pretty," she said.

He kept an artificial smile pasted on his face. She was probably the prettiest, and most empty-headed, female he'd ever met in his life. "You look charming," he said. He frowned. Something was nagging at him. Something Caroline had said. "What did your sister mean by 'this time'?"

Rose blushed and twisted her hands together. "I...I'm not sure you're supposed to know. Papa said it would be best if we all forget the past."

"Does it have to do with Elizabeth?"

"It's such a long time ago," she burst out. "Five years! I can scarcely remember, I was so young then."

He was getting more concerned by the minute. He wanted to shake the little scatterbrain. "Tell me!" he ordered, in his sternest military voice.

Rose flinched at his tone, cowed into obedience. Hesitating at first, she began to tell him a story that made his blood boil with every word she uttered. A story of Elizabeth, standing forlornly at the altar, waiting for some despicable man named Jack. A cowardly bastard who'd left her on the very day of their wedding and vanished God alone knew where.

"Back to England, they think," said Rose. "Jack was an Englishman." She stared at Noël, her eyes wide with child-like naiveté. "Edward is so sweet. The dearest husband in the world. And he says that I'm his light and his life. Why would a man want to give up the joys of marriage? Edward wouldn't. Why would a man want to jilt a girl?"

Noël ground his teeth together. "A *man* would not. What was he like, this...Jack?" He found it impossible even to say the name without feeling sick.

"Oh, he was dashing, and very handsome. Any woman would have been pleased to catch his eye. No one ever understood why he chose Bessie. We thought it might be because of her dowry." She frowned in perplexity. "But then he wouldn't have gone away, would he? And after that, if it was just the money, why didn't anyone else want to marry her? Papa even doubled her dowry to ten thousand." She stopped to contemplate this, then pouted. "Which wasn't very fair to Edward and me, come to think of it. Anyway, I've even heard the gossips say that no man would *ever* want Bessie for a lifetime. Not for all the money in the world! Oh!" She stopped and covered her mouth with her gloved hand, belatedly aware of what she'd said. "But of course *you're* marrying her, and I'm sure it isn't for the money and... Oh, dear..." Her voice trailed off in a helpless bleat.

"Lisbet," he murmured, filled with pain at the thought of Elizabeth's suffering. That was what he'd seen in her eyes, all those times she'd touched his heart.

Still thinking of her own blunder, Rose was now desperately trying to make things right. She began to babble, scarcely pausing for breath. "I didn't mean to suggest that Bessie's dowry... I mean, I'm sure you and she will be sublimely happy. She really isn't so difficult, when you get to know her. I can remember, before Jack, the times when she was very sweet. Oh, *very*. For just weeks and weeks at a time! Just because some people say bad things about her temper, and say she's a shrew, doesn't mean that Bessie—"

Noël fixed her with a baleful glare. "*Taisez-vous!* Hold your tongue, you silly child, and get out of here."

She sniffled, her large eyes filling with tears. "Well, you asked me about Bessie, and I—"

"Enough!" he thundered. "Her name is Elizabeth, not Bessie. Remember that! Now—" he pointed to the door "—out."

She gasped and scurried from the room.

Noël sank into a chair and dropped his head into his hands. Jilted. It was too cruel to contemplate. Even a beautiful woman, much admired, would suffer after such a blow to her pride. He wondered how Elizabeth could ever have gone on. And Babcock, the blind fool, had only added to the insult by increasing her dowry. As though she weren't of value without it. He prayed to God that she didn't know how much Babcock had given to *him*.

And all this time he'd treated her temper as the prickly defensiveness of a fearful woman, unused to a man, ignorant of his kisses or caresses. He'd thought his task was simply to breach that wall of fear with tenderness—patiently and slowly teaching her the joys of love.

But surely that bastard, Jack, had kissed her and held her. Before he'd left her so cruelly. It wasn't knowledge she lacked. No. What he had to teach her was far more important. And far more difficult. He had to teach her to believe in a man again. And somehow he had to capture her rebellious spirit with tenderness and turn it toward him in joyous trust. Or a wall of suspicion and hostility would stand between them forever.

"*Le diable!*" He jumped to his feet and swore aloud, his heart constricting with a sudden chilling thought. She'd sent her mother on ahead. She'd clearly never forgiven Jack—or any man—for what had happened to her. Maybe he was being foolish, but . . . He strode out of the room, found the back door of the church and stepped around into the street. He looked up Broadway, frowned and broke into a run.

Elizabeth stared at herself in the mirror of her dressing table and frowned. What in the name of Beelzebub was the matter with her? Everything was as it should be. Her valises were packed for the wedding trip, the house hummed with servants preparing for the reception in the downstairs drawing rooms, the carriage stood at the door, waiting to take her to the chapel. The bride was dressed in her finery.

It was a lovely wedding gown. Not white, of course. A woman of twenty-five was considered too old to be married in pristine white, whatever her past. It was, instead, a beautiful dress of pale pink satin, with a blond net overlay that fell from a high-waisted bodice. Elizabeth had even bowed to her mother's wishes and allowed the dressmaker to pad the bodice slightly, giving her the fashionably ideal Grecian figure with high, rounded breasts. Her long gloves and slippers were of white satin, and her simple blond lace veil was pinned to a wreath of pink silk roses that encircled her prim topknot.

She scowled at her image in the glass. A mahogany tendril of hair had come loose and was beginning to curl at her temple; she reached for a bit of pomade to slick it back again. She grunted in annoyance, wishing she'd been born with straight hair instead of this russet mop that tended to frizzle unless she kept it under tight control.

"Botheration!" she said aloud. Why was she wasting her energies on something as stupid as hair, pretending not to hear the voice of reason in her head? Think, Elizabeth. *Think.* What did she know of this man, who laughed and joked as though he scarcely had a serious thought in his head, then turned suddenly—frighteningly—angry? Would he be a will-o'-the-wisp as a husband, filled with reckless charm, unfaithful and indifferent to her? Or was that dark, domineering side the true man, showing her what she could expect from their life together?

Then there was the matter of his name. He'd told the vicar he was to be called Noël-Victor Bouchard in the service. He hadn't said a word about his titles. Not General Bouchard. Not Comte de Moncalvo. Simply *Mister* Bouchard. She didn't know about French law. If he didn't list all his names, did that make the marriage less than legal in his own country? Easily annulled? Did he plan someday to sail for France and never return? To find another woman and marry her in his own church, abandoning a woman who had perhaps never been anything more to him than an amusing diversion?

And if he left her—which he surely would someday, since no man could be trusted—how would she hold up her head? Defend her pride? After Jack's betrayal, it would be too much to endure. No. Better to let common sense be her guide, follow her own dictates now, before she was hurt again. She nodded at her reflection and began to unpin her wedding veil. She knew exactly what she would do.

She supposed the idea had been stewing in her brain all week, ever since Mother had pulled her aside and handed her a morocco purse stuffed with bank notes. Saved out of her pin money, she'd said. "When you don't want to ask your husband for unnecessary trifles," Mother had whispered, as though they were conspirators. There was a hundred dollars in the purse. Enough to take Elizabeth far away. Her clothes were already packed, the carriage was waiting. It would be a simple matter to change into her traveling dress now, then have the coachman take her and her things to the City Hotel to catch a Philadelphia-bound stage, or to the harbor and a packet boat heading south. And she'd be free of all her doubts and fears.

"May I be your *femme de chambre* and help you with that veil?"

Elizabeth spun around in shocked surprise and gaped at Noël in the doorway. He was the picture of perfection. His well-tailored blue coat and gray trousers made him look every inch the gentleman without disguising the athletic body beneath. His deep, stiff cravat and snowy collar accentuated the golden bronze of his complexion. And his gaily striped silk waistcoat, like the lock of blond hair falling carelessly over his forehead, seemed to call attention to the more frivolous side of his nature. His smile was gentle. And aware.

Elizabeth gulped, sure that her startled expression had given her away. Does he guess? she thought. "What are you doing here?" Her voice sounded like a croaking frog on a spring night.

"I came to fetch you," he said, striding across the room to scoop up the veil from the floor where she'd dropped it.

She was trapped, her fine plans dashed. That only increased her vexation. "Why should I need fetching?" she snapped.

He laughed. "I was eager to see my bride, you understand." He took hold of her shoulders and gently turned her back to face the mirror; then he moved around behind her. "Hand me those hairpins, *ma chère*."

Reluctantly, she complied, studying his face in the glass as he refastened her veil with deft hands. Curse him, he was *too* lighthearted, too offhand—he'd surely guessed she'd intended to run away.

Criminy! Run away? Quite suddenly, the foolishness of her plan struck her. To run away was the coward's way. Jack had run away, unwilling to face her. To stay, to accept the challenge, the friendship—if not love—that Noël was clearly offering her—that took courage. Courage to overcome the pain of the past. Courage to admit that a part of her was glad for this wedding day. Her eyes strayed to the reflection of his sensuous mouth in the mirror. Courage, most of all, to admit she wanted to feel that mouth on hers again.

He finished pinning the veil, spread it across her shoulders and nodded in satisfaction at his handiwork. "Is it not absurd?" he said with a chuckle. "I almost thought you would not come to the church at all."

That only added to her guilt. Her need to deny what had been in her thoughts. The rash step she'd nearly taken. "Rot and nonsense! Why should you think such a thing?"

"True enough. It is nonsense. For why would you give up the adventure of marriage to me, the excitement of a battle now and then to keep the juices flowing? And for what? The tedium of being a prisoner in your father's house for the rest of your life?'' He pulled her to her feet. ''Come,'' he ordered. ''The carriage is waiting.''

He was altogether too conceited and overbearing. ''A prisoner in my father's house?'' she echoed. ''As opposed to being *your* prisoner?''

''I shall prove a far more loving jailer.'' He held her hands and stepped back to appraise her, his blue eyes sweeping her from top to toe. ''You look very nice. A charming bride.'' His mouth twitched in a wicked smirk. ''However, you might have done without the padding at the bosom. I liked what was already there.''

''Oh!'' The thought that he'd been examining her body for weeks made her redden with embarrassment and fury at the same time. Though she was conscious of his eyes on her as she picked up her wedding bouquet, she ignored him. She steadfastly refused to look at him or speak to him, as he guided her down the stairs and into the waiting carriage.

It was only a few blocks from the house to the church, and they rode in silence. She noticed that he never let go of her arm. His fingers were only a light restraint, but they seemed a reminder that she would soon belong to him.

They arrived at the church. He helped her down, steered her into the vestibule and toward the antechamber. And still he held fast to her arm in that possessive way that was beginning to make her uneasy. His wife. His chattel. She tugged her arm loose from his hand. ''You don't have to hold me,'' she snapped. ''I won't escape before the ceremony.''

''Escape? Why should you? I am not the one who deserves your vengeance.''

His tone was deceptively mild, but his words brought her to a halt. She swung around, her eyes narrowing, and studied his face. His expression was bland; it told her nothing. ''Vengeance? What do you mean?'' she demanded. ''Who do you mean?''

''I mean Jack,'' he said quietly. ''That was his name, Rose said. *N'est-ce pas?*''

He knew. Dear heaven, he knew. She felt as naked as a prisoner awaiting the lash. The complete degradation of her pride was almost too much to bear. Her face burned with shame. And outrage, that Rose should have told him. He'd come to fetch her deliberately, fearing she would jilt him in revenge for Jack. Which, if she admitted it to herself, was what she'd had in the back of her mind from the first. She began to sputter in anger and guilt, the words pouring forth like a bitter tide. "You wretch . . . Jack was my affair. You had no right to know anything about him. To force my sister to tell you . . ."

He grabbed her roughly by the shoulders and shook her. "Listen to me, Elizabeth Babcock. Now that I know the truth, I shall not be Jack's whipping boy any longer. Do you understand? Whatever your lingering wrath for him, you and I start with a clean page. Your father waits in there to escort you down the aisle. *Go to him.*"

She stared, torn with indecision, more than a little frightened. Not "please." Not "will you?" Simply "*go.*" As high-handed as that. She glanced anxiously around her. Perhaps she could still race for the door, regain the carriage and . . .

His hands tightened on her shoulders, but his face relaxed into a devil's smile, the eyebrows arching wickedly. "Unless you prefer me to carry you down the aisle," he offered. "Tossed over my shoulder. It would add a novel touch to the ceremony, don't you think? And give the gossips of New York something new to talk about."

She suddenly remembered how he'd behaved at the reception in Paris, willing to go to any lengths to have his way. And never mind his pride. He was clearly capable of toting her down the aisle in that undignified fashion. There was nothing to do but capitulate, however much it might vex her. She sniffed in disdain. "Don't think for a minute that I'm doing this out of any sense of submission, Mr. Bouchard. You scarcely intimidate me with your threats. It's only that Mother would be heartbroken if her plans went awry again."

He had the decency not to smirk. "Of course."

He waited until she'd gone to her father, then moved down the aisle to take his place before the altar. And when Elizabeth joined him, relinquishing her father's arm to put her hand in his, he smiled in pleasure.

For Elizabeth, there was no pleasure. Only the sense of existing in a dream, in a strange, misty land beyond which waited...what? She shivered. Gone was her independence, gone was her free spirit, given into the hands of a stranger. There would never be excitement for her after all. There would only be the dull routine of a wife—her mother's life, her sisters' lives. Had it ever been what she *really* wanted? Even the first time, with Jack?

Numbly she followed the order of the service, kneeling and standing as she was directed. It was only when the vicar reached the part where she was expected to respond to "Wilt thou obey him and serve him? Love, honor and keep him?" that the dreamy mist was dispelled. She looked at the vicar's kindly face in alarm, then glanced at Noël beside her. Surely that was a self-satisfied grin on his face. She felt the anger building within her, like a volcano ready to erupt. Obey? she thought. *Obey?* By jingo, if she'd stopped to consider it, she would have insisted they remove that horrid word from the service!

"Elizabeth?" The vicar's drooping chins began to quiver at her continued silence. Someone tittered in the congregation. "Wilt thou?" implored the vicar in an urgent whisper.

"If I must," she muttered, scowling at Noël. Then, raising her voice, she said clearly and firmly, "I will." So much for the pinch-nosed gossips who'd said she'd never marry!

She heard a noise from Noël. It sounded distinctly like a snicker; he scarcely seemed able to contain his laughter. The scoundrel! she thought. She moved closer to him and, under the cover of her skirts, kicked him in the shin. As hard as she could. Then she looked up at him and smiled serenely.

He returned her smile, though he dropped her hand from his. She was just beginning to glory in her triumph over him when she felt his hand at her waist, beneath her long, con-

cealing veil. Then, to her complete surprise, she felt the
sharpest pinch to her backside that she ever could have
imagined. She jerked away from him and uttered a squeak
that sounded like a mouse with its tail caught in a trap. How
dare he! It was only the awareness of the congregation behind her that kept her from hurling her bouquet at his
smirking face.

The vicar was beginning to turn pink as he glanced from
one to the other. He hurried through the rest of the service,
breathing what seemed like a sigh of relief when he finally
pronounced them man and wife.

Noël turned to her, grinning and shaking his head. "An
adventure, Lisbet," he said. He pulled her into his arms and
kissed her exuberantly. She was too dazed by the reality of
what she'd done to object.

Above them, in the gallery, the choir burst into song. A
hymn, thought Elizabeth in disgust, that had been chosen
personally—no doubt—by Father. A reflection of his sentiments at her long-hoped-for marriage?

It was Mozart's *Alleluja*.

# Chapter Seven

Alice, Mrs. Babcock's personal maidservant, finished braiding Elizabeth's hair into a single thick plait, stepped back to admire her handiwork and smiled. "There. I'll be going now. You'll find your wedding gown clean and pressed when you return from your honeymoon trip." She nodded toward a small wardrobe in the corner of the room. "I've left out your traveling dress and your necessaries for the morning, and packed the rest. But if you need me tomorrow to help you dress, Miss Elizabeth, I'll come back here to the hotel." Carefully she placed Elizabeth's wedding dress and veil into a hamper, then giggled. "I forgot. I mean *Mrs. Bouchard*. Shall I come back in the morning?"

Elizabeth frowned. She was uneasy enough about tonight, and the mysteries it held; in the morning she didn't fancy seeing a maid who'd known her for years, who might gossip to the rest of the Babcock servants and household. She shook her head. "I won't need you, Alice. No sense in your coming all the way from Warren Street. I'll manage for myself."

Alice giggled again. "And of course Mr. Bouchard can help you. In the morning." Her sly smile faded at the frosty look on Elizabeth's face. She curtsied quickly, picked up the hamper and scurried to the door of the hotel bedroom. Elizabeth could hear her in the adjoining private parlor, setting out the glasses for the champagne that Noël had ordered. In a moment, Alice reappeared in the open doorway. "Shall I close this door for you, ma'am, before I go?"

Elizabeth hesitated. Noël had discreetly left her alone with the maid to prepare for bed while he arranged a carriage for the morning. He'd promised to wait downstairs in the barroom of the Merchant's Hotel for a decent interval of time. Still, she'd have no warning of his arrival when he returned to their rooms. It made her feel trapped and vulnerable. The bedroom door would be a welcome, if momentary, barrier. "Yes," she said. "Please close it." With another curtsy, Alice complied. Elizabeth heard the maid's steps across the floor of the parlor, the click of the outer door, then silence.

She turned to the large standing mirror and examined her reflection. Both her nightdress and its matching wrapping gown were thick with ruffles, an invention that Mother and the dressmaker had hoped would give the illusion of a full, womanly body beneath. She sighed. But nothing could hide her sharp-boned hips, her small breasts. Noël was her husband now. He would want to see her entire body. And how could she bear the look of disappointment in his eyes?

Not even Jack had seen her completely naked that day. She groaned and wrapped her arms around herself, filled with horror and disgust at the memory. How young she'd been, how filled with innocent joy. She'd taken the ferryboat to Brooklyn, to visit Jack at his shipyard. Three days before their wedding, and her heart so bursting with love that she couldn't endure a single day without seeing him.

It had begun to rain heavily by the time she reached the Brooklyn shore; she guided her gig through the rain-slicked streets, her heart beating in anticipation of her welcome. He'd smile and put down his pen; they'd sit in his cozy office and share a pot of tea fetched by his clerk. They never seemed to have much to say to each other. When, occasionally, his silence distressed her, she'd tell herself that he was simply worried, distracted by business matters. Most of the time she was happy just to be with him, to look forward to his sweet kisses, to know that—wonder of wonders!—he had chosen her above all women.

She wasn't surprised to see the shipyard deserted, the halffinished hulk of a ship silent and empty; with this rain, Jack had probably sent the carpenters home ages ago. She jumped from the gig and hurried to the door of the office, holding her shawl over her head to protect herself from the downpour. She burst through the door and threw down her shawl and bonnet, then stood there, dripping on the floor and giggling at the same time. How could a little rain quench her happiness?

John Cochran whirled to face her, a large sheaf of papers in his hand. "Damn, what are you doing here?" His eyes glowed with a strange light and his usually neat black hair was in disarray. Elizabeth had sometimes teased him that—with his dark eyes, thin mustache and swarthy complexion—he looked more like a Spaniard than an Englishman. But today he looked like a wild corsair. "What do you want?" he demanded. He seemed as tense as a coiled spring.

The anger in his voice made her tremble. "Don't be vexed with me, Jack," she began timidly. "I only came to tell you I did everything you asked. I spoke to the rector about the service, and I've had all your shirts laundered. Your blue waistcoat needed mending. The tailor should send it around to your rooms tomorrow." She smiled in wan hope and moved toward him. He hadn't even greeted her with a kiss. "You see what a good little wife I'll make? All these weeks of practice..."

He grunted and continued to sort his papers.

His silence made her feel lonely and bereft. Hungry for his lips, his approval. "Am I not to have even one kiss?" she ventured. Then cursed herself for sounding like a beggar.

He threw the papers on his desk and ran his hand through his thick hair. "For God's sake, Elizabeth, can't you see I have things on my mind?"

The harshness in his tone was a cold hand around her heart. She forced a bright laugh to hide her pain. "My error, milord," she said playfully. "I didn't know that rainy Wednesdays were simply the wrong time to visit. I trust that..." She was suddenly aware that the workroom beyond his office was very quiet. "Where's Haviland? And Marshall?" she inquired, referring to his clerk and his draftsman. Jack usually insisted on a full day's work from them, whatever the weather.

"I dismissed them early." His voice was clipped and firm, clearly forbidding her to pursue the subject.

She was becoming desperate to lighten his dark mood, to win her kiss. "Well, now," she said, consciously imitating Caroline's coy manner, "you don't like rainy Wednesdays. Are you more cheerful on sunny Saturdays? Or have you forgotten, milord, that we're getting married?"

"I haven't forgotten," he muttered. He pulled another stack of papers from a desk drawer and began to leaf through them.

"And how do you feel about cloudy Thursdays? Or windy Fridays? I thought tomorrow we could—"

He scowled. "No. I'll be busy in the next few days. I don't want you to visit me. I don't want us to see each other. I need this time for myself."

Her face fell. "But Jack—"

"Stop looking so hangdog, Elizabeth! I can't abide it when you cling. It's only three days until Saturday."

Even loving him as she did, needing him, there were limits to her tolerance, limits to the abasement of her pride. She drew herself up, smiled with cool indifference. "Whatever you wish, John."

"Elizabeth. Don't be that way." His expression softened, an odd sadness coming into his eyes. "I'm sorry, dearest. Truly sorry. I didn't mean to scold you. Can I atone with a kiss?"

She melted at his words, at his soft gaze, and allowed him to gather her to his breast. And when he bent his head to hers, she knew she'd always forgive him of anything, just for the sweetness of his kiss. She felt the familiar shiver of delight at the warmth of his lips, the strange yearning that rose up within her; it spoke of joys unknown, of pleasures unimagined, of happiness yet to come. She was his. His love. His slave. Now and forevermore.

He lifted his mouth from hers. "Poor Elizabeth." His voice was filled with a deep melancholy. After a moment, he sighed and seemed to shake off whatever was troubling him. He smiled tenderly. "Now be a good girl and run along. It's not so very long until Saturday."

"Oh, Jack, I do love you," she cried. She threw her arms around his neck and kissed him with wild abandon, pressing her body against his in response to her aching need. For a moment he stiffened in surprise; then his arms tightened around her, pulling her more closely to his hard body. She wriggled in pleasure and curled her fingers in his hair. Her breasts tingled where they rubbed against his chest; she moaned softly. When at last the kiss was ended, she turned quickly toward the door so that he wouldn't see her blush. She'd never been so wickedly forward with him. So wanton in her demonstration of love.

"Wait!"

His sharp command stopped her. She turned and stared in wonder. The tenderness had vanished, to be replaced by a strange expression she'd never seen before. His eyes glowed as they traveled over her body, and he ran his tongue across his lower lip as though he were suddenly parched. "Upon my word. What a passionate little creature you are," he said in a rasping voice. "And I never dreamed... All this time..." He held out his arms. "Come here," he ordered. "Kiss me again, like you did just now."

She hesitated, feeling the merest shadow of uneasiness, then moved into his embrace. This time his kiss was more impassioned than hers, hot and possessive; when she gasped in pleasure, he thrust his tongue between her parted lips. It was an exquisite sensation, a delicious intimacy. He'd never kissed her like that before. It was a man's kiss for a woman, not a girl. She could scarcely stand; she feared to lose all control in another moment.

His burning mouth traveled across her cheek to breathe softly in her ear. "Elizabeth." His voice was a husky whisper. "Yield to me. Show me what a good wife you'd make."

She was drowning in her own awakened desires—helpless, frightened, confused. "Jack, I..." Strong hands on her waist, he lifted her, laid her across his desk, raised her skirts to expose her intimate core. Torn between shame and a nameless longing, she had no power to resist. "No, Jack. Please, no," she whimpered, while her betraying body writhed under his caresses and cried out, "Yes!"

He was beyond heeding her. His face was tense with passion, the coiled spring so taut that he looked about to explode. "I want you now," he growled. "It's the least I'm owed." He leaned over and kissed her again. She was vaguely aware that he was working at the buttons of his trousers, but his hungry mouth on hers, her neck, her trembling bosom, drove all thought from her mind. She responded with all the aching passion in her.

It wasn't until she felt his body on top of hers, and a hard, hot...*something* pressing against the naked flesh of her inner thigh that she came to her senses. Desire fled, to be replaced by disgust—horror at what was happening, at what he intended to do. Her body froze in terror beneath his and she uttered a wild shriek. "No!" she cried. With every ounce of strength she could marshal, she pushed him off her and scrambled from the desk, smoothing down her skirts to cover her shameful nakedness, the evidence of her momentary weakness.

"For God's sake, Elizabeth," he choked. He cursed and turned away, bending over as though he were in pain.

"How could you be so vile, Jack?" she cried. "We're not even married yet. So selfish, lustful... Oh!" The more she realized how close she'd come to succumbing to him, the more her anger grew. "What kind of man are you? To dishonor a woman, make her forget herself..."

He finished straightening his clothing, then turned to her. His chest heaved with frustrated passion, and the look in his dark eyes was pure hatred. His lip curled in disgust. "What makes you think you're a woman?" he said.

She gasped in outrage and leapt for him. She slapped him across the face as hard as she could, her savagery springing from a nagging sense of her own womanly failings. Then she snatched up her shawl and bonnet, stalked from his office and bounded into her carriage, cracking the whip over the horse's head with such ferocity that the poor animal snorted and tossed its head wildly.

That was the last time she'd ever seen Jack.

Elizabeth sighed and shook away the painful memory. Noël would be here soon. She glanced across the hotel room at the large feather bed. And she'd be on trial again, forced to prove to herself—if not to him—that she was a woman. She'd failed with Jack. She knew that now. Why else would he have run away from her? After all, there would have been no harm if she'd allowed him to make love to her that day. She would have been his wife before the week was out, in any event. A *true* woman would have yielded—warmly, joyously.

She stared at herself in the mirror. Five years. How much she'd changed. How hard she'd grown. Jack's soft and trusting fiancée was gone. Even if she wanted to yield to Noël, she wasn't sure she was capable of it any longer. The wall she'd built around herself had become too thick. The voice of reason had long since told her that submission to a man was the height of folly. He was the enemy.

She stifled a yawn. It had been an exhausting wedding day, her emotions tossing her about like a ship on a stormy sea. That mad ceremony, the frantic gaiety of the reception—the laughter and joy falling like cold rain on her numbed senses. She wasn't sure she had the strength to deal with her adversary tonight. With a determined nod of her head, she stepped to the bedroom door and turned the key in the lock.

So much for you, Noël Bouchard! she thought.

She'd snuffed every candle except the one by the bed before she heard his step in the other room. She chewed at her lip, torn with sudden indecision. She didn't really want to lock him out, did she? A clean page, he'd said today. Why should she make him pay for what Jack had done? She moved softly across the carpet toward the door. If the key didn't betray her by squeaking, she could have it unlocked before Noël knew what had been in her mind.

There was a gentle rap on the door. "Lisbet? *Ma chère?*" His voice was warm and seductive. Pitched just that way to melt her resistance? she thought, beginning to change her mind. It was a voice of confidence, a smug voice. Surely the wedding night represented an important conquest for a man. Wasn't that why Jack had been so eager for her capitulation that day? So that he could crow his triumph even before they walked down the aisle together?

Still, it must happen sooner or later. And—Lord forgive her weakness—Noël's mouth was beautiful, and his kiss had made her tremble, that long-ago night in Paris. Deciding at last, she reached out to grasp the key. But it was too late. She heard Noël rattle the doorknob and swear softly in French. She turned away from the door. To unlock it now—when he was aware of what she'd done—was to give in, to start her married life at even more of a disadvantage. He'd forced her to go through with the wedding when she'd planned on running away; he had to know that it was a victory for him. But the last one, by jingo. The last one.

Whatever happened tonight, she'd never unlock that door.

"Have I come too soon, Lisbet?"

"No."

"I shall pour the champagne. Will you join me in the parlor?"

"No."

He chuckled softly beyond the door. "Is that meant to be an invitation to join *you?* But you see—" again he rattled the knob "—there are some obstacles that not even love can overcome. You had best unlock the door."

"No." Her voice was stronger, her defiance growing with every calculatedly charming word he uttered.

"You must not be afraid, *ma petite,* no matter what you have heard. I shall give you no cause to fear me."

"I'm not afraid," she snapped. "If it hurt as much as my sisters say, no one would ever get married!"

"They are very wicked to fill your head with nonsense. What else did they tell you?"

"Nothing I didn't already know about a man's animal lusts," she said scornfully. "The look he gets in his eyes when he thinks about...having a woman." The look in Jack's eyes that day.

He muttered something under his breath. "This is very difficult, Lisbet, with the door between us. Come out here. We will sit and talk and drink champagne. Nothing more."

He laughed gently. "I promise I shall keep my 'animal lusts' under control. But let us begin as friends. Come. Open the door, my sweet, fond friend."

She wondered how many women had been seduced by that ring of sincerity in his voice. "Do you think to fuddle me with the champagne, take me off my guard so you can indulge your selfish passions?"

"*Grand Dieu!* You Americans! Is that what you think? Passion is to be shared. It is not a man's privilege alone. But we can share nothing if you insist to behave like a stubborn child. Open the door."

"No," she said airily. "I'm tired. I want to sleep. If you wish to talk, we'll talk in the morning. Good night."

She heard the slam of his hand against the door. "This becomes absurd. You will please to open this door, Elizabeth." He enunciated each word with chilling clarity.

How like him to begin giving orders as soon as he couldn't have his own way, the autocratic dog! Well, she wasn't afraid of him. She wasn't sure what the morning would bring, but tonight she felt perfectly in control with the locked door between them. "I will not," she said. "I believe there's a small settee in the parlor. It may be a little short for you, but I'm sure it will do. There's no blanket, but if you should turn cold during the night, you can always command the fire to burn. You're so good at playing the soldier." She laughed softly, her voice dripping with sarcasm. "And then, perhaps, the heat of your Frenchman's passion will keep you warm. You scarcely need me."

He swore again; then she heard the sound of his footsteps moving away from the door. She stepped closer, straining to hear. There was the pop of the champagne cork, the sound of liquid being poured into a glass. Only one glass. She couldn't believe it. She'd *won*. He'd clearly conceded to her. He'd spend the night drinking, and complain of a headache in the morning, no doubt. But at least he'd leave her in peace tonight.

She crossed the room, kicked off her mules and shrugged out of her wrapping gown. She leaned over the bed, testing its softness with the palms of her hands. It was important to get a good rest tonight. She had no idea where Noël intended to take her on their wedding trip, though from what he'd said she thought it might be a grand hotel in Saratoga Springs. Still, tomorrow could be a long, exhausting day of travel. She pulled back the blanket and sheet, plumped the pillows. A good night's sleep. That was what she needed. She . . .

There was a loud, splintering crash. She gave a squeal of alarm and whirled to see Noël standing in the open doorway. He'd removed his coat and waistcoat, unbuttoned his frilled shirt almost to the waist and rolled up his sleeves. He looked like a pugilist about to engage in a match. He crossed his sinewy arms over his chest and leaned against the broken door, then raised a mocking eyebrow. "Now," he drawled, "shall we continue this battle without the distraction of a damned door?"

She gulped. She'd never seen him shirtsleeved before, with nothing but thin linen covering his broad shoulders and torso. His muscular body was intimidating with its power, reminding her of her own puny weapons—her wit and her sharp tongue. She made a valiant effort to brazen it out. She raised her hands to shield her naked shoulders and stamped her foot. "Get out of here. I'm not properly dressed."

He laughed softly. "You are not properly *undressed,* my angel, but we shall soon remedy that."

Her eyes widened in alarm. "I thought you said you only wanted to talk tonight."

"Ah, but that was when I was speaking to the reasonable Elizabeth. Elizabeth the hellcat does not deserve the same consideration." His voice was deceptively calm and pleasant; the diabolical gleam in his eye seemed a truer indication of his mood. He unwrapped his arms—the sinuous movement was like that of a snake preparing to strike—and stepped toward her. "I insist on my comforts tonight."

She thrust out a defiant chin. "I don't want you to touch me."

"I meant the comfort of a soft bed."

"You may have it, then. I'll take the settee." She started to reach for a pillow, but his low voice stopped her.

"And my wife," he growled.

"Who is neither soft nor comforting," she said with a sneer.

"But who will learn to be both. Beginning now." He stepped closer. "Come to me, wife."

Curse the villain, he meant to have his way in all things! She glanced wildly about. The only object on the bedside table was the candle; if she threw that at him, the room would be plunged into darkness. A dangerous state. And with the bed behind her, and Noël between her and the parlor door, she had few avenues of escape. She decided on a bold attack.

Two chairs and a small table were situated near the foot of the bed. Besides an unlit candle, the table held two cups and saucers on a brass tray—awaiting a pot of breakfast coffee, no doubt. An extravagance of ammunition. She began with the candlestick, a heavy pewter column that whizzed harmlessly past Noël's shoulder and crashed against the wall. She had better aim with the first cup: he had to bend his head to one side to avoid it.

"The more you break," he said, "the less I will have to spend on you. I am sure Monsieur Gibson, the proprietor of this fine establishment, will expect to be compensated—" He broke off to duck the second cup and two saucers, which shattered noisily behind him.

"You wretched man," she said, her lip curling. "You show more concern for the proprietor than for the feelings of your own wife!"

"The proprietor has been unfailingly polite. My wife, on the other hand, still must be taught manners, it would seem. I—*Le diable!*" he swore, flinching in pain, as she swung the tray against his shoulder as though she were beating a rug.

"If you want me to be polite to you," she said, "you'll go away and let me sleep tonight, as I asked." She grasped the dented tray in both hands and raised it over her head, meaning to smash it against his handsome nose.

"Oh, no," he said, and reached out to her. He curled his fingers around her wrists and shook her hands until she dropped the tray. Still holding her wrists, he began to draw her close. "We will begin with a kiss, my sweet Lisbet. After that, how I treat you will depend on your behavior."

She was boiling with frustration and helpless anger, and fought against his iron grip. "Curse you! I won't let you kiss me!" With a savage effort, she tore herself from his grasp and retreated behind the chairs.

He clenched his teeth in anger. "Have you finished your tantrum, Elizabeth? I trust so. Because I have had quite enough. Now you will dance to my tune." With one strong hand, he grasped hold of the chair in his path and lifted and tossed it into the corner of the room to splinter as though it were a piece of kindling. His eyes glowed with a fury she hadn't seen before, a rage she hadn't thought him capable of.

She trembled, filled with genuine terror for the first time. What had possessed her to behave so wildly? He was strong and determined, capable of taking what he wanted. He could break her in half if he chose. And all the time she'd thought she was winning, he'd merely been indulging her temper, allowing her to exhaust herself, like a fly buzzing around a stallion. Now the fly was about to be swatted. She gulped and backed away from him. There was no place to run, no place to hide. Only the bed. Perhaps she could scramble across it, gain the other side. She'd be farther away from the door, but at least the bed would be between her and Noël.

Perched on all fours like a scampering puppy dog, she'd almost made it across to the other side of the bed when she felt his hand grasp her ankle. Ignoring her squeals of protest, he jerked on her leg until she lay flat on the bed, her face buried in the blankets, her hands scratching wildly to find the anchor of the bedpost and pull herself away from him.

"Now you shall have a sample of *my* temper," he said. Though his hand was still an iron band around her ankle, she could feel his other hand on the back of her legs.

He grasped the hem of her nightdress and began to slide it upward. She wriggled in panic, kicked wildly at him with her free leg, and managed to turn herself onto her back.

"Black-hearted scoundrel," she cried, gasping. "Brute! To take advantage of a helpless woman." She kicked again; her bare foot found the side of his face.

He released her ankle, raised himself up on the bed and fell upon her, capturing her hands above her head before she had time to turn them into weapons. "Helpless?" he sneered. "I doubt you were helpless in the cradle. But you will submit to me tonight, by God. My patience is at an end."

Her body went limp, cold with growing dread. "Have you no concern for my feelings?" she choked.

"Feelings? Ha! I was prepared to respect your modesty. Your virginal fears. Not your childish defiance."

She began to struggle again. "Damn you! I won't let you. I hate you. I..."

"*Tais-toi!* Be still!" he barked. His eyes glowed like flame-touched sapphires. While she trembled beneath him— mesmerized by his eyes, the feel of the hard body that covered hers, the frightening power of the man—he took her mouth in a burning kiss.

She didn't know whether it was the heat of their battle that had fired her blood, or the feel of his mouth on hers. But her whole being was suddenly flooded with warmth, a molten tide that surged through her. She heard the sound of her own heart pounding in her temples, a throbbing that was echoed deep within her body's core. She felt weak and vulnerable. Most of all, she felt helpless. To allow him to win so easily, to give in to her treacherous emotions... No! She wriggled and bucked beneath him, aware of the futility of her struggles, aware, as well, that to struggle was the only way to save her pride.

But, dear heaven, his kiss was so intoxicating—his demanding mouth, his scent, the hard, masculine body that pressed her into the bed. Her head was beginning to spin, and still the kiss went on, his tongue forcing its way between her stubborn lips to tease her mouth with silken caresses. She writhed and moaned, no longer sure if her trembling body was rejecting or welcoming him.

Foolish Elizabeth, she thought. It was madness to continue to fight him. He was her husband. She had to face the reality of submitting to him. And the rogue was determined to have her tonight. She tried to tell herself that her surrender would have nothing to do with her own raging hungers. If he overcame her with his superior strength, she could scarcely blame herself. Resigned to the inevitable, she slowly unclenched her fists and arched her body to his.

And then—so suddenly that she could do nothing except lie panting in stunned surprise—he released her mouth and her wrists and jumped to his feet. "*Mon Dieu,* what am I doing?" he muttered.

"Wh-what?" she stammered, feeling oddly abandoned.

"What was I thinking of? Forgive me, my angel. I am scarcely a gentleman to take my dear bride against her will. Come. Up." He reached for her hands and pulled her to her feet.

She frowned in bewilderment at the abrupt change in his behavior. "What is it?"

He was all brisk business. "Come, come. Put on your bed shoes. The floor is covered with cup shards. You might cut your feet."

Dazed—and strangely disappointed—she allowed him to help her into her mules and bustle her into the parlor. He pulled out a chair and ordered her to sit, then turned to rummage in the pockets of his discarded waistcoat.

"Are you mad?" she said. "What . . ."

He cut her off with a wave of his hand and slapped something onto the table before her. She stared, her eyes widening. A deck of cards? He smiled at her look of surprise and reached for the bottle of champagne. "Will you have a drink while we play?"

"Cards?" she squeaked. It was most assuredly disappointment that she felt, her body aching with an unknown loss. "You want to play *cards?*"

"A game of piquet. If we must have war, my angel, it will be safer for both of us to choose this battleground." He grinned and rubbed his shoulder where the tray had struck him. "I am not as young as I used to be. Besides, I remember your boast about playing piquet. For straws, I think you said. What shall we play for?''

"I suppose you'd expect to play for kisses," she said sarcastically.

He managed to look pious and insulted all at once. "*Mais non*. To behave like a lecherous brute? There would be no pleasure to collect those winnings."

"Hmph! What makes you think you'll win?''

He shrugged. "Because I am a man, and so much better at cards than you."

Her eyes narrowed in fury. "By the living jingo! Deal the cards, and we'll see who is the better player."

Noël plucked a handful of straws from the fireplace broom, and the game began in earnest. A mad game, a mad evening, thought Elizabeth, downing the champagne that Noël had poured for her. A perfect ending for a mad day. There was he—one leg draped casually over the arm of his chair, his white teeth clamped around a cigar, his eyes shining wickedly as he shuffled and dealt. And she—nightdress in disarray, the pretty ruffles crushed, unruly tendrils of hair loosened from her braid—acting as though gambling at cards were the most proper behavior for one's wedding night.

He was a superb player, blast him! Not only in the actual play of the cards, but in the preliminary calling, when the players were expected to declare their holdings. His expression blank and innocent, he'd frequently concede points to Elizabeth in the calling and allow her to think she had the better hand, only to drub her unmercifully when the taking of tricks began. It kept her blood stirred, her senses sharp and alert, merely to keep pace with him, let alone to best him. And when she began to flag, protesting the lateness of the hour, he suggested good-naturedly that she'd only proved his theory: that women shouldn't be allowed to play cards, lest it reveal their weaknesses.

"Deal!" she said, slapping down the deck and holding out her champagne glass for more.

It wasn't until they'd been playing for several hours that she began to wonder if he was deliberately goading her to keep her at the card table. It seemed as though every time she hinted that a hand was to be her last, he managed to say something that stirred her ire, pricked her pride so that she felt the need to continue the game in self-defense. She scowled across at him. He didn't seem to be failing. Indeed, as the night went on, every hand that he won seemed to invigorate him more and more. Her own eyes were growing heavy. "Aren't you tired?" she snapped at last.

He smiled and shrugged. "Not a bit. But then, I'm a man. I have seen war and difficult times. That is how it is with men. Far less used to self-indulgence than a woman." His eyes were soft with pity. And male superiority. "My poor Lisbet. Are *you* tired?"

Blast his wicked heart. She'd drop in her tracks before she'd admit to needing more sleep than he did, the black devil! "I can play all night, if I have to." She glanced at her cards. "I call tierce," she said.

"Quinte," he responded. "I have a sequence of five." He waited until she'd reluctantly paid off with a handful of her straws, then smiled in understanding. "Alas. Such bad luck. It may take you all night to win another hand. By which time—forgive me, my angel—the broom may be bald."

That sly insult was enough to keep her playing for another hour. A long, wearisome hour. Her limbs felt like lead, and her thoughts were beginning to whirl in drowsy confusion. Dear heaven, she thought, isn't he tired yet? Doesn't he need to sleep? Sleep. She'd never give in. But perhaps while he went to find another cigar in the pocket of his coat... she'd close her eyes, just for a moment... a little moment...

"Lisbet?" Noël smiled down at Elizabeth and laughed softly. Her arms were sprawled on the table, and her head was resting on her cards. "Lisbet?" he said again, and gave her shoulder a gentle shake. She didn't even move. He pulled out his watch. They'd been playing cards for nearly four hours. He himself was exhausted. He didn't know where she'd found the stamina. Perhaps from that stubborn streak, that will of hers that was determined to win at all costs.

"Come along, my foolish one," he whispered, and gathered her into his arms without disturbing her sleep. She was as light as a drifting petal, and she smelled of lavender. He carried her into the other room, kicking at the bits of crockery in his path, and laid her gently across the bed.

It had been a stupid battle, particularly when he'd lost his own temper. He'd come very close to tearing off her clothing and taking her like some capricious whore in a garrison town. He didn't know what, at the last minute, had prevented him. A sudden flash of insight? The realization that part of her *wanted* him to play the brute, to put him permanently in the wrong so that she would forever have the upper hand? She'd choked on the word *obey* in the ceremony. Clearly, she saw marriage as war, with women as the vanquished. He mustn't fall into the trap of proving her right.

It had been pure instinct that had guided him tonight, but now he saw more clearly: there couldn't be battles if he refused to fight her. No matter the provocation, he could only control *her* temper if he controlled his own. He thought of the coming weeks and chuckled as his strategy began to form in his mind. "I'll conquer you yet, hellion," he murmured. "I'll kill you with good will, Elizabeth Babcock."

No. Elizabeth *Bouchard*. He ran his hand through his hair. Good God, what had he done? The enormity, the wonder, of it overwhelmed him, finally obliterating the sense of unreality he'd carried around with him all day. It might have frightened him in the past, the permanence of a wife, but now it filled him with an odd contentment. Elizabeth Bouchard. He took off her mules, smoothed her nightdress over her slim legs and covered her with the blanket. She was his. Now and forever. He was responsible for this frail creature. It wasn't the same as the financial responsibility he felt toward Martin. That was his own private burden, and one he didn't intend to share with Elizabeth. At least not for the time being. No. His responsibility to Elizabeth went far deeper. Her life was in his hands. It was up to him to make her happy and keep her warm and safe, to teach her to laugh and trust again, if he could. To make her forget that bastard who still seemed to haunt her.

He felt a surge of tenderness, a possessiveness he'd never felt before. Women had come and gone in his life—to be loved with passionate abandon, then forgotten. He couldn't understand why this one was so different. But she was, and had been from the first moment he'd seen her in Paris and longed to drive the sadness from her eyes. He couldn't predict the future. But he knew with certainty that this was right, that this woman *was* his future, and that marriage with her was the best thing he'd ever done.

He chuckled softly. A most lively and challenging future, as well!

She sighed in her sleep and wrapped one slender arm around the pillow in a graceful gesture that he found unexpectedly seductive. Her mahogany curls clung damply to her forehead; he smoothed them back with gentle fingers. He felt a surprising jolt of physical desire, a stirring of his body and senses that astonished him. He'd always found her fiery spirit exciting; when he'd wrestled with her on the bed, he'd wanted her as much as he'd ever wanted any woman, his passion inflamed and stimulated by the wild challenge of the creature.

But this was a different, strange desire, altogether unfamiliar, though just as strong. He studied her as though he'd never really seen her before. The lashes that veiled those beautiful eyes were long and black, resting on the pale clarity of her skin like dark feathers against peach velvet. Her lips—when not compressed in anger—were full and rosy; he remembered the sensuous feel of them beneath his, soft and yielding though she struggled in seeming protest.

He swore softly, his body aching with overwhelming desire. God, he wanted her! But what was he to do? Wake her and take her in all her magnificent fury, trusting in that instinct that told him her desire was almost as strong as his? A fleeting pleasure, for which he'd have to endure weeks of recrimination. No. It was far more exciting to think of her suppressing that volcano and giving herself willingly. A woman who could surrender, trust, accept his lovemaking wholeheartedly as a sign of his affection and concern. *That* was the Elizabeth worth having.

And that would take time and planning. And guile.

He stretched wearily. He'd have to be up early in the morning; there were purchases to be made, messages to send. The hotel in Saratoga would have to be notified.

He scanned Elizabeth's fragile body, lying so defenseless before him. Given his current state of physical need, it would be madness to share the bed with her, to keep from touching her, wanting her. And the settee in the other room was fit only for a dwarf. He picked up a pillow and a small throw that lay at the foot of the bed and found a spot on the floor that wasn't littered with broken porcelain. He lay down and made himself as comfortable as possible. He'd had worse beds when he'd campaigned with the emperor— cold and wet battlefields after a defeat. *This* campaign, he hoped, would end in sweet victory.

## Chapter Eight

"Go away." Elizabeth groaned and slapped weakly at the hand that shook her shoulder with such determination.

"But it is daylight, my angel. Time to be up and about." Noël's voice was far too cheery to be endured. "Come. Greet the morning." He shook her again.

Morning? She felt as though she'd just fallen asleep. Reluctantly she opened her eyes and sighed. The room was bright with sunlight that hurt her eyes; Noël's sunny smile was a further insult. "Go to the devil," she grunted, and closed her eyes again.

"But it is near to eleven, Lisbet. And our wedding destination awaits us."

The black-hearted scoundrel. He'd kept her up half the night, and now he didn't have the decency to let her sleep! She opened her eyes once more and fixed him with a baleful glare. "I intend to stay in this bed for at least another two hours. Nothing will budge me! Do you understand?" Not even a lack of sleep could dull her temper, she thought with satisfaction, and waited for him to concede the field and leave her in peace.

Instead, he smiled that sickeningly tender smile that set her teeth on edge. "Only two hours?" he murmured. "No. It is not enough time, my angel. I shall send the hired carriage away. And leave a message with the chambermaid that we are not to be disturbed until evening." He unbuttoned his coat. "I had not expected my sweet bride to be so eager to fulfill her wifely duty." He pulled off his coat and began to work on the folds of his neckcloth.

She was suddenly very awake and alert. "What are you doing?" she squeaked, sitting up in bed.

He leaned over and kissed her bare shoulder before she was able to pull away. "How coy you women are. You say merely that you wish to stay in bed. How sweetly innocent. Never have I had a more discreet invitation." He pulled off his neckcloth and went for the buttons of his waistcoat.

"Oh, no! I didn't mean that. I..." She gave up with a puff of exasperation. He *would* misread her intentions. Whether it was deliberate, or whether he was too buffleheaded to realize she merely wanted to sleep, she could see by the look in his eye that he was set on his course. Unless she got out of bed. "I've changed my mind," she cried. She threw back the blanket and leapt to her feet before he could remove another item of clothing.

He tried to look disappointed, but the twitch of his lips made her suspect that his behavior had only been a ploy to get her up.

"Must you always smile?" she snapped. It wasn't fair—to be expected to deal with the enemy before she was fully awake.

He shrugged. "I am happy." He watched her put on her wrapping gown and mules, then gestured toward the parlor. "Will you have breakfast first?"

She scowled. "I only have coffee in the morning."

"*Dommage.* I have ordered up the biggest breakfast this hotel can provide. Monsieur Gibson tells me it is the very menu enjoyed by your President, Monsieur Monroe, when he stayed at this hotel, not two weeks ago."

She stamped her foot. "I don't care if President Monroe, his cabinet and half the Supreme Court enjoyed the blamed menu! I only take coffee. First thing."

"I fear you will be hungry, but that is your concern. I shall bring you a cup and keep you company while you dress." His blue eyes twinkled wickedly.

"*Before* I dress," she retorted. "And then you will close that broken door as best you can. I'll not have my modesty compromised merely because you couldn't control yourself last night.''

To her surprise, he didn't even react to her deliberate reminder of his brute savagery. "As you wish," he said mildly. He brought her the coffee, then left her alone to enjoy its restorative powers.

She sighed and put down her empty cup. She was beginning to feel a great deal better. It had been an unfortunate start to the day, but the sun was shining, the birds were singing, and she could sleep in the carriage. By the time they reached their destination, she'd be prepared for a fine supper and the civilities of an elegant hotel. The day would surely end better than it had begun.

There was a pitcher of hot water waiting on the washstand, next to the fresh linens and necessaries that Alice had left out for her last night. She washed herself, brushed her hair into its customary tight knot, put on a clean chemise and stockings. Alice had put her traveling dress into the wardrobe. She was looking forward to wearing it. She'd had it made up just for this occasion: a deep mustard-colored gown of stiff bombazine with crisp vandyked points at the hemline and on the cuffs of the long, tight sleeves. A very proper dress. An elegant gown for travel.

She opened the wardrobe and gaped in bewilderment. Her traveling dress was gone, replaced by an old gown she'd packed up at the last minute, and then only because Mother had thought she might need something cool if the weather should turn stifling. This gown was of soft white muslin, with a high, ruffled neckline, short puffed sleeves, and several deep flounces at the hem. Beside it was an unfamiliar long-sleeved spencer jacket in deep purple silk, a straw bonnet trimmed with silk lilacs, violet kid slippers and a pale, olive-green parasol.

She frowned. But she'd seen Alice with the gold gown last night. Criminy. Noël! She snatched up the muslin gown and jacket and stormed into the parlor. "What is this?" she demanded.

Noël sat at the table, a huge plate of food before him. He chewed a piece of beefsteak with maddening slowness, washed it down with coffee, then smiled. "You Americans have a fine sensibility when it comes to breakfast. It almost redeems the rest of your cuisine. *That*—" he pointed to the gown and jacket in Elizabeth's quivering fist "—is what I should like you to wear today, my angel. I discovered the gown in your portmanteau. Charming in its simplicity. The jacket was a rare find. I had hoped only to buy a pretty shawl when I went to the shops this morning. To my delight, I found a dressmaker whose customer had outgrown the jacket before its completion, and so refused it. A happy circumstance, for which you may thank your slender form. The rest of my purchases followed in joyful succession."

"A jacket? A bonnet? Slippers?" She snorted. "How did you suppose they'd be the proper fit? Because you wished it so?"

"Not at all. I measured you while you slept."

"You *what?*" The thought of the intimacy of it—of him watching her, touching her, while she slept—made her cheeks redden in embarrassment.

"Your foot is the length of my outstretched hand. As for your waist and other measurements—"

"Never mind," she cut in quickly. "I don't think I want to know."

His eyes widened with pained innocence. "I was very discreet."

"Hmph." She brandished the gown and jacket. "And why am I to wear this, instead of what I chose?" The idea of him rummaging through her clothing infuriated her.

"Because I should like to see you in bright colors. That traveling gown..." He made a face. "The color of dying leaves in autumn. I have wondered, from time to time, if it is deliberate. The way you dress. So no one will notice you beside your sisters. Very foolish, my Lisbet. You are a vibrant young woman. You should wear vibrant colors. Now go and dress, *ma chère*. I want to see that jacket next to your eyes."

She felt a stab of pain at his words. Her beautiful sisters. "You dress like a little mouse," Father had often said. "Why can't you look like your sisters? Don't I provide enough money for your gowns?'' She wouldn't endure the humiliating comparison. Not from Father. Not from Noël. She strode to the window and threw up the sash. "Would you like to see what I intend to do with this clothing?" she said through clenched teeth. She raised her arm, poised to fling the offending garments to the street below.

"Wait!" Noël rose to his feet. "Before you do that, you should know that I have packed all the rest of your garments and sent your boxes down to the carriage."

"Then I shall send for them again," she said evenly.

"Alas, no. My pride would not allow it." He sighed, a man in deep distress. "Shall I admit to the world that my wife would not do this small favor to please me? That she prefers the clothing bought with her father's money—not her husband's? Think of how it would look. Think of the shame to both of us."

"Stuff and nonsense!" He had a way of twisting every argument until it became absurd.

"To erase the stain to my pride, it would be best if I had your father's purchases returned to your father's house. All of them." He moved toward the bellpull on the wall. "Let me ring for a porter."

She glared at him in frustration. "You're bluffing."

"*Grand Dieu.* Except at cards, of course, when have you known me to bluff? However, if you still wish to rid yourself of these garments, you will look charming on the street in your chemise. I feel sure of it. Allow me." He pulled the gown and jacket from her hand and made as though to toss them from the window.

"No!" she cried in panic. "Curse you, I'll wear the blamed things!"

He handed them back to her, closed the window and returned to his breakfast table. "I knew I could appeal to your reason, my angel," he said.

"It's only because I'm exhausted from lack of sleep," she maintained stiffly, and stalked back to the bedroom to finish dressing.

She had to admit—when she'd completed her toilette—that he had really chosen rather well. The jacket was snug over her bosom, accenting the feminine roundness of her breasts rather than their size. The deep purple silk looked fresh and young against the softness of the white muslin gown, with its ruffled neckline and skirt. The bonnet was lined with lilac silk that emphasized the striking color of her large eyes. And the slippers were the prettiest things she'd ever seen, with violet ribbons that crisscrossed her foot and tied in a bow at her ankle. She picked up the parasol and returned to the parlor.

Noël stood up and examined her, his eyes so filled with genuine admiration, so intimate in their warmth, that it was all she could do to keep from turning away in a sudden shy fit. *"Formidable,"* he murmured.

Dear heaven, now she *would* blush. She had a mirror. She knew her shortcomings. But his approving eyes made her feel almost beautiful. "Stuff and nonsense," she said, to cover her embarrassment, but there was no vehemence in her tone. And when he again urged her to eat a bit of breakfast to fortify herself against the afternoon's journey, her refusal was gentle and apologetic. "I'm simply not hungry," she said. "It's my way."

While Noël paid the hotel bill, she packed her night-clothes and necessaries. When they settled into the rented hackney, she was surprised to see the coachman turn up Grand Street toward the ferry to Long Island. This was surely not the way to Saratoga Springs. But she was getting too tired to care. She fought sleep for a few minutes, jerking her head upright each time she nodded forward. But Noël's long fingers were at her chin, untying her bonnet ribbons. And Noël's strong arms were gathering her close.

She snuggled against his chest. He was solid and comfortable. There was the warm scent of his cologne in her nostrils. She felt calm, protected. With a gentle sigh, she closed her eyes and slept.

She was awakened by Noël's voice, murmuring her name. "Lisbet. Lisbet, we have arrived."

She yawned and stretched and looked out through the open door of the carriage. They were in front of a high, un-clipped hedge into which was set a rustic wooden gate half obscured with twining roses. Whatever this was, thought Elizabeth, it must be a charming retreat. She anticipated a beautiful old inn, gracious servants, a country garden beyond the hedge.

The coachman helped them from the carriage and tugged politely at the brim of his hat. "I've carried in all your traps, sir. I'll be going now."

Noël paid him, watched the hackney disappear down the tree-lined country lane, then turned to Elizabeth with a smile. "Come along, Mrs. Bouchard."

"But my bonnet..." She wasn't properly dressed to make an entrance at a hotel.

"You don't need to put it on again. Not now." He took her by the hand and led her through the gate.

She gasped in shocked surprise, her heart sinking to the pit of her stomach. Before her was a tiny clapboard cottage with a brick chimney, a little front door, and two dormer windows tucked under a low-eaved roof. A cottage? she thought, taking in the bare clearing, the modest vegetable garden, the siding that needed painting, the faded shutters and shingles. No. Not a cottage. By the living jingo, it was a hovel! "You expect me to stay *here?*" she said, her voice quivering.

He didn't seem to notice her tone. He beamed as though she'd just paid him a compliment on his choice. "Is it not charming?" He pointed to the end of the clearing, where the shrubs grew high and a path led over a small rise. "Just beyond there is the ocean. This belongs to my ship's captain, Steenboch. He has spent the last few weeks in the city, busy with our ship. But you will find it neat and inviting, nonetheless. A woman from the village comes in to clean and tend his garden."

"*What* village?" she demanded. If she was to escape this intolerable situation, it would help to know where she was!

He threw up his hands. "*Hélas.* I have forgot the name."

"No matter. I won't stay, in any event."

He looked surprised. "Where shall you go? And by what means? The carriage will not return for two weeks."

If he thought to outsmart her, he had best think again! "I'll ask that woman from the village to fetch me a horse." She was grateful for Mother's pin money, safely tucked into her reticule.

He tapped at his chin in thought. "Yes, I suppose you can. However, I requested her not to come for at least three days. I wanted to be alone with you, my angel."

"Three days?" she squeaked. "How are we to eat?"

"I had the woman put in a supply of food. You will find the kitchen is quite adequate to—"

"*I?*" She was beside herself. "I don't know how to cook!"

He shrugged good-naturedly. "I'll teach you. We will put some meat on those bones yet."

"You scurvy villain," she muttered. "I reckon you think this is funny. After leading me to suppose we were going to Saratoga—"

"I had planned it. Yes. But then, I am too selfish." He sighed, his eyes as soft and adoring as a puppy dog's. "I could not bear to share you with others. I wanted you for myself alone. For the next two weeks."

"Oh!" The man was impossible! Two long weeks alone with this rascal? She unfastened the spencer jacket and threw it to the ground along with her bonnet and parasol. "I don't want you. I don't want any part of you. I don't want your blasted gifts. If I'm to be your prisoner here, I'll make you regret it! Kindly do not speak to me again." She pointed to the dormer windows. "And there had better be a lock to that bedroom!" She marched to the door of the cottage, then turned back to glare at him. "Did you think I'd tolerate such treatment? Like a docile lamb?" She stormed into the cottage, found a small bench in the corner and sat down, her arms crossed tightly against her chest, her brow dark with frustrated anger.

She was his prisoner. At least until Tuesday, when the woman would arrive to lead her out of... wherever they were. Somewhere on Long Island, she guessed. His prisoner—to torment and tease and bedevil. To confound at every turn, and then smile and pretend that he wasn't aware of his victory. To call her "my angel," while his wicked glance mocked the innocence of the endearment.

But the cruelty of his behavior caught at her heart, driving out the anger. He was a rich and important count. He could have taken her anywhere for their wedding trip. Clearly he hadn't wished either to spend money on her or to exhibit her proudly to others. Instead of a grand hotel, plain Bessie Babcock only deserved this isolated shanty. Was he already sorry he'd married her?

Or was the choice of this place his malicious revenge for last night? She fought back the painful tears. She had never felt so unworthy in all her life. At least not since Jack had gone away.

Noël hurried into the cottage—ignoring her—and went into a second room, which seemed to be a kitchen. She heard him exclaim in delight; then he reemerged. "Good! She brought all that I asked for." He held out his arms. "Come, Lisbet. Don't sulk. Come and see the ocean."

She snorted and tossed her head at him. Be cursed if she'd show how much he'd hurt her!

"If that is what you wish…" He shrugged. "*Eh bien.* To work." He removed his coat and vest, untied his cravat and rolled up his sleeves. He returned to the kitchen and began to carry out supplies: buckets and baskets filled with foodstuffs, a large pot, and a worn quilt that he pulled from the back of a chair. While he came and went, vanishing out the front door for several minutes at a time, Elizabeth surreptitiously examined the room she was in.

It was a simple parlor with whitewashed walls, worn but well-scrubbed pine floors and a brick fireplace; the wooden mantel and doors were painted a soft blue, and a round braided rug covered the center of the room, lending a pastel softness to the surroundings. There was a rocking chair in front of the hearth, as well as several high-backed rush chairs, and an oval table upon which was set an oil lamp and a gleaming copper bowl filled with red cherries. A large dresser against one wall displayed shiny pewter plates, brass candlesticks in a neat row and various stoneware bowls and jugs. It was a humble room, but clean and well-ordered.

Elizabeth remembered that Steenboch was a Dutchman; he was clearly steeped in the tidy habits of his native country. She could see why Noël, no doubt accustomed to the ostentation of a grand château, might find a room like this charming. Perhaps, after all, there hadn't been malice in his choice. Still, he might have considered her feelings and desires before he settled her in this isolated spot.

Noël came bounding into the room. He hurried over to kneel before Elizabeth, his hands on the arms of her chair. His blue eyes shone like warm sapphires and his smile seemed to invite her to share his well-being. "Oh, Lisbet. Come. It is a beautiful afternoon. We will find driftwood for our fire, and dig for clams. I shall cook you a wedding feast you'll not forget. Come! Kick off your slippers and be a child again with me." His gentle voice cajoled her, the invitation tempting and sincere.

"Well . . ." she began, weakening.

He grinned and stood up. "I will go and open the wine."

Confound the cunning devil. It had been champagne last night. "Is liquor always necessary to a Frenchman's seduction?" she asked. "To make a woman more pliant?" What else could he have in mind but to forestall another battle in the bedroom?

His jaw tightened in anger; he clenched his fists, making a deliberate effort to control his temper. Then he shrugged in seeming indifference. The gesture was more studied than casual. "Please yourself, *ma chère*," he said quietly, and left her alone.

She sat for a very long while, torn with indecision, as the afternoon shadows lengthened across the room. Perhaps she'd been unfairly suspicious of his motives. But to yield now . . . She stirred in her chair. It was still quite warm, despite the lateness of the afternoon. It would be cooler out of doors. Coolest of all by the sea. And if she put herself at some distance from Noël, he couldn't misunderstand and think she'd given in. It wasn't *his* ocean, after all!

She went out into the yard. The purple jacket, the bonnet and the parasol had been laid neatly across a bench. On impulse, she picked up the parasol. Only because the sun was still warm, she told herself. Not because it was dainty and pretty and he'd given it to her. She followed the path to the rise at the end of the clearing and walked a short distance, noting how the shrubbery became more sparse and the earth beneath her feet gradually gave way to sand.

After a few more steps, she frowned and stopped. The sand had begun to fill her slippers. She knelt, pulled off slippers and stockings and left them beside the path. She could fetch them later. She continued on her way, enjoying the feel of the warm sand between her toes—the sense of having cast off a bit of the prim Elizabeth with her shoes.

She climbed a small hill and found herself unexpectedly at the crest of a dune, looking out onto the open ocean. It was breathtakingly beautiful. The gentle waves lapped the shore, and the clear blue sky stretched as far as she could see. The line of dunes dropped abruptly, creating a sheltered overhang.

Noël had laid out his supplies at some distance down the beach, where several large, flat boulders created a natural table and a circular hearth, within which he'd already built his fire. The quilt was spread on the sand nearby. Noël was nowhere in sight.

Elizabeth opened the parasol, found herself a secluded nook under a dune and sat down. Yes. This was much better. So cool and refreshing.

In a little while, Noël appeared, swinging down the beach with a bounce to his step. He had removed his shoes and stockings and rolled up his trousers to the knees; his blond hair, caught by the ocean breeze, swirled carelessly across his forehead. He looked like a schoolboy playing truant and enjoying every minute of it. In his hands he carried a bucket and a large clamshell. Every few moments he would stop, step firmly on the sand with his bare foot, then kneel and dig with his shell to unearth his quarry.

Elizabeth remembered Grandpa's stories of going clamming: the search for the airhole in the wet sand of low tide, the hard stamp to make the clam reveal its presence with a squirt of water, the furious digging to find the elusive bivalve. She'd always thought it would be fun to do someday.

But as the Babcock family had grown more prosperous, such simple pleasures had been considered beneath their social standing. She sighed. Noël seemed to be enjoying himself. Drat! she thought. It was a little late for her to swallow her pride and join him.

He looked up and saw her. But when he smiled, she wondered uneasily if it was a smile of triumph. She tilted her chin in the air to show him she didn't care a fig what he thought. She was here to enjoy the sea breezes. Nothing more.

Ignoring her intended insult, Noël looked into the bucket and nodded in satisfaction. He put aside the clams and applied himself to building up the fire. Elizabeth screened her eyes with the parasol and watched him secretly as he worked—now kneeling to stir the embers, now striding to a nearby dune where he'd stacked his supply of driftwood. He moved with an easy grace, a man comfortable with his body. And why not? thought Elizabeth, aware of her own awkwardness. When that body was perfection itself—broad shoulders, narrow, tapering waist and hips—a person could afford to be unselfconscious.

He set the pot on the edge of the embers and began his cooking, pulling ingredients from the various baskets he'd assembled. Onions, that was sure, thought Elizabeth, watching him grimace and wipe his eyes against his sleeve as he cut and tossed them into the pot. An assortment of vegetables and herbs. Elizabeth couldn't tell exactly what they were from this distance, but there seemed to be a great many tomatoes. To her surprise, he next reached into another bucket and pulled out a large, squirming lobster. He placed it on the rock, pierced it with his knife, then cut it into pieces, returning them to the bucket and repeating the procedure with a second lobster. He gave the ingredients in the pot a stir, then stretched out on the quilt to rest from his chores, supporting the back of his neck with his crossed arms. He glanced back at Elizabeth and grinned. As though he were perfectly aware that she was watching him.

She didn't know why she was giving him any notice, making him think for a minute that she took the least interest in what he was doing. Resolutely she turned her back on him and concentrated on the breaking waves at the other end of the beach.

The sun was now quite low in the sky. The freshening breeze blew off the water, wafting the scents of the stew pot to her nostrils. She inhaled deeply. It smelled delicious. She was aware that her stomach was beginning to rumble with hunger; she cursed her foolishness in refusing his pleas to eat this morning. But she wasn't about to *ask* him to share his supper—not when she'd repeatedly rebuffed him with such vehemence.

She remembered the cherries on the table in the cottage. Not a very adequate dinner, but better than nothing. And perhaps she could find a biscuit or two in the kitchen. The village woman would have left food for several days. She closed her parasol and stood up, brushing the sand from her gown. She prayed he wouldn't call out anything that might humiliate her before she could make her retreat.

His quiet voice at her back was so close that she jumped. "I have made far too much supper to eat alone," he said. "I know you have no appetite, *ma chère,* but perhaps I can prevail upon you. It would be a pity to waste the food. Don't you think so?"

She turned, expecting a smirk of victory on his face. Instead, his eyes were dark with a sincerity that heartened her. There would be no loss of pride in giving in. And Lord, it did smell tempting! "A pity to waste it. Yes," she agreed. "Not that I'm hungry, you understand. But perhaps I can force down a mouthful or so." She followed him to the quilt and sat as he directed.

From one of his baskets he produced two large bowls into which he spooned the contents of the pot: a thick, reddish broth filled with seafood and what appeared to be chunks of Indian corn. "You had best let it cool," he said. "We can begin on the bread. And the wine," he added, his voice a little too nonchalant. "That is, if you think you can trust me."

She felt herself blushing with shame. "That wasn't a very nice thing for me to say."

He smiled wryly. "No, it was not. There are many things I have done in my life, but to muddle a woman with drink in order to seduce her has never been one of them." He cut a slab of bread from a large round loaf and handed it to her. "For the sauce. The way we do in my country."

She smiled uncertainly, dipped the bread into the steaming broth and took a tentative bite. Then another, with less hesitancy. The broth was delicious—warmed with the taste of simmered tomatoes and garlic and onions, herb-fragrant and heavily spiced. Accustomed to the rather bland English cuisine of the New York society in which she moved, Elizabeth thought she'd never tasted anything so wonderful in her life before. It seemed to call up visions of exotic lands and sun-drenched shores. Of spice islands and burning sands. She stared at Noël in amazement. "But where did you learn to cook like this?"

"All over the world. When you travel as I have, you learn to manage with whatever the land has to offer. Your American lobster is the finest in the world. Not even my native Brittany can compare. And I have a fondness for your Indian corn."

She frowned at the bowl before her. She'd eaten lobster many times before, but never in the shell. It had always been buttered or sauced and cut into bits by some cook long before it reached her plate. "How are we to eat this?" she asked.

He grinned and handed her a sharp knife. "You can dig out the clams and lobster meat with this," he said. "For the rest, you must use your fingers, and drink the broth from the bowl. This is a peasant dish. We shall have no tableware or crystal goblets here."

She hesitated, then followed his lead, picking a chunk of lobster from the bowl with her fingers and sucking the broth from its crevices before seeking the meat within. She wouldn't have thought it possible, that in so short a time she would be able to put aside her proper manners and attack her food with gusto. She'd never eaten with such reckless abandon. And when Noël poured her a mug of wine, she found herself licking the rich broth from her fingers—like a greedy and impatient child—before she picked up the mug to drink.

He smiled in smug pleasure. "It is good, *n'est-ce pas?*"

He had a right to be smug. "It is good," she agreed. She couldn't believe how hungry she was. Nor how pleasant it was to sit and gorge herself on this wonderful feast as the sun fell below the horizon and evening settled on the beach. Her hands were sticky with the thick sauce; it ran down her forearms almost to the elbows. She didn't care. The food was good. The wine was good. She was warmed with a sense of fellowship, sharing Noël's zest in the enjoyment of the meal. They spoke little; it was as though they didn't wish to sully the pure, primal joy of eating.

"Oh, criminy!" exclaimed Elizabeth suddenly. She finished chewing on a chunk of corn and tossed the cob into the fire.

He frowned. "What is it?"

"My nose itches!" She screwed up her face in a grimace and held out her hands. "And look at me. How can I...?"

He laughed and showed her his own fingers, as covered with sauce as hers. "*Hélas.* I cannot help you."

She twitched her nose unhappily. "Am I to suffer forever?"

"No. It cannot be. Wait. I have an idea. Rub your nose against my shirt. The linen is rough." He held his hands out of the way and motioned with his fingers. "Come."

"Oh, that's silly. I..." She hesitated for a moment. But the itch on her nose was maddening. In another minute she'd be forced to scratch it with her sauce-covered hand. She leaned against Noël's chest and rubbed with all her might, sighing in satisfaction and relief. She giggled and raised her head to his face; instantly the laughter died on her lips.

His face was strong in the firelight, his eyes half-closed, his mouth twisted in an odd smile. Her heart contracted within her. Does he want me? she thought. Could that be desire she read on his face? Desire for *her,* when he could have had any beautiful woman he wanted? No. It was absurd. It was only the food and the wine and the lovely night that had beguiled him, as it had charmed her. And he was too frighteningly, intimately, close. She pulled away from him quickly. "Is there another lobster claw in that pot?"

They ate until Elizabeth declared herself defeated and Noël swore he never wanted to look at another clam again. In the darkness beyond the firelight they found the edge of the ocean and bent and rinsed their hands, laughing in delight as the chilly waves washed over their bare toes. They hurried back to the quilt, stretching their feet before the fire to warm them again. From behind them, in the high grasses beyond the dunes, came the hoarse squawk of a night heron, then the unexpected croak of bullfrogs beside a hidden stream. The fire crackled, sending a shower of sparks toward the heavens, and the full moon rose in the distance, an orange globe that hung suspended on the rim of the sea to watch its own radiant reflection. Elizabeth sighed and stared into the flames. It was a night of enchantment.

At last Noël stirred and stretched. "It grows late. And the tide has begun to roll in." He stood up, piled the utensils into a bucket and carried everything—pot, buckets, baskets—to the edge of the dunes. "I can fetch them in the morning." He helped Elizabeth to her feet. He shook out the quilt, tossed it over one shoulder, then stooped and took a small burning branch from the fire. He held it out to Elizabeth. "We shall need light to guide us."

She took the makeshift torch, wondering what *he* intended to carry, since he was leaving their supper remains until morning. She scarcely had time to frame the thought in her mind before he stepped toward her and swung her easily into his arms. "No, don't—" she began.

"It will be much easier. Hold that light so I can see the path. And put your arm around my neck. I should not want you to slip."

She did as he asked, noticing how his hair grazed the back of his shirt collar and brushed seductively against her hand. He smelled of the sea, of smoke from the fire, of his own distinctive masculinity. A musky scent that was more heady than the wine had been, intoxicating her senses. She leaned into the hardness of his chest and closed her eyes. His heart beat next to her ear; his arms were strong around her. She ached with desire.

Too soon, she thought, desolated, when they reached the door of the cottage and he set her on her feet. She had wanted to stay always in his embrace, to be held forever.

"Wait here," he said. "I'll light a candle." She saw the flare of the light through the window; then he returned, took the torch from her and extinguished it in the rainwater cistern. He gestured to her. "Come," he said, and ushered her into the cottage.

Perhaps it's the candlelight, she thought, looking around the room in wonder. But the snug parlor seemed to glow with a soft magic she hadn't been aware of this afternoon. Warm, charming, cozy. And upstairs—her heart began to thump wildly—the bedroom. His arms. His kisses. Overwhelmed by a sudden shyness, she turned away, waiting for his invitation; she started at the sharp clapping sound from the table behind her. She turned to see that Noël had slapped down his deck of cards. She felt a stab of disappointment, followed by the anguish of rejection. Clearly he felt no desire for her. The magic was gone; the enchanted night had turned cold and empty. She stiffened her spine and stood tall, clothing herself in the tatters of her pride. "If that's what you wish," she said coldly.

His voice was as smoky and seductive as his scent. "No, *ma chère*. It is not what I wish. Neither cards nor a battle." He said no more, his silence seeming to demand a response from her.

She fought to keep her voice calm and impersonal, ignoring the storm of conflicting emotions that raged within her. Desire versus pride. Dignity at war with servile surrender. "Very well," she said, with a regal toss of her head. "You may take me to bed."

At her tone, his mouth tightened in a twisted, mocking smile. "How very gracious of you." He leaned over the table and shuffled the deck of cards.

"No!" she burst out. "I don't want a battle, either."

He stared at her, his eyes turned a dark blue. "What *do* you want?"

He asked too much, she thought. Her very soul. She turned her head aside, unable to meet his searching gaze.

She felt his strong fingers under her chin. He ignored her murmured protest and lifted her head to face him. Surely he must know how difficult this was for her. As if he read her thoughts, he grinned suddenly. "I hope you want me as much as I want you, my Lisbet. Or I have wasted my best cooking for nothing."

She wanted to cry in gratitude for his tender understanding. "Yes," she whispered. "I do want—" The words of surrender still caught in her throat. "I want... to be your wife," she finished lamely.

He didn't seem to notice her awkward evasion. "Then come, *ma chère*," he said. He took her hand in his, picked up the candlestick and led her to the staircase that curved behind the chimney to the dormer room above.

It was a small and intimate chamber, with a large feather bed that nearly filled the space between the slanted eaves. In one corner, the coachman had piled their boxes and valises, still packed and forgotten until now. Noël set the candle on an ironbound chest against the wall and pulled Elizabeth into his arms. His kiss was sweet and gentle. And thorough, traveling from her mouth to her closed eyes to the soft vulnerability of her earlobe. She quivered at the touch of his feathery kisses, her body filled with longing. And when his mouth returned to hers, she parted her lips, remembering, welcoming, the sweet invasion of his tongue. She stifled a moan, thrilled by the exquisite sensation, the sensuous exploration of her mouth. She started to raise her arms, to slide them around his neck, but then she stopped. Would that please him? She'd been a disappointment to Jack: he'd called her unwomanly. Was it unwomanly to be forward? But Noël had said he didn't want a dull wife. Her brain was reeling. What *did* a man want? An eager lover? A passive vessel?

She was aware suddenly that Noël had stopped kissing her. Her eyes snapped open to see him smiling in an odd way. The flickering candle picked up the twist of his mouth, the gleam in his eyes. "Are you unhappy to continue, Elizabeth?" he said softly.

"No!" she cried. Had she disappointed him already?

"Good." He put his hands on her shoulders and turned her around; his deft fingers worked at the fastenings at the back of her dress. She felt the cool night air on her bare shoulders and arms as he peeled the gown from her, then the soft, hot touch of his lips at the nape of her neck. His kisses were tantalizing on her naked skin; this time the moan that he wrung from her came forth unchecked. He unpinned her hair and combed his fingers through the heavy tresses, tracing a path down her back to the roundness of her buttocks. An intimate caress that made her legs go weak.

At last he turned her around to face him. His eyes were dark and heavy-lidded with desire. "Put your arms around my neck," he murmured. When she complied, he took her mouth again—in a kiss that was less gentle than before. She clung to him, feeling the hardness of his body through her thin chemise, waiting for his arms to circle her again. But instead of returning her embrace, he began to pull up the hem of her chemise. At the moment the kiss was ended, and before she had time to protest, he lifted the garment over her head and tossed it aside.

"No," she whimpered, and made a pitiful attempt to hide her thin body, wrapping her arms around her nakedness.

"Don't be foolish, my sweet Lisbet." Gently he took her by the wrists and held her arms away from her body. She closed her eyes. She couldn't bear to see the look on his face when he examined her. He would leave now, no doubt, and go and sit downstairs in mournful silence to regret his choice.

Criminy! She gasped in wonder and opened her eyes. He had fastened his mouth on the nipple of one breast, and was doing something with his tongue and teeth that was sending sparks shooting through her body. She writhed under his loving assault, her hands still imprisoned by his. Surely, she thought with the part of her brain that could still function, he wouldn't behave this way if her body displeased him. It gave her heart hope that this night wouldn't end in his disappointment.

He raised his head from her breast, smiled and lifted her in his arms, depositing her in the middle of the large bed. When he stepped back and began to undress, she turned her head away. It suddenly seemed more embarrassing to see his nakedness than to expose her own body to his gaze.

In a few moments, she felt his weight on the bed and turned back. By the dim light she was aware of his looming shoulders, his hard-muscled torso, his strength and power. His perfection. She felt herself grow tense with inadequacy. How could a man tell that a woman was unsatisfactory? At what moment did he know that she wasn't worthy of him? When the act was done? Later? In the cold light of dawn? When would she look into his eyes and see—as she had with Jack—that look of disgust, disappointment, displeasure?

Noël began to kiss and caress her again, but she found it difficult to respond to him, waiting with dread for the moment that she knew must come. *What makes you think you're a woman?* Jack had said. Would Noël use the same words?

His hand had been on her bosom, stroking the gentle curves of her breasts. Now it traced a path down her abdomen to the intimate juncture between her legs. Surely he didn't mean to touch her there! "No," she began in protest. "I don't want . . ."

She could feel him stiffen beside her. "I will not be directed in bed, Elizabeth," he growled.

She didn't like the peremptory way he'd put that. "Am I your property in bed, with no say in the matter?" she asked with a sharp edge to her voice.

He cursed softly in French. "I thought we had left overweening pride outside the door tonight." He started to sit up in bed. "*Eh bien*, shall I go downstairs and bring back the cards, my angel?"

She hesitated, then shook her head. "No," she whispered.

"I promise I shall do nothing that will not please you. Beyond that, you must trust me." He bent and kissed her— so tenderly that her heart melted. "Agreed?" he asked.

"Agreed," she responded, ashamed at her own foolishness. What did she know of making love, that she should give him orders? She closed her eyes and surrendered to his loving attentions. And when his hand again sought her intimate core, one tentative finger slipping within the moist grotto, she allowed it. It was a strange and wondrous sensation, quite unlike anything she'd ever felt before. He made her body feel warm and strangely eager at the same time, content to luxuriate in pleasure yet impatient for something more. When he withdrew his hand, she felt an aching disappointment that was dispelled a moment later. For he had covered her body with his own, and his finger was replaced by something infinitely more satisfying, hard and demanding.

His first thrust brought with it an uncomfortable pressure, then a sharp twinge of pain that subsided almost at once. She opened her eyes in surprise to see him watching her carefully, his body stilled above her. When she smiled timidly to reassure him that all was well, he began to move again. A gentle rocking that stroked the bud of her womanhood with a soft firmness that was both sensual and comforting. She wondered if it was as pleasant for him. But his eyes were shadowed, and his handsome face was twisted in a grimace that might indicate pleasure or anger. After a few moments—during which his driving thrusts seemed to increase in intensity—he uttered a sharp cry, trembled violently above her, then was still.

It was over. She lay quietly, like a prisoner awaiting a sentence, awaiting his harsh words of condemnation. He withdrew, moved off her, took several deep, steadying breaths. Then he bent and kissed her softly on the mouth. "That was very sweet, my Lisbet. You have given me joy tonight."

Oh, dear Lord! He was pleased. She hadn't failed him. Her long-repressed emotions overwhelmed her and she turned away, fighting against the tears that sprang to her eyes. Tears of relief. Of gratitude for this man who had shown her tenderness and kindness. She wept silently, praying that somehow he wouldn't notice and intrude on her chaotic emotions.

"Did I hurt you, *ma chère?*" he murmured at her shoulder.

She gulped back her tears. "No."

"Do you wish a bed gown from your portmanteau?"

"No."

He sighed heavily. She felt his weight leave the bed, and then the room was plunged into darkness, save for the moonlight that streamed through the dormer windows. He returned to the bed and climbed in beside her, pulling up the sheet to cover them both. "Good night, Lisbet."

"Good night," she whispered. She lay for a very long time, reliving the evening with a mixture of wonder and incredulity. She heard Noël's breathing slow and deepen into sleep. And still she was wide awake. He had been *pleased*. She was truly his wife now, and she would never again look at her unbeautiful features in the mirror without seeing a new sparkle in her eyes. She knew it with certainty. She—plain Bessie Babcock—had pleased the most handsome, talented, wonderful man in all the world.

He grunted in his sleep, reached out and pulled her close. She started at his touch, aware suddenly of their shameless nakedness. But his arm was strong and comforting. She'd never realized before how lonely it had been to sleep alone. She nestled into him, feeling the warmth of his chest against her bare back, his soft breath on her shoulder.

She smiled, closed her eyes and slept.

## Chapter Nine

The chirping of birds woke her. She stirred, opened her eyes to a gray dawn, to a shadowed room that seemed for a moment unfamiliar and strange. Then she remembered Noël. The feast on the beach, the tender night of love. Noël. She sighed in contentment. She had only to turn her head to see him beside her. Would he be smiling in his sleep? Would that unruly lock of hair have fallen across his forehead, making him look like an impish little boy as he slept? Noël. She turned slowly, so as not to disturb him.

"Noël?" Her eyes widened, staring at the empty pillow beside her. Where was he? And the sun not even up yet! *Noël?*

She leapt from the bed and snatched up her discarded chemise, hastily covering her nakedness. Perhaps he'd gone downstairs for a drink. She hurried down the steps, still night-dim and cool on her bare feet. "Noël?" No sign of him in the parlor. No sound from the kitchen. The outside door was open. She remembered that she hadn't seen his shirt and trousers when she'd picked up her chemise. She pressed her lips together. She couldn't believe it—Noël had actually left the cottage without a word! She'd give him a bone to pick on for upsetting her like this. But he wasn't in the yard, either. And as she turned toward the beach path, the terror grew in her, along with the awful certainty, the cold truth: he was gone. Like Jack, he hadn't found Bessie Babcock worth his time and trouble. It had been her foolish fantasy last night—inspired by her own overwrought emotions—that she'd pleased him. Clearly, it wasn't so. He'd only been pleased that the night hadn't been a total catastrophe.

In a frenzy of panic and self-doubt, she careened onto the beach, casting her eyes wildly around her. Noël sat in the shelter of one of the dunes, his arms wrapped around his bent knees, and stared out at the ocean. "Noël Bouchard!" cried Elizabeth, her heart pounding in an odd rhythm of anger and relief. "Why did you—?"

"Hush," he whispered, putting a finger to his lips. Elizabeth's shrill tone had disturbed a spotted sandpiper in its morning search for food; it skipped rapidly down the beach, teetering on slender legs. Noël smiled at Elizabeth and held out his hand. "Come and sit. I did not want to wake you. I thought to return before you opened your eyes." He pulled her down beside him and frowned. "*Mon Dieu,* you're trembling. Here." He put his arm around her and held her close. "We shall soon make you warm again."

She shook free of his arm. "I'm not cold," she said sharply.

He searched her face, his eyes seeming to probe her soul. "My faith," he said at last, "did you think I had gone away for good?"

"Balderdash." She frowned down at the sand. His words had come too close to her pain.

"Then smile at me and wish me good-morning," he said gently.

"Why should I?"

"Because the sun is about to rise, the day will be sweet. And you have a husband who is pleased with the bargain he struck." He put his arm around her again, nuzzled her ear beneath her long, loose tresses. "I like the scent of your perfume," he murmured. "I always have."

"It's only lavender soap," she said. But she found her body relaxing, her scowl fading away. It had been a foolish, a needless, fear that had gripped her. Whatever his reasons for marrying her, he didn't regret it. She sighed and nestled into the crook of his arm.

The tide was beginning to recede in a long, slow hiss of water against fine sand. The air smelled briny, with the tang of seaweed left behind on the beach as the waves washed down to the sea. The rose-streaked sky was filled with seagulls, swooping and diving for clams and stranded crabs along the edge of the shore. It was a glorious morning. Elizabeth was filled with a joy and tranquillity that made her heart swell. All's right with the world, Grandpa used to say, when she sat beside his bed and told him of her day's adventures in the harbor, or listened to his stories of long-ago battles, his childhood in far-off England. All's right with the world.

"I like to come down to the sea at dawn," said Noël suddenly. "It reminds me of when I was a child in Brittany. The land is different, you understand. We have more cliffs near the shore. But the sand—" he ran the beach grains through his fingers "—like this, fine and good. It fills me with sweet memories. There was a rich merchant who lived in a splendid château near us. Monsieur Mansel. He taught me to ride when I was six, and to gamble at ten."

"Not your father?" It seemed surprising, given Noël's wealth and title. Noblemen, it was said, usually passed down their traditions to their sons.

He sighed. "My father never knew how to enjoy life. Always serious. Responsible. Born of a clerk and died a clerk, with so little laughter in his days that it broke my heart."

A clerk. That explained why Noël never seemed to behave like an aristocrat. His title wasn't hereditary, from the days before the French Revolution. He wasn't a parasite who lived off others. Somehow, that made him even more perfect in her eyes. He had won his honors and title, earned his good fortune. "And your mother?"

He shrugged. "I think she thought I would end on the gallows."

"Are they still alive to see your success today?"

"No. But what does it matter?" He laughed; it was a sound that was not as carefree as he tried to make it. "They would still call me a gambler."

It was an awkward moment. She sensed pain in his voice. This was a part of his past that he chose to cloak with indifference. It surprised her, to find such deep feelings behind his laughter. But it wasn't for her to intrude. "The beach?" she prodded, to bring him back to a safer topic. "Monsieur Mansel?"

"Ah, yes. One spring dawn—I must have been just nine—I stole into his stable and made off with one of his horses. A wild, high-strung creature that he had forbidden me to ride, for my own safety. I took it down to the beach and rode it as the sun came up. Back and forth along the sand, with the scream of the gulls overhead. *Dieu!* I can still recall how exciting it was. The danger from the animal, the risk of discovery, the challenge to keep my seat without a saddle."

"No saddle?"

"I did not want to take the time. I might have been found out."

Elizabeth's eyes shone. "How I envy you. I've always wanted to ride bareback and astride, like a man."

He turned to her with a smile. "And why not? You're a fine rider. You can do it. I shall teach you. We will rent horses in the village."

His blue eyes were so warm and filled with affection that she found herself blushing. "If—if you want to," she stammered. "I'd like that. I—" Really, she was behaving like a ninny! "Your Monsieur Mansel," she said quickly to hide her discomfiture, "was he angry?"

"My faith, yes! He thrashed me as thoroughly as my own father would have." He grinned and shook his head. "But I was snared. Not his wrath nor the risk of another beating could deter me. I did it again the next morning. Stole the horse and went down to the beach. I wasn't caught that day. Nor the next. Nor ever, though I rode in fair weather and foul. I think Monsieur Mansel knew what I was doing and told his people to allow it." A heavy sigh. "He sold the animal the following year. He'd had a generous offer for it, and a bad year at the gaming tables. It was the greatest disappointment of my childhood."

Elizabeth blinked, lost in her own memories. Drat! It must be the rising sun that was making her eyes water. No more than that. She brushed away the tears. "I learned early not to expect very much," she said. "Then you can't be disappointed."

His arm tightened around her in a gesture of comfort that was as welcome as it was unanticipated. "But how sad, *ma chère*. You expect nothing, but there is no joy, either."

"Rot and nonsense. Ridiculous sentiment."

"And what taught you to close your heart as a child?" he asked with sympathy.

"Close my heart? You mean face the reality of life." She gazed out at the ocean. Far away, a large vessel moved across the horizon, its broad sails glowing golden in the rising sun. "I remember a party," she said slowly. "Christmas, I think. With grown-ups and children in somebody's parlor. I'd just turned four. Caroline was almost three, I suppose. There were all sorts of games and contests that day. Caroline won one of them. She went to collect her prize, her pretty curls bobbing. It was an apple made of marzipan. I can still see it. Gold and red, with a real holly leaf. It seemed like the most wonderful thing in the world." She looked at him out of the corner of her eye, almost unwilling to continue. "I wanted one of my own. I had a tantrum." She announced it like a challenge, expecting his condemnation.

His voice was soft with understanding. "But that is natural."

"I screamed until they gave me an apple, as well. It wasn't until later that I learned the prize had been given to Caroline as the most beautiful child."

"Oh, my sweet Lisbet," he began.

"Botheration!" she burst out. "I learned two things that day. How to get my way. And that I don't like the taste of marzipan. To this day I despise it." Maybe it tasted bitter all those years ago, she thought, because she hadn't deserved it. "Oh, what does it matter?" she cried. She started to rise, but Noël held her fast.

He tipped up her chin and kissed her softly on the mouth. "I never liked marzipan, either."

Elizabeth gulped. He hadn't told her lies, he hadn't said that she was beautiful or that Caroline hadn't deserved the prize or that life was fair. But she felt warmed and comforted, the pain of remembrance fading before that honest gaze, his tender kiss. She smiled her gratitude.

He stroked her tousled hair and the straggling curls at her temples; then he looked away, his eyes focused on the distant sea. "Why did you weep last night?" he asked quietly.

He was too dangerously beguiling, waiting for a moment of weakness to probe her soul. She pulled back her emotions, shutting him out. "They were foolish tears. They had nothing to do with you," she lied.

"Were you..." He hesitated, his voice less self-assured than before. "Were you disappointed?"

"Oh, no!" she burst out, then cursed herself for revealing more than she'd intended. "That is...I hadn't expected it to be quite as...pleasant as it was." An embarrassing disclosure. She was making a fool of herself.

"Ah, yes. I should have guessed. You were afraid *I* would be disappointed?" It wasn't a genuine question. He seemed to know the secrets of her heart.

She wanted to die then and there. She stuck out her chin in defiance. "I'm sure it never entered my mind," she said with a toss of her head. "What you choose to derive from the...the act is entirely up to you."

She saw the angry set of his jaw, but his voice was benign and reasonable. "And Jack," he said softly. "Was he disappointed?"

It was too much. He came too close. She jumped to her feet, her voice rapid and shrill with the goad of conscience, remembering that awful scene in Jack's office. Her naive stupidity. "How dare you ask? I was a virgin! Couldn't you tell, you... What are you doing?" Her eyes widened in panic. Noël had risen to his feet and was now stripping off his shirt. In the light of day she could see for the first time how strong he was, the powerful muscles that rippled beneath his tanned flesh.

"My angel," he said with a smile.

It was the very endearment, the tone of voice—tinged with mockery and false ardor—that normally would have sparked the tinder of her temper. Except that he had already removed his trousers and was working on the buttons of his underbreeches. "You couldn't... You wouldn't..." she began, then backed away, holding her hands before her to fend him off.

"Wouldn't what?" he asked innocently, and stepped out of his underbreeches.

She gulped. His nakedness was intimidating, his power and size formidable. She decided in a flash of wisdom—occasioned by his taking several menacing steps toward her—that any sharp words would be puny weapons against his brute strength. She turned and fled down the beach. His hard footsteps pounded behind her. She squeaked in terror as he clamped a hand on her wrist, swung her around and lifted her into his arms. She squirmed and wriggled but he held her fast, walking with resolute strides.

"Tell me, my angel," he said, "do you swim?"

Steeling herself to be carried back to the cottage or ravished right there on the beach, Elizabeth was caught by surprise. "Wh-what?" she said.

"Do you swim?" His voice was mild and the smile was still on his face. At her bewildered nod, the smile became a grin. "Good! I thought it would be pleasant for us to have a swim this morning."

Too late she realized his intentions, the direction of his purposeful steps. She felt herself tossed into the air—arms flailing wildly—then felt the cold shock of the water that engulfed her. She sputtered and splashed and finally struggled to her feet. The hip-high waves lapped softly against her body. She surveyed her ruined chemise, the dripping ends of her curls. "Look what you've done! And my hair..."

He stood on the beach laughing, his arms crossed over his chest in smug satisfaction. He bent and picked up a sliver of driftwood and waded into the water to stand before her. "Your hair is very charming that way. But if you wish it to stay dry while we swim..." Swiftly he gathered up her tresses and twisted them into a knot on the top of her head, threading it with the twig to hold it. "The women of Japan do this. With beautiful carved sticks. I shall find a captain who is going to the Orient and have him bring some back for you. As for this..." Over her protests, he pulled off her wet chemise and tossed it onto the beach. "I never yet saw a fish with a bathing dress. Now." He kissed her softly, stared at her with that warm, blue-eyed gaze that made her insides melt. "You do swim, *n'est-ce pas?*"

How could she fight an adversary who refused to fight back? She relaxed into a smile. "Yes. My grandfather used to take me to the marine baths. At Arden's Wharf, near the Battery."

"Your grandfather? The one who taught you to play piquet?"

"He was my best friend. We did everything together until he had an accident that left him bedridden. And then I'd sit beside his bed and we'd read and play cards and laugh..."

"How your eyes shine when you speak of him. I think he must have loved you very much, Lisbet."

She blinked furiously. Even after twelve years, she still missed Grandpa. "Criminy!" She brushed impatiently at her eyes. "Do you want to swim or not?"

He grinned and stared down at her naked breasts. "If we do not swim, I shall have to make love to you."

"Then we'll swim." She slammed her palm against the water, sending up a spray that drenched him, then escaped his retaliation by diving into an oncoming wave. They swam and frolicked as the sun rose in the sky and the air grew warm, now challenging each other to a race, now swimming far out to ride the crests of the waves. At last Noël sighed and brushed back his dripping hair. "Enough. My leg is tiring. An old war wound," he explained.

She'd seen the numerous scars on his leg, but had said nothing. Clearly he'd forgotten that he'd told her about his wounded leg when they'd waltzed in Paris. To speak of it now would be to acknowledge that she was aware of his masquerade. And until he himself was ready to reveal his true identity, she preferred to keep silent. "I've had enough, too." She followed him onto the beach, noticing that he'd begun to limp slightly, favoring his injured leg.

She shivered in the morning air. "You must wear my shirt," he insisted, wrapping her in the garment. They retrieved the rest of their clothing, and the pots and supplies they'd left on the beach the night before.

By the time they reached the cottage, Elizabeth was nearly dry and squirming. "Drat," she said. "The salt itches."

"Of course," he said. "You are too fair. Too soft-skinned. There's a little stream just behind here. Wait." He vanished into the cottage and emerged with a bucket and a large towel. He led her to a small creek, hidden by trees and banked with wild roses in bloom and amethyst-colored milkweed blossoms. The water of the creek was too shallow for bathing, with slippery moss-covered rocks that gave few footholds. Gingerly Noël stepped into the middle of the creek, using the bucket to splash his body with clear water. He scrambled out, wrapped the towel around his waist, then knelt and brought up a fresh bucketful of water. "Now you," he said. "Take off the shirt."

She did as he asked, but she eyed the bucket uneasily. "Is it cold? Is it—" She gasped in shock as the water cascaded down her shoulders and breasts in a chilly flow.

"One more," he said. "To get off all the salt."

"Oh..." she groaned, but allowed him to repeat the dousing. She shivered and closed her eyes, feeling refreshed as he began to towel her body dry. It was all so unreal, so wonderful. To swim naked with a man, to be free of her clothes and her constraints on a beautiful summer morning with the birds singing. To be bathed and dried tenderly, as though she were a beloved child. To... She blinked open her eyes, aware suddenly that the toweling had stopped. "Noël?"

He was staring at her lips, his eyes a hazy blue and half-closed. His breathing was deep and labored, and when she allowed her eyes to stray to that part of him that had recently been covered by the towel, she drew in a sharp breath of surprise. He was erect, poised, waiting. She returned her glance to his face. He shrugged in apology, a wry smile twisting his mouth. "You are very desirable at this moment, Lisbet. Sweet and fragile." He caressed her bare shoulder.

She sighed angrily and shook off his hand.

"You find it an insult. But why?"

"Men are lustful animals," she snapped. "That's all they want."

He shook his head. "You say it like a catechism. As though you've been repeating it for years."

She hadn't thought it possible, but she suddenly found herself confessing the deepest secret of her heart. "I'm sure that's why Jack left," she said bitterly. "Because I wouldn't let him. He tried to, just before the wedding. And I refused. Then he vanished." She lifted her chin and stared at Noël, defying him to give her pity.

Instead he frowned and took her by the shoulders, his hands less than gentle. "I do not want to hear of this Jack anymore," he growled. "I'm your husband now. And I want you. I do not consider it lust, but a natural act between a man and a woman. All the more natural when she is his wife. You had best resign yourself to that." He took her mouth in a hungry, demanding kiss. She tried to resist for a moment, but his mouth burned on hers, his tongue thrusting against her closed lips with such insistence that she was forced to part them and welcome his invasion. At the soft caress of his tongue, she shivered in unexpected pleasure, her body awakening to desire. She returned his kiss with passion, boldly placing her hands against his bare chest. The touch of his warm flesh only inflamed her the more. She stroked the firm planes of his breast; her fingers tingled with the scratch of the blond hairs that thatched his chest, the sensual hardening of his nipples.

Panting, he broke away from her, put his strong hands at her waist and lifted her off the ground. "Wrap your legs around me," he said in a throaty murmur.

She did as he asked, curling her arms around his neck, as well, to receive the thrilling reward of another kiss. She cried out in exquisite joy as he lowered her onto his hard shaft and she felt herself filled and possessed by him. Last night it had been strange and new, this feeling. Today she had only to surrender to her body to enjoy the full measure of what it meant to be a woman. He moved her up and down on him in a pounding rhythm that grew in intensity, that thrilled her with a blinding, mind-shattering passion until she was pure sensation. She moaned aloud, rocking her hips to meet his every impassioned thrust. Her body was a volcano—taut with tamped fires that built and built in hot waves of pleasure to the final violent, wrenching explosion. She uttered a great, sobbing cry and collapsed against Noël's neck, clinging to him while the world stopped spinning and the fires slowly died.

After a while she opened her eyes and lifted her head from his shoulder. "My stars," she said. Her voice trembled as uncontrollably as her body still did. "I've . . ." she rubbed the flesh of his shoulders, "I've scratched you most dreadfully. I don't know how it happened. I . . . I don't remember doing it . . ."

He laughed softly. She noticed he was trembling as much as she. "*La petite mort*. The little death, we call it in my country. When your soul leaves your body for a moment to fly free." He lowered her to the ground, set her on still-unsteady feet, and kissed her again. Then he grinned. "Now, my bride. Are you hungry?"

Hungry? By jingo, she'd never felt so hungry in her life! It was a new and exciting sensation, to look forward to food. She smiled back. "Ravenous!"

"Good! It is a good thing to have appetites. Without them, life is gray. Now, we shall find something to wear in our valises, and then I will teach you to make the best omelet you have ever tasted."

"And coffee. I still need my morning coffee."

He nodded. "And coffee. Then I think we shall go back to bed for the rest of the day."

"Bed?" She hesitated. It seemed somehow improper to spend the whole day in bed. "That's truly what you want to do?"

He lifted his hands and rubbed his palms against her breasts, chuckling with delight when she gasped and shuddered in pleasure at the exquisite feeling. "For the joy of discovering the passion in the woman I married, I would fight off a regiment of Prussians at the gates of Paris who tried to keep me from her bed."

She giggled. "That's very gallant. Still...the day-time...to go to bed..."

He frowned a warning. "It's either bed or piquet."

"Bed," she said quickly.

"Unless you intend to lock the door again," he teased.

"Don't," she said, feeling her face burning with shame.

"Why *did* you lock me out, Lisbet?" he said softly. Despite his gentle smile, his eyes revealed betrayal at her act.

She stared at him in confusion and humiliation. What had been in her mind, to be so cruel? He hadn't deserved it. "I don't know!" she cried.

He pulled her into his arms. "Don't lock me out again, Elizabeth," he said soberly. "Closed doors resolve nothing. If we are to make a life together—"

"Why did you marry me?" she blurted, giving voice to the fears that still haunted her.

"For many reasons, some of which I do not understand myself. But I do not regret it."

His words were genuine, and his eyes were filled with a sincerity she couldn't doubt. Oh, Lord, she thought. Could she believe him, trust him? Allow herself to be happy with this man? She looked away from his penetrating gaze. It was too soon to hope. Too soon to give in to her budding feelings of wonder and joy.

"Kiss me, wife."

"What?" His voice had become altogether too autocratic. She looked up at him, prepared to do battle.

"I said kiss me. I will be obeyed." His mouth twitched in a sudden smirk. "It was part of your vow. Unwilling, perhaps. But you've sworn it."

She wasn't about to concede *everything*. She put her arms around his neck, but pulled her head back for a moment when he would have kissed her. "I'm only doing this because *I* want to, you understand."

"Of course," he said with mock solemnity, and pressed his burning mouth to hers.

She couldn't believe it possible, that her body could want his again so soon. She rubbed her breasts against his chest and trembled with renewed desire. She hesitated, then slipped her hands around his waist to the tight firmness of his buttocks, kneading the solid flesh and pressing him close to her own throbbing loins in a primal need that was as old as time itself.

He stiffened in surprise at her bold caress. And when he lifted his head from hers, his eyes were filled with wonder and delight. *"Formidable!"* he crowed. "I think your Jack was an imbecile!"

## Chapter Ten

"Enough, *ma chère*. It grows too hot." Noël slid from his horse, pulled his handkerchief from his trouser pocket and mopped his damp brow, his bare chest and shoulders. The beach sand was already hot on his shoeless feet this morning, and it was likely to become more so as the scorching day progressed.

Elizabeth shook her head and clutched the reins of her own horse more firmly. "Just once more, Noël. Down to the point and back."

"No."

She tossed her dark red curls. "I'll go without you, then. So you can just take that look from your face."

He suppressed a smile. "What look?"

"That exasperated-husband look. I can almost hear you saying it: 'And *obey*, wife?' "

He laughed aloud at her expert mimicry. "Go and take your last ride, you vixen, or I'll pull you from that horse and make love to you right here and now."

"Mmm." She purred like a cat. "For that I could almost forgo the ride. *Almost,*" she added hastily as he reached for her. She wheeled her horse around and smiled over her shoulder. "I'll be back in a few minutes."

He watched her go with a mixture of pride and wonder— her bright curls flying, her checkered gingham dress pulled high above her bare knees to give her the maximum control of the animal. She'd only been riding bareback for three days, yet she sat the horse with a sureness that seemed to have been bred into her.

He sighed in contentment. Was it only a week since he'd brought her here, expecting a war every step of the way? Instead, he'd watched her come to life, like the sleeping princess in the fairy tale. Every day revealed a new and delightful Elizabeth. She abandoned her severe topknot in favor of loose curls and replaced her most proper gowns with the simplest dresses she could find in her wardrobe. She laughed, she wrestled good-naturedly with the pots and utensils as she tried to cook, she ate even the humblest meals with gusto. She swam naked with no shame for her slim body and dug for clams like a happy child.

And she loved with a passion that took his breath away. He had opened the door, to be sure, but—from that wild coupling beside the stream—she'd joyously embraced her sexuality. It was as though all the intensity of her former pain and rage and hot temper had been completely channeled into a new and wondrous direction. Now he could scarcely touch her or kiss her without seeing desire in her beautiful eyes. And his own body responded with a hot urgency that astonished him. He'd never been so besotted in all his life, so enchanted with a woman's fiery spirit. He laughed softly to himself. It was a wonder he was even able to drag himself out of their bed each morning! He wanted nothing more from his days than to enjoy her sweet body, to touch the spark that would ignite that wild passion once again. She was the most exciting, sensual woman he'd ever known, a tigress *in* bed, as well as out of it. And all that with a modest figure that wouldn't turn most men's heads. Who could have believed it? Bouchard, he thought, you're a lucky devil to have found her.

Still, there was a part of her that yet resisted, a part of her that still seemed haunted by Jack, by the past, by her lingering self-doubt. She'd surrendered her body, but he knew she wasn't quite ready to surrender her heart. That fierce, frightened, wary and independent heart. It would take more time. More patience. More trust.

He didn't think he should tell her about Martin. Not yet. The boy, after all, was his burden and responsibility. As soon as he made a little money on his venture, he could put some aside for Martin's future. There was time later to consider whether it was wise—for the boy's sake—to acknowledge him openly. As for taking him back from Adam ... he wasn't sure yet whether Elizabeth would be willing or able to mother another woman's child. Yes. He'd give himself more time to make his decisions, more time to learn about the remarkable creature he'd begun to realize he'd married.

She came galloping up the beach, a shout of triumph on her lips, reined in her horse and fell into Noël's arms. "Oh, that was glorious!"

He stared at her violet eyes sparkling with joy and felt an answering surge of happiness that almost overwhelmed him. "*Je t'aime. Je t'adore!*" he cried impulsively.

Elizabeth stiffened in his embrace. I love you, he'd said. I adore you. But what did it mean? Was it only the beautiful morning, his own joy of life, that had wrung the words from him? He'd never said them before, in French *or* English. Did he truly love her? The words had been uttered in such a carefree, jaunty manner. As though he weren't sure himself that he meant it. Jack had said the words, and they'd meant nothing. And now Noël was gazing intently at her. Waiting, no doubt, for her response.

Oh, Lord, she thought. It was too soon, too new, too frightening and wonderful. And how could she bear it if it all turned to ashes? Wasn't that the way of love? The way of men? She smiled thinly. "What a funny language you have. 'Je t'adore' always sounds like 'Shut the door'." Don't ask for more, Noël, she thought.

He brushed a gentle finger across her lips, as though he understood and forgave her silence, then bent and kissed the spot where his finger had been.

Would she ever tire of his kisses? It seemed as though each new day of lovemaking only increased her desire, until she could think of nothing except lying with him, giving and receiving pleasure. She returned his kiss with burning

ardor, and rubbed her breasts against his bare torso. Her
thighs still tingled from the feel of the horse's flanks between them, and a new, more urgent tingling had begun
within the very core of her eager body. She clung to Noël in
savage delight, boldly slipping her tongue between his lips
as he had done, exploring a new and wonderful sensation.
He groaned and held her more tightly, his arms a sweet
prison.

At length, gasping, he thrust her away. "You're a glut-
ton. Do you never get enough?"

"No." She grinned and looked suggestively at the flat
beach.

"The sand is too hot. And we must get the horses into the
shade." When she pouted, he caressed her buttocks through
her thin skirts. "The bed will be cool."

Leading the horses, they started back to the cottage. "It
will be very hot today, I think," he said. "I remember once
in Tahiti..." He began to tell her a story of his travels. She
listened, starry-eyed. It never ceased to thrill her—the places
he'd been, the things he'd seen. The most exciting stories
she'd ever heard had been Grandpa's tales of fighting in the
Crimea. But Noël had seen the whole world.

"How wonderful it must have been," she cried. "How
heart-stirring!"

He stopped and smiled down at her. "I thought so then.
But it is nice to contemplate settling down. We wander the
earth when we do not know what we seek. But when we
think at last that we have found it, it is sweet to anticipate
quieter joys."

Her heart thumped at the misty tenderness in his eyes.
How wise he'd been to choose the splendid isolation of this
cottage over the sophisticated pleasures of a grand hotel.
They shared lovely, serene days. Nights of passion. Laughter and joy. And when the village woman came late every
afternoon to bring supplies and clean and wash up, Elizabeth found herself resentful of the intrusion on their paradise.

There was an unfamiliar horse tied up at the cottage. Elizabeth couldn't imagine who would come calling. "A visitor?" she asked.

Noël grunted, a worried frown creasing his brow. "It's Steenboch." He pointed to the battered felt hat hooked onto the saddle. "That's his hat. Why the devil is he here?" Hastily he donned his shirt, and he and Elizabeth slipped into the shoes they had left at the door.

"M'soo Noël. Lady." Captain Hessel Steenboch jumped to his feet as they entered the cottage and nodded a greeting. Elizabeth had met him once before, at the shipyard: a large, grizzled old salt whose rumpled and lined face looked as comfortably well-worn as his clothes. Clearly his Dutch love of order didn't extend to his person. Except for the sailors' queue hanging down his back, he could have been taken for a rough denizen of the streets, a peddler of old clothes, someone's jolly uncle. According to Noël, he'd had a colorful past; he'd been taken prisoner by Malay pirates off the coast of Sumatra and had fought against the British when Dutch Java had been occupied during the Napoleonic Wars. By sheer luck and good seamanship, he'd escaped from Batavia with his ship, only to have it destroyed in a storm.

"Is there trouble?" asked Noël.

"Far from it, *m'soo*. The work goes quickly. I need you in New York this week." He launched into a discourse on the happy progress of their venture.

Listening to their conversation, Elizabeth felt her heart sink. The ship's repairs were finished, the cargo of furs was already arriving from Ohio. Now there was the matter of the crew to be hired, supplies for the voyage, the purchase of foodstuffs as additional cargo to be traded in the West Indies. All requiring decisions and disbursements from Noël. And how much sooner than she'd hoped would he be gone to France? "You don't need me here. I'll go upstairs," she grumbled.

"Lisbet. *Ma chère*." Noël took her by the hands and gazed at her in understanding. "We will talk of the future, I promise you. But now we have a guest. Go and put on your

apron and show the good captain what a fine housewife you
have become.''

She hesitated, reluctant to start a quarrel over the change
of plans. Not in the face of Noël's obvious solicitude. ''Very
well.'' She went into the kitchen and began to prepare their
noon meal. It was too hot to do much cooking. She looked
in the cool root cellar off the kitchen and found a piece of
smoked ham, a little butter and cheese, a pitcher of ale tied
up in a damp cloth. From the garden she took a small head
of lettuce and an onion, and dressed them with vinegar and
piquant spices, as Noël had taught her. Mrs. Miggs, the village woman, had brought a fresh-baked cherry pie. They'd
have it for dessert, that and coffee—Noël always liked coffee at the end of his meal. Elizabeth built a small fire in a
corner of the hearth, ground the beans and put on the coffee. In one short week she had come to enjoy her culinary
chores, experimenting boldly and tasting each dish as she
prepared it or set it out; Noël always laughed and accused
her of eating everything before he could even get close to the
table.

But today she felt no joy in her work. Their sweet idyll
was over. She'd already overheard Noël speak of returning
to the city on Monday instead of Friday. If all went well, he
and Steenboch planned to sail for France in just two weeks.

She carried plates to the parlor and began to set the table
for three, but Steenboch rose from his chair and shook his
head. ''No, lady. I shall not stay. Much to do to prepare for
M'soo Noël's return.''

She smiled thinly. ''It goes well, then? Your venture?''

Steenboch lumbered toward the door. ''As I knew it
would.''

Noël laughed. ''Liar! Was it only a few weeks ago that
you swore we'd have to turn to smuggling contraband to
succeed?''

''Well, I...'' Steenboch muttered and grunted and
shrugged his shoulders. ''I had faith in you, *m'soo.*''

Still laughing, Noël held out his hand. ''I'll see you in the
city in two days' time, then.''

Elizabeth returned to the kitchen for the dishes of food, then lifted her apron to wrap it around the handle of the coffeepot. Noël was alone in the parlor when she returned, but she kept her head averted, unwilling to look at him. They hadn't quarreled all week, but she knew that if she raised her head he'd see all the hurt and anger in her eyes. She put down the pot, then cried out in pain and surprise when her apron slipped and the hot handle burned her fingers.

In a second, Noël was before her. Tenderly he lifted her hand and kissed her fingers, then let his soft lips travel to her palm, her throbbing wrist pulse, the hollow in the crook of her elbow. Elizabeth gasped and trembled at the sensual tickle of his lips against her flesh. Her body was suddenly filled with a hot fire that made her forget her burning fingertips.

"*Formidable,*" murmured Noël, and gathered her into his arms. He kissed her mouth and neck while his hands tugged at her skirts to raise them up to her waist.

She mumbled a feeble protest. "The coffee will grow cold."

"I like it cold." He stroked her flanks and bare thighs, then pulled her hips close to his own impatient loins.

Her voice shook, her body one long ache of desire. "But, Noël, we should . . ." They should be talking of his leaving, of her pain at seeing him go. Not making love as though everything were settled between them.

"We should do as our hearts dictate, *ma chère,*" he whispered, and pulled her down to lie beneath him on the rug. As always, he made love to her with a passionate intensity, a rapturous haste; she moaned and writhed and cried out with the joy of exquisite feeling. With the knowledge that her body was never more alive than when he sought and found the trembling, eager, throbbing core of her and united it with his own burning manhood.

They climaxed together with a great blended cry of ecstasy, then lay entwined, too spent to move, too contented to spoil the moment. At last Noël stirred, opened his eyes and smiled down at her. "My pretty Lisbet."

This was the one thing she couldn't bear from him. Lies. "Don't," she said, and tried to push him from her.

"Don't you know how lovely you become when you make love?" he said. "Your eyes are always beautiful. But when we have made love, they become as dark as a king's velvet robe, and as soft. Royal purple. And your skin glows with life, and your lips are fragile and full and... *Grand Dieu*, it makes me hungry just to look at them." He bent and inhaled her lips again, then lifted his head and grinned. "How I enjoy to make love with you!"

"Hmph! You needn't look so smug." She pretended disdain, but her heart was singing. He'd called her pretty. Lovely. She knew it wasn't so, but she knew that it wasn't a lie, either. She was pretty to *him*. That was all that mattered.

"What is this 'smug'?" he said. With his French accent, the word sounded like "smoog."

Elizabeth giggled. "Self-satisfied."

"Well, why should I not be so? You are a passionate woman. I am a fortunate man."

She wriggled beneath him, already eager to make love again. "Do you think if we stay here, like this, just for a little while, that you could...?"

He laughed and rose from the floor, straightening his clothing as he did so. "I am a fortunate man. But I am not the eighth wonder of the world, my greedy Lisbet! We will eat, and then we will go to bed again."

She stood, smoothed down her skirts and ran her fingers through her unruly mop of russet hair. A saucy reply hovered on her lips. Then unhappy reality intruded, and her smile faded. They had so little time before they would be parted. "Oh, Noël," she cried, "hold me!"

He held her in his arms; his voice was soft against her ear. "Lisbet. Come to France with me. Sail with me. I know it will not be an easy voyage, but I want you with me."

Sail to France? To be with him and to share in the excitement of the voyage? Her joy was complete. She didn't know whether to laugh or cry, her heart so filled it was close to bursting. "Yes," she whispered. "Yes, I will."

He lifted her from the floor and swung her around. His eyes shone with happiness. "Oh, Lisbet! It will be an adventure! I shall teach you to climb the rigging. And when we get to France..."

"Shall I..." Would he acknowledge her as his countess in France? "Shall I meet your friends?"

"My friends? *Grand Dieu,* you will meet my family! Nothing less."

She laughed shakily, relief washing over her in a warm tide. They wouldn't be parted after all, they would laugh together and make love aboard ship and... "Your cabin is very small, I remember."

"No matter. I've already told Steenboch to build in the largest bed it will hold."

"The largest bed? Oh!" She put her hands on her hips. "You were very sure of my answer, you arrogant dog!"

He frowned and crossed his arms over his chest like a stern officer, though his eyes twinkled merrily. "You forget I can always insist that you *obey* me, wife."

She tossed her head in pretended disdain. "Balderdash! And if I still refused? What would you do then, you tyrant?"

He shrugged his shoulders. "*Eh bien,* what could I do? I am a Frenchman, after all. I should need to find another woman to come with me."

The laughter died on her lips. She turned away. "Don't make jokes like that!"

"Lisbet. *Ma chère.*" He pulled her into his arms, smoothed the frown from her brow and kissed her softly. "Surely you are not jealous."

"I think I am," she muttered.

He grinned. "That must mean you love me." He laughed, but his eyes were serious—waiting, hoping, for her final surrender, no doubt.

A surrender she couldn't yet give him. She smiled stiffly, the expression frozen on her face. "Love you? We've only been married a week. I've taken longer to decide on a saddle before I bought it!"

## Chapter Eleven

"Oh, Noël, will they never go home?" Elizabeth sighed and looked with despair toward the few guests who still lingered in her parents' drawing room.

Noël smiled, his eyes twinkling. "You cannot wait to get into bed with me. Is that it, *ma chère?*"

Elizabeth rapped him playfully across the knuckles with her fan. "Hmph! Don't be 'smoog.' I just can't wait to get out of this *gown.*" She made a face and wriggled in discomfort. It really was a bother. The gown had been made less than a month ago as part of her wedding trousseau, but the blamed thing seemed too tight. If she and Noël weren't sailing for France on tomorrow's tide, she'd send the dress back to Mrs. Hudson, the dressmaker, with a sharp note of rebuke.

It was a minor vexation, to be sure. And insignificant when weighed against all the wonderful events in her life. Her trunk was packed and waiting to be carried down to *L'Espérance* in the morning. The start of a glorious future. And, since their return from Long Island a week and a half ago, every day had been filled with excitement. She had watched with pride as Noël negotiated the best prices for flour and cheeses from the Mohawk Valley, salt beef and pork—perishables to be sold in the West Indies; chatted with some of the newly hired crew as they loaded the ship; admired the snug cabin that would be their home for the next month or so. And now this lavish farewell party. Mother and Father's proud tribute to their daughter's happiness—as well as the opportunity for them to prove to their set that their "unmarriageable" daughter had made the best catch of all.

And Noël hadn't disappointed them. He'd been his most charming all evening—attentive, thoughtful, loving. Most of all, loving. He'd pulled her into the shadow of the draperies to kiss her when no one was about, whispered, "*Je t'adore,*" in her ear while they waltzed. And though they both laughed and shared the by-now-familiar joke that the French words sounded like "shut the door," Elizabeth suspected that it was only a joke to Noël so long as she still declined to swear her love in return.

She looked at him standing beside her, handsome and elegant in his evening clothes. Tonight, my dearest one, she thought. After they'd made passionate love and she was lying in his arms and they began to speak of the adventure of the voyage together—as they had all this week. That was when, at long last, she would tell him what he wanted to hear. She loved him. The past was gone, the ghost of Jack was finally buried. She was sure of it. And she was Noël's, with all her heart and soul. Open, trusting, unafraid.

She frowned at a heavyset matron across the room and clicked her tongue. "I swan, Elvira Beedle will be the last to go! She's always afraid she'll miss a bit of gossip."

He chuckled. "I like Elvira Beedle. Thanks to her, will there be a soul in all of New York City tomorrow who doesn't know that Noël Bouchard is in love with his wife?"

Her breath caught at the tenderness in his eyes. "Don't look at me that way. It's positively immoral, the ideas you put into my head."

He grinned and dropped his voice to a seductive growl. "I know. And I can scarcely wait. I—*Nom d'un chien!* There is your Monsieur Lawson. I thought you said he could not come tonight."

"I didn't think he would. He was waiting for one of his ships to come in and unload." It really was quite curious, she thought. Mr. Lawson was still dressed in his business clothes—rumpled from a long day's work—and his graying hair was tousled. It was clear he hadn't come to enjoy the party.

He carried a piece of paper in his hand, which he held in front of him as though it burned his fingers. Scowling, he hurried over to Josiah Babcock and thrust the paper under the other man's nose. More curious still, thought Elizabeth. For Josiah Babcock's face turned as red as his hair, and his loud exclamation—"Damn!"—could be heard all the way across the room. He snatched the paper from Lawson and stormed over to them, elbowing past a small cluster of guests to plant himself before Noël.

"Now, you scoundrel," he said, "would you care to explain *this?*"

Elizabeth looked at the paper quivering in her father's fist and felt her blood run cold. It was a page from a recent London newspaper, clearly just come over on Lawson's ship. It was a gossip column; someone had circled the first item with a black pencil.

"Your correspondent," it read, "having recently returned from Paris, can report that the capital is buzzing with news of the lavish soirée that the Count and Countess of Moncalvo will be giving to celebrate the recent safe birth of a daughter, Gabrielle. Monsieur and Madame de Moncalvo—he is General Bouchard, and a Councillor of State to His Majesty the King of France—are already the parents of two sons."

Noël slapped his palm with his fist. "A girl!" he exclaimed, clearly delighted. "Good for Charmiane."

Josiah Babcock was sputtering with rage. "You find that cause for joy, you damned bigamist?"

"*Pardon?*" Noël frowned in bewilderment. "Bigamist?"

Elizabeth struggled against her tears. Hadn't she always expected a disappointment someday? Her happiness had been too sweet to last. But to learn he had a *family*—! "How could you break my heart?" she whispered.

"Lisbet. Why do you weep?"

"Go back to your wife and children," she choked. "Cursed be the day I met you."

"*My* wife and—? But certainly not! It is *Adam's* wife and children. My brother Adam. My twin. I told you..." He studied the faces of the curious guests who had crowded near and were now passing the newspaper among themselves and muttering ominously. "You cannot have thought... *Grand Dieu!* You thought I was Adam? All of you? Lisbet? But that is absurd. I told you who I was the day I came here. Myself. Noël Bouchard."

Mr. Babcock made a growling sound in his throat. "You're not General Bouchard in disguise? You're not the count?"

Noël continued to look perplexed. "I never said I was!"

"You don't have a wife in France?" Babcock went on, his eyes cold and hard.

"The only wife I have is the only one I ever want." Noël started to slip his arm around Elizabeth's waist, but she shook him off.

"Confound it, man," said Babcock, "why did you let us think that you were your brother, the count?"

"*Mon Dieu!* I had no idea that was what you thought. Why should you come to such a conclusion?" He laughed softly. "It is really quite amusing. And I think Adam will find it so."

Twins? It couldn't be, no matter what he said. Elizabeth frowned at him. "But General Bouchard told me in Paris about the wounds to his leg," she said, her voice bitter and accusing. "And I've seen your scars. What lies do you have to explain that?"

He swore softly in French. "I had forgotten I spoke of my wounds that night." He smiled sheepishly. "But you see, I *was* the man in Paris. I confess it. Brother Adam did not wish to leave his wife just before her confinement. I took his place at the reception. A harmless masquerade. We have done it in the past. Who would have thought...?" He shrugged his apology. "But I am Noël Bouchard. Not Adam Bouchard. And I never claimed to be anyone but who I am since the first moment I arrived on your shores."

Josiah Babcock looked nervously around at the assembled guests. At Noël's explanation, they had begun to smile and chat among themselves: Twins! What an amusing case of mistaken identity. Who had started the foolish rumor in the first place? Babcock breathed a sigh of gratitude at their good humor—the family's social standing was saved. With a broad grin, he clapped Noël on the shoulder. "Well, after all, it was *our* error, not yours." He beamed at his daughter. "And it doesn't really matter which Bouchard you are. You've made our Bessie happy. That's our only concern."

Limp with relief, Elizabeth felt her heartbeat slowly return to normal. She would have died if her faith in Noël had been shattered. She smiled her reassurance at him, and even slipped her hand into his as they bade the last of the guests good-night. "Thank the good Lord they're gone at last," she breathed as she and Noël made their way upstairs to their bedroom.

Noël laughed and closed the door. "Madame Beedle could scarcely wait to go. I feel sure that the first light of dawn will find her on the street, ready to go calling and spread the news of my 'unmasking.'" He shook his head. "I still cannot believe it—all this time you thought I was Adam! The great General Bouchard. *Grand Dieu,* I fear the highest rank *I* reached in the army was lieutenant. As for a title, the only names I have ever been called were 'scoundrel' and 'rogue.' And then mostly by jealous husbands all over the world eager to protect their wives."

All over the world, she thought, remembering his tales of remote lands. "But have you no permanent home?" she asked, an unwelcome thought beginning to whisper in her brain.

"I never thought to want one," he said with a shrug. "I stay with Adam sometimes, when I visit France. But otherwise..."

The unwelcome thought had become a silent cry of pain and dreadful certainty. No home. No permanence. All those bank loans. His talk of money as though he had very little. She'd thought it was just his democratic manner. But now she understood clearly. He was penniless, as well as devil-may-care. She turned on him, her eyes flashing in accusation. "You *needed* my dowry, didn't you."

He scowled at the hostility in her voice. "I never spent a dollar of it. Nor did I intend to. Didn't your father tell you?"

"But you wouldn't have married me without it. Would you?"

He tried to gather her into his arms. "Lisbet. Don't do this."

She slapped at his hands. "Curse you! *Would* you have married me without my dowry?"

He sighed. "I'll not lie to you. I would not have chanced it. No. Not with everything riding on this venture. I saw your dowry as insurance. I still do. For your comfort, should I fail."

Oh, the smooth-talking villain! How gullible she'd been—believing his eyes, his soft words. Had she learned nothing from Jack? Oddly, she felt more cold contempt than pain. "You're a fortune hunter. You're no better than the rest of them!"

"Damn it, Lisbet! I cared for you long before we married. My feelings had nothing to do with your dowry. I thought you understood that."

"Bah! How easy it was for you to swear your devotion, with the shine of my father's gold to blind you."

He clenched his fists and drew a deep breath. "It is very difficult to keep my patience when you choose to be foolish and stubborn. But I cared for you even from the moment I saw you in Paris. My heart ached for your lonely pain."

"Pity for an old maid?" she sneered.

"Perhaps it was. At least that night. But was it so wrong of me? Pity is not a cruel emotion, but soft and filled with tenderness. As I felt for you."

She remembered what he'd said about Elvira Beedle. "And tonight? All your loving attentions? Was that more pity? Or a performance, for the benefit of the guests?"

"Yes!" he answered impatiently. "It was as much for them as for you. Those people have treated you unkindly in the past. It was not to be endured any longer. I wished, for your sake, to put the lingering, ugly gossip to rest. To show them what I thought you, at least, already knew. That you are dear to me.''

"Or was your behavior tonight because you didn't want anyone to suspect what a charlatan you are? A shallow fortune hunter! And all the time you allowed everyone to think you were the rich Count de Moncalvo in disguise!"

He swore under his breath and paced the room. "*Quelle absurdité*. Will you persist in this? I tell you I had no idea that—" He stopped and stared at her, his eyes filling with the light of sudden comprehension. "Name of a dog! You wanted to be a countess. You *expected* to be a countess. Did you fancy there was a château and a diamond tiara waiting for you when we reached France? Was that my attraction for you? The reason you accepted me? You and your title-hungry family and friends? Was that all you saw when you looked at me? My *brother's* name and fame and fortune?" His voice was dark and bitter.

"I can scarcely blame you for trading on his reputation," she countered. "After all, what did *you* have to offer? With all the money you squeezed out of my father, you couldn't even manage a proper honeymoon trip!"

He ground his teeth in fury. "Have you no control over your vicious tongue? Will you now pretend that there was no joy for you in what we did? No love?"

Her pain and anger had carried her far beyond reason and common sense. Her world of happiness had crashed to earth, and the splinters were like sharp daggers in her heart. Daggers that she would turn on him—the source of all her grief. "What do *my* feelings have to do with any of it? You had what you wanted. Twenty-five thousand dollars, and a warm body in your bed. You call it love? I call it greed and lust!"

"You will have your pride at all costs?" he asked, fighting to keep calm in the face of her savage attack. "Even if it destroys us both?"

"What do you know of pride? You allowed yourself to be bought by a rich man as a toy for his daughter! The pity of it is that I accepted so readily. Surely I might have found a better husband to buy than a scoundrel who had to hide behind his brother's name!''

"Now, by *le bon Dieu* . . ." he swore, and clutched her wrist in a hard grip.

She cried out in pain and tore herself from his hold. "Will you break my bones to prove your mastery as a man, my husband?''

He took a steadying breath and pulled her fiercely toward him, his hands like bands of steel on her arms.

She shivered in genuine terror at the determined look in his eyes. "No!" she cried. "You *wouldn't*. You—''

There was a loud rap on the door, and muttered conversation beyond the paneling. "Bessie?" Josiah Babcock's voice rang out. "Bessie, are you all right?"

Noël relaxed his grip, released her, and ran his hand tiredly through his hair. "She is unharmed, *monsieur*,'' he answered. "And will remain so.''

Elizabeth bit her lip, weak with shame that her family should be privy to her humiliation. But their nearness, at least, would ensure her safety. She gave vent to one last cutting insult. She glared at Noël, her body quivering in outraged pride. "Harm me?" she sneered. "You'd scarcely harm the goose that laid the golden eggs. *N'est-ce pas,* my fortune-hunting husband?'' She smiled in mockery and waited for his angry retort.

Instead, he reached out and stroked the side of her cheek. It was so surprising that she flinched, half expecting a blow. But Noël's eyes were as deep a blue, and as troubled, as a stormy sky. He wore a look of resignation, rather than anger. "I'd begun to think I had found a love like no other,'' he said sadly. "A pure and burning passion.'' He sighed. There was finality in the sound. "But there is a dark side to you, Lisbet, that I do not like. A cruelty in the words you speak. A need to hurt, lest you be hurt yourself. I do not understand it. Perhaps you have not laid the past to rest, after all. But I shall be your scapegoat no longer.'' He crossed the room and picked up his top hat. "I will spend the night in a hotel and return tomorrow for my trunk and boxes. Unless I feel more hope for us in the morning, I in-end to sail for France without you. When I return, we can decide if we are to live in peace as husband and wife. In the meantime, I want the peace of solitude. *Adieu.*'' He clapped his hat on his head and strode to the door. He flung it open and left the room, nodding to a scowling Mr. Babcock and a white-faced Mrs. Babcock as he passed.

"Bessie?" began Mrs. Babcock in a quavery voice.

Behind her, Elizabeth could see Rose and Edward. Curious, and perhaps a bit smug and superior. It was too much to bear. She rushed to the door and slammed it in all their faces. "Leave me alone!" she cried. She threw herself on the bed and gave way to her tears, to her old doubts and fears. He *had* married her for her money, no matter how he denied it. And now he intended to leave her here to deal all alone with her pitying family and neighbors.

"No, damn you, Noël Bouchard," she whispered, lifting her face from her tear-stained pillow. "I'll make you pay first. Just you wait and see if I don't!"

Elizabeth mounted the steps of the house on Warren Street, paused and brushed the dust from her gown. Would this July heat never end? It had been an exhausting, oppressive morning. It seemed as though every citizen and shopkeeper were content to sweep his sidewalks without first sprinkling them with water, as the city ordinance required; her gown was filthy, and she'd breathed in and tasted enough dust to fill a desert.

The bells from St. Paul's Church began to chime. Elizabeth counted them out. Twelve o'clock. If she were really lucky, Mother and Rose would be gone by now, off on their usual round of social calls and shopping. She'd sit in her room, take off her dusty shoes, drink a mug of cool cider. And wonder—as she had during her long, lone morning's ramble through the city, her mind in a turmoil—if she'd done the right thing by going to Stephen.

It had been humiliating to endure his smug condescension. He and Caroline had left the party early last night, but he'd already heard the story of Noël's false identity. He could scarcely wait to use it as just another example of his superior male wisdom. "I never trusted that man from the first," he said. "Damned lying Frenchy. Well, I tried to warn you, upon more than one occasion. But you would have your stubborn way. A headstrong female inviting your own destruction."

"He didn't intentionally deceive us, after all, Stephen," she said grudgingly. "We deceived ourselves." Though she still couldn't forgive Noël in her heart for all the pain he'd caused, her sense of fair play and decency made it difficult to accept Stephen's theory of a deliberate deception.

"You may believe that," he said. "Our friends may believe it. But not I. Well, what do you intend to do about the scoundrel?"

"He's still my husband," she snapped. "And exactly the same man he's always been!" No, not quite, she thought bitterly. Before last night, she'd looked at him and seen a god, a perfect man. But gods didn't need to marry for money; gods didn't have feet of clay. She sighed. There was one small blessing, at least. No one had heard Noël's threat to leave her behind in New York. She didn't know how it could be arranged, but she knew she must sail with him at all costs—if not for the sake of their marriage, at least for her pride and dignity among people who already had reasons aplenty to jeer her. Well, by jingo, she'd give them no more cause.

It was just unfortunate that *L'Espérance* was due to sail this afternoon. It gave her so little time to plan, to decide. "Stephen," she said at last, "I haven't come for your reproaches. I came because I wanted to know—" she twisted her fingers together in a gesture of uneasiness and agitation "—if it's possible to delay a ship's sailing? Only for a day or two, of course." Perhaps in that time she and Noël could come to some sort of agreement.

"I assume you mean Bouchard's ship." At her nod, he rubbed his chin in thought. "Well, I don't see how it can be done. Not when it's loaded and ready to sail. I assume there are proper bills of lading for the goods he's carrying."

"Of course."

"I have a friend in the Custom House. But his concern is with incoming goods, not outgoing."

She hesitated. It was wicked and reckless of her, she knew. But she was desperate. And how else was she to delay Noël? "Well," she said, "I *did* hear my husband speak of contraband with his captain. It might have been only talk, but..."

Stephen's ferretlike eyes narrowed, and he broke into a smile. "I quite understand, my dear," he said. "That's a different situation entirely. Well, you may depend upon me to relieve you of your burdens. It's not a woman's place to worry her head over men's affairs." He patted her hand. "Go home and have a cup of tea. I'll take care of everything."

Elizabeth sighed and lifted the heavy knocker on the front door of her house. She'd walked aimlessly for hours, filled with doubts and regrets. And a lingering anger. She couldn't forgive Noël, no matter what she told herself. Still, short of a craven—and completely false—apology to her husband for last night's quarrel, how was she to persuade him to take her to France? She rapped sharply on the door and brushed past the parlormaid who opened it for her. "Bring some cool cider to my room, please," she ordered, starting up the stairs.

"But, Mrs. Bouchard..."

She turned. "Whatever it is, Molly, can wait. What I need right now is a cool drink." She continued on to the bedrooms on the third floor and pushed open her door.

Noël was there, seated at a desk in the corner of the room. At Elizabeth's entrance, he put down his quill pen and stood up. "I had hoped to be gone before you returned," he said. His voice was drained of all emotion. "I could think of nothing more to say after last night. You accused me of marrying you for your money. I could say the same to you. You wanted money *and* a title. I regret to have disappointed you. Perhaps if we are apart for a few months, we can both decide what it is we want from our union."

She was beginning to regret a great deal, not the least of which was her wild temper. "But, Noël..."

He held up his hand to cut her short. "I have sent on my luggage to the ship. This is all that remains to be settled." He pointed to the paper upon which he'd been writing. "It is a letter addressed to the president of the Manhattan Bank, giving you sole access to your dowry of fifteen thousand dollars. It was always meant for you." He sighed. "But I see from the look in your eyes that you will never believe that. Your dowry may be intact. Your trust in me is not. Perhaps my absence will encourage you to remember our happy days together." He reached for his hat on the table, then turned to her with a sad smile. "I shall miss making love to you, Lisbet," he whispered.

His melting eyes still had the power to make her knees weak. "Noël, can't we speak of this before you go?"

He shook his head. "There were too many ugly words spoken last night. I had thought my love for you would conquer your rage. But you proved to me last night that you still prefer war, my angel. I cannot be bothered. I have seen war—real, and terrible. It is a travesty to measure it against the ravings of a spoiled child whose feelings have been hurt."

"Oh!" She didn't know if it was the contempt in his voice or his insult in calling her "my angel" that triggered her wrath. She leapt toward him to slap his face, but he parried the blow with an upraised arm.

"Another tantrum?" he growled.

She bit back a cruel retort and turned away, silently cursing her ungovernable temper. She hadn't meant for this to happen. She'd wanted to make peace today.

The parlormaid's voice sounded from beyond the closed door. "Excuse me, ma'am, but there are gentlemen below."

Elizabeth threw open the door and glared at the girl. "I'm not at home to callers," she snapped.

Molly looked distinctly uncomfortable. "They've come to talk to *Mr.* Bouchard, ma'am. And it's...the police."

Noël frowned. "Send them up."

The man who strode into the room was tall and lean, with a sharp nose and a downturned mouth that seemed permanently frozen into its unhappy position. Behind him were two constables of police. He marched purposefully to Noël and nodded. "Mr. Noël Bouchard? I am Jasper Gore of the United States Custom House. I'm afraid I must put you under arrest."

"*Le diable!* For what reason?"

"There has been a report that you harbor contraband aboard your ship."

"A damnable lie! My cargo is legitimate. My papers, they are in order."

Gore looked skeptical. "You well may say so. Nevertheless, we have reason to suspect otherwise. We've impounded your vessel and intend to search it diligently. In the meantime, it's necessary for you to be detained at Bridewell."

"No!" Elizabeth shook with outrage. To lock Noël in Bridewell, a prison for felons and common criminals...! "He was not to be arrested," she cried, without thinking. "Merely delayed!"

At her words, Noël stared in disbelief. "This was *your* doing?"

"N-no, I..." What could she say? She cringed before the look in his eyes, then turned on Jasper Gore in a fury. "You villain! Why must he be arrested?"

Gore frowned, his sad mouth drooping further. "He's a foreigner, ma'am, flying a foreign flag. We've had too many troubles with fly-by-night foreigners making free with our laws, crowding into our good American cities and filling our streets with their foreign yammerings." His sharp nose twitched in righteous American pride and indignation. "And until we can be sure that Mr. Bouchard doesn't intend to take advantage of our goodwill, we must detain him."

"For how long?" growled Noël, curling his hands into fists.

"That's not for you to question. A day or so, perhaps. Now, Mr. Bouchard, if you'll come along quietly? It would be a shame if we should have to manacle you." Gore's tone seemed to suggest that was exactly the treatment he felt was due a foreigner.

For a moment, Elizabeth feared that Noël intended to fight his way past the constables; then he relaxed his rigid frame and nodded to Gore. "If I may be permitted to take leave of my wife."

Gore returned the courtesy with a little bow. "Of course."

Despite the hard look in his eye, Noël was surprisingly gentle as he took Elizabeth by the arm and led her to a corner of the room. He bent and kissed her formally on both cheeks, in the French manner. His expression was distant, his mouth twisted in an odd grimace. She couldn't tell if he was sad or angry. "Goodbye, Elizabeth," he said. "I shall not return from France, I think. There is nothing for me in this land."

Her mouth went dry. "Not return? What do you mean?"

"I've wasted my time trying to win the love of a woman whose heart is still too filled with anger and malice. If my trading venture is successful, despite your clumsy attempt to destroy me—" he acknowledged Gore's grim presence with a quick glance "—I'll send you a large settlement."

The reality of his intentions was too much to bear. Not again, she thought. Not again! She stamped her foot in helpless rage. "No! I won't have it. You *will not* abandon me."

Now she saw the fury behind his cool façade. "Abandon you?" he said through clenched teeth. "Name of a dog! It is taking all my power of will to keep from throttling you for what you have done! My ship ransacked, the sailing delayed. Prison, God knows for how long! And for what? Because you feared I wanted you for your money? It scarcely seems a fair trade, *n'est-ce pas?*"

"I didn't mean for all that to happen," she cried.

He raised an eyebrow in sharp mockery. "That was what I said the day I killed my first enemy soldier. But he was dead all the same. And a part of me rejoiced. As you do now, I think, however much you try to deny it." He sighed. "Tell me, do you hate me for myself? For what you see as my deception because of my brother? Or am I merely the substitute for Jack? For all men who have tried to enter that cold spinster's world of yours?''

She caught her breath. She could almost hear Jack's insult echoing through Noël's words of scorn: *What makes you think you're a woman?* ''Damn you!'' she shrilled, and struck him across the face as hard as she could.

He laughed softly, bitterly, lifted her hand to his lips and kissed it. His cheek glowed red from the marks of her fingers. ''Thank you for that,'' he said. ''It will be much easier now to forget you.'' He turned to Gore. ''I am ready, *monsieur.*'' He put his hat on his head, set himself between the two constables and left the room without looking back.

Elizabeth sank to the floor and buried her head in her arms. She was less than a woman. She was a monster who had conspired to destroy the one person she loved in the whole world. And he would never forgive her.


Noël raised his coat collar against the driving rain and glanced back at the closing door of Bridewell. If he'd had to spend another night in that hell of a prison, he'd have been ready to commit murder. One night had been more than enough, crowded with thieves and violent felons while his brain ached with worry over what was happening on *L'Espérance.* He had no doubt that Gore's search would be unrestrained and thorough—the man's contempt for ''foreigners'' had been ill-disguised.

''Come this way, Mr. Bouchard, sir. Cap'n Steenboch told me to wait with a hackney.''

Noël grunted and followed the young seaman through the wooden paling that surrounded City Hall Park and onto the rain-soaked cobbles of Broadway. ''How fares the ship?'' he asked, ducking into the waiting carriage.

''They finished their search this morning and finally let us back aboard, just afore the rain started. We been stowing the goods since then. But it's a kettle of fish, I can tell you.''

Noël frowned. ''What do you mean?''

''They wasn't too gentle about it. Every barrel was opened, and every crate. There's oil-paper bales thrown all over the deck, and some of 'em was cut open, like they figured to find treasure.''

"*Le diable!*" Noël pounded his fist against the side of the carriage. "But those are bales of flour! And in this rain..."

"I know, sir. Cap'n's been riding us hard to get 'em below. But we're shorthanded. We lost Pease and Ingham."

"What do you mean, lost them?"

"When they saw the constables, they took to their heels. Cook says they was wanted in Boston for nimming a horse and wagon."

Noël swore aloud and stared out the carriage window at the steady rain. There wasn't a break in the clouds; it would last all day. The ride seemed to take forever, and his patience was exhausted by the time they finally arrived at the wharf where *L'Espérance* was tied up. Heedless of the downpour, the crew swarmed the deck in a frenzy of activity, rewrapping bales, nailing shut casks and barrels and crates. It looked to Noël as though Gore's men had piled the whole of the ship's cargo on deck; Captain Steenboch's roared commands above the sound of the drumming rain attested to the urgent need to seal and stow the goods before they were soaked and ruined.

Noël raced for the deck, throwing aside his coat and hat as he ran. He hoisted a crate of salt pork on his shoulder, noticing a gaping hole in the side that seemed to have been made with a hatchet. Damn Gore, he thought. Damn all narrow-minded, proud Americans who couldn't see the larger world beyond their own shores! He passed the crate to a seaman waiting in the open hatch, then wiped the rain from his face and reached for another crate. He worked until he was soaked to the skin, till his muscles ached from lifting, till his empty stomach reminded him he hadn't eaten all day.

But at last it was done. The cargo was safely stored again below decks. As night fell, Noël sat in his cabin with Steenboch, wolfing down a hastily fetched meat pie and assessing the damage to their venture.

"The furs are safe, M'soo Noël. But we lost at least a quarter of the flour to the rain," said Steenboch. "Cheeses should hold, unless the bastards cut into the rind." He muttered a few curses in his native tongue. "Don't know how much water got to the pork, but if the weather turns cool, we might reach the West Indies before the meat begins to stink."

"What if we make for the Bermudas instead of Guadeloupe? It shouldn't take more than ten days, if the wind is fair. An English port instead of a French one, but we'd get there sooner, and save our cargo, perhaps."

"Why can't we replace some of the spoiled foodstuffs, *m'soo?* Only yesterday, old Elliott down on South Street asked if we needed more flour. Been a good growing season. Elliott's warehouse is filled to the rafters, and he's willing to sell cheap."

Noël reached for the bottle of cognac on the table. "Tomorrow is Sunday. We'd have to wait another two days before we could leave this accursed city. Besides, there's not that much money left, except for the banknotes I left with you."

Steenboch snorted in disgust. "Almost gone now. I had no choice. Gore claimed to find fault with our papers, and only a large payment, he said, would put things to rights."

Noël swore in half a dozen languages, then returned to the French of his conversation with Steenboch. "I wonder how much will find its way into the United States Treasury, and how much into the pockets of that flag-waving pig." He downed his cognac in a gulp and poured another glass. "I suppose it's too much to hope that Pease and Ingham left before you gave them any advance on their wages." He looked at the gloomy expression on Steenboch's lined face and sighed. "I thought not." He sighed again. "Two men gone. Can you manage shorthanded?"

"I've done it before."

"This is a damned sorry way to start our venture."

They stared at the flickering oil lamp on the table between them, lost in their own dark thoughts. At length Steenboch arose. "The morning tide, *m'soo?*"

Noël nodded. "The morning tide, Hessel."

"I'll tell the men. Get a good night's sleep."

Noël laughed sardonically and raised the bottle of cognac. "I intend to."

After Steenboch had left the cabin, he stood up and stripped off his damp clothes, then fetched dry garments from his trunk. His leg had begun to ache, and he found himself limping as he made his way around the cabin. It took another two glasses of cognac before he could bring himself to lie down on the large bunk bed. The bed he would have shared with Elizabeth. It seemed too large, too empty, now.

He rubbed his hand across his eyes. *Elizabeth.* How could she have done it? Hadn't she known, hadn't she understood, how important it was for him to succeed? Had it been so simple for her to crush his hopes and dreams? In all his vagabond life, the good times and the bad, no one had ever set out deliberately to hurt and destroy him. Until now. He'd had friends and enemies—people he'd charmed, people who were indifferent, people who wished him ill. But, great God, he'd never known *hatred* before.

And surely she hated him, to have done this. Hated him with a blinding passion that admitted no logic or sense. "*Why,* Lisbet?" he whispered, feeling a terrible contraction around his heart. What had he done? He hadn't played her false. He hadn't claimed to be Adam. He hadn't married her for her money; he thought he'd been quite sensitive to her wariness on that score, assuring her he'd never use her dowry.

Elizabeth, his wife. His beloved. The past few weeks had been among the happiest of his life. He'd nurtured her fragile self-confidence—at first as a kindness, and then for the joy of watching her bloom. The heart-stirring wonder of being rewarded a thousandfold by a passionate creature, a woman who'd excited his soul and spirit, as well as his body.

And then, one day, he'd known he loved her. Like a warm ray of sunshine, it had flooded his being, illuminated the darkest recesses of his heart, overwhelmed the devil-may-care Noël who had laughed his way through life. He didn't know how it had happened, but more and more he'd found himself acknowledging feelings he'd always pretended weren't there. He'd even been fool enough to think he'd won her. That she'd begun to trust him, love him, though she couldn't say the words yet.

And then she'd repaid his love with hatred and betrayal. Well, it was over. He'd go to France, resume the wandering life that had suited him before. And forget her—if he could.

In the dark, he groaned and closed his eyes, fighting against bitter tears. Now he knew why he'd never let himself love before. There was too much pain.

Henceforth, the only women he would allow in his life would be the kind of women he'd known in the past—empty, shallow, useless. And if he ever read anything deeper in their eyes, he would turn and run, for his sanity's sake.

For his heart's sake.

# Chapter Twelve

"Boy, I'll give you five cents if you get me home." In the light of the flickering street lamps, the wobbling drunkard cast long, grotesque shadows across the cobblestones and the few lingering rain puddles. His top hat was crushed, and he clutched a small flask in one hand.

Elizabeth pulled her visored cap lower over her forehead and shook her head. "No, sir. I'm wanted home, sir," she said in as deep a voice as she could manage.

The drunkard grumbled softly, staggered to the nearest lamp and wrapped himself around the post. "Sniveling milksop. Go home to your mama, then. If I get lost...your fault..."

"Yes, sir," agreed Elizabeth without stopping. She hitched up her wide-legged trousers in what she hoped was a masculine gesture and hurried past the man as fast as she could go. In the daytime, dressed as a lady of quality, she found it easy enough to hold her own against the lowlifes who frequented South Street, the rough sailors and intoxicated gentlemen who'd fallen on hard times. But at three o'clock in the morning, the dockside—with its taverns and cheap rented rooms spilling ruffians and their women onto the pavement—was forbidding and dangerous. Even for what appeared to be a thin, harmless boy in threadbare clothes. It had been a trial for Elizabeth to convince the clerk of the secondhand shop that it was perfectly normal for a young woman to buy clothes for her manservant. A simple jacket and trousers and cap.

She shifted her small satchel from one shoulder to the other. She'd only had room in the satchel for a change of linen and one gown; she'd packed the white muslin dress with its purple jacket that Noël had chosen for their wedding trip. She hadn't even found space for a bonnet or a second gown, but she did have her pin money. Perhaps Noël would put in at Norfolk for a day of shopping on the way down to the West Indies.

That is, if Noël would ever forgive her.

The things her family had said after Noël's arrest had infuriated her. Father had come from the bank at Mother's summons, his face red with anger. It had taken him no time to decide that Noël had, after all, deliberately let them think he was his brother the count. And that, to his regret, he himself had allowed his friends to make loans to the scoundrel on the strength of his recommendations. In vain Elizabeth had reminded Mr. Babcock that every banker in the city had been willing to give Noël money on the forcefulness of his arguments alone, no matter who he was. Mother had wailed about the disgrace—her son-in-law in prison on suspicion of smuggling—and had taken to her bed with a glass of orange-flower water laced with ether to calm herself.

After hours of sharp argument, Elizabeth had finally persuaded her family—including a smug Rose and a falsely sympathetic Edward—that Noël's arrest had been a mistake that would be quickly put to rights. As soon as her husband was cleared and released from Bridewell, they would proceed with their plans to leave New York together. She assured them that the best thing they could do to save their reputation—and hers—was to invite Elvira Beedle to tea, express their confidence in Noël, and squelch the ugly gossip at its source.

Stephen was another matter. Elizabeth had stormed into his office and demanded that he speak to that wretched Jasper Gore; her husband was to be released from prison with all haste so that he might begin his voyage without further delay.

Stephen threw up his hands in exasperation. "Oh, the fickleness of women! I only did as you asked, Elizabeth!"

She stamped her foot. "I didn't ask for him to be arrested!"

He shrugged. "Well, it's too late now. It's out of my hands entirely. You'll have to wait until Gore finishes his search."

It had taken the rest of the day and into Saturday morning before Gore and his men had left *L'Espérance*. In the meantime, Elizabeth had tried to see Noël in Bridewell, but had been turned aside at the door. She didn't know if that had been Noël's request, but she feared it was so. If only she could make him understand that it was *Stephen's* doing! She had only wanted to delay the sailing so that they might be reconciled.

The bare masts of *L'Espérance* suddenly loomed before her—dark bones under a dark sky. This seemed like such a coward's way, to sneak aboard his ship. But if she waited until the morning to come openly and beg to be taken with him, and he should refuse... The whole city would learn of it then, and her humiliation at Jack's abandonment before the wedding would be nothing compared to the shame of a deserting husband. No. She couldn't endure that. This was the best way. She'd left a note behind, explaining to her parents that she had wanted to go aboard the ship well before it sailed. Under the circumstances, she didn't feel the need for a lingering farewell. She'd passed off her scanty packing as Noël's desire to buy her a complete new wardrobe as soon as they reached France.

She found a rope ladder hanging over the side of the docked ship, mounted it with care and peered over the edge of the deck. The seaman on watch sat on a barrel in the bow of the ship and played softly on a small harmonica. He seemed absorbed in his tune and the still night; Elizabeth was able to climb aboard without alerting him. She crept to the ship's boats that lay alongside the mainmast, untied a corner of the canvas cover on one of them, crawled inside and made herself comfortable. She hoped Noël would be glad to see her and forgive her. But it was sensible to stay hidden until they were well under way and it was too late to turn back.

In the darkness, she yawned. She'd been so nervous about leaving her house in the middle of the night that she hadn't once closed her eyes. And the long walk through the darkened streets of the city had tired her further. Well, she had time for a few hours' sleep. Surely the deck noise in the morning would waken her. She settled against her satchel and fell into a troubled sleep filled with dreams of Noël and Jack and heartbreak.

"Look smart, boy!"

"What?" Elizabeth groaned and sat up in the little boat. The sun glared in her eyes, and her stomach was queasy from the rocking of the ship.

A sailor in a striped jersey shirt leaned above her. He grinned, revealing a large gap in his front teeth. "Look smart, says I," he said. "Bestir yourself."

"What d'ye have there, mate?" A second seaman lumbered over to join the first. At the sight of Elizabeth, he slapped his knee in delight. "Be hanged if it ain't a stowaway!"

Toothless grinned again. "Skinny little weasel." He reached down to Elizabeth and grasped her shoulder. "Well, come on, boy. Cap'n will want to see ye. He don't much take to stowaways."

She shook him off and rose proudly to her feet, stepping onto the deck with as much dignity as she could manage. Her neck had a crick in it, and she was desperate for a cup of coffee. "Don't touch me," she muttered. "I don't have to mind the likes of you."

"You be a saucebox," he replied, scowling. "I think when Cap'n's through whalin' the tar out o' ye, I'll have a go meself." He curled his fingers around Elizabeth's ear and gave her a tweak that made her cry out.

"Stop! That hurts!"

"Aye," he said complacently. Despite her furious struggles and squeaks of protest, he kept a tight grip on her ear, forcing her down the hatchway to Steenboch's cabin. He knocked on the door and opened it at Steenboch's command. "Cap'n," he said, "can you use a cabin boy? We found this 'n sleepin' in the jolly boat." He pushed Elizabeth ahead of him into the cabin.

Noël and Steenboch were standing at a table, poring over charts. Noël raised his head, and his face darkened at the sight of Elizabeth.

Steenboch's mouth twitched in a half smile of recognition. He nodded to the sailor. "Thank you, Gilchrist. Go, now." He turned to Noël. "Shall I leave you and your lady alone, *m'soo?*"

"No." Noël strode to Elizabeth, took her firmly by the elbow and steered her across the passageway to his own cabin. He closed the door with an ominous snap and turned to face her, his eyes like blue ice, cold and hard. "Now," he said, "what the devil are you doing here? I thought it was over between us."

She cringed under the malevolence of his gaze and stumbled over her words. "You're still my husband. I wanted to... to be with you. To help you. To—"

He laughed; it was a sharp, ugly sound. "*Help* me? You have ruined my life. My future. What is left for you to do?"

"Ruined? But it was only two days—"

"And half the foodstuffs, spoiled in the rain. Thanks to your malice."

She gasped. "I didn't know!"

"Your American officials were very thorough in their destruction of the cargo. But if we can reach the Bermudas without any mishaps, I might not be completely ruined. Does that disappoint you? Did you hope to see the fortune hunter drawn and quartered by his creditors?"

"I told you, I didn't know! I merely asked Stephen..." She stamped her foot. "Oh, *damn* Stephen's blockheadedness!"

"How convenient to have someone to blame," he sneered.

"Noël," she said, her eyes pleading, "you must understand. I'm so sorry for what happened. I never meant to hurt you. I only wanted to delay your departure so we'd have time to mend our quarrel.''

His handsome mouth twisted in the mockery of a smile. "How tenderly you say that, my angel. Do you mean to tell me you love me now?''

She hesitated. It was clear he didn't love *her*. He probably never had. And the words stuck in her throat. To confess her feelings to a man who'd as much as said their marriage was over . . . She bit her lip and stared at the toe of her heavy shoe. "Perhaps . . . a little,'' she whispered.

She could feel his eyes on her, but she dared not lift her head. Would he be pleased at her confession? Or arrogantly triumphant? "I see,'' he said at length. "You are not quite sure. *Eh bien—*'' a heavy sigh ''—perhaps I was too hasty. When I return from France, we shall try to begin again. In the meanwhile, we are only a few hours out. I'll have Steenboch turn about and return you to your family and friends in New York.''

"No!'' she cried. "No, I can't face them. Not after Jack!''

"Ah . . .'' He exhaled a slow, rasping breath. "Now we have the truth at long last. We do not speak of love here. I am, and always will be, a fortune seeker in your eyes. Worthy only of your contempt. But you will do anything to keep us together. To keep the truth from those gossips back in New York. If my hopes and plans are destroyed through your interference, what does it matter? If you must creep aboard this ship dressed as a *gamin*, what does it matter? And that sweet apology, your beautiful eyes seducing me. It meant nothing, but what does it matter? And your soft confession of love—'' he swung his hand against the cabin wall in a violent slap that sounded like the clap of thunder ''—what does it matter? It is only important that I allow you to stay with me. That your pride is maintained at all costs. Is that it? Is that it? Will you do anything to save yourself from being shamed again?''

"Noël, please . . .'' The way he put it, everything was twisted and ugly.

His hands shot out and clamped her shoulders in a savage grip. "Damn your lying eyes," he growled. "Will you do anything to save your pride?"

Her heart ached, and her life was a shambles, and all she had left was her pride—as much of it as Jack had left her. "*Yes,*" she said defiantly.

"*Mon Dieu,* such sublime self-interest." His eyes burned with an anger that was more terrifying than anything she'd ever known. "So be it. You may stay on the ship. But let me tell you, Elizabeth Bouchard, how it will be between us," he said. "We will continue to pretend we have a marriage for as long as you please me. Thanks to your plotting with Stephen, we are shorthanded on the voyage. Every man must do the work of two. Well, then, you came aboard as a cabin boy. You'll work as one. You will help the cook and mend my clothes and scrub the decks. You'll serve my meals and tend my cabin. You'll run and fetch and carry. And if a sailor vomits in a storm, you'll clean that up, as well!"

She tore from his grasp and glared at him. "You craven bully, I'll not be your slave!"

"This is my ship, hellion, and you'll do as you are told—if I have to take the 'cat' to you! By God, your pride will cost you dear, I promise you. You'll be a cabin boy by day. And if I want you, damn it, you'll be at my beck and call by night!"

She was shaking from head to foot, but she found the courage to defy him. She never wanted to make love with him again. In his arms, his strong embrace, she forgot everything. And she didn't ever want to forget the ugly words that were now burned into her brain: Noël Bouchard had married plain Bessie Babcock for her money, and nothing else. Taking her to bed had merely been a bonus for him that he'd repaid with pitying kindness. "I'll not be your mistress," she said bitterly. "Not anymore."

His voice had risen in fury during the course of their argument; now he seemed to make a conscious effort to control his temper. "I would have to suffer a moment of weakness before I'd even want you," he said, his lip curling. "Until that unlikely moment—" he pointed to the large railed bunk against one bulkhead ''—that is my bed. You will sleep in a hammock in the corner, as befits your station.''

''I won't be treated this way.''

Before she realized what he was doing, he had reached out and pulled the cap from her head. Swiftly he unpinned her topknot and ran his fingers through her hair until the tresses lay full around her shoulders. ''If you are wise, you will obey my every command. And with a smile on your face. I intend now to introduce you to your shipmates as my wife. Would it not be better for your pride if the crew thinks you have chosen to help out of love and loyalty to your husband? As long as we can choose the farce we are playing, humble acceptance is the wisest role for you. If not, there are ways to make you obey,'' he added ominously.

She was caught in a trap, and the brutish devil knew it. She didn't mind making a scene to have her way, but she couldn't win in the present circumstances. And she wasn't of a mind to be chastised before the whole crew, if that was what he intended. ''You bastard,'' she muttered.

He laughed sharply. ''Not I. I may be a villain and a scoundrel, a 'money-grubbing fortune hunter,' as you would put it in your charming way. But in one thing, at least, my rich and titled brother and I are equals—we shared a legitimate birth.''

She shrugged. ''Alas. I'll have to think of another name to call you.'' She made an exaggerated bow and smiled her defiance. He wouldn't break her. ''Now, master,'' she said, ''set me to my chores and I'll work with a will.''

At least, helping the cook, she might finally get her cup of coffee!


''Have another cake o' bread, ma'am, afore ye dump them slops.''

''Thanks, Cooky.'' Elizabeth accepted the hard biscuit with gratitude, dipping it into her grog to make it soft. It seemed as though she couldn't get enough to eat lately. It must be the salt air and exercise. Eight days out of New York, and she was eating as much as the hardest-working seaman aboard ship. Not that she wasn't doing her share, and then some! Noël, the wretched villain, had become a slave driver, finding fresh chores for her the moment she stopped to catch her breath!

"It will be nice to see you in a gown when we reach Bermuda, ma'am."

Elizabeth finished her hardtack, downed the last of her grog and smiled at the ship's cook. She plucked at her worn shirt and trousers. "This is easier to work in, Cooky. But it will be nice to wear a gown again." If her gown would still fit her. She was sure she'd gained a great deal of weight from all this eating: even the loose trousers had begun to feel snug. She didn't think she could be pregnant; she'd had her monthly courses too soon before the last time she and Noël had made love. And Lord knows a body couldn't get pregnant just from wanting...

She felt herself growing warm all over. That was the worst part of this dreadful voyage, so different from the adventurous, romantic trip she and Noël had originally planned. Not the exhausting labor. Not the need to keep her temper in front of the crew, no matter how often Noël provoked her, to pretend she obeyed him—how she hated that word!—out of willingness. Not even his hostility and contempt. But the hunger, the wanting of him.

It was an agonizing temptation to be near him, to watch him strip off his shirt and wash his muscular torso after a long, hot afternoon in the rigging. To hand him his towel or dry his back if he demanded it of her, to pull off his boots and tend to his every need—save one. She ached with desire, remembering the feel of her eager, naked breasts against that virile chest, the burning kisses and the nights of wild passion.

*Weak,* Elizabeth thought. To be a slave to your desires. To desire a man who doesn't want you.

She bent and lifted the bucket of kitchen refuse, wincing when the rope handle rubbed across the blisters on her palm. Blast Noël. Though he'd been a tyrant all this week, angry and cruel and disagreeable below decks, he'd played a cunning part for the benefit of the crew. It was "my angel" this and "my dear wife" that, and how was she to fight it without appearing to be a shrew? And so, this morning, when a gaff line had slipped and he'd called out, "Give me a hand with this, my angel," what could she do?

She sighed. Well, the blisters would heal. But she'd never forgive him for any of this. She hadn't deserved it. *She* was the wronged one, not he. And the only thing he'd suffered—the night in Bridewell, the loss of a few barrels of flour—had been as much Stephen's fault as hers.

She mounted the aft ladder to the deck, leaned over the stern railing and tossed the contents of her bucket into the wind. Then she set down the bucket and scraped back the sweat-damp hair from her forehead. Botheration! she thought. No matter what she did with her hair, it simply refused to behave. She'd put it into a single braid down her back, but that hadn't kept the front pieces from coming loose and blinding her in the midst of her chores. She hadn't thought to pack any pomade. And when she'd asked Noël, all he could do was suggest unpleasantly that she use a bit of stinking whale oil grease, as the seamen did. In a moment of desperation, she'd finally taken a scissors and cut a thick fringe of hair across her forehead. It kept the tresses out of her eyes, but the pieces frizzed and curled every which way until she thought she'd go mad.

She bent again and picked up the bucket, then trudged slowly back to the galley. Hours of work yet, and her back already ached. Thankfully, they'd be in Bermuda in another two days, and she could sleep in a bed again, instead of that blamed hammock! Not that she'd ever lower her pride enough to tell *him* of her distress.

Twilight was beginning to fall on the sea when she carried Noël's supper to him and knocked at his cabin door. She entered, set down the tray near the door and turned to leave.

He looked up from the table where he'd been working. His sun-bleached hair was spun gold in the light of the oil lamp. "Stay," he said.

"There are pots to be scrubbed," she insisted. "I couldn't help Cooky with them this afternoon, because the blasted sail you gave me took too long to mend."

He laughed, a sharp, ugly bark. "How your mother would rejoice to see you, needle in hand. Perhaps after this a lady's workbasket will not seem so unpleasant."

"Merely because I know how to sew doesn't mean I'll ever enjoy it. There are many things I've done since I met you that, in retrospect, didn't please me at all. They were unpleasant and boring." She hoped he understood her meaning, the insult behind her words.

"Still the sharp-tongued virago, I see." He smiled coldly and put aside his papers. "Bring my supper here, then fetch another tumbler from the shelf." He indicated a second chair. "Sit."

"But the pots—"

"Cooky has had some experience in the art of potscrubbing. He will endure without you." He reached under the table and brought up a bottle of cognac, which he placed before him. "I feel like getting drunk tonight. And I want company."

"May I be permitted merely to watch?" she said with a sneer.

"No." He pulled the cork and poured a generous measure of liquor into their glasses. He finished his drink quickly and stared at Elizabeth. "Well?" he challenged. Reluctantly she emptied her tumbler, then watched with a sinking heart as he refilled their glasses to the brim. "Again," he insisted.

Elizabeth scowled at him and raised her tumbler. "To your health. What was it Stephen once said about you Frenchmen needing your tipple?"

He saluted her in return. "To your venom, which never flags. Drink up." He downed his cognac in several gulps and poured himself another glass. "Finish your drink," he ordered, "and take more."

He was in too vile a mood to argue with. She did as he bade her—shuddering as the liquid burned her throat—then asserted her independence by pushing his bowl under his nose. "Don't forget your stew while it's hot," she said sarcastically. "I cooked the fish myself. I even refrained from adding poison."

"Sewing. Cooking. You are becoming everything a woman should be." He pushed away his supper and smiled at her, his eyes dark. "Including spiteful, selfish, deceptive—"

"As to deception, I had a good teacher, monsieur le Comte de Moncalvo," she added with malice.

"You still choose to nurse that grievance, I see. What a bitter disappointment it must have been, to lose your expected title." His mouth twisted in mockery. "I can scarcely blame you for wanting to ruin me in revenge."

"I didn't ruin you. You ruined yourself. It's a pity you didn't spend my dowry when you could. Then you wouldn't have had to give it back. How that must have pained you."

He shot her a savage look, but his voice was controlled. "You Americans. Everything with you is money. Your dowry. The fortune you thought to gain by marriage to me." He sighed, a deep sigh filled with regret and disappointment. "Well, perhaps it is the way of the world now. To measure a man by his money." He stared darkly into the flickering lamp, then sighed again and poured himself another drink.

The cognac was beginning to go to Elizabeth's head. The cabin had become dark and shadowy. In the golden glow of the lamp, Noël's face was soft-edged and handsome, shimmering through the gauze that the liquor had dropped before her eyes. His mouth was wide and firm, the upper lip chiseled into a perfect bow. As he'd begun to speak again, he had lapsed into his native language, his normal constraints released by the drink. The speaking of French required more mobility of the lips and mouth than the speaking of English—an exaggeration that only made Elizabeth more aware of his soft lips, the seductive glimpses of his tongue behind white, even teeth. She hated him for tormenting her, for making her want him so much.

"Is your brother very rich?" she asked. At his surprised expression, she shrugged. "I'd like to know what I lost."

Only a twitch at the corner of his mouth acknowledged the cruelty of her words. He emptied the rest of the cognac into his glass and gazed morosely at the amber liquid. "He's very rich, he's very successful, he's well loved."

"And his wife?"

"She is beautiful. An aristocrat of the *ancien régime*. And she adores him."

"He has everything, then."

"Yes. But he earned it. And suffered for it. I can't begrudge him, nor envy him. Serious, sober Brother Adam. Perhaps it was always ordained. He was meant to be the successful one, the responsible one. From the time we were children. 'Why can't you be more like Adam?' Maman would say. She was always so worried for me." He laughed softly, sadly. "Sometimes I used to imagine I was a changeling child. A will-o'-the-wisp dropped secretly into the midst of a proper, hardworking bourgeois family. Ah, well..." He downed the last of his cognac and leaned back in his chair. He stared at her, his look so deep and intimate that she squirmed in her seat. His tongue flicked out to stroke his lower lip, and his long fingers began an impatient tattoo on the table.

"Take off your clothes," he growled at last.

"What?" She jumped to her feet, trembling.

He rose in his turn, towering above her, powerful and menacing. "I want you," he said. "God knows why. You're the most impossible, exasperating woman I have ever known. And you'll probably hate me more in the morning than you do now. But I'm willing to chance it." He swayed slightly and passed his hand across his eyes. "It must be because I'm drunk. Now do as you're told. Take off your clothes."

She stamped her foot. "I shall not! This is one time you won't get humble obedience, husband."

His eyes glowed with anger, the deep blue at the heart of a flame. "Obedience?" he sneered. "You sharp-tongued cat! I doubt you even know the meaning of the word. But I want you in my bed tonight. I've had enough of denial, of sleepless nights listening to you breathing in the dark. Of remembering the feel of your body under mine. There are damn few things you're good for, besides malice, but one of them is—"

She refused to let him finish. With a shriek, she hurled the remains of her drink in his face.

"*Le diable!*" he exploded, and dragged her into his arms.

The tumbler fell from her hands and crashed on the floor. His mouth ground down on hers in a kiss so savage and passionate it took her breath away.

She moaned and clutched at his neck, her nails digging into the firm flesh. Her mouth remembered. Her hot, eager body remembered. The rekindled fire raced through her blood, throbbed and pounded in every vein, and sought and found its hearth in her moist inner core. She tugged at Noël's shirt even as his frenzied hands tore the rough clothes from her body. They seemed to dance a wild, mad dance of desire, writhing out of their clothes as they made their frantic, breathless way to the wide bunk. And then she was in his arms, and he was lifting her, holding her, tossing her onto the bed with a haste that sprang from all-consuming passion, not anger. In the space of a heartbeat, he was beside her on the bed, clasping her in his fervent embrace.

She matched his impatience with her own. The hot kisses, his breathless, murmured endearments—"*ma chère,*" "sweet Lisbet"—weren't enough. She wanted to feel him within her, to be filled, possessed, by his need. She curled her hand around his pulsing manhood and guided him to her. He groaned in pleasure and plunged—in a fierce, savage attack that wrung from her a cry of ecstasy. Again and again he thrust, inflaming her senses, carrying her to that sweet realm—the little death, he'd called it once—that brought with it paradise, oblivion, glorious release.

When it was over they lay exhausted, still locked in an intimate embrace. Elizabeth felt close to tears. Tears of tenderness and gratitude. She didn't know how much longer she could have endured without his lovemaking. She was aware that he was now leaning heavily on her, his head tucked in the curve of her neck. His breathing had the deep rhythm of sleep. Her own eyes were growing heavy; they'd both had too much to drink. She moved beneath him, try-ing to extricate herself.

He stirred, lifted his head, stared at her with the heart-breaking eyes of a wounded animal. "Why, Lisbet?" he whispered. "*Why?*" He rolled off her, curled himself into a tight knot of pain and fell into a deep sleep.

Why, indeed? She climbed out of the bunk, picked up the several pieces of the broken tumbler and retrieved their scattered clothing. She extinguished the lamp, hung it from its hook on the rafters and crept back into bed beside Noël, pulling up the blanket to cover them both as they lay.

Why? Why had she deliberately given him pain? If she put aside her own disappointment for a moment, she had to admit the truth to herself: no matter how she tried to cast him in the role of deceiver, she knew in her heart that he'd never lied about the count's title and fortune. He'd been in-nocent, and she knew it. And the dreadful thing about the whole muddle was that he'd almost come to believe that *she* was the fortune seeker, wanting him only for his name and riches. Stupid, cruel Bessie, she thought, to let him think so. Didn't she know how that felt, the pain of wondering if you were wanted for yourself alone?

But had she chosen to be understanding? No. With her vile, intemperate words she'd chosen to wound him fur-ther. It was hard to keep convincing herself that he'd mar-ried her for her money—if that were the case, he could have stopped being kind the moment the bank notes were in his hands. But had that stopped her from continuing to accuse him of being a money-grubbing fortune hunter? From pre-tending that she thought he'd only returned the dowry to her out of guilt? Oh, no, Elizabeth, she thought bitterly. Not you. She'd betrayed him at every turn, then told herself that *he* was the villain.

At every turn. Yes. Including the near-ruination of all his plans, the humiliation of his having to spend a night in prison, the blackening of his good name before folks who'd had nothing but praise and admiration for him in the past. And that had been the cruelest of all. And the most ugly and deliberate. Yes. *Deliberate.* Noël had known it, had seen it in her eyes the day Gore had arrested him.

If she hadn't meant to hurt him—in that dark corner of her heart that she tried to keep hidden even from herself—why had she gone to *Stephen* to stop the ship's sailing? She had known that Stephen didn't like Noël, that he'd be ruthless in whatever he did. She could have gone to Father to intercede, to plead her case with her husband. Or kindly Mr. Lawson, who had always been fond of her. He would have had dozens of more benign ways to delay *L'Espérance.*

Noël had called it malice, and it was so. How could she blame him for his anger and want of mercy during this voyage, when she'd torn out his heart in a hundred ways and never realized it until now? "I love you," he'd said. A tentative, budding love, perhaps—but she'd repaid it with cruelty.

She groaned aloud. What anger, what misplaced rage, kept preventing her from following her heart? But of course she knew. It was the ghost of Jack, the ghost of her past, still dragging at her, like a heavy chain around her heart. Would it always be so? Would she never be free? Free to trust a man? Free to turn to Noël and say the words she knew he wanted to hear?

Weeping, she wrapped her arm around Noël's shoulder. He turned in his sleep and pulled her into his warm embrace. *I love you, Noël.* The words were there, trembling behind her closed lips. Would it be so difficult to whisper them aloud?

Instead she sighed, turned away from her husband and buried her face in her pillow. "Why?" she murmured to the darkened cabin, the down-filled pillow. "Why did you do it, Jack?"

# Chapter Thirteen

She awoke to the tossing of the ship, a great heaving swell that had her clutching the railing of the bunk for support. "Noël?" she said, alarmed.

He stood in the center of the room, braced against the table as he hastily donned his clothes. "It is a good one," he muttered. "It blew up about an hour ago. Steenboch should have wakened me sooner." He sat down to put on his boots.

"What can I do to help?" She scrambled from the bed and reached for her clothing, then stopped, aware that he was staring at her naked body. It was a look of such intensity, such desire, that she found herself blushing. She wrapped her arms around her breasts and smiled shyly at him, hope and yearning bright in her eyes. "Noël," she whispered.

He dropped his gaze, turning his head away from the sight of her. He finished pulling on his boots and stood up. "Nothing is settled yet between us, you understand. One night of drunken madness..."

She gulped back the sudden rush of anguish. Would he now deny the emotion they'd shared, as though what had happened had only been an animal need? "I'll come on deck as soon as I've dressed," she said.

He turned to the door. "You'll stay below. The galley fire will be out, but Cooky can use help to bring food to the men when they have a minute to eat."

"But..."

His jaw hardened. "You'll stay below, I said!" He turned on his heel and left the cabin.

The storm seemed to be increasing in violence. The empty cognac bottle had fallen off the table and now rolled from one side of the cabin to the other with each pitch and toss of the ship. They'd been lucky all week; the weather had held, with clear beautiful days and star-filled nights. But today nature was demanding payment for those clear skies.

Despite the movement of the ship, Elizabeth managed at last to put on her clothes. Perhaps, if Cooky didn't need her, she'd go and look for bandages and rum. She'd heard lots of stories at the wharves about ships in a storm—there'd be more than one injury before the wind blew itself out.

A sudden, terrible crashing sound from the deck above made her cry out in alarm. Surely something dreadful had happened and she'd be needed topside. She hurried forward to the main hatch. Foaming seas cascaded down from the opening and made her ascent slippery and terrifying. She was drenched before she even reached the deck.

The scene on deck was one of chaos. The ship rose and plunged through gigantic waves that washed over the bow and swept the length of the ship, pouring into hatches and picking up loose debris on the way. The crew had managed to furl most of the sails against the storm; the wind and scattered rain howled through bare rigging. But the square-rigged topsail on the mainmast, its sails still set, had caught a sharp gust of wind as the men were struggling to clew up the canvas. The topmast had cracked and come crashing down; the deck was a confusion of broken spars and tangled ropes and trapped men.

Noël stood in the midst of the turmoil, feverishly hacking at the lines to free the sailors. Other crewmen hauled on the ropes that kept the masts steady, taking up the slack each time the ship pitched, lest the masts come toppling to the deck. Elizabeth inched forward from one handhold to another, looking to be useful in some way. Noël glanced up and shot her a savage look that was more intimidating than the storm. He shouted something that was carried off by the whistling wind, drowned by the pounding seas.

She ignored him. She could deal with his anger after the storm abated. She saw that several water barrels, lashed to the starboard railing, were beginning to come loose. She grappled with the wet ropes, tugging at them with all her strength. The rough hemp scraped her hands, and the rain pelted her face. It was all she could do to keep her balance each time a fresh wave rolled over the deck. She felt helpless, struggling against the overpowering elements. And when a particularly furious gust of wind caught her and nearly swept her over the side of the ship, she abandoned her task and merely clutched the ropes for dear life. She was suddenly, frighteningly aware of how stupid she'd been.

She looked up. Gilchrist, the carpenter—the seaman who'd found her in the jolly boat that first day—was there. Next to Cooky, he'd become her best friend aboard ship. He smiled his toothless smile and leaned toward her ear. "Never 'e fear, ma'am! I'll help ye below," he shouted above the storm.

He reached out to take her arm. At that moment, one of the heavy water barrels tore loose. It lurched forward and crashed against Gilchrist, then scudded across the deck on a wash, smashed through the railing and fell into the sea. Gilchrist was bent over, clutching his arm, his face twisted into a grimace of pain. He sank to the deck, crawled toward the main hatch and disappeared below.

Elizabeth felt strong arms clamp around her waist. None too gently, she was lifted, tossed over Noël's broad shoulder. He carried her below deck to the door of their cabin and set her roughly on her feet. His face glistened with rainwater, and his blond hair was plastered to his forehead. He glared at her and bared his teeth in an angry snarl. "I do not know whether you're fearless or just stubborn!"

"But the water barrels..." she began in her own defense.

He swore softly. "The least of our worries. It's not as though we have been a month out with no supplies in the hold, damn it! Scarcely worth the risk of lives! Now. There is enough work to be done here. Will you stay below, or must I lock you in the cabin?"

She jutted her chin in anger, defying him. "You wouldn't."

"If I had the time," he growled, "I'm not sure I would not hang you from the rafters by your hair for what you have done! Now go forward and see if you can help Gilchrist. Pray we have not lost the services of the best carpenter around."

That chastened her. Whatever had happened to Gilchrist, it *was* her fault. "You needn't be a bully," she grumbled. "I'm going."

She found Gilchrist with the cook, patiently submitting to the painful examination of his arm. The bone of his forearm seemed to be broken; Elizabeth helped Cooky to bind it, cringing with guilt every time the carpenter groaned.

"Not yer fault, ma'am," he reassured her. "Might o' happened to anyone when them barrels went. Now, if you can brace me shivered arm, I'll be headin' for the bilge pumps. I still got one good sail to flap!"

The storm raged for hours. Elizabeth worked tirelessly, fetching supplies from the storeroom, bringing a piece of hardtack, a dried apple or a tankard of ale to a hungry seaman, even giving makeshift relief to the occasional scratch or cut. But by midafternoon the wind was slackening, the rain was spent, and the dark clouds had begun to break up. Cooky was able to light a fire again. The crew gathered in the forecastle to eat a hot meal, change into dry clothes and tend to their injuries in earnest. Except for Gilchrist, and a young seaman whose leg had been impaled by a splintered yard, no one had been seriously hurt. After a brief respite, they'd begin their work again: the deck would have to be cleared of broken spars, the rigging disentangled, the sails reset.

Noël was the last to come below. His eyes glazed with fatigue, he stumbled into the galley for a mug of hot rum, then limped off toward his cabin. Elizabeth followed silently. Ignoring his muttered protests, she helped him off with his boots and his wet clothing. She toweled his hair with tender concern, then knelt before him to dry his feet. She felt very humble, and a little frightened, aware that their relationship had—in some strange, indefinable way—moved to a new plane. Whatever happened between them in the next few days would somehow color the future of their marriage.

She rubbed his legs with the towel, unconsciously stroking more gently each time she touched one of the several raised scars along its length. "Your poor leg. Does it hurt very much?"

He sighed wearily. "I'm too tired to notice."

Saber cuts, he'd said once. "It looks dreadful," she said, grimacing as she imagined the repeated slice of the blade into sinew and muscle.

He stood up and pulled on the pair of fresh underbreeches she'd fetched from his sea chest. "I regret I am as imperfect of body as I am of character," he said dryly.

Stupid choice of words, Elizabeth, she thought. She hadn't expected him to misunderstand and take it as a criticism. "I—I didn't mean that," she stammered.

He seemed too tired, too discouraged, to care what she meant. "*Your* scars don't show," he said. "But I, at least, have learned to live with the occasional pain."

There was something so sad and final in his tone—as though he'd already given up hope for them. He sighed again, shuffled to the bunk and collapsed across it.

She sat beside his sleeping form for a long time. He seemed unable to relax even in sleep. He stirred and murmured aloud, words and phrases that Elizabeth had difficulty understanding, though the worry and distress behind them was clear enough. "Oh, Noël," she whispered, "forgive me for all the cruel things I've done and said."

*The Hope*, he'd called his ship. She should have understood from the first how much it had meant to him. But all the while he'd been struggling to make a go of his shipping venture, she'd thought only of her pride, her own injured feelings, seeing dark and sinister motives behind his wish to marry her. Well, it would be different from now on. She'd be a good wife to him. The wife he deserved.

She stirred in her chair. She could sit here all afternoon just watching him, but there was work to do. She returned to the galley to help Cooky until all the men were fed and had gone back to their chores.

The cook handed her a plate of beans and a mug of ale. "Cap'n's topside, ma'am. He won't stop to eat."

"I'll bring it to him." She climbed the ladder way and found Captain Steenboch forward, barking orders in his guttural voice. While the twilight still held, the sailors swarmed over the deck, clearing the debris and making order out of chaos. Steenboch grunted his thanks at the proffered food and proceeded to shovel the beans into his mouth with a ravenous haste that astonished Elizabeth. She took back the empty plate and handed him his drink. "I hope you don't need my husband soon, Captain," she said. "He needs his sleep."

Steenboch nodded. "Aye. That he does. Done the work of three men since we've come aboard."

"Yes. You're shorthanded, I understand. Gilchrist told me two men deserted before we sailed."

"Aye. Showed a clean pair of heels, they did. But we were short before then. Only had fifteen men to start. Ship this size can take twenty."

"Why didn't you hire more, then?"

"Not enough money, M'soo Noël said."

"Not enough money? But that's absurd! What about all the loans?"

"It takes a heap of money to outfit a ship, lady. And not even M'soo Noël could squeeze another penny out of the bankers."

She was getting an education in the real world. "And that talk of smuggling—it wasn't a joke, was it?"

It was clear Noël hadn't told Steenboch about her part in his arrest. "Glad I listened to *m'soo*, now. If we'd been caught with contraband, it would have meant prison for both of us. And the key thrown to the fishes! *M'soo* was even thinking to risk his luck at the gaming tables to give us a little money for insurance."

"Gambling? But why? When he had fifteen thou—" She stopped. Her dowry. Why, in Noël's great need, his desperation, hadn't he used her dowry? Because, Elizabeth, you fool, she answered herself, he swore he wouldn't. Instead, he'd worked like a dog, driven himself to succeed on his own terms. For her. For their future together. Her heart swelled with love. How little she'd understood of the man she'd married.

Steenboch finished his ale, wiped his mouth against his rumpled sleeve and handed the mug back to Elizabeth. "Glad you're aboard, lady. I never knew why *m'soo* changed his mind about taking you. Always thought it was a good idea, from the first. Well, not my affair." He grinned, a broad smile that added to the creases on his lined face. "But you're the finest cabin boy I've ever seen on a ship of mine."

Filled with an odd sense of pride, she returned his smile. "Thank you, Captain." She turned to go, then stopped and frowned at him. "By the way...who's Martin?" It had been the only clear word in Noël's sleep-drowned ramblings, a name he'd repeated several times.

"Martin's his son, lady. His son in France."

She felt her heart go cold. "His...son?"

"Aye. I remember when we first met, *m'soo* and I. I'd just been stranded in New York without a ship. He talked about the boy. How he'd given him to his brother to raise. But when I met him again this spring, he told me how he'd decided to find a mother for his boy. Reclaim him if he could." Steenboch nodded his head in approval. "Found a good woman in you, lady."

She didn't know how she could endure the pain. Noël had talked about the children he'd hoped to have, the children they'd raise together. How was she to know that he meant another woman's child? A child he'd never even bothered to tell her about! She began to tremble—out of anger or grief, she couldn't tell. But she couldn't stay here, with Steenboch staring so intently at her. "Cooky will want me," she mumbled, and hurried below.

She told herself she must remain calm, wait until Noël had given her an explanation. But by the time she'd paced past their cabin door for the tenth time and finally heard him stirring within, her rage was almost beyond containing. She burst into the cabin and slammed the door behind her. "When did you intend to tell me?"

Noël looked up in surprise and finished buttoning the cuffs of his shirt. He scowled. "Tell you what?"

"Martin. Your son." She spat the words. "You talked in your sleep."

He looked disconcerted for a moment, then shrugged. "What was there to tell? Adam adopted him. He is none of your concern."

"That's not what Steenboch said! He said you were looking for a mother for the boy."

"That was just talk when we were in our cups. Wine-begot dreams. Steenboch does not understand."

"But I do. You'd hoped to find a mother for your child. A spinster who'd be so grateful for a husband she wouldn't mind raising another woman's child. Was that it? How many women refused the offer before you met me and decided to marry first and tell later?"

His jaw tightened in anger. "The boy thinks he is Adam's son. He's happy and thriving. I saw no reason to change anything so long as my fortunes were subject to the whims of fate."

He was so controlled it only added to her fury. "And his mother. Didn't she want the brat?"

His eyes flashed a warning. "My son Martin is three and a half," he said evenly. "Sweet, wise and blameless. His mother was a whore. A camp follower. Cold and unfeeling. She did not want him. Nor me, it would appear."

Had that been said with regret? She felt a sharp twinge of jealousy. "Did you love her?"

He swore softly in French. "It was a long time ago. During the war. Men were dying around me every day. What the devil is love in those circumstances? You live while you can."

Surely it was an evasion. "You *did* love her."

"No! But the *boy* is precious to me. As for his future . . . I wasn't about to be hasty. Not until I knew your mind. Martin is happy with Adam and Charmiane. Why should I tear him from that life to give him to a woman who is not sure she wants the father, let alone the son? I had begun to think you cared for me. I intended to broach the subject of Martin on our trip to France.'' He laughed bitterly. ''That is, until your malice in going to Stephen made it clear that—''

''Cared for you?'' she cried, interrupting him. ''What did it matter to you? You thought you had everything in me! The plain spinster who'd raise your child out of gratitude. Give you her money out of gratitude.''

He grunted in exasperation. ''Are we to argue over the damned dowry yet again? I wanted *you*, Elizabeth! Will you never understand that? If I had wanted money, I knew half a dozen rich widows I could have charmed out of their inheritances. Without giving up my freedom. And if my concern had been Martin alone, I could have hired a nursemaid!''

She was sick with jealousy at his words, remembering the effect of his devastating charm on others. Remembering her own susceptibility to it. ''How many women *have* you known? Your rich widows, your camp followers, those silly creatures back in New York that you flattered and danced with—Oh!'' Her eyes filled with tears of helpless rage. ''How many women did you leave behind in France?''

''Elizabeth, stop this!'' he ordered. ''How can you be jealous?''

''How many, you honey-tongued lothario?''

''*Merde!*'' He threw up his hands. ''You are impossible! Hundreds of women,'' he said sarcastically. ''Hundreds! Is that what you want to hear? Every size, every shape. And do not forget the ones I met on my travels. Who knows how many bastards I have put on this earth? Is that what you want to hear, you hotheaded little fool?''

''And how many did you love?'' she asked, the word a bitter taste in the back of her mouth.

He struggled for control. He reached out and put a gentle hand on her arm. ''None of them, Lisbet. I swear that. Not even Martine.''

*Martine.* Elizabeth's blood turned to ice. He'd named his child after his woman. And now he had the effrontery to tell her he hadn't loved the creature? She pushed away his hand. "Save your oaths for someone who believes them. How can I trust anything you've ever said?"

"I have not lied to you," he growled.

"No," she responded, her lip curling in scorn. "You simply forgot to tell me you had a son somewhere. How many other children have you abandoned on your careless way?"

His face turned white. "Elizabeth, I warn you . . ."

Her pain was tearing her apart. He'd never wanted her for herself. He'd only used her. Used her money. She was simply another one of his many women. Seduced by his charm into overlooking the cold truth. In her agony, she lashed out blindly, as though she could release her own pain only by inflicting it on him. "How lucky for you that your brother is so rich," she said coldly. "To shoulder your burdens, when you couldn't be bothered."

He shut his eyes and clenched his hands into fists. "No more," he whispered, his voice strained with anguish.

"What would you have done without your brother and his good name? All those bank loans. All those people in New York falling at your feet. Do you think, if they'd known who you *really* were—"

"*Silence!*" he roared. His eyes sprang open, and he raised his fists above his head. For a moment—trembling in fear—Elizabeth thought he'd strike her. Then he drew a shuddering sigh, lowered his hands and turned away from her. He stalked to the corner of the cabin, his shoulders rigid with anger. He snatched up Elizabeth's hammock, strode to the door and gave a curt bow.

"The bed is yours, *madame*," he said stiffly, and left Elizabeth to her remorse.

## Chapter Fourteen

"For the Lord's sake, Noël, please talk to me!" Afraid to look at her husband, Elizabeth turned and stared out the window of the dockside inn, watching the ships move across the turquoise waters of the Great Sound into the shelter of the harbor. The town of Hamilton was bright and clean, its whitewashed sandstone buildings sparkling under the morning sun; since Hamilton had only been named the capital of Bermuda two years before, half the buildings were still as shiny and new as fresh-minted coins. Elizabeth sighed. She'd yearned for adventure, to see strange ports. But where was her joy now? Without Noël's laughter and *joie de vivre* to buoy her spirits, the lovely view before her might just as well have been a gray, chilly November in New York.

Noël's voice behind her was cool, distant and faintly mocking. "Talk to you? But I have been talking to you for the past two weeks, my angel."

She clenched her fists in helplessness. It was useless to try to reach him. Since their last dreadful quarrel aboard ship he seemed to have built a wall around himself—an invisible barrier against which she battered in vain. He spoke about trifles and deflected her attempts at serious conversation. He never raised his voice. He smiled in unconcern. He called her "my angel" and cavalierly took her arm to cross the street and bought her a parasol to shield her from the hot sun.

But he slept on the floor in the corner of their room at the inn. And the eyes he turned to her were dead.

It had taken her days of bewilderment, an agonized searching of her soul to finally understand the terrible wrong she'd done him. Not her going to Stephen. Not even her hot temper when they quarreled. She supposed that a part of her had realized he was strong enough to overcome her thoughtless words and unmeant cruelties. But—to her grief—she'd struck out once too often and blindly hit a secret, fragile place in his heart. Without even being aware of it at the time.

She'd thrown his brother in his face. She'd as much as said he couldn't compare to Adam. His twin, who was rich, successful and—if she'd realized from some of the things he'd said—his parents' favorite. She knew how that felt, didn't she? The pain of measuring oneself against siblings who seemed to be more blessed by chance or by nature? Why should it be different for him? Because he was handsome and cocksure and seeming carefree? But perhaps Monsieur and Madame Bouchard had preferred the sober, industrious qualities of his brother.

She turned around to face him at last, praying he'd accept her sincerity. "I didn't mean what I said when we quarreled. On *L'Espérance*. The bankers in New York...the people who were nice to you... It wasn't because of Adam. Truly. It was because of *you*. Your determination to succeed in the venture. That's what everyone saw."

He shrugged; it was a lazy, Gallic gesture of self-assurance. "Of course. It was Adam's name, perhaps, that opened the door. But it was my charm that won the day. Adam could not have succeeded so well."

"Not at all," she agreed. "That's what I've been trying to tell you. Why, these past two weeks in Bermuda I've heard nothing but praise."

He looked pleased and leaned forward in his chair. "Is that so?"

"Oh, yes!" She was warming to her theme. Perhaps at last she could breach the wall. "You drove such a hard bargain selling your goods on the wharves... So shrewd." Steenboch had crowed with delight in the telling. The ship had been unloaded of its foodstuffs in no time, and an ad-

vertisement of the sale put into the *Bermuda Gazette*. De
spite the damage they'd suffered in New York, Noël ha
salvaged most of the goods and managed to sell them out
right at a large profit or trade them for coffee, sugar an
indigo that would join the furs bound for France. The re
pairs to the ship's mast were finished, the new cargo wa
even now being loaded, and Noël hoped to leave Bermud
at the beginning of the week. "You're a born trader," sh
finished warmly.

"Or a mad gambler." His smile deepened, his expressio
bordering on smug conceit. "And so, you have heard noth
ing but praise these past days?"

"Indeed, yes. Oh, I'm so proud of you, Noël."

"From whom?"

"What?"

"From whom did you hear the praise? A shopkeeper
perhaps? A fish-seller on the quay? That half-wit peddle
who sold us the sugarcane on Front Street yesterday?"

How could she have been so blind? He wasn't pleased a
her words of admiration. She saw now that his smile wa
coolly indifferent, as mocking and detached as though h
were watching a farce that faintly amused him. "But it'
so!" she cried in desperation. "I only wish I had half you
competence."

"*Mon Dieu.* Such fulsome praise," he drawled. "Suc
easy flattery. Next you will try to tell me that you did no
marry me because of Adam's title and fortune."

"Of course not!" She stamped her foot in frustration.

He finished his breakfast coffee, leaned back in his chai
and examined her as though she were a trifling obstacle i
his path. "But then why did you accept my offer?" h
asked. "Was it that you were tired of being a spinster?"

Her heart sank. If she'd seen hatred in his eyes, she coul
have dealt with it, could have found a way to win him back
If there was passion, some feeling for her. *Something.* Bu
it was clear he didn't care enough to be angry any longe
She sighed. "It's as good a reason as any." She reached fo
her purple jacket and shrugged into it, fluffing the whit
muslin ruffle of her dress over the jacket's neckline. "I'r

ff to the shops. The gowns I ordered should be ready this morning.''

He uncurled himself from his chair and stood up, reaching into the pocket of his trousers. ''Do you need more money?''

''No. I have enough, and to spare.'' That was certainly true. He'd insisted that she not stint on a new wardrobe, and had left bank notes beside her bed every night after she'd gone to sleep. She hadn't used any of Mother's pin money; in view of Noël's difficult mood, she'd be afraid even to tell him of it! ''You've been more than generous,'' she added.

His mouth twisted in a sardonic smile. ''But since I'm so successful in the eyes of the Bermudians—is that not what you said?—I can afford it.''

Blast him! He meant to repay her in kind for the hurts he'd given her. Well, by jingo, she could be as cold and unfeeling as he! ''Do you want me to go to France with you?'' she demanded. She wasn't a helpless ninny, after all. There's a merchantman in the harbor. The *Sea Venture*. Bound for New York tomorrow afternoon. I've already spoken to Captain Forbes. There's a place for me aboard, if I want it. If you don't want me on *L'Espérance*.''

''Go back to New York alone, my angel? But think of the shame of it! We would be the laughingstocks of your society.'' He smirked. ''Upon my return from France I should be forced to pretend to be my brother again. And I've grown tired of the role.''

She ignored that. It was more important to learn the inclination of his heart, if she could. ''Then you *want* me with you?'' she persisted.

He smiled, his bland expression telling her nothing. *Pourquoi pas?*''

''But we can't go on like this!''

He shrugged his shoulders in a gesture of sublime innocence. ''Like what?''

She gnashed her teeth. It was like having a discourse with a stone wall! She looked scornfully at the bedding rolled up in a ball in the corner of the room. ''Surely you don't intend to sleep on the floor for the whole of the voyage.''

"Of course not."

"Will you return to your hammock in Steenboch's cabin? Or is it to be mine again?"

"No."

She threw up her hands in frustration and despair. "Dagnation! No, *what?*" she cried.

He clicked his tongue. "Will you never learn to curb your temper, my angel? We shall sleep in the bunk together, of course. I on my side, you on yours. For the comfort of the bed, you understand. Nothing more."

The memory of their nights of passion flooded into her brain, washing away her defenses. "Is that all you want?" she whispered, then lowered her head so that he wouldn't see the sudden rush of tears to her eyes.

"What else can I want? There are two reasons for taking a woman to bed. For pleasure, of course. But you have told me upon more than one occasion that you find me a lustful rogue. A— What did you call it? A lothario, with far too many women in my past. Should I risk to offend you again? Never. As for a man's other reason, it is to have children. And you made it clear on *L'Espérance* that you think I already have one child too many." He stared hard for a moment, as though he meant his words to penetrate; then he grinned wickedly. "Of course, remembering your passion for me, I might be in danger beside you in the bunk."

She reached for her reticule and parasol, her hands shaking in fury. "We'll hang my hammock in its usual corner," she snapped. "At all costs, let us avoid the temptation of an encounter that would surely disappoint us both!" She turned on her heel and stalked from the room, nodding brusquely to Captain Steenboch, who had just emerged from his room next door.

The innkeeper—a transplanted Yorkshireman—met her at the door of the common room below. "Will you want a horse to ride this afternoon, ma'am?"

"Can you hire for me that roan gelding from the livery stable? The one I had before? If not, I'll want a cabriolet instead. And supper in my room, as usual."

A lonely supper. As usual. Breakfast was almost the only thing she had shared with Noël since *L'Espérance* had come limping into Hamilton Harbor two weeks ago. They had gone their separate ways by unspoken but mutual consent. Once or twice he'd invited her to join him for supper. But she'd stared into his cold and mocking eyes and refused. It was less lonely to depend on herself than to spend her days with a stranger. She'd ridden out alone to explore the islands, following sun-baked roads that meandered through gentle hills and cedar-filled valleys luxuriant with tropical vegetation. She'd walked along the sandy beaches, stared for hours at the deep purple seas that changed to brilliant blue and turquoise in the shoals, climbed the gray coral cliffs and refreshed herself with the oranges and limes that grew wild on the island. She'd shopped in Hamilton, or gone over to St. George's Island to stroll in the park of the old Government House. And always alone.

Steenboch was gone most of the day, seeing to the ship's repairs, the stores, sails, cordage and provisions needed for the long voyage across the ocean. Noël concerned himself with the cargo and with interviewing seamen. A carpenter with a broken arm was useless, and Gilchrist would need to be replaced. Then there was the other sailor who'd been hurt during the gale, as well as the two deserters, Ingham and Pease. Noël hoped to find half a dozen able-bodied men for the job.

He never returned to their room until it was very late and she was already in bed. And then she always pretended to be asleep. It was easier that way. She knew from the things Steenboch said that Noël spent his nights carousing in the public houses and gambling heavily and successfully. He'd even been invited to several gentlemen's clubs to play cards. She always knew, in the morning, if he'd been lucky at the card table—there were a few more bank notes beside her bed. It made her feel dog-cheap, like one of those coarse women who frequented the grogshops along the wharves. But she had no one but herself to blame. Too often she'd measured him in terms of money; why wouldn't he feel the need to prove himself by how much he gave her?

Her gowns were finished and waiting for her when she called in at the dressmaker's shop. She tried them on, nodding her approval at the fit and workmanship. A pale gray poplin gown with a deeper gray pelisse to match, and a simple dress of white dimity, worked all over with white embroidery. She had the dressmaker wrap them in a neat parcel to be sent round to her room at the inn; then, at the last moment, she took off her purple jacket and added it to the package. The day was growing quite warm.

It was too early to go back to the inn. Noël might still be there, with his mocking smile. She couldn't endure more of his torments today. She wandered aimlessly down the streets, finally stopping at a shop that displayed several elegant shawls in its window. Without her jacket, she felt underdressed. She went inside and poked through a wide selection of shawls until she found one to her liking. It was a fine silk sarcenet, the color of old wine. She held it up and gestured to the clerk at the other end of the shop.

"Oh, no, my dear. Not that color. Perish the thought." The voice was feminine and faintly breathless, as well as an odd mixture of clipped British and soft French.

Elizabeth turned to the woman behind her. She was a handsome matron of middle years, with a proud carriage and pale yellow curls that peeked from under the edge of her black silk bonnet. "I beg your pardon?" said Elizabeth.

The woman frowned and shook her head, though her gray eyes were filled with laughter. "That color makes you look like a beldam, my dear. I absolutely forbid you to buy it."

"But, I..." Elizabeth was too surprised to do anything except stare and stammer.

The woman smiled. "You will forgive me, my dear. It's a privilege of growing older. The right to speak one's mind." She reached out her gloved hand and resolutely pulled the shawl from Elizabeth's limp fingers. "Now, let us find the perfect one for you." She began to search through the profusion of shawls, all the while giving Elizabeth a brief history of her life.

Her name was Marianne Cooke. She had been born in the West Indies, the daughter of a French planter. When the

Revolution had come to the island of San Domingo in the summer of 1793 and engulfed her family in death and destruction, she had escaped the flames and horror of Port-au-Prince on a Spanish vessel. Within a week of having lost everything most dear to her, she'd found herself in Bermuda—an orphan, a destitute refugee, a terrified young foreigner of sixteen.

"And then, my dear, I met Samuel Cooke. He was old enough to be my father, but he was the kindest man I ever knew. We had a long and happy life together before he died last year, and raised reasonably civil children. Not as attentive to their mother as they might be, but then, I forgive them. And you, my dear? Tell me all about yourself."

Elizabeth smiled thinly, feeling dazed and overwhelmed. It was impossible to resist this lively, forceful woman. "I'm Elizabeth Bouchard from New York," she began hesitantly. "My husband's ship—"

Mrs. Cooke's eyes lit up. "Ah, yes. The clever and audacious Monsieur Bouchard, about whom all the men are talking. He's outsmarted them in trade and outplayed them at the gaming tables. But no one knew he had a charming wife."

Elizabeth felt a pang of regret. How foolish she'd been. While Noël seemed to have made an impression on half the islanders, she'd chosen to go her solitary way. She felt the need to say something in her own defense. "I prefer to be alone," she said. "I know little of his business. And I don't care for the way he amuses himself," she added primly.

"Very shortsighted of you, my dear. I didn't care a fig for the writings of the British wits—give me Beaumarchais any time—but I went to literary readings once a month with my husband. Just to please him. The more one gives up in love, the more one gains."

Elizabeth frowned. The woman was really quite presumptuous to lecture her so. "If you'll excuse me, Mrs. Cooke..."

The elder woman shook her head. "No, no. You mustn't be offended, my dear. I told you, it's the privilege of age to be quite shameless." She held up an embroidered shawl of clear aquamarine blue. "Now," she said, "this is the one you must buy."

Elizabeth relaxed into a smile. How could she be angry with someone who radiated such goodwill and cheer? "It's very kind of you, but I never wear that color."

"Why ever not?"

"Because it's too showy for a plain woman to wear."

"Plain? You're not at all plain, my dear." Mrs. Cooke took her by the chin and turned her face this way and that, examining her minutely. "Fine bones. Beautiful eyes. Superb complexion. I see you've caught a bit of the sun on your cheeks. It's very becoming. We must do something with your hair, of course."

Elizabeth pulled away from her and self-consciously smoothed the curly tendrils of hair at her forehead. "Perhaps it's your climate," she said by way of apology. "The pomade doesn't seem to hold it properly here."

"No. You need more curls, not fewer. Then your face will be even more pretty."

To Elizabeth, the word was a war cry. "Pretty?" She snorted with indignation and picked up the wine-colored shawl. "With my looks, I'm better off with this one."

Mrs. Cooke raised a delicate blond eyebrow. "Doesn't your husband's ship possess a looking glass, my dear?" She pulled Elizabeth to a large mirror at the end of the shop and pointed. "Look. Is that a plain face?"

Elizabeth stared, seeing herself with fresh eyes. She'd never been much for mirrors, spending only as much time before them as was necessary to straighten a hem or smooth a wild curl into place. Now she examined her reflection as though she were appraising a stranger.

And surely it *was* a stranger who looked back at her out of clear violet eyes. Though she'd been aware that her figure had grown rounder as she'd gained weight, she hadn't noticed what it had done to her face. Her cheekbones were still sharp, but the rest of her face had filled out, with softness that only served to emphasize the fine bones, the delicate pointed chin. The sun had given an apricot tint to her normally creamy complexion, and her deep red hair

urling softly around her face, had been bleached to a bright
opper. "Thunderation," she whispered, almost breathless
t the transformation. "I believe I *am* pretty."

"And it's time you met some of the folk on the island. I
hould be pleased to receive you at Fairhaven, my house
ear Tucker's Town. Come for tea this afternoon. Four
'clock. Where are you staying?"

"The Pembroke Arms."

"Good. I'll send a carriage around to pick you up. Bring
our husband. Tell him I haven't spoken French in years and
ook forward to a jolly conversation."

"But . . ." Elizabeth felt caught up in a whirlwind.

"You'll have a delightful time, my dear. I never invite
oring guests." She pushed the blue shawl into Elizabeth's
ands. "Buy this. And wear it." She frowned. "Are you
raveling with a maid?"

"No."

"Then I'll send the carriage at three. I have a clever girl
vho can do wonders with hair!"

"Your husband's ship sails at the beginning of the week,
understand, Mrs. Bouchard."

Elizabeth nodded at the elderly gentleman—a doctor that
Marianne Cooke had introduced her to—and took another
ip of cedarberry wine. "If all goes well, Dr. Simmons, we'll
lepart for France on Tuesday next."

"It's a pity your husband couldn't be here today. I made
is acquaintance the other night at a gentleman's club. And
ow we islanders are to lose you before we've scarcely come
o know you."

"A dreadful loss, Simmons." A young dandy stepped
orward, introduced himself and reached for Elizabeth's
and to bring it to his lips. He was fair and handsome, and
is eyes shone with admiration as he allowed his gaze to
ravel over Elizabeth's face. "What shall we do when this
harming creature has left us?"

I don't believe this, Elizabeth thought. Not any of it. It
vas something she'd dreamed of, watching her sisters at
parties and balls. To be the center of attention, to have

masculine eyes follow her as they had when she'd made her
way through Mrs. Cooke's drawing room. It wasn't just her
new coiffure, though the bright curls that bobbed against
her forehead and cheeks framed her face in a soft halo. It
wasn't her dimity gown, with the low neckline that showed
a graceful swell of bosom, a newly rounded form. It wasn't
even the aquamarine shawl draped seductively about her
shoulders to emphasize her extraordinary coloring, her large
violet eyes. It was a *feeling*.

I feel pretty, she thought, and so they see me as pretty.

She remembered the way Noël charmed a roomful of
people. It had nothing to do with his good looks. Not really. It was his thoughtful compliments, the manner in
which he smiled, how he looked at everyone as though they
alone existed for him—an intimacy, a caring that was re-
flected back to him in the way he was treated by others. And
she was discovering that it wasn't difficult to do.

She smiled warmly at the young dandy. "I feel sure that
when I'm gone, sir, you'll not want for tender attentions
from others. Not you. Such a charming gallant."

He beamed at the compliment and stroked his mustache.
"As much as it pains me to leave your side for a moment,
dear lady, may I fetch you another glass of wine?"

"Please."

He moved away to the other side of the room, but his
place was immediately taken by two more men who demanded an introduction from Dr. Simmons. They chatted
amiably for a while and were joined by others. Several of the
men had met Noël, either in the course of business or across
a card table: all expressed dismay that he'd wished to keep
his lovely and charming wife to himself. Elizabeth found
herself laughing and blushing by turns, which only made her
more attractive, as one of the gentlemen was at pains to
point out.

Her only regret was that Noël wasn't here with her. She'd
found him at dockside and told him about Mrs. Cooke and
the tea party at Fairhaven, but he'd refused to come, on the
grounds that he still had to find a carpenter to replace
Gilchrist. Upon reflection, Elizabeth didn't know whether

she wanted him here to share her happiness or to suffer pangs of jealousy at her success with other men.

At last the press of people and the unremitting attentions of the gentlemen began to exhaust her. It was too new, too overwhelming. She fanned herself and smiled at her circle of admirers. "If you'll forgive me, gentlemen, perhaps I'll step out onto the veranda and enjoy the cool breezes for a little while."

"You're staying in Hamilton, Marianne tells me," said Dr. Simmons. "Haven't been there much myself this summer. Too dashedly hot in town. Do you find it so?"

"It's certainly hotter than New York, even at this time of year."

The doctor sighed. "I'll be glad when the summer's gone. We've had too much sickness in this heat. Too much yellow fever coming in on foreign ships. Begging your pardon, ma'am. I didn't mean your husband's. But it's a worry." He sighed again. "I look forward to the October gales to blow the summer's fevers out to sea."

"Now, Simmons," said one of the other men, "you'll frighten our lovely visitor with such talk." He offered Elizabeth his arm. "May I escort you out to the veranda, ma'am?"

Elizabeth took his arm and allowed him to lead her out onto the balcony. Mrs. Cooke's house was a large whitewashed edifice set on a hill and surrounded by lush greenery and beds of bright tropical flowers. This side of the house faced the ocean, and Elizabeth took pleasure in the cooling breezes that ruffled her curls. She was content just to enjoy the view, the softness of the late-afternoon sun over the sea. When her escort offered to fetch her another glass of wine, she welcomed the opportunity to be alone for a few minutes. "Tea," she said, "with milk and sugar. And perhaps a biscuit or two." It would take him longer to bring those things than wine, and she could enjoy the serene vista in solitude.

If only Noël were here, she thought. If only she knew what to do to recapture the loving magic, the enchantment of their days at the beachside cottage. If only...

"I must meet the charming young woman about whom everyone is talking."

Elizabeth jumped at the sound of the deep masculine voice behind her, and turned to stare into dark, expressive brown eyes.

"Upon my word. Elizabeth Babcock," said Jack. "What are you doing here?"

## Chapter Fifteen

She was numb. A frozen statue where, a moment before, had been a living woman. Her hands were cold. Her heart was a block of ice. She closed her eyes against the sight of John Cochran. "Go away," she whispered.

"Elizabeth. Look at me," he pleaded.

Reluctantly she opened her eyes. He was as swarthily handsome as he'd always been. The chiseled features, the neat mustache, the dark eyes and hair—though he'd begun to gray at the temples since she'd seen him last. She despised every bit of him. "Go away," she said again, through clenched teeth. "Or I'll have one of those gentlemen throw you out of my presence."

"I beg you, let me apologize."

"For what? For turning tail and running like a miserable coward?"

"Oh, God," he groaned. "Forgive me. It was more than cruel of me. It was unspeakable." His anguish seemed genuine, though it might only have been a guilty conscience.

"You might have written. You might have left a note," she muttered. She was beyond even rage.

"I was too ashamed."

Ashamed? she thought bitterly. She could tell him what shame felt like! "Get out of my way," she said, moving toward the balcony door.

He blocked her path. "No. Let me speak. It was for the best. You must understand that. We would never have been happy together, Elizabeth. And now you're a married

woman. Elizabeth Bouchard, Marianne tells me. I'm happy
for you. I think I met your husband last week. At the shipyard. A fine man. A much better husband than I would have
made.''

"I have no doubt of that," she said coldly.

"Elizabeth. It was a long time ago. I wronged you terribly. But the past is gone. What can I do to make amends?"

"Tell me why."

He scowled at the toe of his boot. "I just couldn't go
through with it. And I couldn't face you."

There had to be more to it than that! Everything about
him—his tense posture, his shifty glance—screamed the
word *lies*. "Did you ever love me?"

He reddened beneath his tan. "I ... I was very fond of
you." He raised his head and stared at her boldly. The
searching appraisal was filled with curiosity—and admiration. "I could love you now. The last five years have taught
me much about my heart. About what I lost when I left
you."

"How touching," she said with a sneer. "You could have
returned, if I was so precious to you."

"I couldn't. Not with the war. I was here in Bermuda. I
have a shipyard here, you know. And we were at war with
the United States."

"Oh, what does it matter?" she said tiredly. She'd imagined this scene a thousand times. She'd pictured herself
screaming, attacking him, destroying him as he'd destroyed
her happiness, her peace of mind—even with Noël. But now
that it had happened, she felt nothing. Not hatred. Not even
the need for vengeance.

No, she thought. That wasn't so. There was still one thing
unsettled: the one dark thought that had tormented her all
these years. The need for the answer to her question. *Why*.

She'd always told herself it had simply been a whim of
his, a spur-of-the-moment decision because she hadn't suc-
cumbed to his desires that day. But now, remembering those
last few moments in his office, she was sure that something
quite specific had happened to drive him away. He'd dismissed all his workers early. Odd, and not at all like him.

She'd found him going through his papers, as though he were planning to take them with him. Even the words he'd used when he'd wanted her to make love—"It's the least I'm owed"—were the words of a man who planned to leave. No. There was a better reason than impulse. There had to be. And, by jingo, she'd learn it, no matter what it took. No matter what craft or guile. And then she could lay it to rest once and for all, and make a fresh start with Noël, if he'd let her.

"Can you ever forgive me?" Jack said again.

Not in a thousand years, she thought. But she smiled tentatively, as though her heart were softening. "It was dreadfully cruel of you, Jack. But you're right. It was a long time ago. And perhaps, as you say, it was for the best."

He breathed a sigh of relief. "My dearest Elizabeth. How generous you are." He seized her hand and pressed it fervently to his lips. "I shall never forgive myself for letting you go. It has weighed so heavily on my conscience." His dark eyes searched her face, dropped to the soft curve of her bosom. "Damn, but you've blossomed. I envy your husband."

If she was ever to learn the real and true answer to her question, she'd have to win his confidence, make him think she still cared for him. She remembered one of Caroline's favorite tricks. She lowered her head and gazed at him through her long lashes. "Why should you envy him?" she murmured. She hoped he read it as a clear invitation.

His eyes widened in surprise and pleasure. "Elizabeth! Can I hope for more than just your forgiveness?"

She rapped the sleeve of his coat with her fan. "You're very hasty after five years, Jack," she chided gently. "Be content with my forgiveness for now."

"I haven't forgotten the passion of your kisses," he murmured. "They've haunted my memory. Kept me sleepless till dawn, wondering what it would have been like to . . ."

The wretch! The nights of grief when she'd hugged her pillow and imagined him in her arms. "I've wondered, too," she said with feigned tenderness.

"May I take you back to your inn?"

"Yes."

"May I take you to supper?"

"No." Let him yearn for her through the long night. She'd arrange a rendezvous for the morning. From the hungry way he was beginning to look at her, she thought she could wring the truth out of him in no time.

After taking her tea, she made her farewells to Mrs. Cooke, thanked her and promised to see her again at least once more before she sailed. She went out into the soft twilight and sat beside Jack in his open carriage.

"Are you expected back at once?" he asked. "I'd like to ride for a little while and learn what your life has been like these past years."

"I'm not expected, no." They drove through the dusk, the sky streaked with pink and filled with the evening songs of exotic birds. He seemed more interested in telling of his life than in hearing of hers. She let him talk—as much out of curiosity as anything else. He told her of his lonely struggles to start up his shipbuilding enterprise again, the difficulties engendered by the war and the American privateers who'd captured many a good Bermuda vessel.

It astonished her, the number of dispassionate conclusions she reached on their long ride through the hills. To begin with, he was boring and uninteresting, frightfully self-absorbed. She wasn't sure she liked him very much besides. Even if she didn't compare him unfavorably with Noël, there was little in his demeanor or personality to recommend him. Yet all this time she thought she'd loved him once.

Perhaps her "love" had been a combination of her own insecurity, awe at his extraordinary good looks, gratitude that he'd chosen her—and her unexpectedly sensuous nature, responding to his kisses. She wondered idly if she still would.

It was dark before they rode into the courtyard of the Pembroke Arms. She'd already arranged to meet Jack for morning coffee near the market house on Front Street. He helped her from the carriage, then put a hand on her arm when she would have gone into the inn. "Don't go yet," he said. "I can't get enough of you. You've become the most enchanting creature in the world."

"What was I like in the old days, then?" She could remember. Poor Bessie Babcock. But it would be instructive to hear what he had to say.

He stroked the side of her cheek. "Shy. Eager to please me. Hot-tempered from time to time." He smiled. "But I always knew how to calm you down by promising a kiss."

Though it seemed a pleasant memory for him, it brought her no joy to recall her weakness, her willingness to bend to his needs for the sake of a kiss. For the crumbs of his affection. "I was younger then," she said.

His eyes burned into hers, black as a raven's wing by the dim light of the courtyard lamps. "And now I'm the one who sues for *your* favors," he said, his voice husky with desire. "You have me in your power, Elizabeth. That last day, that last kiss, has tormented me for years. That tantalizing glimpse of an Elizabeth I hadn't known existed. Is she still within you, that woman of passion?"

"Do you want to kiss me now?" she asked suddenly. Let him humble himself, let him beg for a kiss, she thought, as I used to do.

"Dearest Elizabeth," he said, and reached out to take her in his arms.

"No!" She held him at bay, determined to wring the last drop of humility out of him.

Again his arms reached for her, and again she pushed him away, this time taking a large step backward.

Nothing, she thought. She felt no passion, no desire for this man. No urge to do his bidding for the reward of a kiss. She felt disgusted and faintly sick to her stomach. It was only by reminding herself that she hoped to lead him into a confession that she resisted the impulse to spit in his face. "Tomorrow at ten," she whispered, and hurried inside. I'm free of your power at last, Jack, she thought with a surge of fierce, exultant pride.

She mounted the stairs to her room. Noël, casual in shirtsleeves, leaned against the open doorway, his arms crossed over his chest. "Where have you been, my wandering angel?"

She felt a momentary shiver of fear. He was too nonchalant, his smile too devil-may-care, his pose too indolent. She glanced toward the end of the corridor: one window overlooked the courtyard of the inn. She chewed at her lip. Had he seen Jack's pursuit of her? She couldn't be sure. There was nothing to do but brazen it out. "I told you where I was going. Mrs. Cooke's, for tea."

He shook his head. "No. I was there." He shrugged at her startled expression. "Why should it surprise you that I'd want to be with my lovely wife?" He took a moment to appraise her. "And you do look lovely. That coiffure suits you."

His compliment seemed genuine. She felt more guilty than ever about the scene with Jack, whether he'd seen it or not. "Thank you," she murmured.

"But you were not at Mrs. Cooke's. I purposely put off my interview with a new carpenter so that I might join you. *Hélas*. When I arrived, I found that my dear wife had left with a Mr. John Cochran." His mouth twisted in an ugly smile. "Was he the reason you look so beautiful today?"

If she had any sense, she'd tell him everything. But her affair with Jack was her own, to be resolved in her own way. Besides, Noël's overbearing manner had set her teeth on edge. "Mr. Cochran merely offered to escort me home," she said.

"All this time?"

She stamped her foot. "I won't be interrogated this way! We drove to the South Shore to watch the sunset." A lie, of course. She had watched the sunset; Jack had watched her with his rapacious eyes. She squirmed uncomfortably under Noël's searching gaze. The only way to protect herself was to attack first. "Do you think I'm trying to make you jealous?" she asked scornfully. "In retaliation for all your women?"

"Are you?"

"Don't be absurd."

"I trust not. I have met this Cochran once or twice. Scarcely worthy of you, my angel. The man has no backbone." He shrugged. "Well, it does not matter. You will not see him again."

"Is that an order I'm expected to obey?"

He smiled coldly. "Yes."

"Go to the devil." She swept past him into their room and tossed her shawl and fan across the bed.

"Someday we will deal with your willfulness, wife. But for now, I'm expected at cards." He buttoned his vest, threw on his coat and picked up his top hat. He gave a mocking bow, "Don't wait up for me," then he was gone.

He came in very late and very drunk. His boisterous laughter, blending with Steenboch's guttural voice in the corridor, woke her from a deep sleep. The laughter subsided, and then she heard the clink of glasses from Steenboch's room next door. Evidently Noël hadn't yet got his fill of carousing, she thought in disgust. Well, his head would throb in the morning, and he'd have no one but himself to blame! She turned over in bed and went back to sleep.

She awoke several times during the night. And though there were no sounds from Steenboch's room after a while, Noël's bedding remained folded neatly in the corner. Well, she thought, perhaps he fell asleep on Steenboch's floor, the drunken lout!

She awoke once more at dawn to the sound of footsteps beyond her door and the soft whinny of a horse from the street outside her window. She jumped out of bed, dashed to the window, and was just in time to see Noël climbing into a waiting carriage. She threw her shawl over her nightdress and hurried out to the corridor. She nearly collided with Steenboch.

"Lady," he growled politely. He tugged at his broad-brimmed hat and continued toward the staircase.

"Wait!" she cried. "Where are you going?"

His normally pleasant face was dark with an impenetrable expression. "An appointment. M'soo Noël."

She frowned. The sun was barely up. "So early?"

"Can't stop to talk," he said. "We'll be late." He tipped his hat again and clattered down the stairs.

The more she thought about it, the more uneasy she became. Steenboch was angry with her. She'd have sworn to it. But it wasn't like him. He was Noël's trusted confidant. He probably had a clear understanding of what was happening between her and her husband. Yet he'd always seemed, if not unaware of their difficulties, at least neutral. But not this morning. What had she done to earn his enmity? Concerned now, she rang for the chambermaid.

The girl shuffled into the room and bobbed politely. "Yes'm?"

"Was that my husband who just left in a carriage?"

The girl looked uncomfortable. "Yes'm."

"Do you know where he went? Don't be afraid. I'll give you a penny if you tell me the truth."

"I heard him ask the master if the coachman knew the way to Cobb's Hill."

How strange, thought Elizabeth. She'd ridden up to Cobb's Hill on her travels around the island. It was a wild, windswept area that gave way unexpectedly to a secluded dell. A pleasant morning's ride, but scarcely a place to meet on business. "Why would he want to go to Cobb's Hill?" she mused aloud.

"It's where all the gentlemen go, ma'am."

"Go for what?" It was a romantic spot, but she didn't think that was Noël's purpose. Not at this hour of the morning, and with Steenboch in tow!

The girl began to back nervously out of the room. "We're not supposed to know. The gentlemen don't like it noised around."

She was filled with sudden dread. "Is that where they go to *duel?*" At the maid's reluctant nod, Elizabeth uttered a cry. "Oh, my God. Noël! Quick, now, girl. Go and tell the innkeeper to get me a horse as soon as he can. I want it waiting when I come down. Do you understand?"

She threw on her clothes, gulped down a hastily fetched cup of coffee and dashed out to the saddled horse. The town was just beginning to stir, and the clatter of her horse's hooves through the quiet early-morning streets was a sharp tattoo of foreboding. What madness had possessed Noël?

It was a long, steep climb up Cobb's Hill, and her heart was heavy with dread. Let him be safe, she prayed. But safe from whom? Who had he angered? One of the merchants, who'd resented his hard bargaining? An adversary across the card table? She didn't know whether she was just frightened, or angry at herself for not having been his companion these past two weeks, despite his mood. If she had, at least she might have known something of his business on the island.

Ahead of her, near the rise of the hill, was a small open carriage. She slowed in surprise when she saw the occupant was Dr. Simmons. He frowned and brought his carriage to a halt. "Go home, Mrs. Bouchard. This is no place for you."

"What's happening?" she demanded. "Is my husband fighting a duel?"

"I was sent for, in case I was needed. I would have been here sooner, but I was busy delivering another Jennings baby."

In case he was needed. That was too awful to contemplate. "Please tell me what happened. I beg you."

"I was at the club when your husband came in last night. He went at once to John Cochran and demanded satisfaction of him. There were no other words spoken between them, so your reputation is safe. But John seemed to understand the reason for the challenge." He sighed. "A stupid business, this. Go home, ma'am."

Her heart sank. Noël had seen Jack in the courtyard, and had misunderstood. But she loved him, whatever his feelings for her. And she wasn't about to see him killed over the likes of Jack Cochran! It had been folly not to tell Noël everything the moment she'd come in last evening.

She kicked at her horse's flank. "I'm off to stop the fools if I can, Doctor. Pray you'll not be needed." She raced ahead, following the road until it dipped to a wooded valley, then turned off into the trees.

She was just emerging into a large clearing when she heard the report of a pistol, followed immediately by the sharp crack of another. Noël and Jack stood facing each other at some distance, smoking pistols in hand. As Elizabeth watched, Jack crumpled to the ground. His seconds rushed forward to catch him as he fell.

It took her only a moment to see that Noël was unharmed. And another long, panic-filled moment to realize that if Jack were to die, she'd live with the torment of her self-doubts for the rest of her life. "No!" she cried. She slid from her horse and raced across the field toward him.

"Elizabeth!" Noël stopped her and clutched at her arm, his eyes blazing with savage anger.

She was weeping hysterically now, filled with relief for Noël's life, fury at the stupidity of it, terror that Jack might die without telling her—a wild confusion of emotions that left her trembling and half mad. She struggled in Noël's fierce grasp. "Let me go!" she cried. "You...you risked your life! For what? Your pride? A stupid scene? This was *my* affair, not yours! Blast you, if you've killed him..."

He stared at her, his lip curling in disgust; then he pushed her away. "Do as you wish, *madame*," he growled. "I'll not stop you." He signaled to Steenboch to bring him his coat.

She had only one thought now. To reach Jack's side. She fell on her knees before him, cringing at the sight of the blood that stained the shoulder of his white shirt. With shaking hands, she tore open the shirt. The bullet seemed merely to have gone through the flesh and muscles of his upper arm, but she had little experience of these things. She looked anxiously at his seconds. "Is it serious?"

One of the men shook his head. "I don't think so, ma'am."

Thank God, she thought, feeling her pounding heart slow to a semblance of normalcy. "I passed Dr. Simmons, coming up the hill. He should be here soon. In the meantime—" she looked down at Jack, who had begun to weep in pain "—will you let me speak to Mr. Cochran alone, please?"

The two seconds made Jack as comfortable as possible, then stood up and bowed. "Your servant, ma'am."

"Elizabeth." Jack brushed at the tears in his eyes and smiled weakly at her.

A blubbering baby, on top of everything else, she thought contemptuously. Noël was right. The man had no backbone. "Be of good cheer," she said. "You'll be mended in no time."

"I'd suffer the torments of hell for you."

A high-sounding offer, she thought, in view of the fact that Noël had merely winged him!

"You're here with me, not with him," he went on. "Does that mean we can begin again, Elizabeth dear?"

"All I want to know is why you left me."

He looked away. "I told you . . . it was best . . ."

"Damn you, I want the truth!"

He sighed, wincing at the pain in his shoulder. "Yes. You deserve the truth." He closed his eyes, then covered them with his hand, as though to shield himself doubly from her probing gaze. "Caroline and I . . . were lovers," he said reluctantly.

"*What?*" She rocked back on her heels, doubting the words she'd just heard.

"This is so difficult. Forgive me, Elizabeth. We met soon after your sister had married Stephen. But he was suspicious. Always jealous of her. After a while it became almost impossible to steal a few minutes together. He didn't like to see me near her. At parties and dinners. Anywhere."

She groaned. "But if you courted her sister, it was natural for hostesses to seat you with the rest of the Babcock family. Natural for you to take your fiancée's sister on errands. Dance with her at balls. Is that it? Is that what was in your mind?" When he nodded, she felt sick. "How convenient that Stephen and Caroline lived next door on Warren Street. And whose idea was it, this clever scheme of yours?"

"Elizabeth . . . dearest . . ."

"Look at me, you coward. Open your eyes and look at me! Whose idea?" Caroline couldn't have been so cruel. Not her dear sister.

He dropped his arm and stared at her, his eyes dark with shame. "It was my idea. You mustn't blame Caroline. She was very uneasy. Very unhappy about it. I swear that."

"But why me? Why didn't you choose Rose?"

"She was only seventeen. And besides, Caroline was jealous. Afraid I'd..." He squirmed, plainly aware of what he'd revealed.

"Fall in love with the *beautiful* Babcock sister?" It was one more turn of the knife. "Tell me, did you ever intend to go through with the marriage?"

"Yes."

"Of course. You were talking about buying the house across the street from Caroline, I remember. How easy for you both." She laughed bitterly. "What spoiled your plans? Did you and Caroline have a falling-out?"

"Stephen found out. I don't know how. He came to me and threatened me with ruin. Your brother-in-law has powerful friends."

"So I've learned. To my husband's sorrow. But you didn't suffer very much. You left your debts behind and managed to start a new business here. Eh?"

Jack cleared his throat in embarrassment. "I had help from Stephen. He...paid me never to communicate with Caroline again."

Elizabeth remembered how distraught her sister had been at her jilting. She'd thought it excessive then, coming simply from Caroline's fear of public shame and the wagging tongues of the neighbors. Poor, bewildered Caroline. How much more *she* had suffered, when one came to think of it. She'd been abandoned—with never an explanation—by a man who'd truly loved her. And Stephen, that hypocrite. Dissuading Father from going after Jack. From suing for breach of promise. Swearing to Elizabeth—his eyes warm with sympathy—that she was better off without the scoundrel. Well, that was true enough, at least.

"And that last day," she said, "when you tried to dishonor me in your office. You were planning to leave then, weren't you?"

"That was thoughtless of me, to treat you so. I was angry. And unhappy, you understand."

"And if you'd left me with a child that day?" she asked in disgust. "Did you think of that?"

"Elizabeth." He put his hand to his injured shoulder and pouted. "Don't chide me. No matter how villainous I've been. Not when I'm in such pain."

She stared at him, seeing him clearly for the first time. *This* was the man she'd allowed to destroy her life, her marriage? The man who'd loomed large through her days and nights, who'd haunted her and kept her from giving Noël all her love? She felt no satisfaction at his injury and suffering. The man was no giant brought to his knees. He was a weak and insignificant worm, a coward and a cheat who'd carried on a tawdry love affair with her sister. "It had nothing to do with me," she said in wonder. "Not any of it. You left me at the church, would have dishonored me out of childish disappointment—and it had nothing to do with *me*."

"Forgive me, dearest. I was blind and stupid then. Unaware of the treasure before my eyes. But things will be better now. I'll make amends to you, you'll see. I'm so very sorry."

She laughed—a sharp, brittle laugh. "Why should you apologize? I'm grateful you left. The thought of spending the rest of my life with you turns my stomach."

He frowned in bewilderment. "But you care for me! You always did...."

She rose to her feet. She was tired and drained, still trying to make sense of it all. She stared down at him, at that handsome face, twisted in pain and blighted hope. "I wouldn't have been as generous as my husband," she said.

She sighed heavily. She was dazed, incapable of feeling anything yet. She stumbled toward her horse. She had to be alone. To sort out her thoughts. To rethink the past, her relations with her family—so patently false, it now appeared. To root out the last bit of hatred and anger in her heart.

"Elizabeth." Noël loomed before her, his blue eyes dark and clouded.

"Please, Noël. Let me be alone for a while," she begged.

He raised a mocking eyebrow. "Alone? Haven't I left enough of Mr. Cochran to please you?"

Her head was spinning. "What are you talking about?"

"Your sensibilities for Mr. Cochran."

Sensibilities? She was numb. Why didn't he leave her alone? "You don't understand," she said impatiently. "I've waited five years to get answers, and you nearly ruined everything with your idiotic duel." She brushed past him and grabbed for her horse's reins.

"Do you not intend to stay and comfort your lover, *madame?*" His voice behind her dripped with sarcasm.

It was too much! She whirled to face him. "Lover?" she cried. "*Lover?* I'll despise Jack Cochran till the day I die!" She leapt onto her horse, kicked it savagely in the flank and galloped away through the trees.

Noël stared at her retreating figure. Jack? John Cochran was *Jack?* The man who— He raced to Cochran, knelt before him and put his hand to his throat. "What did you tell my wife?"

Cochran groaned. "Let me be, Bouchard. Haven't you done enough?"

"I allowed you to shoot first, *monsieur,*" he snarled. "Your trembling hand was your affair, not mine. Now—" he tightened his grip on the man's throat "—are you the man called Jack? The damned fiancé who abandoned Elizabeth five years ago?"

"It was a mistake. I told her . . ."

It was taking all his will to keep from throttling the bastard. "What did you say to her just now?"

He listened in horror as Cochran reluctantly told his story, imagining the pain with which Lisbet must have received each fresh revelation. To be used as a stalking-horse, to think she was loved, and then to learn he'd never cared for her. To discover her own sister's treachery, her brother-in-law's silence when one word would have eased her agony. He closed his eyes, tasting the bitterness of her grief.

No. More than grief. Her behavior today made it clear that Jack had harmed her far beyond what he'd imagined.

The wound ran deeper than Cochran's bloody shoulder, the scar more livid and angry than those half a dozen saber cuts had left on him. His dear Lisbet. He would have to love her a great deal to wipe out the hurts of the past, and the fresh wounds she'd received today.

He stood up and scowled down at Cochran. "You may thank your God, *monsieur*," he growled, "that I do not kill you now."

He thought at first to go after Elizabeth at once, but then he changed his mind. He had to admit he was angry that she hadn't told him who Cochran was. Angry at himself, as well, for not confronting her the minute he'd seen her descend from Cochran's buggy, instead of going off to throw his glove in Cochran's face. In his present mood—and Elizabeth's—they would only quarrel again. Best to give her time to be alone, to deal with her humiliation in solitude. The agony of once again being second-best to one of her sisters. A few hours for the raw pain to subside. He left Cochran to Dr. Simmons and crossed the clearing to Steenboch and his waiting carriage.

Steenboch scowled at him. "Well, have you resolved anything by risking your life? It wasn't *you* she comforted! If I may make so bold, M'soo Noël, your lady needs a good dose of strap oil."

He clapped his hat on his head. "You're a loyal friend, Hessel, but stay out of this. What my lady needs is what I have not seen fit to give her these past weeks." All the love that was in his heart. The tender care that would make those violet eyes laugh again. As he'd made them laugh that long-ago night in Paris, when they'd danced. Had he forgotten the joy of courting her, of winning her trust? He'd acted like a stiff-necked fool ever since they'd come to Bermuda, ignoring her, nursing his own wounds behind a mask of callous indifference and mockery. Pretending he didn't notice how his behavior hurt her.

Well, things would be different now. It was a long voyage to France. With a large enough crew that he didn't have to work himself nearly to death aboard ship this time. He'd take her to bed morning, noon and night, if he had to. Until she understood that she was loved. Until her wounds had healed. Until she could tell him what he was sure he'd read in her eyes—that she loved him. He chuckled softly. That should please Steenboch, who was as meddlesome as an old crone when it came to his marriage, and had chided him for that separate hammock on the trip down from New York.

Hell, he didn't have to wait until they sailed to start his campaign of sweet seduction. "Hessel," he said, "please find me a lonely stretch of beach that would be suitable for a picnic supper. Someplace where the lady and I will not be disturbed. Meanwhile, I will consult with our host, the good innkeeper, to see if he can cook me up something delicious for tonight."

Steenboch followed him into the carriage and shook his head. "Now?"

"Why not? I want to be at the inn, in any event, when Madame Bouchard returns."

"Did you forget about Jacob Murray?"

"*Le diable.*" Murray was the carpenter he'd planned to interview yesterday. After he'd sent his message canceling their appointment, Murray had responded by requesting that they meet this morning at his lodgings. "Can you not meet him, Hessel?"

"*M'soo,* if you want to be ready to sail by Monday or Tuesday next, I haven't much time to buy provisions and see them stowed. And you need to sign for one more load of coffee today."

Ah, well. His plans for tonight would have to wait for a little while. "The boardinghouse of Monsieur Murray is near to the coffee warehouse. Meet me there in an hour, and we will go together." There was time. Given Elizabeth's distress, he guessed she would need to ride for a long time; it would be almost noon before she returned to the inn, he supposed.

The boardinghouse—a dingy old structure—was located down a narrow lane in the old section of Hamilton. By the look of disappointment on the landlady's face when he declined her offer of a room, Noël suspected that Murray was almost the only lodger in the place. At the woman's direction, he climbed the stairs to a room at the end of the corridor.

Jacob Murray was a thin man, far too frail-looking to seem capable of heavy carpentry. He'd come up on a ship from Barbados, bound for Philadelphia. But his family was in England, and he welcomed the chance to return to Europe on Noël's ship. Noël had met him a week before on the wharf.

Murray glanced apologetically around his shabby, dimly lit room, which was in disarray and smelled faintly of vomit. "Forgive the state of the room, Mr. Bouchard, sir," he said, "but I aren't been well. Not to worry, though. I'll be on my feet afore you can say Jack Robinson. You'll get a full day's work from me. Hale and hearty, I always been, till t'other day, when I had me a mess of turtle soup. Didn't sit well, and that's the God's truth. But sick or well, I'm the finest carpenter you'll ever have, and no mistake!" His eyes shone with enthusiasm.

Or drunkenness, thought Noël. The man's eyes were distinctly bloodshot even in this gloom, and his hands shook as he held out a chair for Noël. Maybe his sickness had less to do with turtle soup than with West Indian rum. Still, he owed the man a fair hearing. "Who have you sailed with?" he said.

He was sorry he'd asked the question. Murray launched into a rambling discourse, stopping now and again to "wet his whistle," as he put it, from a jug of water on the table.

After a while, Noël stopped listening. There was only one thought on his mind. He didn't care if he hired a broommaker who'd never seen the inside of a forecastle. He only wanted to be with Elizabeth. To hold her, to kiss that vulnerable mouth, to press her trembling, naked body to his and... Damn! He was getting hot just thinking about her. "Yes, yes," he said impatiently, interrupting Murray. "I think you will do. Twenty-four dollars, American, in advance pay. Come to the quay on Monday morning. Captain Steenboch will sign you on."

"Thank'ee, Mr. Bouchard, sir." Murray began to shake violently. He stood up, tried to walk to the door to open it for Noël, then collapsed in a heap on the floor, twitching and uttering little yelps and grunts, like a dog having a nightmare.

"*Merde!*" Noël dropped to his knees and examined the man. What a blind fool he was! If he'd had his wits about him, he'd have noticed the yellowish tinge to the man's skin, even in this half-light. He put his hand to Murray's face; the flesh was hot and dry. He lifted him carefully and carried him to the bed, then pulled out his handkerchief, moistened it in the jug of water and laid it across the man's forehead. As soon as Steenboch arrived, they could notify the authorities of another case of yellow fever.

No! What was he thinking of? Murray's ship from Barbados might have brought the infection with it. There could be an epidemic on Bermuda like the one that had wiped out more than thirty thousand French troops in San Domingo in 1802. He still remembered how it had destroyed the Emperor Napoleon's hopes for an American outpost. And if the governor of Bermuda decided to quarantine all the ships in the harbor for the time being, there'd be no escaping the pestilence.

He freshened the compress on Murray's forehead and covered his quaking form with a blanket, thinking it was possible that he himself was a dead man already. He'd spent nearly an hour in the unwholesome atmosphere of this room, breathing in God alone knew what. He almost laughed aloud at the irony of it. Had he survived the deadliest war in the history of mankind only to be felled by a fever?

His musings were interrupted by a soft knock on the door. "M'soo Noël? Are you there?"

He leaned close to the panel of the door. "Hessel. Listen to me. Are you quite alone? No one is there to hear?"

"No. The old woman went across the street to buy a pint."

"Good. Listen." Urgently he explained the situation to Steenboch. Whatever happened, he wanted Elizabeth safely off the island before anyone knew of Murray's illness. "Captain Forbes is sailing for New York this afternoon on the *Sea Venture,* is it not so? Put my wife aboard. I shall wait here until you come and tell me that the *Sea Venture* has cleared the harbor. Then we can decide how we are to inform the authorities."

Steenboch swore softly. "How am I to get your lady aboard?"

"Tell her I think it is for the best. She is to go back to New York and wait until we return from France. Assure her that we *shall* return. I think she has money, but give her more. I will not have her stay with her family. She is to take lodgings somewhere, and leave word at my bank where I can find her. Tell her, if she has ever trusted me, to trust me now." A vision of Elizabeth's haunting eyes rose before him. It could be months before he saw her again. It could be... never. "Tell her I love her," he choked out.

A long silence. Then: "Shall I tell her about Murray and the yellow fever?"

"Yes. *No.*" He could just see Elizabeth, stubbornly jutting out her chin at the mere idea of running from danger. And if she knew how much he loved her, she'd never go. "Tell her nothing of my feelings. Nor of Murray," he said. "Wait a moment, and I'll write you a letter to give to Captain Forbes. Let her read it when she is out to sea."

"But what shall I tell her in the meantime?"

*Grand Dieu,* but he couldn't think straight. "Tell her... tell her I am angry because of Cochran. That I shall forgive her when I return. Yes. That will send her away. Tell her I order her to go, as her husband. Be as harsh as you must. My letter will put things to rights."

"Your lady is willful and headstrong, *m'soo,* as well you know. What am I to do if she still refuses?"

"Damn it, Steenboch, do what you must! By whatever means, get her on that ship. Now wait for my letter."

He found writing materials on a shelf and sat down to compose his thoughts. It wasn't easy—to tell her how much he loved her, knowing he might never see her again. How could he tell her of the loneliness he'd felt all his life—and called it independence and self-sufficiency? Loneliness that had been a vague ache of dissatisfaction, no matter what he did, until he'd met her? How to put into words the heart-stopping joy of seeing her smile? The pain of watching her weep? He scribbled simple words of love, hoping they'd be enough. He prayed she had learned to love and trust him a little. She was not to be troubled about leaving him on the island with the fever. God had protected him before, and would do so again.

He sealed the letter and slipped it under the door to Steenboch, then listened to the man's retreating footsteps. It was very quiet. Jacob Murray had ceased his fevered thrashings, and was now sleeping quietly, his jaw slack. Noël replaced the compress, then went to stand at the window and gaze out at the sun-baked street below. He'd never felt more alone in his life. If only he could hold her once more. If only they hadn't parted in anger on Cobb's Hill. Well—he sighed and shook off his melancholy—he would have to keep a sweeter memory in his mind until he saw her again.

"For the last time, Captain Steenboch, I will *not* go back to New York. You can just go and tell that to my husband." Elizabeth scowled at Steenboch and poured herself another cup of tea. Dagnation, why couldn't the man leave her alone? She'd come back from her ride still filled with confusion, hoping to have a few hours to sort out her thoughts before Noël returned.

She knew she loved him. She thought perhaps he cared for her, in spite of everything. He'd said they would sleep together in the bunk on the long voyage back to France. Surely such proximity would lead to passion, and passion to love. But for tonight, it was important to talk about Jack. To clear the air. Noël must be made to understand that yesterday's buggy ride with her former fiancé meant nothing.

She'd hoped to have the afternoon to plan what to say to her husband. Instead, she'd been interrupted by Steenboch's knock on her door almost as soon as she'd sat down to lunch. And now he was telling her that Noël wanted her to go back to New York after all. To find rooms and wait for him, as though her wishes didn't even matter. And the cowardly Frenchman didn't even have the nerve to tell her in person, but had to send this rumpled emissary! "I won't go back," she said again. "I had more cause to be angry about Jack Cochran than he did."

"*You* didn't risk your life on a foolish duel like *m'soo* did."

"You're still blaming me for that, aren't you? Well, I didn't ask him to duel. He's your friend. Why didn't you stop him?"

Steenboch glowered at her across the table. "He said it's for your own good. To leave Bermuda now."

"Hmph! So he says."

He sighed, trying to be reasonable. "Please, lady, don't make this difficult."

She tossed her head. "I intend to sail on *L'Espérance*."

"And if I forbid you to come aboard? I can do it as the captain."

"I have friends among the crew. And I'm already very good at being a stowaway. Remember? Tell me," she added sarcastically, "does he have a woman waiting for him back in France?"

"Ach!" He threw up his hands in disgust. "I knew this would happen." He slammed his large hand down on the table. Elizabeth's teacup rattled violently, spilling the hot liquid into the saucer. Steenboch looked uncomfortable. "Beg your pardon, lady." With movements that were surprisingly deft for his awkward bulk, he picked up Elizabeth's cup and saucer, emptied them into the slop bowl and poured her a fresh cup. "Will you be guided by your husband in this, lady?" he asked, handing her back her tea.

"No."

"So be it." He rose, sighed again and walked to the window, watching morosely as she finished her lunch.

She stared at him and blinked. She really felt quite peculiar. A strange heaviness, a feeling that she wanted to lie down and sleep forever. She put down her cup and rubbed her hand across her eyes, then looked up at Steenboch. She could scarcely focus on him for the mist that dimmed her eyes. "How very odd..." she mumbled.

"I'm sorry, lady," he said gently. "*M'soo* thought you might be reasonable and do as you were told. But I knew you'd be too stubborn for anything but the strongest persuasion."

She forced herself to look at him, to fight the darkness that was closing in on her. He seemed to be holding something in his hand. A small glass vial. Quite empty.

She awoke to a gentle rocking and sat up. "Criminy," she moaned. Her head was pounding. She looked around her. She was on a bed. In a ship's cabin. "Oh, no!" she cried. He couldn't have. He wouldn't have! Her heart sank. In the middle of the room was her luggage, the pile of boxes topped by her parasol and reticule. She eased her way out of the bunk and opened her reticule. It was stuffed with bank notes.

The cursed villain! she thought. He'd abandoned her again, no matter what he might tell himself. He wasn't about to forgive her for Jack. Not yet. She clutched her aching head. Maybe they weren't that far from land yet. She climbed up on deck and gazed with dismay at the islands of Bermuda, already fading into the horizon and the evening twilight.

"Mrs. Bouchard."

She turned to see Captain Forbes beside her.

"I trust you're feeling better, ma'am," he said. "I was alarmed when Captain Steenboch brought you aboard, but he assured me it was a temporary fit that would pass."

Yes, she thought bitterly. But I only have fits when I drink tea with Steenboch!

Forbes held out a letter. "I was to give this to you when we reached this latitude."

She took the letter and stared at the name written on the outside. In Noël's handwriting. "Lisbet." Blast him! He had the gall to call her by his pet name after what he'd done to her? Thrown her aside so that he could go off to France and carry on with all his other women? Without even a goodbye? In a fury, she tore the letter into a hundred pieces and tossed them to the foaming waves. "I'm going to my cabin, Captain Forbes,'' she said through clenched teeth. ''I'll stay there till we reach New York. If any man aboard ship intrudes upon my solitude, I'll personally impale him on the end of my parasol!'' She turned about and stormed back to her cabin.

Her proud carriage held until she'd slammed the door behind her. Then she bent over and vomited into her washbasin.

Louisa Rawlings

I'll see these till we reach New York. If any man aboard
begins trying to get too soused. The merchants inspire him
whichever of my pleasing. The turned about and started
for her room.

Her proud carriage faltered as she reached the door,
and she put...

# *Chapter Sixteen*

"**O**h, Bessie! I don't know why you choose to live in that
awful boardinghouse. Your room is still waiting for you
here."

Elizabeth smiled tolerantly at her mother across the
luncheon table. "I do wish you'd try to call me Elizabeth,
Mother. Noël doesn't like the name Bessie. And Mrs. Bradish's boardinghouse isn't awful at all. It has a lovely view of
the Battery and Staten Island across the water."

"It's dashed expensive, I hear." Mr. Babcock frowned
and motioned to the maid for another helping of cold veal.

It certainly isn't cheap, thought Elizabeth. Not at two
whole dollars a day for a private parlor, a bedroom and Mrs.
Bradish's indifferent cooking. "Noël thought it would be
best," she said. "And it's only until he returns from France.
After that, I'm sure we'll buy or rent a house and I can send
for the rest of my things."

Rose dabbed delicately at her mouth with her napkin. "I
don't know why he sent you home from Bermuda. My Edward wouldn't have done such a thing," she added, looking pleased with herself. "Would you, dearest?" She smiled
at her husband, who grunted and continued to eat.

Elizabeth had been surprised to find Edward between jobs
when she'd come home. Mother had taken her aside and
begged her to say nothing. Edward had left Mr. Scantlebury's employ and was now looking for a "business
opportunity." But in the few visits Elizabeth had made to
her parents' house since her return from Bermuda a week

and a half ago, Edward had seemed to be doing nothing more than lazing around the Babcock house and feeling sorry for himself. "I told you, Rose," she responded to her sister, "there was a bad storm on the way down to Bermuda. Noël thought I'd be safer here in New York than going all the way across the sea." A glib lie, and she'd learned to tell it well.

Mr. Babcock cleared his throat. "How are you managing, Bessie? *Elizabeth*. Do you need anything?"

"Of course not. Noël provided very well for me. He was quite shrewd in his dealings in Bermuda."

"I swan," said Rose, her perfect mouth twisting into a sour pout, "you've spoken of nothing except that husband of yours since the moment you arrived."

"Why shouldn't I? I'm very fortunate."

"Well, marriage certainly agrees with you," said Mrs. Babcock. "You've changed, and for the better. But then, I knew it would be a good match. Didn't I tell you so, Mr. Babcock? I think our Bessie has done very well for herself."

Yes, I *have* changed, she thought. She felt it in herself. Whether it was the freedom that came with the final closing of Jack's door, or the secure feeling of belonging to someone, she didn't know. But there was a serenity in her she hadn't known in years.

Mr. Babcock looked pleased. "I think you're very fond of your husband, Elizabeth."

She returned his smile. "I love him," she said simply, knowing, even as she said the words, that it was true. No matter her hurt at Noël's sending her back to New York. But did he love her? She spoke of him constantly to her family, she talked with confidence of plans for the future, but in her heart she wondered if there was anything left of their marriage. She'd attacked him too many times. Said too many hurtful things.

"I wish we could persuade you to come to the Park Theater with us tonight," said Mrs. Babcock. "I've invited Caroline and Stephen...."

"No." Elizabeth shook her head.

"But why not? You've refused to see them since your return."

"I haven't refused to see them, Mother," she lied. "I happened to be busy each time they called." She couldn't yet bring herself to face Caroline. No matter how often she tried to tell herself that the deception had been Jack's idea, she couldn't forget that her sister had allowed her to be used and hurt. It was a selfishness, a callous cruelty, she'd never before been aware of in Caroline. She wasn't quite ready to forgive her yet.

As for Stephen, she'd gone to see him the second day after her return from Bermuda. She'd confronted him with the whole story, accused him of destroying her happiness and keeping her in an agony of uncertainty and doubt for five years. To her surprise, he hadn't shown a bit of remorse. To the contrary, he considered that he'd done her a favor by saving her from an unprincipled man, a dishonest, loveless marriage.

"Besides, Elizabeth," he'd said, his ferretlike eyes glowing in righteous pride and sanctimony, "you should thank me for my restraint. I could have exposed Jack openly as a scoundrel and a wolf in sheep's clothing. The whole story would have come out, you would have been shamed all the more—and estranged from Caroline, as well."

There was no arguing with his logic. How could she make him suffer for having hurt her, when he was too blind and self-interested to know he had? She'd left his office with nothing but contempt in her heart.

"I know why you don't want to see Caroline and Stephen," blurted Rose. "Stephen told me that you'd somehow got it into your head that *he* had something to do with Noël's arrest."

Elizabeth shrugged. It wasn't worth quarreling over. Not anymore. And she wasn't about to tell them the whole story.

"Well, if you won't come to the theater," said Mrs. Babcock, "do you want to go shopping today?"

"Oh, yes! I'd like..." Rose began, then sighed unhappily at her husband's warning glance. "Never mind. I'd rather spend the afternoon with Edward. Who needs a silly old gown anyway?''

Mrs. Babcock ignored her youngest daughter's glum expression. She smiled at Elizabeth. "But you and I, dear—?"

There might have been a time when Elizabeth would have welcomed her parents' attentions, their interest in pleasing her above her sisters. But it was a question of too little, too late. She felt strangely detached from them all. "I can't," she answered. "I happened to meet Mr. Lawson on Broadway yesterday. He asked me to come for tea this afternoon. Besides—" she indicated her deep peach flowered-silk gown "—I've already had several dresses made up this week. I don't need anything more."

Mr. Babcock stood up. "Well, it's time I was getting back to the bank. Can I give you a ride to your boardinghouse, Elizabeth?"

"Drop me at Front Street, Father. I'd like to take a long stroll, and then go straight to Mr. Lawson's."

The weather was still warm for September, but a refreshing breeze blew off the water as Elizabeth turned onto South Street and headed toward Mr. Lawson's office and countinghouse. As usual, the streets near the harbor were dirty, with pools of stagnant water, carcasses of dead animals and all manner of garbage. Pigs and dogs wandered free, rooting among the piles of rubbish, searching for a morsel. Elizabeth covered her mouth and nose with her gloved hand. Was it only her imagination, or was the stench getting worse? Only this morning, an English traveler had put a letter into the New York *Post,* declaring that this city was the filthiest one in the whole of the United States!

Of course, her sudden sensitivity to familiar smells might have something to do with her condition. She'd begun to suspect it that last week in Bermuda. And during the long, queasy voyage home. She suspected, as well, that her lingering anger at Noël was because she hadn't had the chance to tell him about her condition before the wretch had had his henchman spirit her aboard the *Sea Venture!*

She thought he'd be pleased about the child. She *hoped* he'd be pleased. But oh, the long, lonely wait before he'd return and she could tell him! It would be almost the end of November, she reckoned, before *L'Espérance* sailed into New York harbor.

Lawson greeted her at the door and ushered her into his comfortable office. "Well, my dear," he said, admiring her silk gown, "you look splendid. Makes a man wish he were thirty again. Come in and tell me all about your adventures in Bermuda."

"I did very little except enjoy the countryside. Noël was the one." Her eyes lit up just speaking of him. "You wouldn't believe the profit he made on the flour alone!"

Lawson sighed. "I wish I still had his youth and enthusiasm. Only this morning, one of my ships came in. I should take charge of the unloading. Get the goods properly into my warehouse. But you see? I much prefer to have tea with a charming young woman and let my agent see to the ship's cargo." He sighed again. "If I had any sense, I'd retire to my farm and cultivate apples. But your husband, Mrs. Bouchard...there's a fine man. I thought so the minute I met him. A man of conviction and persuasion. I think he would succeed at whatever he did. And this latest news, his courage and daring on your behalf...you must be quite touched by it."

She stared. "What courage?"

"But you had to know. In Bermuda. The yellow fever."

Her heart stopped. "Is he well?" she whispered in dread.

"Yes, of course. I thought you knew. The news from the islands came on my ship this morning. It seems that your husband risked arrest for concealing the presence of yellow fever on the island. At least until you'd escaped the danger. It's all they're talking about in Bermuda, I hear."

"I never knew," she gasped. "I didn't see Noël before I left. Perhaps he didn't want to frighten me by telling me." And perhaps he'd told her in the letter she'd so rashly and stupidly destroyed. Trust me, he'd begged through Steenboch. And she'd ignored his plea. "*Would* they have arrested him?"

"Yes, indeed. When a quarantine is declared, no ships can go in or out of the harbor until the danger has passed.

Mr. Bouchard had knowingly allowed you to go, nursing the sick man in secrecy until you sailed. A serious charge, if proven. I understand there was talk of confiscating his ship and his cargo. A foreigner, flying a foreign flag, after all. Some of our British cousins have little use for the French. Not after Bonaparte, naturally enough.''

She was growing more and more uneasy. "He didn't lose his cargo, did he?" The ruin of all his plans? It mustn't be!

"No, no. Put your fears to rest, my dear. It seems he made a great many friends on the island who were willing to vouch for his character."

"And they let him sail for France?"

"I should think so. The quarantine was lifted, I understand, when no further instances of yellow fever appeared. The sick man came from the West Indies. He must have caught it there."

She leaned back in her chair and closed her eyes. "Oh, thank goodness Noël is safe," she breathed.

"What a fortunate young woman you are, to know such devotion."

She opened her eyes. "Devotion?"

"A man doesn't often risk everything, unless he's a fool. Or deeply in love."

She smiled wonderingly at him. "Do you think so?" At his nod, she felt herself turn red. "And if he ... challenges someone to a duel?"

Lawson smiled, a gentle smile of understanding. "He did that?"

"On Bermuda," she whispered. "Because of a misunderstanding." Her face was now on fire.

"Dash my wig!" he said, slapping his thigh. "There's a man after my own heart. Old-fashioned chivalry. He won, I trust."

"Yes." She was suddenly overwhelmed by the urge to cry. Oh, Noël! He *did* love her, and everything he'd ever done had affirmed it over and over again. If only she hadn't been too pigheaded to see it. She ached with the need to see him, to tell him of her own deep, abiding love, of their child in her womb. "Mr. Lawson," she said suddenly, "do you have a merchantman leaving for France within the week?"

He looked mystified. "Yes. The *Princeton,* sailing for Le Havre in three days."

She threw back her head and laughed. She felt young and giddy and foolhardy. And very much in love.

"Mr. Lawson," she said. "Can we talk a little business?"

"It will rain tonight, Hessel. Mark my word." Noël gazed out the tavern window at the stone quays that lined the Le Havre waterfront. "Do you still want to go to Paris for a few days?"

Steenboch stirred in his chair and finished the last of his wine. "You know October. The sun could shine tomorrow. And I haven't seen the old city in many years. Had friends there once. You don't need me on your coattails. You have your family to crack a bottle with."

Noël laughed. "You'll always be a sailor. You start getting restless when you're on land for more than a week. How did you suffer it? All those years as a landlubber in New York?"

Steenboch rose and clapped his broad-brimmed hat on his head. "Did a deal of fishing." He scratched at his grizzled chin. "You won't need me before Monday, then?"

"No. We won't begin loading the new cargo until Tuesday. I only have my meeting this afternoon with Duval. The hold is clean, the sails are mended, the barnacles scraped away. We can all take a few days of rest. We've earned it." He watched Steenboch lumber out of the tavern, then tipped back in his chair, a contented smile on his face.

It had gone well. Even better than he'd hoped. The coffee and indigo had fetched top prices at auction. As for the furs, that trapper of his in Ohio had an eye for real quality; he had new orders from half a dozen hatters in Le Havre. And a cargo of good French porcelain and silks ready to transport back to the United States. His future looked bright. Only last week a ship had brought news that the Americans had broken ground for a canal from Lake Erie o the Hudson River at Albany. In a few years he could look forward to his furs getting to port in no time. Perhaps on the next voyage to France he could rent a warehouse and hire an agent. That way, when a cargo was unloaded, he could sell it at leisure, waiting for the best price. He smiled more broadly, thinking of his grand plans. If Lisbet were here, she'd accuse him of being smug again!

Lisbet. God, how he missed her. His body ached with desire. But more than that, his heart ached to hear her laughter, to see the lively spirit in those glorious eyes. Damn! he thought. It would be another sleepless night.

Off in the distance, he saw a ship moving past the stone jetties and into the harbor. She flew an American flag. He couldn't see her name from here, but maybe in a little while he'd go down to her berth and see if there was any news from New York. He had a sudden wistful thought, a flight of fancy: the captain of the ship would smile and say, Mr. Bouchard, I have a message from your wife. She loves you.

"May it be so, Lisbet," he murmured, then smiled sheepishly at the odd stares from the nearby patrons. "Come," he said to one of them, a young man who had already yawned several times in boredom, "will you join me for a game of piquet, *monsieur*?" He still had several hours to kill before he was to meet with Duval, the importer. At the young man's nod, he pulled the deck of cards from his waistcoat pocket.

They played for an hour or so; by the time the young man finally stood up and announced his intention to go home— a number of francs poorer—Noël saw that the American ship had already reached its berth and was beginning to unload its passengers and supplies. He paid for his wine and sauntered out to the quay, picking his way past a jumble of lines and boxes and crates, of bustling seamen and sober merchants. The American ship was a trim schooner. Fast, from the look of her. Rigged for speed. A real beauty.

*Mon Dieu!* He started at the sound of a familiar sharp voice, and turned to see Elizabeth coming down the gangway and berating the man who accompanied her.

"And I tell you, Captain Kendall," she was saying, "tea doesn't vanish from the storeroom for no reason. You might at least question your steward, since he has the keys!"

Noël stared in astonishment and wonder, his heart catching in his throat at sight of her. She was even lovelier than he'd remembered. Her limbs were soft and rounded, her bright hair—in that coiffure he'd so admired that last day in Bermuda—was seductively curled around her face, and her violet eyes were clear and dark beneath the shade of her straw bonnet. The color of her gown—a pale yellow—made her look as fresh and radiant as a sunbeam. He stepped forward. "Name of God, Lisbet," he said, with more impatience than he'd intended, "don't scold the man. It is *his* ship, after all."

She turned, saw him, seemed about to respond to him. Then she glanced at the captain and dismissed him with a wave of her hand. "I'll speak to you in the morning, Captain Kendall."

"Ma'am." The captain bowed and returned to his ship.

The more Noël thought of it—her appearing here in Le Havre—the more his astonishment turned to outright anger. "What the devil are you doing here?" he demanded. "Did I not order you back to New York?"

At his autocratic tone, the beginnings of a smile on her face turned to a frown. "I didn't want to stay there. I wanted to find you."

"And so you disobeyed, and decided to follow me? Did you not consider that I might have left Le Havre by now? Great God, Elizabeth! We could have been following each other around the world for the next two years!"

She tossed an insolent shoulder in his direction. "I never thought of that," she sniffed. "I came because I wanted to be sure that you love me!"

He threw up his hands in exasperation. Could she understand nothing? "Of course I love you! Did I not say it often enough in my letter?"

She had the decency to look abashed. "Well, you see, I was angry at you...." she said, a little more calmly.

"*Le diable!* You did not read it?"

"Don't be absurd. How could I, when I'd already torn it into a thousand pieces and thrown it into the sea?"

He swore softly. Would there ever come a time again in his life when he could remain calm and removed from his emotions? This devil in skirts had managed to burrow herself permanently under his skin, until he was helpless, raging like an idiot.

She seemed to sense her advantage. The angrier he became, the more serene she grew. "Is there anything else, my angel, that is troubling you?" she asked with cool sarcasm.

"Yes, damn it! Why did you not tell me of Jack, the minute you met him again?"

"I'd only met him that afternoon. Besides, it was my affair."

He shook his head vigorously. "No. *Ours.* For as long as we are together, we share our burdens. I would have allowed you to learn the truth from Cochran, by whatever means. But you should have told me!"

"You would have 'allowed'?" She snorted with indignation. "How kind of you. Just because I love you, it doesn't mean I have to jump into your pocket every time you call!"

He stared at her, his anger draining away. She'd said "I love you." It had been spoken so naturally—as though she weren't aware that it was the first time she'd told him. He was suddenly filled with happiness and desire, a longing for this woman that was joy and pain and wonder all at once. He reached out and put his fingers across her mouth, stilling her further tirades. "Just for once, wife," he said, his voice husky in his throat, "be quiet."

He pulled her into his arms and soothed his hunger with her honeyed lips. He kissed her over and over again, thrilling to her impassioned response, to the eager body that pressed to his. He dragged off her bonnet and tossed it to the ground so that he might hold her face between his hands and stroke the downy cheeks, kiss the shell-like ears. He was trembling with the wonder of their love. "*Ma chère,*" he breathed at last. "My pretty Lisbet. How I have missed you."

"*Am* I pretty?" she asked, her voice soft and hesitant.

"Foolish question. I told you so a long time ago."

"I thought you were just being kind."

"Let my eyes be your mirror. You grow lovelier by the day."

She blinked back the happy tears. "It must be because I love you so." A sudden breeze sprang up and blew her bonnet into a dirty puddle. She wiped at her tears and began to laugh. "I believe that makes *three* hats of mine you've ruined."

He grinned. "We shall buy more. In the meantime, I have among my luggage several bundles of fine silks. And the newest patterns from Paris. You shall be the most exquisitely dressed woman in all of New York." He held up a warning finger. "But I will not let you see them until you say it again."

She didn't need to be told what he meant. "I love you," she whispered, and threw her arms around his neck. "*Je t'aime. Je t'adore.*"

His face darkened, remembering the sea of pain she'd had to cross before she could say those words. "That bastard Cochran. And Stephen. I intend to call him out as soon as we return to New York."

"No. Let it be. I don't want Caroline ever to know. It's Stephen's place to tell her, if he has the courage. If not..." She shrugged. "I feel no malice for either of them. Not anymore. Now..." She looked up at him, and a wicked gleam appeared in her eyes. "I didn't come all this way to talk about Jack. Or Caroline and Stephen. Do you have lodgings? A room?"

"Yes. At *La Reine de la Mer.*"

Her expression grew more cunning still. "Does it have a bed?"

He laughed in delight. "Hussy! If I had the time, I should take you right here on the quay. But, alas, I must meet with an importer in a little while. Go to my room and refresh yourself. I will come to you as soon as I can." He hailed a passing fiacre, bundled her aboard with her luggage, and sent her off to The Queen of the Sea.

He watched the carriage disappear down the street, then smiled. His wife was here. His wife loved him. His shipping enterprise prospered. Everything was perfect.

Everything, of course, except the matter of what to do about Martin.

# Chapter Seventeen

Elizabeth smiled in blissful pleasure and sank lower into her bath. She lifted a dripping arm and gestured across the room to the little maid who was busy opening boxes and trunks. "Yes. The velvet gown," she said in French. "If you will be so kind as to lay it out for me. You'll find stockings and black kid slippers in the small portmanteau." She sighed in contentment and looked around Noël's lodgings. A comfortably furnished room, and almost as fine as some of the hotels in Paris. Noël must be feeling quite prosperous, to spend his money so freely.

It made her heart swell with pride. Once, in a moment of anger, she'd falsely and cruelly accused him of trading on his brother's name for his success. She prayed that his good fortune in Le Havre had washed away the sting of her ugly words.

She watched the maid set out the rest of her clothes, then stepped from her tub into the waiting bath sheet. She allowed the maid to dry her, then sat in a chair, wrapped in her towel, while the girl combed her hair. She didn't know whether she should dress yet. If Noël came, it would be for nothing. She'd only have to dress again. Afterwards. She felt herself growing warm with the thought of making love to him.

He burst into the room without knocking, threw down his hat and glared at the maid. "You. Out." She scurried away.

Elizabeth stood up, wrapped the towel more tightly around her body and pretended to pout. "Not a very sweet beginning for a seduction, *monsieur*."

He planted himself before her, arms folded across his chest, and scowled in silence.

Criminy! she thought. What's the matter? "Well?" she began.

"I have just come from Captain Kendall," he growled. "*Who* is the owner of the *Princeton?*"

She gulped. She'd hoped to break the news to him diplomatically. "Well, you see...we are, my angel. That is...we own part of it, and will own the rest someday, according to the terms I arranged with Mr. Lawson." She smiled uneasily, gauging his mood.

His hands curled into angry fists. "And what did *we* use to pay for it?" he asked sarcastically.

Drat! she thought. Perhaps, after all, she should have gone to Father for a loan. Her throat suddenly felt dry. "My dowry," she croaked.

"What?" His roar was like the bellow of a bull.

"It was mine to do with as I pleased," she said in her own defense.

"It was yours to keep you from starving if this whole scheme should come to nothing! Of all the foolish, irresponsible things to do!" He swore in French. "I thought I was the gambler, but *you*—! All it takes is one storm at sea, and our future is lost, our fortunes gone."

She was beginning to regret her impetuous arrangement with Lawson, but she wasn't about to admit it to Noël! She faced him defiantly. "Well, now we have *two* opportunities to succeed."

"And two to fail. Did that never occur to you?"

"You said, down at the quay, that you expected us to share our burdens! Well, what do you think I've done, you blockhead?"

His eyes glowed with fury. "You have made a decision of great importance without even speaking to me of it. You should have told me first!"

"Ha! The way you told me about the yellow fever? Why didn't you tell me before you sent me away?"

"Why? For another battle? Another tantrum? And no assurance that you would do what is best? I love you, Lisbet, but sometimes I do not understand why. You are stubborn, difficult, bad-tempered...." He threw in a few uncomplimentary French adjectives. "You never do as you are asked—out of perversity, I think it is! On Bermuda, I asked you to trust me and go home. You would not, and defied Steenboch and me. On the ship, in the storm, I asked you to stay below. You would not, though you might have been killed on deck! From the first, I asked you to trust my love and put aside foolish thoughts of fortune hunters. *You would not.* Your heart was filled with suspicion and anger. And Cochran. How dare you keep that secret from me, when our happiness was in the balance? And to spend an evening alone with him—with everyone knowing it! *Dieu!* Headstrong, willful..." He swore again, pacing the room in anger, as though he were gathering fresh grievances against her. "You tore up my letter without reading it, spent every penny we have on another ship, let your temper lead you into folly on more than one occasion! *Grand Dieu,* you try my patience as no woman ever has before!"

That was the final insult! She stamped her foot in indignation. "If you wanted a meek rabbit, you should have married a meek rabbit!"

He stared, the anger fading from his face. Then he began to roar with laughter, shaking his head in amusement and disbelief. "I have confounded myself, it would seem. Ah, well, *le bon Dieu* knows I always dreaded a dull wife."

She felt her own wrath draining away, to be replaced by a deep tenderness. It was fear she'd read in his eyes behind the anger, if only for a moment. Fear not for himself, but for her, who might be left destitute if he failed. "I love you, Noël Bouchard," she whispered. "I'm sorry about the ship. It *was* stupid of me to use all our money. Foolhardy and reckless."

"We shall manage," he said. "No matter what happens."

"I'm sorry about everything. For making Gilchrist get hurt, for going to Stephen and having you arrested. For all the mean things I said to you about Adam and your son. For all the trouble I've been."

His eyes were warm with love. "And all the joy, *ma chère*. I should not have given it up for half the treasure in the world."

She still felt a lingering guilt over her past behavior. She'd bedeviled him at every turn, crossed him constantly, refused to give him her love or her trust. Somehow she wanted to let him know how much she regretted that. How much she was determined to guard her temper from now on. To swallow the cruel, careless words that had too often hurt him.

Her eyes lit upon her clothing, laid out by the maid. She remembered something Noël had said once. Yes. It would be a fitting, symbolic gesture. She bent, picked up one of her slippers, and held it out to him. "Should you ever feel the need to use it..." She smiled shyly, her eyes shining with love and hope. Take me in your arms, she thought, and tell me I'm forgiven.

He hesitated, searching her face, then took the slipper from her hand. Without a word, he crossed to the bed, sat down and beckoned to her.

Her blood ran cold. "Noël?" He couldn't mean to... He wouldn't!

There was no laughter in his eyes. "Come here, wife."

She jutted her chin in defiance. "For heaven's sake, Noël, didn't mean..."

"That you were sorry?" he finished. "That you have no regrets for your willfulness?"

"Of *course* I'm sorry, but..."

"Then come here."

Curse him, how could he be so calm? She bit her lip, torn by indecision. It was a dilemma of her own making. A grand gesture that had produced the reverse of what she'd confidently expected. By offering him the slipper, she'd indicated her willingness to submit to his will, no matter what. A pledge of her love and devotion. To defy him now would be to mock the pledge, to deny the sincerity of her love. But to submit... She gulped at the painful thought. Drat! She knew his temper could be as towering as hers. Why had she foolishly assumed he'd accept the slipper merely as a gesture of humility? A symbol of deserved punishment, not the reality! She took a deep breath to give herself courage, then crossed the room to stand before him.

His expression was unreadable. She prayed he wasn't too angry, that a few gentle slaps of the slipper would satisfy him. To her dismay, he reached out and tore the towel from her body, leaving her naked and frighteningly vulnerable. She feared he didn't intend gentleness, after all. He intended her to be thoroughly chastised.

He patted his lap. "Here, *ma chère.*"

She made one last desperate attempt to save herself. "Noël, I love you," she cried.

He stared, nodded in acknowledgment and patted his lap again.

She considered having a tantrum, but changed her mind. A fine beginning, after she'd resolved to guard her temper! Besides, it was clear there was no escaping him. And a childish outburst would only increase his wrath.

She sighed. The sooner this was over with, the easier it would be. "You're a brute, you know," she said sulkily, and laid herself across his knees. He put his hand firmly on the middle of her back to keep her from wriggling. She'd never felt more helpless in all her life. She clutched at the bed with tight fists, in cold dread of what was to come. She squeezed her eyes shut and held her breath, anticipating the first sharp and painful crack of the slipper.

His knees, beneath her bare abdomen, began to quiver. At the same moment, she heard the soft plop of the slipper as it hit the floor. Her eyes sprang open. She felt herself being turned and cradled in his arms until she was staring up into his laughing face. His body shook with merriment.

"And *obey,* as well?" he asked. "At least some of the time, Lisbet?"

She gasped. She didn't know whether she was relieved or vexed at his good humor. "You wretch! You frightened me for nothing! You never would have struck me."

He chuckled. "But of course not. Still, I was mindful of the gesture. And the lessons to be learned. Let us both remember this day. In the meantime..." He smiled down at her naked body and ran his hand across her breasts. "I have better things to do when you are in this state." He stroked her bosom, her belly and rounded hips, praising her body with the sensuous touch of his hand. She shivered in remembered pleasure and forgave him everything. "How round and full you have become," he said. "You always pleased me, but now you are perfection. What a sweet pleasure it is to make love with you." He kissed her with passion, then lifted her from his lap, placed her across the bed and swiftly shed his clothes.

They made love with all the reckless joy they'd known in their days and nights at the beachside cottage. A wild, ecstatic fusion of bodies and souls that left them both drained and sated, gasping in each other's arms, unwilling to be parted.

At last Noël stirred. "I must go back to the harbor to see Duval. When I heard about the *Princeton,* I was so angry I put off my meeting. He will be impatient now, I fear."

She stretched languidly and sighed. "Must you?"

He climbed out of bed and began to put on his clothes. "Does the *Princeton* have a cargo to take back to New York?"

She frowned and sat up. "I don't know. We'll have to ask Captain Kendall. I don't know if Mr. Lawson has an agent here, but I don't think so."

"Then that will become my responsibility, as well, *n'est-ce pas?*" He laughed at her look of consternation. "Do not make faces, my angel. You will have to accustom yourself to my preoccupation with work. We have bought not merely another ship, but more burdens."

"Which I intend to share. Remember? That's what you said. By jingo, I'm not a helpless female!"

He smiled wryly. "That is true enough, God knows!"

"Then I'll want to help and share and work alongside you. And sail with you sometimes."

"And so you shall, my Lisbet." He leaned over the bed and kissed her exuberantly. "By my faith, let other men be content with homebodies! I have a prize. A woman without equal!" He reached for his hat. "I will see you in an hour or so. *Dieu!*" He snapped his fingers in recollection. "It nearly escaped my mind—we are to have guests tonight for dinner. I had told the landlord to make preparations for a good dinner in a private dining room. Have him set a place for you now." He threw her a kiss, put on his hat and bounded from the room, all youthful enthusiasm and joy.

Her heart swelled with happiness. Could she want for anything more? Drat! she thought suddenly, slapping her forehead. She still hadn't told him about the baby!

"Your guests are here, *madame.*"

Elizabeth nodded at the maid. "Thank you." She patted a last copper curl into place, stood up and smoothed the skirt of her azure velvet gown. The guests had arrived and Noël still hadn't returned? Well, she was inclined to forgive him. His appointment with that importer must be taking longer than he'd expected. And the good Lord knew that her arrival today had thrown his plans into a hurly-burly!

But when she followed the maid into the private dining room, acknowledged the presence of a woman seated at the table and saw Noël standing at the window, she was less inclined to be generous. "Dagnation, Noël, you might have come to fetch me yourself!"

The man at the window turned. He smiled, bowed stiffly. His expression was formal, distant, proper. "*Madame.* I trust we have not come too early."

Elizabeth smiled in her turn. Not in a million years would she mistake the differences. Not after the intimacy of living with Noël. "You are Adam, of course," she said, reverting to French out of politeness. *"Monsieur le comte."* She nodded at the woman. "And you are *madame la comtesse?"* Then, realizing that Noël wouldn't have had the chance to tell them of her arrival, she held out her hands in welcome. "I am Elizabeth. His wife," she explained.

"Please. Call me Charmiane. We are family, is it not so? And this is your brother Adam, not *monsieur le comte."* Charmiane rose from her chair and came forward to kiss Elizabeth on both cheeks. She was exquisitely beautiful, with the grace and natural ease of a woman unaware of her charms. Her pink satin dress set off her pale complexion and raven hair to perfection. Noël had said she came from an aristocratic family before the Revolution; there was a fineness in her bearing that attested to her upbringing. "But we didn't know you'd be here, Elizabeth," she said. "Noël didn't tell us."

A hearty laugh came from the doorway, followed by Noël's deep tones. Even his voice was different from his brother's, thought Elizabeth. More easy, with laughter in it. "Noël didn't tell you, dear sister-in-law," he said, "because *Noël* didn't know." He slipped his arm around Elizabeth's waist and kissed her on the neck. "Do you remember, Charmiane, you once wondered what kind of woman would catch me at last? I'll tell you." He kissed Elizabeth's neck again, a great, happy smack of his lips that made her blush and giggle. "A devil," he went on. "A maddening creature who does exactly as she wishes."

Elizabeth tossed her head, choosing to ignore the gibe. "And I wished to come to France."

"Ah, well." Noël sighed. "Since my wife is here, brother, perhaps it's just as well you ignored the request in my letter."

Adam looked mystified. "Indeed I did not. I changed my itinerary especially on your behalf, so that Charmiane and I could spend a few days with you here in Le Havre. Since we couldn't persuade you to come to Bonneval."

"No, no. I meant the part of my letter that asked you to bring several charming and agreeable women with you. To keep me company." He tried to maintain a serious expression, but the corners of his mouth insisted on twitching. "After all, it's what my wife expects of a lecherous Frenchman."

Charmiane put a gentle hand on Elizabeth's arm. Her gray-green eyes were soft with understanding. "I hope you know by now that your husband only pretends to be wicked."

Elizabeth smiled in reassurance. How kind of the woman to be concerned, lest she misunderstand Noël's teasing. "I know him better than you think," she said, and broke into a grin. "He *is* wicked. Completely unredeemable. And it's time you knew it." She swept her arm toward the table in a gesture of hospitality. "Come. While we eat, I'll tell you exactly what occurred that night at the Hôtel de Ville, when Noël pretended to be Adam."

Adam scowled and cleared his throat as he held out a chair for Elizabeth. "It might be instructive. Bazaine said very little about that night, but I was of the opinion that Noël compromised my good name."

"Only a little," laughed Noël. "Just enough to counterbalance your stiff neck."

Supper was a rollicking affair. With great good humor and high dramatics, Noël told the story of that night, while Elizabeth interrupted from time to time to remind him of some forgotten point. And to "keep him from glorifying his role," as she explained to a laughing Charmiane.

Noël shook his head. "I thought you were the most impossible woman there, Lisbet." His eyes warmed with love. "I think I began to fall in love with you that night."

Elizabeth snorted. "No doubt that's because I was the only woman who was willing to tolerate your outrageous behavior."

Charmiane reached across the table and put her hand over Adam's. "What is there about a ball that makes the Bouchard men so susceptible? That's where Adam and I fell in love. At a ball." She smiled at Elizabeth. "How nice to have something more to share, my dear sister, than two men with the same face. We shall be good friends, I think."

Elizabeth nodded in agreement. She liked her new family. Charmiane was gentle, kind and straightforward. Adam had a sobriety about him—as though he felt the need to preserve his dignity, to live up to his title. But it was a very endearing quality once one saw past his stiff bearing to the warmhearted man beneath. Elizabeth remembered with amusement that Noël had captured that side of his brother perfectly the night of his masquerade.

"I do wish we could persuade you to come to Bonneval," said Charmiane at last. "You haven't seen our daughter yet, Noël. Gabrielle. She's smiling and laughing now. Such a joy! I think Fabien is jealous of her. He clings to me when Madame Nogare brings Gabrielle into the room. But Martin..." She smiled fondly, her eyes misty with remembrance. "Do you know, I found him last week standing by Gabrielle's cradle? All alone. He was telling her a fairy story, one of the ones I tell him before he goes to bed. All tender whisperings and solemnity, as though he was sure she understood every word." She looked at Noël, her voice soft and pleading. "Oh, do come and see the children before you go back to the United States."

Noël frowned. "I don't know. I planned to sail in a week."

Elizabeth shook her head. "But how can we, Noël? Don't you want to oversee the *Princeton*'s unloading? And at least have some say in her new cargo? Besides—" she affected a pout "—I've decided to be difficult. I want to stay and visit with Charmiane and Adam for a few days." And she wanted to see Noël's son. To meet him. It was strange that Noël didn't seem as eager. "Please say yes, my angel."

"Well..." said Noël, weakening.

"You can't leave," said Charmiane. "Not till after the twenty-seventh. It's Martin's birthday."

"That settles it," said Elizabeth. "We'll stay." Noël nodded reluctantly. "Besides," she went on, "we can always send *L'Espérance* home with Captain Steenboch next week, and return ourselves on the *Princeton* when she's ready to sail.'' She'd have to remember to have a large bed put into the main cabin of the *Princeton*. Though of course that idea might occur to her lusty husband, as well!

''*Two* ships?'' asked Adam. ''I thought you had only one.'' He shook his head, his eyes filled with wonder and pride. ''My God, Noël, I don't know how you've managed to succeed so well in such a short time.''

''Let's not sell the skin of the bear before we've killed it, brother. It will take a few years before I can feel we're comfortable.''

''Still, who would have thought—of the two of us—that you would have had our bourgeois ancestors' business sense?''

''You're not exactly struggling yourself,'' said Noël dryly.

''It's very easy to make money once you have it. My windfall of diamonds was sheer luck. A dying émigré and a sympathetic cavalry officer. It could have been any soldier besides me. And I've had Bazaine all these years to invest for me. But *you* ...'' Adam shook his head. ''Father and Mother always called you a reckless gambler. How little they understood. Maybe that's what it takes to succeed in this new world. That kind of courage.''

Noël shrugged; it was a sublime gesture of nonchalance. ''Don't strain the point, brother. I don't have anywhere near your success, no matter how you had your start.''

Listening to the conversation, Elizabeth wanted to throw something at Noël. Couldn't he hear what Adam was saying? Couldn't he hear the admiration—and, yes, the *envy*—in Adam's voice? She thought of herself and her sisters. What is it about siblings, she thought, that makes one think the other is better? That uses the other one as a foolish, unfair measurement, when the other might be feeling the same insecurity and doubt? ''You'll have a great success one day, Noël,'' she said confidently. ''So there's nothing more to be said about it.''

Noël stared at her. Her heart caught at the look. Surely he'd heard the love in her voice, the unshakable strength of her faith in him. The mask of indifference faded from his face. He muttered a soft oath, rose from his chair and came around to stand next to Elizabeth. He nodded at Adam and Charmiane. ''Pardon me,'' he said, and bent and kissed Elizabeth on the mouth. A long, tender, lingering kiss. And then another.

''Really, Noël,'' said Elizabeth, as soon as she could catch her breath. She felt herself blushing in embarrassment. Whatever else Noël's kin were, they were accustomed to civilized, aristocratic surroundings. It didn't seem right, to kiss so shamelessly before a count and countess. ''I'm sure your family is used to more discreet behavior in company.''

She expected Charmiane to agree with her; instead, her sister-in-law laughed. ''Don't be fooled, my dear. Adam may seem proper and sedate, but I assure you there's a wicked streak in the whole family. He pinched me as the landlord showed us to this room this evening. And defied me to show the slightest reaction.''

Adam wriggled uncomfortably in his chair, his face turning red. ''Charmiane...'' he warned.

Noël threw up his hands and crowed with delight. ''Good for you, brother! I like to see evidence of your human side.''

''Hmm. Yes. Well...'' Adam growled. ''So. You see a solid future for yourself with this shipping business?''

Noël smirked at his brother's instant change of subject, but chose to let it pass. ''A few successful voyages with no serious mishaps, God willing. Then I think I'll be well on the way.''

''I'll drink to that,'' said Adam, and toasted his brother in the wine.

Elizabeth thought she'd never had a happier evening in her life: to be with Noël, to share his contentment and confidence, to feel the deep, strong love that passed between the brothers. Her heart was filled to overflowing.

Too soon the evening ended. They said their farewells, making their plans for Noël and Elizabeth to visit in a few days' time. It had begun to rain—a soft autumn downpour that swirled beyond the windows and pattered against the glass. While Adam went below to see that his carriage was brought to the door of the inn, Elizabeth and Charmiane stood on the stairs, saying their last goodbyes.

"I'm so glad for you both," said Charmiane, kissing her tenderly. "I've known Noël for as long as I've known Adam. But I've never seen such a look in his eyes. Such serenity and joy. As though his wandering soul had come home at last. I think he must love you very much."

Elizabeth nodded, too moved to answer. She hurried back to Noël, her heart as eager for him as her body.

He stood at the window, staring out at the rain. She was tempted to pass a teasing remark, but something about his carriage, the set of his shoulders, stopped her. "Noël?"

He didn't turn, and his voice, when he spoke, was muffled. "It's too late," he said. "I have lost him."

For the first time, she was aware of the heavy burden he'd carried all this time. His pain and guilt over giving up his son. Her heart ached for him, understanding clearly his torment. That's what love is, she thought. Not merely to laugh together, but to grieve together, as well. To give each other strength. "No, you haven't. We'll take him to live with us."

"I meant to speak of it tonight. That was why I invited Adam and Charmiane here. But I could not. God help me, I could not!" He turned to face her. His eyes sparkled with tears. "How could I ask for the boy's return? He's not my son anymore. He belongs to Adam. To Charmiane. How can I take him away from the only life he has ever known? The only father?"

"Don't, Noël." That was why he hadn't wanted to see the boy. Because he had already made this painful, heartbreaking decision. "Noël. *Mon cher,*" she whispered, and ran to clasp him in her arms. She'd never felt more needed. More helpless.

He buried his head against her neck. She felt the wetness of his burning tears. "It seemed so simple at the time," he said hoarsely. "So sensible. He was just a baby. My conscience scarcely raised its head. But now... Oh, God, Lisbet. What am I to do now?"

She kissed him on the mouth, smoothed back the hair from his forehead. "Now we'll go and visit him, and wish him well on his birthday. And decide what's to be done next."

He crossed to the table and poured himself another glass of wine, drank it slowly to steady himself. He laughed bitterly. "I don't even know if that is his birthday. We could only guess, Charmiane and I. Martine had run away and married. There was no one to ask. His mother abandoned him even before his father did."

"It's as good a date as any." She took him by the hand and pushed him into a chair, then sat on his lap, her arms around his neck. "Listen to me, Noël Bouchard," she said. "There's no point in blaming yourself now. You didn't abandon him. You gave him to people who could love him. What you did was best for the boy. Certainly at that time. Doesn't that show your love, you foolish man? Let him stay where he is for now. Perhaps in a few years, when he can understand better, he'll learn the truth. He'll know that you did what you did out of love."

He thought about that, then sighed. "Of course. It's for the best. You are wiser than I am, *ma chère*. When he's older, he can come and stay with us in America, for a time."

"Of course. And in the meantime—" she laughed softly and put his large hand on her belly "—you'll just have to be content with *this* child. I've been bursting to tell you all evening."

He stared, his blue eyes bright with wonder and joy. "Ours?" he choked.

"Well, I should hope so! You certainly had at me often enough!"

He shook his head. "Never enough. When? The baby, I mean?"

"It's too early to be sure, but probably the end of April."

"Oh, God," he said, and held her close in his embrace. "What did I do to deserve you?"

She smiled her love and devotion. "Wicked man," she said softly, "you put on your brother's uniform, and danced your way into my heart."

## Chapter Eighteen

'Bessie... I mean *Elizabeth,* I want you to make your husband promise that *L'Espérance* won't sail until after Christmas." Mrs. Babcock cast a pleading look at her daughter.

"Of course not, Mother." From her seat at the foot of her own dinner table, Elizabeth surveyed her guests. Mr. and Mrs. Babcock, Mr. Lawson, flushed with the success of the *Princeton's* first voyage under Noël's stewardship, Rose and Edward. And even Caroline and Stephen.

Elizabeth and Noël had talked about her sister and her husband at some length, and had finally decided that they'd simply pretend—for the sake of family harmony—that Jack had never happened. "After all," Elizabeth had said, "it ended happily for us and miserably for them. Can't we afford to be generous?"

She motioned for the manservant to refill her guests' wineglasses and bring out the dessert. This was her first real dinner party, and it was a success so far. All the more remarkable since she and Noël had been back in New York for less than two weeks. But their rented house on Pearl Street had come comfortably staffed and furnished with marble fireplaces, walls hung with East India papers, elegant and tasteful furniture, competent servants. And tonight, to ward off the dark and frosty December evening, wood fires burned cozily in every room and wax candles scented the air, casting golden glimmers on crystal and silver and soft vel-

vet draperies. Noël had even spent hours with the new cook
to ensure that the evening's menu—turtle soup, roast lamb
and potatoes, followed by a burnt custard cream—was up
to his French standards. The house was perhaps larger and
more luxurious than they needed, but Noël had taken such
delight in it that Elizabeth hadn't had the heart to dampen
his enthusiasm.

She smiled across the table at him, then turned to Mrs.
Babcock. "We wouldn't miss your Christmas dinner for
anything, Mother."

"Besides," said George Lawson, "he can't go too soon.
I don't intend to lose my new partner until he's bargained
for a good cargo for the *Princeton*'s hold." Lawson smiled
at Elizabeth. "If you're not married to the most charming
and persuasive man in all of New York, I'll eat my cocked
hat. I don't know how he does it, but—"

Mr. Babcock beamed as though the compliment had been
directed to him. "I always knew it. That's why I convinced
Elizabeth to marry him." He turned to Noël. "So, my boy,
you plan to go to Savannah?"

Noël nodded. "It will mostly be a speculative voyage. I
explained to Monsieur Lawson that it might be worth our
while to see if we can establish a regular run to the southern
ports. There is a great deal of interest in France for American cotton."

Mr. Lawson beamed. "You see what I mean, Babcock?
This partner of mine will make me a rich man one of these
days. And the ink scarcely dry on our agreement!"

Elizabeth marveled at the change in Mr. Lawson. He
seemed to be infused with Noël's enthusiasm, making plans
for the future, discussing a full partnership that would
eventually allow Noël to take over all of his ships. Ever since
they'd returned from France with an exotic cargo beyond
Lawson's expectations—auctioned at a huge profit by
Noël—Elizabeth hadn't heard a word from him about re-
tiring or growing old.

Caroline looked across the table and fluttered her eye-
lashes at Mr. Lawson. "I'm sure you've always been such

ssful . . . George. I've watched you around your ships. All
at to-do with cargo duties and harbor fees and all the rest.
find it so interesting. You must be terribly clever to man-
ge so well.''

Seated beside her, Stephen stiffened, his hand curling into
fist around the stem of his wineglass. "You don't know a
amn thing about shipping, Caroline," he said with dis-
ust. "And you care even less. So leave *George* alone."

Caroline's lip trembled. She looked like a child who'd
en caught doing something she ought not to do, thought
izabeth. She felt a twinge of pity for her sister. There was
desperation in her flirtation that Elizabeth had never no-
ced before. Did she need the reassurance of every man's
dmiration? Even a comfortable, fatherly man like George
awson?

And Stephen, tormented with jealousy. Not without rea-
n, she realized. If Caroline had had an affair with Jack,
ere must have been other men. Relationships that went
yond coy smiles and harmless flattery. Elizabeth won-
red how many of Caroline's lovers Stephen had had to
y off. Poor, pitiful Stephen. Poor, unhappy Caroline.
nd to think she'd admired her sister's marriage once upon
time!

Not that Rose was any more fortunate. After much tear-
l pleading by Mrs. Babcock, Josiah Babcock had been
rsuaded to take Edward into the bank with him. But at the
lary of a junior clerk until he proved his worth. Rose cast
sidelong glance at her husband, then sighed. A martyr's
gh. "I don't see how we can enjoy Christmas this year,"
e said. As usual, her mind was still dwelling on the pre-
ous conversation. "Not when Edward and I can hardly
fford proper gifts for each other."

Edward stopped eating his burnt cream long enough to
peal to Mr. Babcock. "Your daughter saw a bewitching
nnet in a shop the other day, sir. If you could see your
ay clear to a small advance . . . at least until after Christ-
as."

Mr. Babcock's eyes flashed dangerously. "Confound i she'll do without. As for you, young man, you spend to much and work too little!"

Rose looked as though she were about to cry. Quickl Elizabeth glanced across the table and signaled to Noël. H nodded. She rose to her feet, smoothing her skirts. "La dies, shall we retire to the parlor and leave the gentlemen t their whiskey and cigars?" Noël rose and bowed as the la dies left the dining room, promising that the men would joi their women shortly. A gracious speech, thought Eliza beth, in view of the fact that Noël considered the Englis and American practice of segregating the sexes after dinn to be barbaric.

Behind her, she heard a snatch of conversation. "Yo wife looks radiant tonight, Bouchard," said Mr. Lawson.

Before the door closed, she heard Noël's warm laugl "*Monsieur,* my wife has always been radiant to me."

Am I? she thought. The creature was still so new—tha pretty woman who smiled back at her from the mirro There was a large looking glass in the parlor; she took moment to assess her reflection as she passed. Her gown wa certainly radiant, made up from the fabrics and patter Noël had bought in France. A handsome dress of lavende blue twilled silk. Her braided hair and loose curls at the sid were caught up with ribbon bows of the same blue. The la est coiffure from Paris, which Charmiane had shown her Bonneval. Her pregnancy hadn't yet begun to show itself her abdomen, but her limbs were round and soft, and h bosom swelled in a graceful curve. Noël had given her matched set of gold-filigree-and-amethyst jewelry that he bought in France before they left: a comb for her hair, necklace, two bracelets, a brooch and a pair of danglir earrings. She found herself smiling, remembering the honeymoon and the purple jacket. He always seemed t know what would suit her looks best.

She settled herself comfortably in a chair near the ser ing table and poured coffee for her mother and sisters. Ro took up her workbasket and pulled out a bit of embroider

wning over the stitches. Mrs. Babcock had brought her
itting. She worked in silence for a few minutes, then
nted her work in her lap and pursed her lips at Eliza-
h. "Now, while we're alone, I must scold you, Bessie!
. Babcock doesn't agree with me, but I'm plumb set
ainst your travel on *L'Espérance* in your condition. And
the dead of winter. The very idea!"

"Oh, Mother. I'll only be five months along when we go.
d it's not as though we're crossing the ocean. We'll only
gone a few weeks, and they say it's warm in Savannah."
e was bubbling with excitement over the trip. Noël had
ured her that she'd find the southern cuisine very much
her liking. "After that, I swear to stay in New York until
baby is born. And Noël will be with me." He'd prom-
d to stay ashore until her confinement, letting Steenboch
d Kendall sail out on trading runs. She grinned, her eyes
ning. "But if he goes to China next year, he's promised
take me!" An adventure, Lisbet, he'd said once. And she
uldn't imagine a single day of boredom with him, ever.

Caroline slumped in her chair, her mouth twisted and
uty. "You should be glad you're having a baby, instead
making plans to gad about the world with your hus-
nd. You don't deserve it!"

Mrs. Babcock looked shocked. "Caroline, what an un-
d thing to say to your sister!"

"Yes," said Rose, her eyes wide and innocent. "I don't
ve a baby yet, either. But *I'm* not jealous of Elizabeth."

"And maybe you're not barren, either!" blurted Caro-
e. "That's what Stephen calls me, though I'm sure it's not
fault!" She tossed her head—a sad, defiant gesture.
nd who wants a baby anyway? They only drain you of
r looks."

here was an uncomfortable pause, occasioned by Car-
ne's unexpected confession after all these years. The
avy silence was punctuated only by the soft click of Mrs.
bcock's knitting needles. Elizabeth racked her brain to
nk of words of comfort for her sister. But what could she
? Perhaps for Caroline, losing her beauty had become

her greatest fear. The reason for her constant flirting, h
need of men's attentions—as well as her husband's jea
ousy. To give herself the sense of womanliness that s
would never find through motherhood.

Just then the door to the parlor opened and Noël led t
men into the room. Elizabeth's heart lifted. He always ha
the power to thrill her with his presence—a brilliant sun th
eclipsed every other planet in the room. While the other m
settled into chairs, he took his coffee from Elizabeth an
lounged against the mantel. And watched her.

Oh, she knew that he smiled at others, spoke, turned I
head. But he was watching her all the same, sending a s
cret message of love and desire that made her burn wi
longing and wish everyone would get up and go home th
minute!

"I've been telling Noël," said Mr. Babcock, "that I thin
you ought to buy a house and settle down. None of th
rented nonsense."

"Oh, I'm sure we shall, someday, Father."

"Where would you live?" asked Mrs. Babcock.

"New York. For Elizabeth," said Noël.

At the same moment, Elizabeth—thinking of what wou
please Noël—had said "France." They looked at each oth
and laughed in delight.

Noël shrugged. What did it matter where they lived, wh
they had each other? "*Eh bien,* wherever it is, it will be
sight of the sea. Yes, my Lisbet?"

She nodded. "With a stable full of horses." They'd nev
talked about it, but somehow, whenever she thought of
house of their own, she always pictured it overlooking t
sea. And long bareback rides across a wide beach. She mig
have known that she and Noël were so in tune that he'd ha
the same daydream.

"Oh, choose France," said Rose. "Then you can send
the most beautiful gifts all the time! Like that lovely je
elry."

Caroline frowned at Stephen, making an ugly crease on her perfect brow. "It was a gift from her husband," she said pointedly.

Elizabeth stared at her sisters in wonder. What had she ever seen in them to envy? They were merely human. And really quite sad and empty. Wanting *things*. Wanting constant attention. But their lives were meaningless without love and happiness. And the beauty that they so valued would fade soon enough. And then what would they have? She felt a deep sadness for these women who had never learned to seek for contentment within themselves. She remembered what Mrs. Cooke had said in Bermuda: The more one gives up in love, the more one gains.

She sent a secret look to Noël, praying he'd understand and forgive her actions. She reached down to her wrists and unclasped her bracelets. "Here," she said, holding them out. "For you, Rose." She pulled off her earrings. "Caroline? Please take them." She looked at Noël. He was smiling his approval.

"But you can't, Bessie," fluttered Mrs. Babcock. "You can't give away your jewels!"

"Why not, Mother?" she asked with a gentle shrug. "Why do I need them? A woman is beautiful who shines with the jewels her husband gives her—the jewels of his loyalty and devotion, his ever-abiding love."

"*Formidable!*" Noël set down his cup and saucer with a crash, strode across the room and pulled Elizabeth from her chair. She was too stunned to resist. He swept her up into his arms and turned to their guests. "You will excuse me. Please stay as long as you like this evening. Entertain yourselves. Help yourself to more coffee. Madeira and cognac are on the sideboard. Whatever you wish. Cards? Backgammon? Draughts? You have only to ask a servant."

"But what are you doing, man?" said Stephen with a scowl. "You can't just leave us alone. Are all you Frenchies so ill-mannered?"

Noël grinned, though his voice was like steel. "Someday, my fine brother-in-law, I shall have to teach you to be more amiable. But for now—" he settled Elizabeth more firmly in his arms "—I am taking my beautiful wife to bed."

Mrs. Babcock looked scandalized. "The very idea!"

Mr. Babcock frowned in warning. "Hold your tongue, Mrs. Babcock."

Noël bowed with as much grace as he could manage with Elizabeth in his arms. "Thank you, *monsieur,*" he said solemnly. Then he looked down at her and winked.

It was all she could do to keep from laughing hysterically. She leaned her face against his chest as he carried her from the room. She wasn't embarrassed—living with Noël had taught her to put aside false modesty. But she really didn't want her family to see how glad she was to quit their company this evening!

Noël took the steps two at a time to their bedroom, then set her on her feet. His eyes searched her face, scanned her body with an intimacy that made her shiver. "You are indeed beautiful, *ma chère.* And glorious in that gown. But I shall take it off you as fast as I can. What do you say to that, my angel?"

She giggled and threw her arms around his neck. "Shut the door," she whispered.

\* \* \* \* \*

**THREE
UNFORGETTABLE
KNIGHTS**

First there was Ruarke, born leader and renowned warrior, who faced an altogether different field of battle when he took a willful wife in *Knight Dreams* (Harlequin Historicals #141, a September 1992 release). Now, brooding widower and heir Gareth must choose between family duty and the only true love he's ever known in *Knight's Lady* (Harlequin Historicals #162, a February 1993 release). And coming later in 1993, Alexander, bold adventurer and breaker of many a maiden's heart, meets the one woman he can't lay claim to in *Knight's Honor,* the dramatic conclusion of Suzanne Barclay's Sommerville Brothers trilogy.

If you're in need of a champion, let Harlequin Historicals take you back to the days when a knight in shining armor wasn't just a fantasy. Sir Ruarke, Sir Gareth and Sir Alex won't disappoint you!

## IN FEBRUARY LOOK
## FOR *KNIGHT'S LADY*
## AVAILABLE WHEREVER
## HARLEQUIN BOOKS ARE SOLD

---

If you would like to order *Knight Dreams*, Harlequin Historical #141, please send your name, address, zip or postal code, along with a check or money order (please 38 not send cash) for $3.99 for each book ordered, plus 75¢ ($1.00 in Canada) postage and handling, payable to Harlequin Reader Service to:

**In the U.S.**
3010 Walden Avenue
P.O. Box 1325
Buffalo, NY 14269-1325

**In Canada**
P.O. Box 609
Fort Erie, Ontario
L2A 5X3

HHSB93

## OFFICIAL RULES • MILLION DOLLAR BIG WIN SWEEPSTAKES
### NO PURCHASE OR OBLIGATION NECESSARY TO ENTER

To enter, follow the directions published. **ALTERNATE MEANS OF ENTRY:** Hand-print your name and address on a 3" ×5" card and mail to either: Harlequin Big Win, 3010 Walden Ave., P.O. Box 1867, Buffalo, NY 14269-1867, or Harlequin Big Win, P.O. Box 609, Fort Erie, Ontario L2A 5X3, and we will assign your Sweepstakes numbers (Limit: one entry per envelope). For eligibility, entries must be received no later than March 31, 1994 and be sent via 1st-class mail. No liability is assumed for printing errors or lost, late or misdirected entries.

To determine winners, the sweepstakes numbers on submitted entries will be compared against a list of randomly preselected prizewinning numbers. In the event all prizes are not claimed via the return of prizewinning numbers, random drawings will be held from among all other entries received to award unclaimed prizes.

Prizewinners will be determined no later than May 30, 1994. Selection of winning numbers and random drawings are under the supervision of D.L. Blair, Inc., an independent judging organization whose decisions are final. One prize to a family or organization. No substitution will be made for any prize, except as offered. Taxes and duties on all prizes are the sole responsibility of winners. Winners will be notified by mail. Chances of winning are determined by the number of entries distributed and received.

Sweepstakes open to persons 18 years of age or older, except employees and immediate family members of Torstar Corporation, D.L. Blair, Inc., their affiliates, subsidiaries and all other agencies, entities and persons connected with the use, marketing or conduct of this Sweepstakes. All applicable laws and regulations apply. Sweepstakes offer void wherever prohibited by law. Any litigation within the province of Quebec respecting the conduct and awarding of a prize in this Sweepstakes must be submitted to the Régies des Loteries et Courses du Quebec. In order to win a prize, residents of Canada will be required to correctly answer a time-limited arithmetical skill-testing question. Values of all prizes are in U.S. currency.

Winners of major prizes will be obligated to sign and return an affidavit of eligibility and release of liability within 30 days of notification. In the event of non-compliance within this time period, prize may be awarded to an alternate winner. Any prize or prize notification returned as undeliverable will result in the awarding of the prize to an alternate winner. By acceptance of their prize, winners consent to use of their names, photographs or other likenesses for purposes of advertising, trade and promotion on behalf of Torstar Corporation without further compensation, unless prohibited by law.

This Sweepstakes is presented by Torstar Corporation, its subsidiaries and affiliates in conjunction with book, merchandise and/or product offerings. Prizes are as follows: Grand Prize—$1,000,000 (payable at $33,333.33 a year for 30 years). First through Sixth Prizes may be presented in different creative executions, each with the following approximate values: First Prize—$35,000; Second Prize—$10,000; 2 Third Prizes—$5,000 each; 5 Fourth Prizes—$1,000 each; 10 Fifth Prizes—$250 each; 1,000 Sixth Prizes—$100 each. Prizewinners will have the opportunity of selecting any prize offered for that level. A travel-prize option if offered and selected by winner, must be completed within 12 months of selection and is subject to hotel and flight accommodations availability. Torstar Corporation may present this sweepstakes utilizing names other than Million Dollar Sweepstakes. For a current list of all prize options offered within prize levels and all names the Sweepstakes may utilize, send a self-addressed stamped envelope (WA residents need not affix return postage) to: Million Dollar Sweepstakes Prize Options/Names, P.O. Box 7410, Blair, NE 68009.

For a list of prizewinners (available after July 31, 1994) send a separate, stamped self-addressed envelope to: Million Dollar Sweepstakes Winners, P.O. Box 4728, Blair NE 68009.

SWP193

# ROMANCE IS A YEARLONG EVENT!

Celebrate the most romantic day of the year with MY VALENTINE! (February)

CRYSTAL CREEK
When you come for a visit Texas-style, you won't want to leave! (March)

Celebrate the joy, excitement and adjustment that comes with being JUST MARRIED! (April)

Go back in time and discover the West as it was meant to be . . . UNTAMED—Maverick Hearts! (July)

LINGERING SHADOWS
*New York Times* bestselling author Penny Jordan brings you her latest blockbuster. Don't miss it! (August)

BACK BY POPULAR DEMAND!!!
Calloway Corners, involving stories of four sisters coping with family, business and romance! (September)

FRIENDS, FAMILIES, LOVERS
Join us for these heartwarming love stories that evoke memories of family and friends. (October)

Capture the magic and romance of Christmas past with HARLEQUIN HISTORICAL CHRISTMAS STORIES! (November)

## WATCH FOR FURTHER DETAILS IN ALL HARLEQUIN BOOKS!

# HISTORY IN
# THE MAKING!

Join Harlequin Historicals as we celebrate our 5th anniversary of exciting historical romance stories! Watch for our 5th anniversary promotion in July. And in addition, to mark this special occasion, we have another year full of great reading.

- A 1993 March Madness promotion with titles by promising newcomers Laurel Ames, Mary McBride, Susan Amarillas and Claire Delacroix.

- The July release of UNTAMED!—a Western Historical short story collection by award-winning authors Heather Graham Pozzessere, Joan Johnston and Patricia Potter.

- In-book series by Maura Seger, Julie Tetel, Margaret Moore and Suzanne Barclay.

- And in November, keep an eye out for next year's *Harlequin Historical Christmas Stories* collection, featuring Marianne Willman, Curtiss Ann Matlock and Victoria Pade.

**Watch for details on our Anniversary events wherever Harlequin Historicals are sold.**

## HARLEQUIN HISTORICALS . . .
### A touch of magic!

HH5TH